Texas Told'em: Gambling Stories

Texas Told'em: Gambling Stories

Laurie Champion, Editor

INK
BRUSH
PRESS

ISBN 978-0-9827514-1-1

Library of Congress Control Number: 2010939032

Ink Brush Press
Temple, Texas
www.inkbrushpress.com

Acknowledgments

The following stories collected in *Texas Told'em* are reprinted from earlier publications:

Michael Kardos's "Two Truths and a Lie" appeared in the fall 2010 issue of *PRISM international*.

Terry Dalrymple's "Services Rendered" appeared in *New Mexico Humanities, volume* 31 (1989): 49-66.

Eugene Cross's "Eyes Closed" appeared in the spring 2006 issue of *Callaloo*.

Adam Berlin's "O'Kaye in the Ninth" appeared in *Writers for Racing Project* (Sept./Oct. 1996): 45-55.

Sheila Thorne's "The Numbers Angel" first appeared in the 1999 issue of *Primavera*.

In a much revised form, "Cassidy's Gamble" appeared as a chapter in Clay Reynolds's second novel, *Agatite* (St. Martin's Press, 1986).

"Smoke," by Maureen A. Sherbondy, appeared in the 2009 issue of *The Petigru Review*, sponsored by the South Carolina Writers' Workshop.

Jeff W. Bens's "Golden Day" appeared in *New England Review*, volume 29. Copyright 1997 by Jeff W. Bens. Reprinted by permission of the author.

As editor of this book, I am grateful to all the contributors for sharing their love of writing in this volume, for their patience, and for their support during the process of putting together the anthology.

I owe special thanks to Jerry Craven for his guidance and help, to Doyle Brunson for his willingness to contribute the introduction, to my daughter, Bracha Berkson, for her support and help editing the volume, and my husband, Bill, who has been playing poker much longer than I have been writing. He checked the gambling details for accuracy and fact-checked the stories. Thanks also to my son, Billy Brumley—the only person I know who really understands the concept of "implied odds"— for his support and for his interest in the project.

An inexperienced poker player, I've lately been dabbling in Texas hold'em tournaments. Call it beginner's luck or the luck of the Irish, but I somehow managed to win second or third several times in a row. I told my father that I couldn't figure out what was keeping me from winning first. "After all," I said, "with a name like *Champion*, we must be champions."

He explained the concept of increased hand value in head's up poker and concluded, "Besides, you're just gonna have to take a chance."

I dedicate this book to my father

Jerry Champion

whose poker advice echoes the many life lessons he's taught me, one of which is the way he has encouraged me to take risks.

CONTENTS

Introduction

Doyle Brunson

I once claimed that the ideal poker game was one where you didn't look at your cards. To illustrate my point, I told about the time I got knocked out of a Texas hold'em tournament with a queen-eight. But I could've just as easily been holding a seven-deuce because the decision wasn't based on my cards. I thought I could win the pot right there, so I pushed all in. Someone called with a pair of jacks. It baffled me how he could make that call, but he did. I'd made a bad read, but I was still correct to play the situation rather than to focus on the cards. Most of the hands aren't shown in a poker game. You raise, you bet, then you bet again. So when I said that I didn't need to see my cards, that's what I meant.

The characters in the stories you're about to read don't need to look at their cards either because they're playing the game of life. Told from uncommon perspectives, the stories explore both ordinary and extraordinary truths about human conflicts and dilemmas. Amidst the world of brightly-lit casinos, smoke-filled poker rooms, and crowded racetrack stands, they show the ups and downs not only at the tables but also in daily life.

The last decade has brought a huge rise in poker's popularity. In 2008, "poker" was Lycos search engine's number-one-searched term, placing it in the top spot three years in a row, ahead of contenders "Paris Hilton," "Britney Spears," "MySpace," and "YouTube." Poker champions have become household names, and players such as Johnny Chan, Scotty Nguyen, Phil Ivey, and Jennifer Harman have reached celebrity status. Arguably the best woman poker player in the world, Annie Duke was a contestant on Donald Trump's *Celebrity Apprentice*, where she competed for charity against such luminaries as Joan Rivers, Dennis Rodman, and Clint Black. In short, poker's in. It's *all in*.

Nicknames such as The Kid, The Mouth, Poker Brat, Unabomber, and Una-bombshell have become the iconic aliases of the twenty-first century. And given the flourishing popularity of televised poker tournaments and

Internet access to live poker, we thus find at the tables the same timeless themes found in fiction—competition, rivalry, suspense, love, envy, trickery, loyalty, and victory. Even the legendary feat of William Tell is echoed in Chris Ferguson's uncanny ability to slice a piece of fruit in half with the toss of a card.

Throughout my years of playing poker, I've learned about cards and about life. As these stories remind us, playing is about the game, but it's also about the people. The players are poker's ace in the hole, as are the characters in *Texas Told'em.* "Beer, Poker, Pool" is made up almost exclusively of dialogue between two close friends. They banter, laugh, tease, and cajole each other, all the while betting on everything from a challenge at the pool table to whether or not they can tell the difference between two beers. In "O'Kaye in the Ninth," an afternoon two men spend at the race track shows more about the depth of their friendship than it does about betting the horses. I've played poker for many decades, and I treasure the friends I've made while sitting at the tables.

The sort of friendship we had in the old days was different from the kind in today's poker world. I started playing in small games at colleges then moved on to bigger games held in north Fort Worth, an area that could be a tough place because of the thieves, robbers, and worse, Some of the crowds were rough, but they made for some good poker games. I first met Sailor Roberts in Fort Worth, and we started traveling together. We were playing in bigger games around Texas when we hooked up with Amarillo Slim, and three of us became partners. We watched out for each other. We had to take chances with hijackers, cheaters, and the police, so we had to watch each others' backs.

Back then, we developed long-lasting friendships, and our word was our bond. When we borrowed money from each other or lost a bet we always paid when we said we would, even if it meant selling some of our assets. Sometimes, all you had was your word, so we gambled based on trust. Even today, once you lose your reputation, that's it. Nowadays, in the upper crust of gambling, we deal in such high stakes that we can't talk about it because people think we're lying. No one believes the big figures that go back and forth between us and the trust we have amongst ourselves. Real gamblers can be trusted, and trust leads to friendship.

Sentiments expressed between the characters in "O'Kaye in the Ninth" and "Joyriders" remind me of my friendship with the late Chip Reese, who just might have been the best poker player ever. We went in together in some far-fetched business ventures. But none were successful, so we always came back to poker. When we played in the same game, we didn't take winning or losing personally because we both knew the object of the game was to just win the other players' chips. And just like the friends in

"Beer, Poker, Pool," when we weren't playing poker together, we bet on almost anything.

One insight the stories in this book show is the inclination of gamblers to be superstitious. In "The Inevitable Big Win," the main character has a change of heart when she recalls fond memories of her grandmother, who "had always spoken of signs—emblems of good luck, symbols of bad luck." Likewise, a woman in "The Numbers Angel" uses numerology to place bets at the craps table. The young boy in "Wann's Gambler" sees his father as "after the fact" superstitious. He blames his losses on others for misplacing his lucky pen, putting a hat on the bed, or opening an umbrella.

I have known gamblers who wouldn't change their clothes when they were on a winning streak. Black cats, spilling salt, walking under ladders, etc., are supposed to be unlucky. I don't really believe in that stuff, but I must admit I've still got my lucky charm Casper, a card protector with a picture of Casper the Friendly Ghost. As a joke, I started asking Casper to bring me luck, and strangely enough, the things I asked for usually came to pass. When the media showed pictures of him at the poker table, he became a celebrity in his own right. I sold Casper to Howard Lederer, but on the condition that I got to keep him until I died. My daughter Pam used Casper in a World Poker Tour tournament. She won. After that, she held onto Casper and outlasted both me and my son Todd in five consecutive tournaments. The media zoomed in on her during these tournaments as she'd hold Casper and proclaim, "I'm the last Brunson standing!" She then asked on national television for Howard to let her keep Casper forever. After relentless pleading and much negotiation (after all, I'd given my word) I bought back the rights to Casper from Howard and kept him in the Brunson family.

It wasn't superstition but sentimentality that brought Casper home to stay. We wanted to keep Casper because his place in our lives had evolved from humorous superstition to heartfelt sentiment. That good luck charm became part of our family's story.

And that's what real gambling is all about. If you play enough over the years, the games become about the interesting people you meet, the exciting adventures you experience, and the valuable lessons you take from the table. Laurie Champion has collected in *Texas Told'em* the tales that make the best "gambling" stories. These stories have little to do with the cards we're dealt, the horse that wins, the dice we roll, or the Lotto ticket we choose. They're about winning, about losing, *and* about how you play the game.

That's Life, Folks

Sugar Britches

Andrew Geyer

Being a mailman sometimes put Corlis Holybee in delicate situations. Throughout the day, he intruded into the space of many creatures such as dogs, cats, and people. He'd always heard that dogs were the postman's biggest adversaries, but he soon found out people were the true menace. Some folks treated Corlis like their government-issued whipping boy, hurling obscenities at him for not delivering their expected checks. Others called the post office to complain about such untrue acts as Corlis stomping through their flowers or driving on their lawns with his mail truck. Still others called in to report having witnessed him sitting in his mail truck doing nothing for thirty wasted taxpayer-subsidized minutes—something Corlis liked to call *eating lunch*.

Being the seat—and by far the most populous town—of a brush-country county in Southwest Texas, and hence the station through which the mail for all the smaller towns in the county was processed, Jordan had a large and bustling post office, and an assortment of mail routes. All the mail routes had various pluses and minuses. Some were in-town, which involved a combination of driving and walking. Some were rural, which involved driving only. Despite the fact that the in-town routes forced Corlis to intrude into the space of the greatest number of people, which meant being subjected to the greatest amount of unearned harassment and unfounded complaints, it was the in-town routes Corlis liked best.

Truth be told, the delicate situations he sometimes found himself in as a result were about the only interesting things that ever happened in Jordan.

Sugar Britches would certainly fit into the interesting category.

On one of the in-town routes where Corlis carried mail lived a woman named Selma Berry. Some of the mailmen called her *Sugar Britches*. She weighed between three hundred and four hundred pounds and had a hard time getting around—so much so that she had to use a heavy duty scooter to leave the house.

Corlis would never forget the first time he'd been assigned the Sugar Britches route. It was his first day soloing as a mail carrier, and he'd been taking special care with every detail.

The first thing that had struck him funny, as he sorted the mail for his route, was that the only mail in one of the delivery bundles was flyers and letters from gambling casinos. There were a dozen of them, six flyers and six letters, all from casinos in Shreveport. He rubber-banded together flyers from the Eldorado Resort Casino, the Gold Strike, Hollywood, Lucky Jacks, Sam's Town, and the Silver Star, all of which promised discount rooms, player's club perks, and even free food and entertainment if Selma Berry would just grace their particular establishment with her presence. Not that Corlis would ever open anyone's mail. These flyers were printed on both sides, and as Corlis packed them into her delivery bundle with a half-dozen letters from the same casinos, it would've been impossible for him not to notice what they said.

The second thing that had struck Corlis funny was the mailbox itself. As he walked up the concrete ramp onto the front porch, he caught sight of what looked like a miniature slot machine on the wall next to the front door. The box was nickel-plated, with the house number—777—in shiny red letters where the spinning wheels would've been on a real one-armed bandit, and with a nickel-plated handle that Corlis had to pull to open. When he pulled the handle, the mailbox made a ringing sound as though Corlis had just hit a payout.

The ringing had scarcely ceased when Corlis heard a woman's voice from inside call out, "Could you bring my mail in to me?"

Which brought Corlis to the third thing that had struck him funny, although he guessed *bizarre* might be a better word for it. Being, he liked to think, a helpful person—and having taken note of the wheelchair ramp that led up onto the porch—Corlis was happy to oblige.

"Happy to oblige, ma'am," he said.

Besides being helpful, Corlis was curious to see in the flesh the owner of the slot-machine mailbox and the recipient of all those casino lures. He opened the screen door and stepped, mail in hand, into the smell of stale cigarettes and fried bacon. Once his eyes adjusted to the dim interior light, he noticed a profoundly obese woman, dressed in nothing but an overflowing and quite revealing black negligee, lying on a sagging couch.

"Come closer, darling," the woman said, "and allow me to show the depth of my gratitude."

Stunned as much by the idea of all that gratitude as by the sight of all that exposed flesh, Corlis froze. The only sounds in the room were the labored breathing of the woman he assumed was Selma Berry and the creaking of the couch as she reached a bloated hand in his direction.

"No thank you, ma'am," Corlis stammered finally, his polite Church of Christ upbringing coming to his rescue. Then his practical armor crewman training took over. He fired the mail in her direction and advanced to the rear, stumbling out the door and down the wheelchair ramp into the blinding Southwest Texas summer sun.

Despite a couple of wrong turns and a good bit of backtracking, Corlis somehow managed to make it through the rest of his route. The only other time he could remember his brain feeling this scrambled was after his tank had taken an artillery hit during Operation Desert Shield. Corlis would never forget the *spang* of hot metal ricocheting off the armor of his M1A1, or the bleary deaf-and-dazzled sight of the desert afterwards with all those oil wells on fire in the gathering darkness.

When Corlis finally pulled his mail truck back into its spot behind the post office, the postmaster was waiting for him in the parking lot.

"Corlis," the postmaster said, "is there anything you'd like to share with me?"

"Well, I—"

"Because there's a lady over on South Prospect Street who called in and said you tried to force yourself on her."

"Oh my God."

The postmaster was lean and grizzled-looking, the twice-decorated veteran of an infantry unit in the Vietnam War, and his grip felt firm and steady on Corlis's elbow as the older man led Corlis to the back door. When they stepped through into the sorting area, Corlis saw that all the other mailmen were waiting for him with huge grins on their faces.

"Bring my mail in to me," someone said in a wheezy falsetto.

Corlis felt his jaw drop.

"Come closer, darling," the postmaster said with a slow smile, "and allow me to show the depth of my gratitude."

"But," Corlis stammered, then stopped. "How—"

"We've all had a brush with Sugar Britches's gratitude," the postmaster said, and his smile turned into a belly laugh that spread to every mailman in the sorting area.

As the laughter died down, they led him around the corner into the postmaster's office where there was beer on ice. Then they all sat around and drank cold beer and told their own Sugar Britches stories. Apparently, Selma Berry and her see-through negligee had been a rite of postal passage for the past five years.

"Now that you've lost your Berry cherry," they said, "you'll be okay."

When the beer was gone and the crowd had dwindled down to just Corlis and the postmaster, the older man gave Corlis that slow smile again.

"We've got a running Texas hold'em tourney here in the sorting room on Sunday nights. Hundred dollar buy-in. Winner gets to choose his mail route for the week. Loser gets Sugar Britches. You interested?"

"Yes sir," Corlis said. "You bet."

The following week, Corlis was once again assigned the Sugar Britches route. And he was a hundred dollars poorer for the privilege. Corlis spent his driving time Monday morning trying to figure out how he'd managed to lose his buy-in so quickly—it had taken less than an hour—but his walking time was wholly devoted to coming up with a plan to avoid another glimpse of naked gratitude. Finally, as he approached 777 South Prospect Street, he stealthily crept along the hedge on the side of the yard. He slipped up the ramp and crossed the porch on tiptoes. Instead of pulling the handle on the slot machine mailbox, he slipped the rubber band holding together Sugar Britches's delivery bundle over the handle. Then he turned and ran.

This strategy got him through the rest of the week. But the following Monday found Corlis right back on the same route, down another hundred dollars. And just like the week before, he was mystified by the speed at which he'd lost. It seemed like all he ever managed to win was blinds, and it was a quick slide from short-stacked to pot-committed to done for the night.

He'd even managed to earn a nickname: *Short Stack*.

There was one interesting thing, though, that he had discovered as a result of his second hundred-dollar debacle. This Monday, just like last Monday, Sugar Britches's delivery bundle contained—in addition to all the usual enticements from Shreveport casinos—a check from PartyPoker.com. After rubber-banding the check in with Sugar Britches's mail, making good his escape once he'd slid the bundle onto the handle of her slot machine mailbox, and finishing the rest of his route, Corlis did a fast web search, logged onto PartyPoker.com, and checked out the site. Although he was too cautious to play online with real money, he spent a couple of hours on their free poker trainer. The next night he logged on again, and subsequently spent every evening that week sharpening his Texas hold'em skills. Then on Sunday night he walked into the sorting area with two hundred dollars in his pocket and some swagger in his step—with the result being that he managed to lose his buy-in and his rebuy in half the time it had taken him to lose just the buy-in the past two weeks.

Corlis also managed to earn himself a new nickname: *Dead Money*.

Seeing another payout check from PartyPoker.com in Sugar Britches's Monday delivery, Corlis resolved to double his practice time before the upcoming tourney. There wasn't much of anything else for Corlis to do in Jordan anyway. He lived with his mother, an early-onset Alzheimer's victim who spent most of her time watching reruns of crime dramas on cable TV. Truth be told, the Alzheimer's was almost a blessing for his mother, who hadn't done much of anything except go to church and watch crime drama reruns in the three months since Corlis's father died. Because she could never remember whodunit, no matter how many times she had seen a particular episode, she was never bored. Corlis, on the other hand, spent the majority of the time he wasn't actively caring for his mother surfing the web. This had become much more enjoyable since he'd gotten his job at the post office. He'd traded his old desktop computer for a state-of-the-art laptop with his first paycheck from the USPS, and purchased wireless networking hardware and software with his second. The wireless network had proved a particular blessing because it allowed him sit out on the front porch while he practiced his poker game.

He had just gone all in on a set of queens in a poker-trainer game of Texas hold'em when he caught sight of Sugar Britches at the Panther Mart across the street. There was a handicapped van that went around to the houses of the homebound and drove them to run their errands in town. Corlis's mother sometimes took the van to church. As he watched Sugar Britches—in an olive drab dress that looked like an Army tent—roll out the front door of the Panther Mart with a fistful of Lotto tickets and a carton of smokes, Corlis hit a fourth queen on the river. If he'd been playing for real money, he could've retired at twenty-nine. What he did instead was wait until the handicapped van drove off in the direction of the high school, and then log off and trot across the street to the Panther Mart to ask about Sugar Britches's gambling habits.

The cashier, a tattooed, pierced, and unwed mother of three named Rosemary—who was surprisingly attractive, and who Corlis had graduated with from Jordan High School eleven years before—was only too happy to fill Corlis in on the Lotto strategy of "Miss Selma." Apparently, the *Sugar Britches* nickname had not spread beyond the post office.

"Miss Selma," Rosemary said, "comes in every Tuesday and Friday and buys a hundred tickets for the next night's drawing. Half her numbers are pre-selected on the pick 6, and half of them are quick picks." Here Rosemary paused, looked across the beef jerky and the pre-paid phone cards on the counter, and met Corlis's eyes.

Despite his determination to get the low-down on Sugar Britches's gambling secrets, Corlis felt his heart skip a beat. Rosemary had captivating blue eyes, the color of robins' eggs. And although none of her kids were Corlis's, he'd been captivated by those robin's-egg eyes more than once.

"So she does everything the same way, every time?" Corlis asked, looking down at the beef jerky and trying to refocus on Sugar Britches.

"Well, not quite everything," Rosemary said. "Usually, Miss Selma pays for her numbers with winnings from the previous drawing. But she has hit a few of the bigger payouts, ones she had to go to Austin to collect on. Every time she does, Ms. Selma takes the Lotto money and heads to Shreveport to play poker."

This brought Corlis's eyes up off the beef jerky. "What does she say about playing poker?" he asked eagerly, gripping the counter with both hands as he connected the Shreveport lures, the Lotto tickets, and the payout checks from PartyPoker.com.

"Not much of anything about poker," Rosemary said. "But Ms. Selma always says the same thing when she hits a big payout."

"What's that?" Corlis asked, his grip on the counter white-knuckled now.

"'You have to bet big to win big, darling.'"

It was a revelation. Sunday night, after practicing five hours a day on the PartyPoker.com poker trainer for the remainder of the week, Corlis put five hundred dollars in his pocket and headed for the post office—and managed to go through the whole five hundred in about the same time it had taken him to go through a hundred in week one. It seemed like every time he went all-in, he went down on a runner; and every time he bluffed, everybody at the table called or raised.

Corlis also managed to earn a nickname that, for the first time, brought unfriendly snickers from the other mailmen: *Rebuy*.

But the postmaster said he felt so bad about Corlis losing all that money—even though the postmaster had taken the vast majority of it himself—he offered to send somebody else on the Sugar Britches route.

"No sir," Corlis said, thinking about the payout check Sugar Britches got every Monday. "I guess I'll take what I got coming."

The next morning Corlis was at work early, sorting mail. Sure enough, just like every other Monday morning, Sugar Britches had a check from PartyPoker.com. Corlis slipped the check into his pocket, then rubber-banded together the usual flyers from every Shreveport casino, and went about his route the same as always. But this time, after Corlis had slipped up the ramp and tiptoed across the porch, he pulled the handle on that one-armed bandit.

Almost before the ringing stopped, he heard a woman's voice call out from inside. "Could you bring my mail in to me?"

"Happy to oblige, ma'am," Corlis said.

He opened the screen door and stepped inside, smelling again the mix of stale cigarettes and fried bacon. Huge, pale white, naked beneath that same sheer black negligee, Sugar Britches stretched a bloated hand in Corlis's direction.

"Come closer, darling," she said, "and allow me to show the depth of my gratitude."

"I didn't come in for the gratitude," Corlis said. "And I'm not here just to bring in your mail. I'm here to ask you a question."

The couch groaned in protest as Sugar Britches levered herself into a sitting position. She narrowed her eyes at Corlis.

"All right, darling. Fire away."

Corlis pulled the PartyPoker.com check from his pocket and slipped it into Sugar Britches's outstretched hand. "How do you win?" he asked.

"No, I don't think so, darling." She set the check down on the end table next to the couch, then pulled a cigarette from a pack next to the check, lit up, and blew smoke in Corlis's direction. "I don't see a percentage in answering that. Of course, if you'd come a little closer, we might be able to work something out."

"I can't come any closer," Corlis said, trying not to think about what all that flesh was doing underneath that negligee every time Sugar Britches made a move. "Anyways, not for that."

"What else have you got to offer?" she asked, blowing smoke.

"If you'll answer that one question for me, I'll answer as many for you as you like."

"Done! Come back tonight after you finish your route."

Corlis went through the rest of his route feeling almost as scrambled as he had the first time he'd laid eyes on Sugar Britches. He parked the mail truck and headed home, fed is mother, got her in front of a *Law and Order* marathon on TBS, and then drove back across town to Sugar Britches's place on South Prospect.

It felt strange pulling up in front of her house instead of creeping along the hedge. It felt even stranger knocking on the screen door instead of pulling the handle on her slot machine.

"Come in, darling," he heard from inside before he'd even finished knocking. "And bring your question with you."

Corlis walked inside, smelling again stale cigarettes and fried bacon, and wondering whether he'd be having another encounter with that black negligee. Sure enough, once his eyes adjusted to the dim interior light, he saw Sugar Britches naked under her see-through nightie. This time, though, there was a card table in front of the couch she was reclining on, and a chair on the far side of the table.

"Have a seat, darling. Make yourself at home."

"Thank you, ma'am," Corlis said, sitting down in the chair and looking at everything in the room except the vast expanse of flesh across the table. He admired the expensive laptop computer on the table in front of him. He noticed the deck of cards with the GOLD STRIKE logo next to the laptop. He studied the photos on the wall of Sugar Britches, younger and thinner, standing in front of legendary casinos he'd heard of but never seen: Horse-shoe, Golden Nugget, Four Queens, Circus Circus, Flamingo, MGM. "So," he said, still not looking at her. "How do you win?"

"No, darling," Sugar Britches said, and laughed a little. He heard her light a cigarette, inhale, and blow smoke. "You first. But before we begin, please fetch me a Coke from the fridge. Feel free to get one for yourself."

"Yes, ma'am," Corlis said. He fetched the Cokes and opened Sugar Britches's can for her before he handed it across the table. "What do you want to know?"

"Do you have a girlfriend?"

"No," Corlis said.

"Have you ever had a girlfriend?"

"In high school."

Sugar Britches laughed again. "If you want to get details, darling, you're going to have to give details yourself."

Corlis took a long sip of Coke. "All right. I had a girlfriend in high school. We got engaged just before I enlisted in the Army. Even though the only thing I ever wanted to do was fly helicopters, I picked an armor MOS so I could be stationed in Texas when I finished training. She didn't want to be far from her folks. When I shipped out to Kuwait for Operation Desert Shield, she said we'd better put the engagement on hold. By the time I got back, she was married to somebody else. I've been with other women since, but I wouldn't call them girlfriends."

"What does that mean?"

"A dinner here, a couple of movies there. They were always a letdown. Except for Rosemary."

"Rosemary?" she asked.

"You know her. She's a cashier at the Panther Mart."

"I do indeed, darling. What a lovely girl! And always so sweet. What was that like? Rosemary, I mean."

"About like you and the mailmen, I expect," Corlis said. "That is, if any of them ever allow you to show the depth of your gratitude."

"Let me tell you something about those mailmen, darling." She took a deep drag and blew smoke all over Corlis. "They may laugh at me, but you'd be surprised at how many of them ring the bell on my slot machine when they're out on their routes."

"The postmaster?" Corlis asked.

"Yes."

"Did you teach him how to win?"

"Yes."

"Will you teach me?"

"That depends, darling, on the level of detail with which you answer the rest of my questions."

"Then let me save you some trouble. I grew up in Jordan. I've spent my whole life, minus an eight-year stint in the army, here. My dad had owned the Panther Mart, back when it just sold gas and groceries. I used to work there when I was growing up. I enlisted when he was forced to sell."

"Forced to? Why?"

"Because he refused to gamble. My father was a devout Church of Christ member, not one of those 'Do as I say, not as I do' types. So he refused to sell Lotto tickets. That meant he lost a lot of his trade to the station down the street. It was run by another Church of Christ member who not only sold Lotto tickets, but also sold beer on Sunday mornings in violation of the blue law."

"You don't go to church anymore, do you?"

"No."

"Neither do I, darling," she said, and blew smoke. "What does your father do now?"

"Not much of anything. He's dead. That's why I got out of the Army. I had to come back here and take care of my mother."

'What's the matter with your mother?"

"Alzheimer's."

"I'm sorry. What did you do in the Army?"

"Liberated a monarchy from a dictatorship, for one thing, riding across the desert in an M1A1 pumping DU ordnance into Iraqi tanks. I spent the rest of my time at Fort Bliss, making trips back and forth across West Texas to watch my father die. But it was the Army that helped me land the post office job. That and the Gulf War."

"What's it like to ride in a tank?"

"I assisted in target detection and identification. I operated the main gun controls and firing controls. In other words, I identified bogeys and blew the hell out of them."

"How did you feel about that?"

"It beat the hell out of changing my mother's diaper. Now it's your turn."

"Fair enough. But before we start, tell me about the tourneys at the post office."

Detail after humiliating detail, including the nicknames, Corlis filled her in on his miserable performance on Sunday nights—culminating in his five-hundred-dollar loss the night before.

"I can tell you this right now. You need to stop playing cards and start playing poker. The smarter you play, darling, the luckier you'll be."

"So how do I do that?"

"How much money did you bring?"

"None. I didn't figure I needed any."

"It's probably better that way." She took a chip rack from beneath the table and gave each of them a thousand dollars. Then she picked up the GOLD STRIKE deck and started dealing Texas hold'em. In less than fifteen minutes, she had all his chips. But she didn't say anything for a long time.

"So?" Corlis finally said.

"So you have a tell, darling. No, that's not exactly accurate. You have a lot of tells. I always know when you have a hand, and when you don't."

"How do I fix it?"

She pulled another cigarette from her pack, lit up, and blew smoke all over Corlis.

"Stop doing that," he said, "or I'm out of here."

"Tell me the truth. Do you want to become a gambler, darling? Or do you just want your money back?"

"My money, and my self-respect."

"That's good," she said, and blew smoke all over Corlis again. "You're not a gambler by nature."

"What does that mean?"

"That means I knew you wouldn't go anywhere if I blew smoke all over you again, darling. You'll have to go against your nature to win."

"Excuse me?"

"Whatever you'd usually do, do the opposite. I mean that quite literally. If you'd normally check, go all in. If you'd normally muck, bet. If you'd normally go all in, just check or call. If you'd usually sit and stare across the street pretending to look at your computer, get up and go talk to that girl."

"That's it? That's all I have to do?"

"No. Come back next Monday and let me know how you do this Sunday night."

Monday morning Corlis was at work early, sorting mail. Just like every other Monday, Sugar Britches had a check from PartyPoker.com. Corlis bundled the check in with the usual mailings from Shreveport. When he got to 777 South Prospect, he walked boldly across the front porch and pulled the handle on that one-armed bandit.

"Come in, darling. And bring my mail with you."

He opened the screen door and walked into the smell of stale cigarettes and fried bacon. Once his eyes adjusted to the dim interior light, he caught sight of Sugar Britches in her black negligee, sitting on the couch and leaning over her laptop computer.

"So?"

"So I won."

"And?"

"And here's your mail."

10

Corlis stepped in close and handed Sugar Britches her delivery bundle. "Thank you, darling."

"No, thank you," he said. "I've got my money back, and most of my self-respect. And I've retired from Texas hold'em."

"Hmm . . . So what will you do now?"

"Deliver mail. And spend more time across the street at the Panther Mart."

"Not a bad idea, darling. I rather like her."

"So do I."

Two Truths and a Lie

Michael Kardos

So in walks my composition teacher on day one wearing Levi's 501s and a tweed blazer. Blue collared shirt unbuttoned just enough for the orange N-C-E of his PRINCETON t-shirt to peek through. His hair is messy, intentionally so. I'm around guys quite a bit, what with my boyfriend being the president of Phi Delta Mu, and I know what real scruffiness is all about. This isn't it. He tosses his briefcase on the desk and studies us for a moment, running his fingers through his hair, and I want to pat him on the shoulder and tell him to drop the act. It's the 90s, not the 60s. This is no peace rally. All the contrived nonchalance in the world isn't going to change who he is, an adjunct instructor who needs to wear his credentials on his t-shirt, nor will it change who we are: the unimpressed, the hung-over, products of the public school system, dull and unmotivated as cows, heads down and grazing our way toward graduation from Jersey Central College.

He scribbles his name on the chalkboard—Buddy Munson—then asks us to move our chairs into a circle, because at some point someone must have told him that rows are for dictators, while in a circle everybody has an equal voice. This is obviously bullshit. You throw my family in a circle, my mother will still rule the roost. She'll still make my father feel like shit for losing all that money in Atlantic City, and she'll continue to remind me at every opportunity that my best and only hope is to marry Richy Rich. That's what she calls him, though his real name is John. Short for Jonathan Alexander Garwood III. John's father owns a chain of mattress stores, but he's an older man, past sixty, and John would have to commit some major felonies not to be running the family business in five years.

In order to become acquainted, Buddy has us play a game where we each have to tell two truths about ourselves and one lie. The class will guess which is the lie. By the end of the game, we're supposed to have bonded. As if before taking on such colossal matters as *Writing the Personal*

Narrative and *Understanding Academic Discourse*, it's vital to know that Sheila, for instance, got knocked up at prom, or rides a Harley.

I'm the only senior in a class of dopey freshman. For four years I've put off this requirement on account of how stupid it is. So now that I'm just nine credits shy of a degree in psychology, I've got to take a class aimed at teaching me how to write a college paper. Total waste of time, and all I can hope for is entertainment value. But the freshmen don't even understand how Buddy's game is meant to be played, that the idea is to tell *interesting* things about yourself. The first kid, a fat boy who squints, goes, "I'm left-handed. I'm from Cleveland. I wear contact lenses."

Buddy sighs. "So which do you suppose is the lie?" The game goes on, each kid telling truths that could be lies and lies that could be truths—*I'm majoring in business, I have two brothers, I play the tenor saxophone, my birthday is in June, I ate Chinese food last weekend*—but we're not learning a damn thing of substance about anyone.

When it gets to my turn, I tell three lies. I look around the circle of my classmates and say, "I've had three abortions. I stole my mother's wedding ring last summer to buy crystal meth. I have an ashtray fetish and love to lick out the ashes." I saw that in a documentary in my Abnormal Psych class.

It's a brilliant moment. The kids don't know what to say. I can almost hear their brains groaning to a start, like metal on metal. Buddy winks in my direction, so either he's hip to me or hitting on me, and frankly either one will make the semester a little livelier.

"Maybe you should just tell us," one of the girls says. Chickenshit.

I go, "Maybe you should guess." But when nobody does, I tell the class that the lie was having had three abortions. I fold my hands on my desk and smirk. "I've only had *two* abortions."

I could have gone with the ashtray licking. What matters is they believe the wedding ring story to be true. It'll keep class interesting. I like the idea of these kids checking their pockets and the zippers on their backpacks, counting and recounting the cash in their wallets.

When we're done with the game, class is nearly over. Before dismissing us, Buddy tells us to write a short story for next Monday. Any topic. Five pages. All the freshmen start moaning, but I'm thinking: piece of cake. I'll turn in the same story I wrote last year for my creative writing class. Father loses life savings at the blackjack table while devoted family thinks he's putting in overtime at the tire factory. Bankruptcy ensues. Family sells house, moves to a dreary rental on the business loop. Son shaves head, joins the Marines. Daughter foregoes dreams of a college that actually rejects some of its applicants. Begins dating fraternity brother, spends all her time at the frat house. Drinks too much beer and vodka one night, lands in the hospital, nearly dies.

"But what do we write about?" some girl asks.

Buddy says, "Only two stories have ever been written." Then he writes on the board:

1) A stranger comes to town

2) A person travels to a strange and unfamiliar place

"Every story," he says, "is some variation on these two themes." He nods like he's just said something important, but I'm thinking he's wrong. In my story—hell, in my life—where's the stranger? The only stranger I've met lately is him, the instructor, and he doesn't carry anywhere near the sense of menace or mystery that a word like *stranger* evokes. And as for an unfamiliar place, nothing is remotely unfamiliar about the damn Central College, where as a child I took ballet lessons, and piano lessons, and karate, a school that ever since I can remember has hocked itself on Sunday afternoon television:

> *Your own future, your own Central College,*
> *A place for fun, a place for knowledge.*

I'm convinced that Buddy is way off-base—only two stories, yeah right —until twenty minutes later when I arrive at the Phi Delta Mu house to find somebody I've never seen before up on a ladder, scrubbing the windows over the front door. He's older than I am, but not *old*. Buddy's age, maybe, and rail thin. His pants are tattered and too short, and his canvas sneakers are coming apart. Even though it's January in Jersey, the guy's face is shiny with sweat from working hard. His shirt could be wrung out.

As I come closer to the ladder his scrubbing speeds up (all men are show-offs), and some of his greasy sweat lands on the stoop beside me. Is this my stranger? It would figure. "Hey"—I look up and point at him—"watch where you're dripping."

He glances down and mutters, "Sorry." He's got green eyes and isn't bad looking in a stray-dog, underfed kind of way, and from the way he avoids my gaze, I believe he *is* sorry. As I leave him to go inside, he starts scrubbing like a madman.

In the frat house, John and his buddies have cleared out all the furniture and the foosball table and the projection TV from the common room and are setting up the boxing ring.

"Who's the stranger outside?" I ask.

"His name's Gunnipuddy," John says, tugging the ropes tight around the ring."

Well, that's a stupid name." Because I'd rather my stranger have a name like Hank or Rusty.

"Get used to it," he says. "He's our new maintenance man."

By maintenance man, he means janitor. He means toilet scrubber. Puke mopper. And it's about time. It's only been a week since the old maintenance man quit without warning to buy an RV and retire in Georgia, but the brothers aren't the sort to pitch in when it comes to cleaning, and the house is filthy even for itself.

My stranger doesn't know it yet because it's only his first day, but cleaning the windows is going to feel like a day off compared to cleaning the house after a Phi Delta Mu party. And in just two nights the frat house will be crammed with hundreds of drunk and stoned undergrads, each having paid twenty bucks to enter the boxing pool. Sixteen contestants—all frat brothers—will face off in a single-elimination tournament of one-round bouts. By the end of the night, one boxer will be named champion, whoever has bet on him will win half the cash, and the other half will go to the fraternity's chosen charity, breast cancer awareness.

Boxing Night might not seem like the wisest event for a fraternity that's perennially on the brink of losing its charter. But it's become a significant university tradition and the biggest fundraiser on Greek Street. Everybody knows that on the first Friday night of spring semester, you come to Phi Delta Mu and put down your twenty bucks and catch some live boxing action. And in nearly a decade, nobody has gotten too badly injured. Banged-up, sure. Bloodied, sure. But the fighters are all friends, more or less, and they all wear mouthpieces and headgear and groin protectors. Anyway, the guys love their cuts and bruises, because they are battle scars that can be shown off long after the event is over.

John is favored to win. His payout is a meager three-to-one. For weeks the guys have sat around at night, setting and re-setting odds. The same guys who flunked trig have suddenly become as skillful as actuaries, creating probability tables on their computers, arguing late into the night about setting lines and spreading risks. Most of the boxers come in at five-to-one, seven-to-one, ten-to-one. The long shot is a kid in my psych classes, Leon, who is short and bow-legged and possibly asthmatic, and who gets so excited when telling you about hallucinatory mushrooms that spit collects on his upper lip. Leon is paying fifty-to-one.

Dozens of students, maybe even hundreds of them, have already paid their twenty bucks. I've bet on John, of course, and will jump around like wild for him publicly, but I also placed twenty on Leon because, hell, I could use five hundred bucks.

At lunch, when I tell John about playing Two Truths and a Lie in my composition class, he doesn't get how funny it was. He swallows the last of his meatball sub and goes, "You seem pretty hung up on this teacher. Are you *into* this guy?"

Oh, and John can get jealous for no reason at all. Have I described

Buddy as attractive? As tempting? Just the opposite. He is the worst sort of dork—the sort that pretends not to be.

"Trust me," I tell him. "When I decide to make a man out of Buddy boy, you'll be the first to know."

A few laughs escape from the next table. We're in the tap room of Phi Delta Mu, and at noon the tables are occupied by big beefy guys eating big beefy lunches. John doesn't like the brothers knowing we have a relationship where I can bust his balls in good fun. Or maybe we don't actually have that sort of relationship. John has a lot going for him—amazing body, relief pitcher on the baseball team—but his sense of humor is lacking. I've explained this to my mother, but her sense of humor is lacking, too. Anyway, I've never minded a jealous boyfriend.

At least he's predictable. *That* I like. He'll put hot sauce on his three hardboiled eggs every day till he dies. You'll find him opening night at any new Steven Seagal movie, and on nights when we've been drinking, he'll always force me to down two tall glasses of water before going to bed. He'll rub my shoulders after I've taken a hard exam. He'll buy me a dozen red roses on Valentine's Day. And most importantly, he will *not* stupidly put at risk everything that is supposedly important to him. John and I aren't perfect together—maybe from time to time I ask myself if this is all there is—but at least I know what I'm dealing with.

John gets up from the table with his protein shake (he's off beer until after Boxing Night), goes over to the jukebox, and starts flipping through the song list. Screaming guitars begin to play. Metallica, I think. The jukebox is filled with songs that make you want to conquer weaker people. John stands there facing it for a moment, nodding in time with the beat. Then he's back at our table again, scooping up our drinks. "Come on."

I get up and follow him. "Where are we going?" I ask, though with a coy lilt because I know exactly where we're going. John leads me through the house, to the staircase. One of the brothers, coming down the stairs, goes, "Be careful, Garwood. That's bad luck before a fight."

"Fight isn't until Friday," John says, and punches the other guy on the shoulder as we pass.

As president of the fraternity, John has the largest bedroom, up on the third floor, overlooking the soccer fields. The first time he led me up here during a party was pretty exciting. It still is. Spring nights, the breeze blows in and chills our sweaty bodies, and mornings I wake up to the sweet, yeasty smell from the bread factory a mile away. Spring isn't for a few months yet, but this afternoon is warm enough to use John's clanky fan, which he keeps on a milk crate by the bed. It's a terrific bed, queen-sized mattress, a million springs, courtesy of his dad. John and I both have 1:30 classes, but we can fit a lot of activity into an hour.

* * *

After my dad lost all that money, the whole family started going to see Herve, our therapist. This was before I started college and decided to major in psychology and came to understand that Herve had been practicing his own brand of Client-Centered Therapy, originally developed by Carl Rogers in the 1950s. I didn't understand that by having us remove our shoes and by playing George Benson CDs in the background, Herve was creating a "growth-promoting climate," and that by parroting back everything we said with a voice so calm you wanted to elbow him in the teeth, he was showing respect for our feelings and expressing "unconditional positive regard." I also didn't know that Client-Centered Therapy was almost completely out of favor by then, except with therapists who were lazy or hippied-out or both. I just thought, considering what we were paying him, that he ought to do more than repeat all of our bullshit back to us.

That was on Monday nights. On Thursdays we went to a support group where other dads and moms whined about gambling away their life savings. We met in the private room at the rear of Ino's Pizza, so that Ino, first-generation American and Lotto addict, could dart back and forth between the meeting and the kitchen.

The room throbbed with fear and desperation. Voices quavered. Sobs arose from nowhere. They were a sorry lot, these people, and I felt that my own family was far superior to them. My dad wasn't violent or even an asshole. He had coached my softball team in the sixth through eighth grades. In high school, he had done my chemistry homework for me. He hadn't ever imposed a curfew on me or my brother, Paul. All he did wrong was lose a lot of money. We had to move out of the house. We had to sell a car and some jewelry. Still, aren't we taught that money isn't everything? That it's the root of all evil? So there you go, I remember thinking. My dad might have screwed up, but he had cleansed my family's souls in the process.

Mom didn't regard Dad as any soul-cleanser. Growing up, Mom would always laugh at Dad's corny puns. His goofy charm made her smile. Not anymore. Frown lines formed around her mouth. Her eyes darkened a shade. Then again, it was mostly her money that Dad had lost, inheritance from her parents.

I'm making it sound as if I was completely accepting of my dad's vice. Not so, apparently. Because when it was my turn to speak, I stood and told the group gathered at Ino's Pizza that I'd give ten dollars to whoever could guess what color panties I was wearing. "Come on, people," I said, walking around the room like I owned it. "What's the matter with you? I'm paying out ten bucks here. Where else are you going to get something for nothing?"

Dad sucked his teeth. Mom shot me a murderous glance. The air was heavy, I remember, everyone snickering and sighing and whatnot, though some of them, I'll bet, were itching to guess a color. My brother took me by the arm and led me outside behind Ino's. We lit up cigarettes, and I laughed until I cried, and Paul skipped the laughing part and went straight to crying, and he told me how lucky I was to be leaving for college in half a year, and I said I wasn't going anywhere, dummy, because there wasn't any money for that anymore, and he said that he was thinking of joining the Marines or something so that he could get out of the house, which he did.

* * *

I get home in the late afternoon as the sun is coming down over the Ford dealership across the street. I shove open the front door because it doesn't sit right in the door frame. Nothing in this rental house works the way it's supposed to. But when we moved, Mom and Dad said *no apartment*—that was where they drew the line—so here we are, the lone residence on the business loop. Two-bedroom house with cracked siding and rusty water and a heater that runs too hot or not at all. Shag rugs that reek of cat piss. Bathtub stained fungus-green. And our neighbors: two parking lots.

I dig around my bedroom closet for my box of old schoolwork. The story I wrote last year for my creative writing class was called "Betting It All." The facts I included were essentially true, but I skipped over the parts that made me look bad. For instance, I avoided everything about therapy and the support group. I included the part about my spending the night in the hospital, because my story needed a climax. But mainly it was just a lot of preachy nonsense about how Mom's behavior toward my dad was just as lousy, in its own way, as his own behavior had been, and how the daughter got psychologically screwed in the end, embittered and unable to trust another human being. Rereading it now, I know I won't hand it in again. The story is melodramatic and whiny. Undoubtedly it got an "A" not because the teacher found it insightful or clever or because of its refreshing turns of phrase, but because the punctuation and spelling checked out, which, at Central College, a place for fun and a place for knowledge, is the best that our teachers can hope for.

But also, I feel done with this particular family drama. Beyond it. Four years since we sold the house, and Mom hasn't eased up at all. Last month my dad fell on the ice in the parking lot at work, and ever since, Mom has been calling him Klutz and Screw-up. But if she wants to keep torturing him for past failures, and if he's okay with the arrangement, then who am I to pass judgment? In June I'll be done with Central College, and I swear you'll hear the sound of rubber meeting road. You'll see me not looking back. Maybe John will come with me wherever it is I go, but whenever I picture the open highway, my only companion is a box of mix tapes.

I decide to write a new story for Monday, one that looks to the future rather than the past, about a woman who starts a new life by making off with a stolen sports car, an Alfa Romeo spider convertible, and she drives west from Jersey to California, robbing banks and evading the law and breaking stereotypes and hearts.

I tear a blank sheet of paper out of my notebook and lean back in my chair, thinking about how my heroine will steal that car. When I hear my parents shove open the front door, I get up to say hello and maybe get some cookies from the pantry to help me to think better. Seeing them, I stop in my tracks.

I need to back up.

Ever since I was a kid, Dad worked in the accounting department at the tire factory. But after the whole losing-the-house incident, Mom quit her job in real estate and started working there, to—right in Dad's department, to keep an eye on him. (At the time, Herve suggested that maybe Mom had overstepped some boundary. Maybe she ought to trust Dad a little more than that. That was when we stopped seeing Herve.)

So when Dad fell on the ice last month outside the factory and broke his wrist, Mom told me—with characteristic empathy—that she'd witnessed firsthand his "latest display of grace." When they got home from the hospital, I found a magic marker in the kitchen drawer and signed my name, Alice, on the cast they'd put over his hand, and I drew a heart over the "i."

When I tried to hand Mom the marker, she said, "Forget it. I might write something I'll regret."

Cruel, but typical. What I'm getting at is that I thought my family had come to work as follows:

A) Four years ago, Dad lost a lot of money
B) Ever since, Mom has made Dad pay, which was unfair because
C) What was in the past was in the past

What I see in the doorway, however, changes everything. Mom is carrying Dad's suit jacket and white button-down shirt and tie. Dad's got on just his dress pants and a white undershirt. His right arm is still in a cast. But now his *left* arm—which for the past month he's been forced to drive with and eat with and do everything else with—now *it's* in a cast, too. The new cast goes up past his elbow and is hanging in a sling. For a second I think he really *is* a klutz. But the weather has been so warm, there isn't any ice to slip on. He's standing there with the strangest look on his face—an embarrassed grin, if I had to name it—when suddenly the answer comes to me, like it must for a detective or a code-breaker. Dad didn't fall again.

He never fell in the first place. Which means that I've completely missed D:

D) Daughter is an idiot

Seeing him standing there with two casts is almost comical. Almost. Because you get casts put on when your bones are broken, and if dad hasn't been breaking his own bones, then we've entered a world where people are breaking them for him. It's the world of mobster movies. This is hard for me to get my head around. My dad works in a tire factory. He wears a tie and sits at a computer all day long. He understands chemistry and cooks a good bacon and potato soup.

"I want the truth from you," I tell him. "So start talking."

Mom goes, "Take it easy on him, Al. Your father fell."

"He fell? I'd like to know how he fell!" I'm feeling hysterical. "Tell me exactly how he fell!"

"What do you mean, how? Your father fell down. And you're being very loud."

"*Tell me how!*" I scream. When my dad winces, I lower my voice and say to him, "Or maybe you'll tell me the truth. That somebody . . . *did* this to you."

We stand there for a minute while Dad decides what to do. Then he says, "This is part of life, too."

If his words were meant to be wise or somehow comforting, they aren't. "I'm going to be sick," I announce.

I'm not being dramatic. I run to the bathroom, kneel by the toilet, and get sick. When I feel like I won't puke anymore, I flush the toilet, then move the clothes that Mom has soaking in the sink over to the bathtub so I can rinse out my mouth and brush my teeth. My mom opens the door and comes into the bathroom.

"Are you all right?" she asks as I'm spitting toothpaste. As usual, shirts and pants and underwear are hanging up all over the bathroom, drying. For a while we had a clothes line out back, but people kept stealing our things.

"You lied to me," I tell her. "I thought you were being such an asshole."

"We didn't want you involved," she says.

"And *him*," I say, loud enough for my dad to hear. "He needs help. He needs a whole goddamn team."

"Actually," he calls from the other room, "I need money. Come here, honey, let me get you a glass of water."

But I don't want anything from anybody, so I leave the bathroom and walk straight out the front door and away from the house, which I immediately regret because it's gotten really cold outside. Sure enough, a few seconds later my dad is hurrying after me with my coat.

"How could you keep gambling after losing our house?" I ask him after putting the coat on. "What the hell were you thinking?"

I don't expect an answer. I don't get one. We walk in silence along the small perimeter of slushy dead grass bordering our rental property, and once we've completed a loop we head to one of the parking lots, which this time of day is mostly empty. I want my dad to cry. I'm not sure I've ever seen him cry before, and right now would be a good time. I want him to crave my pity, to need it as much as he needs to play craps or poker or bet on the Rangers or whatever he does.

Finally he stops walking and rests his right arm, heavy from the cast, on my shoulder. He's looking out across the road, where the lights from the car dealerships glow a misty orange. "Sometimes, honey, I have this fantasy where I win enough money to fix all the problems I've ever caused. I buy your mother an even bigger house than the one we had. A better house. And things are so good."

"Dad."

"Alice, listen to me a minute." Now he's looking at me. "We have a butler. A private chef. A three-car garage. And I buy you the nicest jewelry you ever saw. A pearl necklace and diamond earrings. And your brother, when he comes home on leave, there's a Porsche parked in the driveway waiting for him."

As he shares this fairy tale, it dawns on me how naïve I've been, thinking all this time that losing our stupid house was *the* event, *the* towering symbol of how out-of-hand things have gotten. Losing the house always felt like rock bottom. *My dad lost our house,* I told John on our second date, a fact that felt important and shocking when I said it. *My dad lost our house*, I told my friends at the moment when I most desired their deepest pity. But now it seems that losing the house was just a rung down a ladder to some subterranean place I've never even considered. There's still a wife to lose, isn't there? And friends. A career. Me and Paul. There's still money to be borrowed and lost, and then more money, and when he can't repay it there are still other bones to break. And after he's been humiliated and broken and crushed for long enough, after he's lost everything and *still* craves the action, there's a bed in the middle of the afternoon on which he can sit and put the end of a gun to his temple or in his mouth, and he can weigh the relief that would come from pulling the trigger against the image of me and Paul and Mom in a funeral home, looking at his closed casket because of what he's done to himself. And *that*—sitting on that bed and making that sort of decision—is what you call rock bottom. Until then, Dad isn't done yet. This thing hasn't run its course. Not by a long shot.

I also should have known from being a psych major, as well as a human being, that people don't change without really wanting to. And even if you do want to change, the odds are strongly against you. No addict worth a lick would ever bet on his own recovery. It's like Newton's Law, how once you're already in motion you tend to keep going the way you're going. Dad will always feel the tug of beating the odds, and John will always be the favorite, and people like my stranger Gunnipuddy will always be cleaning other people's toilets.

My dad is still going on and on about his stupid fantasy, so I tell him to shut up already. Then I ask, "Is your score settled now? Now that they've broken your arm?"

"Wrist, honey. Just the wrist." He's trying to be funny. When he sees it's not working, he lifts his arm off my shoulder and looks at me. "I'm afraid it doesn't work that way."

"You mean you still owe it?"

He nods.

"Can't Mom pay it?"

"She doesn't have that kind of cash."

"What kind of cash?"

He shrugs. "Fifteen thousand."

"Jesus, Dad, you're in some real trouble."

His laugh can probably be heard all the way across the parking lot. It's a dark, angry sound, unlike any I can remember my father making before.

* * *

Because it's the first week of classes and nobody's got any real work to do, practically the whole fraternity is hanging out in the common room. Guys are making use of the boxing ring, jumping around, tackling each other. A few have gloves on and are sparring. They all love it, you can tell. That boxing ring fulfills a thousand childhood fantasies of being strong, being the center of attention, being all-American. Every guy in the place seems to have invited his girlfriend over tonight, and you'd think it was a scheduled party, so many people are hanging out drinking and smoking cigarettes and shouting. Even Leon the long shot is in the ring. Getting used to the feel of things. He looks detached from the scene, though, as if watching wild animals on a nature show. Seeing me, he calls out, "Hey, Alice, how about you and me go a few rounds right now?"

He's kidding, but I'm tempted to take him up on it because I feel ready to punch somebody. "Where's John?"

"The gym. I swear, he's taking this too seriously." And then with an *oof!* Leon gets sacked to the mat by Roy, who played offensive line in high school and is twice Leon's size.

I go to the tap room, pour a beer, and take it upstairs to John's room.

I lie in his bed and think about my dad as he stood there in the doorway, wearing two casts, a pained and embarrassed grin on his face. I think about hunting down my brother, because this seems like the sort of crisis he ought to know about. But you can't just dial him up in East Timor. You have to send a letter, and he won't get it for weeks. So I focus on the more urgent matter of how the hell you get your hands on fifteen thousand dollars.

Even though John's family is rich, I can't ask him for that kind of money. I just can't. But a five-hundred-dollar bet on Leon at fifty-to-one, split evenly with the breast cancer people, would still give Dad close to what he needs. It's a gamble. And super ironic, gambling to save the gambler. Other thoughts swirl in my head, too, like the fact that my father is out of his fucking mind, and that even if he pays off this particular debt he still won't have learned his lesson. But it's all about priorities. And the first priority is to stop whoever keeps breaking my dad's bones from breaking any more of them.

When John gets home I put off what I know I have to do, and not until morning do I finally ask him for the money. It's hard, asking him, because I'm very particular about being independent and self-reliant, etc., and it's even harder telling him, when he asks what I need the cash for, that it isn't any of his business. I'm not trying to be rude or distant with John. But he isn't family, just my boyfriend. I'd always told him that my dad's gambling problems were ancient history. Now I feel ashamed not only for my dad, but for myself, for believing that a handful of sessions with Herve and a few months at Ino's Pizza magically cured him.

John is brushing his hair in front of the mirror. When I ask him to lend me five hundred dollars, he sits down on the bed. "You're pregnant," he says.

I deny it, and he doesn't press the matter. He just says okay and squeezes my shoulder and goes sort of pale. He assumes I'm pregnant and not telling him the truth, and that I'll deal with it on my own.

* * *

Leon never should have entered the match. He can't weigh more than 130 pounds, and you can tell from the spazzy way he plays pool or foosball that he was picked last for any number of teams growing up. So it's hardly a surprise when, just hours before the event is to begin, he chickens out.

He explains with great passion—tears are in his eyes—that he won't fight his own brothers, even for a cause as worthy as breast cancer awareness. Nothing to do with being afraid, he says. "Hell, I'll take a beating if that's what needs to happen. But the brother-against-brother thing. I just can't abide it, morally."

Nobody believes him for a second. Leon, like all the rest, was walking around campus all week with visions of being a champion. But after standing in the ring and watching the others spar, he has come to understand that his fifty-to-one odds are, if anything, extremely generous.

"People have already bet on you!" John tells him. "Lots of people. You can't drop out now."

"Sorry, guys," Leon says. "I'm out."

"Well, shit." John looks at me. "Where are we going to find another fifty-to-one shot?"

Dozens of heads swivel in unison toward the new maintenance man, who has just come around the corner into the common room holding a broom and dustpan.

"Forget it," says Rick, one of the odds-makers. "That man is no fifty-to-one shot."

"Hey, G.," John says, "how tall are you? Six feet?"

"Six one," Gunnipuddy says.

"What do you weigh? Two bills?"

"Less."

"Ever box before?"

"No."

"See?" John says to Rick. "Man's never boxed before." Then he explains to Gunnipuddy about Leon dropping out of the match. "We need a replacement. You're it."

Gunnipuddy looks at the ring again. "Nah, I don't think so. You guys look pretty serious about this, and I'm no fighter."

"Come on, big guy," Leon says, now that his replacement is in sight. "It's for charity. And it'd really be helping us out. It'd really show your commitment to—"

"No fucking way," I tell the room. "He said he doesn't want to fight." My own words surprise me, since I have more to gain than anybody by having Gunnipuddy take Leon's place. Betting on Leon, I was throwing my money away. At least Gunnipuddy might stand a chance. Still, I don't like them strong-arming him. These days, straight-up honesty is sitting a lot better with me than strong-armed manipulation. "Gunnipuddy, you don't have to do this. We'll figure something else out."

"Whoa, wait a minute, Alice—maybe he *wants* to fight," John says. "We use soft gloves." He tosses one over. Gunnipuddy catches it and presses it with his thumbs. "See? And we really need you."

Gunnipuddy slides his hand into the glove and punches his other palm a few times. "I won't be any good. I've only ever hit one guy before."

"Well, maybe it's time to hit another," John says. "Anyway, you don't have to be good. You're the long shot."

"And you say you need me to do this?"

"We do," John says. "The fraternity needs you. We're all on the same team here."

If I were Gunnipuddy I'd be pissed at having to listen to such horseshit. The man signed on for janitorial duty, not this. He takes the glove off his hand and tosses it back to John. "Okay."

Suddenly they're all clapping him on the back and making him feel like a million bucks. They put him up on the scale and ask him about himself so they can introduce him properly when it's his turn to fight.

Four hours later the common room is packed with people I've never seen before and people I see all the time, everybody shouting and drinking beer and spilling beer and dancing and hitting on one another and shoving one another and working themselves up for the event. I know John can take care of himself, but I'm worried about my long shot. I need him to win, but I also want him to win. He might be my stranger who waltzes in and saves my family without even knowing it, but from his perspective Phi Delta Mu is the strange place that he's come to visit. I'd like his story to include a victory like this one.

Everybody gathers around the ring and the music shuts off, and one of the brothers, dressed in a tux jacket, bow tie, and blue jeans, welcomes everybody to Boxing Night. He thanks everyone for their contribution to breast cancer awareness and promises a spectacular night of boxing.

And because of the seeding process, where the long shots meet the favorites in the first round, right off the bat Gunnipuddy gets matched up against the man most favored to win. John.

In this corner, the announcer is saying, wearing the brown shorts, hailing from right here in Breakneck Beach, weighing in at 179 pounds, is the challenger, Gunnipuddy. Who, by the way, is looking out at a sea of strangers, pale and afraid.

And in the other corner, wearing blue shorts, stands my boyfriend, whose eyes are as focused as when he's about to throw a pitch, whose protein shakes are looking like they've paid off, and who, it is absolutely clear, is about to pound the hell out of my poor stranger.

In the instant before the bell rings, I have a fantasy where Gunnipuddy wins round after round, defying the odds, culminating in my winning fifteen thousand dollars, which I use to bail my father out of his predicament. My father turns his life around, I graduate summa cum laude and get a high-paying job in California, my mother gets promoted to vice president, she and Dad buy the old house back, and my brother parleys his military career into a successful run in the state Senate. Every long shot comes in. A beautiful fantasy.

Then the bell rings, and people start cheering, and Gunnipuddy actually lands the first punch. There isn't much force behind it, but one of his long arms connects with John's chest. Then John slaughters him.

Gunnipuddy was right—he's no fighter. He arms hang at his sides, useless, and John is landing some fast and hard blows. To the body. To the head. Last year John couldn't enter Boxing Night because of a sprained ankle. Watching him now, I'm impressed with his strength. I really am. But it's also horrifying, watching this guy I've been sleeping with for two years hit another person so hard. "Fall down!" I'm shouting, but Gunnipuddy stands there, arms dangling, staggering but stupidly upright, and only when a punch to the chin sends him spinning does he land on the mat.

Soft padded gloves, my ass. I crawl into the ring and kneel over him. When I touch his face, his eyes open. The idiot is smiling up at me. It's unsettling—his lips are swollen and his eyes are unfocused, plus that head of his keeps bleeding. When I yell for somebody to call 911, it's like that dream when you're yelling something important but nobody can hear you. It's so loud in there that in the end I have to leave Gunnipuddy alone on the mat to call for help myself. The ambulance seems to take forever to arrive, which is just as well since the guys insist on moving Gunnipuddy outside and away from the hundreds of drunk, underage undergrads. So they half-carry, half-walk him out to the street, and tell the EMTs that they found him out here all smashed up. The EMTs look skeptical, but they strap him to a gurney and carry him away. I'm embarrassed to say, none of us rides with him. He is still a stranger to us.

I sleep in John's bed that night even though I'm angry at him. For what exactly, I'm not sure. Still, I face away from him. "I'm not a bully or anything," John tells me, rubbing my back. "It's boxing. You have to make the other guy go down." I don't say anything. I just lie there looking at the window, where outside it's dark. "We were wearing gloves," he says. His fingers feel soft on my skin. He could have just come from a spa. "Sometimes people get hurt even when you take precautions. It's boxing. Things happen."

* * *

In my dream, my parents are murdered and my brother refuses to fly home for the funeral. Then I sleep for a few hours without dreaming. When I awake again it's still very early, but lighter, and all I hear besides the birds outside is the unlikely sound of the downstairs bathroom being cleaned. The digital clock on John's night table reads 7:05 a.m. I slide out of bed and put on a pair of my shorts and a t-shirt that are on the floor, and I go downstairs. The boxing ring is still there, along with countless plastic cups and bottles on tables and the floor and on bookshelves and on the television and every available surface. The house smells sour but is absolutely still except for the sounds coming from the bathroom. I tap on the door and then walk in. Gunnipuddy, bless his heart, is mopping the tile floor.

The bathroom smells industrial and lemony. Gunnipuddy has on blue jeans, a white t-shirt, and his canvas sneakers. His right eye is swollen shut and purple, and there's a bandage taped to his forehead. When he sees me he smiles, then winces, then smiles again, then winces again. This could go on forever, so I say, "You should have slept in. I think the guys would understand."

He looks down and seems intent on getting the stain out of a particular tile, scrubbing back and forth, but I think it's just a flawed tile. "I couldn't sleep. How was the rest of Boxing Night?"

"You sort of put an end to it. If you want to know the truth, the guys were pretty mad at me for calling an ambulance." When Gunnipuddy looks confused, I explain, "They're afraid of getting booted off campus."

"Oh, sorry."

"Don't be. Does your head hurt?"

"Not really," he says. "I'm on some good medicine. I'm okay."

"How many stitches you got under there?"

"I don't know. A few. I keep thinking about last night."

"You're probably better off not thinking about it," I tell him. "I never saw anybody get beat up like that before. It was scary."

"No, not the fight," he says. "I was thinking about . . . I mean, the part where you. . . ."

I know that gaze. He's taken a beating, he's had stitches sewn into him, but I don't want him to think things that are untrue. So I shake my head. "Don't get any ideas. I didn't want you to get killed, is all. Jesus, don't think it meant anything."

Then, feeling like I've been too harsh on the poor sucker only hours after being beaten to a pulp, I make the ultimate sacrifice. I take a scrub brush out of a metal bucket, get down on my hands and knees, and start scrubbing the floor underneath the sinks. Holy shit, don't ever clean the floor of a men's room if you don't have to. Suddenly I understand the value of a college education, even from a lousy place like Central College. Anyway, I'm scrubbing away and trying to think of something to say that won't give Gunnipuddy the wrong idea. "Where did you work," I ask him, "before coming here?"

He seems to like that question, because he whistles and goes, "Oh, I've had lots of jobs. I left Breakneck Beach at fifteen and didn't come back until recently, so I've done about everything." He tells me about bussing tables in Cape May and cleaning office buildings in D.C., and a summer gig he had raking the beaches in Nags Head, North Carolina. "For a while I cleaned up waste sites. That wasn't such a good job, but it sure paid well. I got a bad cough in my chest and had to quit."

He stopped mopping the floor while he talked to me. Now that he's done talking, he starts mopping again.

"All your jobs involve cleaning up after other people. Do you love trash or something?"

He laughs. "No. But most people don't like it more than I don't like it, which means that there's usually a job for me when I need one."

He passes the mop several times over the world's most putrid section of floor tile. There's no word for the color.

"This place gets pretty disgusting," I tell him. "I guess you're finding that out."

He shrugs. "I like it here. I could stay here a while." It was as if he didn't remember that eight hours earlier he'd been beaten nearly unconscious.

"Even after what happened last night?"

His fingertips move instinctively to the bandage, then down again to the mop. "Look, this might sound dumb to someone like you, but I like how the guys were talking about how everybody was on the same team. You know?"

I *knew* he'd hooked into that line of bullshit, and I'm angry at the brothers for honing in on the guy's loneliness and using it against him. "They didn't mean it," I tell him. "Christ, I'm sorry to break this to you, but they just needed another boxer. You know that, don't you?"

He nods, thinking to himself. "Maybe."

"I mean, some of them aren't bad guys, but they aren't looking for new friends."

"But if I didn't fight, they'd have held it against me for as long as I worked here. That's no way to start a job. Especially a job with good pay, and room and board. I mean, I hope to stay here a long time, you know?"

I smile and say, "Well, I hope you stay a long time, too."

This felt like the right thing to say until the second it was out of my mouth. I immediately recognize it for the mistake it is. Gunnipuddy gives me that intense gaze again, and our nice conversation is derailed.

"You do?"

I shrug, trying to downplay my words. But the shrug feels staged. "Yeah, sure."

Well, no way should I have reaffirmed it. Because suddenly Gunnipuddy is kneeling beside me, right by the urinal, and—whammo!—kissing me on the mouth, and since I'm down on my haunches, I sort of tip over backward and then I'm flat on my ass, on a part of the floor that hasn't been cleaned yet. I get so mad I fling the scrubber at him, but I miss, and it skims across the tile floor and comes to rest by the heating vent.

"God dammit," I say. It actually wasn't a bad kiss. The angle was about right considering how quickly he moved in, and his breath was surprisingly minty. "Didn't I just tell you not to get any ideas?" I stand up. "Are you stupid or something?"

He goes, "Oh, man. I'm so sorry. Oh..." And he gets up and runs—literally runs—out of the bathroom. I follow him, but he's already out the frat's front door, running like police dogs are chasing him. Which makes me sad, because while he shouldn't have done what he did, it wasn't *that* big a deal. What if it was the boldest thing he's ever done? I wouldn't want him to think he should never take a chance or be spontaneous or whatever. For all I know, Gunnipuddy hasn't kissed many girls before, and now I've tainted the whole experience for him.

I hoped that would be the end of it, but a couple of hours later Gunnipuddy goes and, like an idiot, tells John. All I can figure is that in the story that Gunnipuddy tells himself, he's probably noble. As long as you're the hero of your own story, you might as well be a noble hero, right?

I was in John's room trying to phone my parents. Trying, but failing, because ever since my dream last night I've developed this crazy and irrational fear of calling home. But *is* it crazy? *Is* it irrational? I'm afraid of an unfamiliar voice answering the phone and giving me terrible news. I keep dialing six digits, then hanging up. Finally, I give up and head downstairs, and when I get to the TV room, there's John, his forearm up to Gunnipuddy's throat, saying, "I swear I'll make that other eye blacker than the first, you son of a bitch." That's where Gunnipuddy's nobility has gotten him.

"I stepped over the line," Gunnipuddy says. "I know that I did."

"You fucking leapt over it," John tells him, "and now you're gonna pay."

But John isn't a violent guy, just jealous, and overprotective, and sometimes quick to anger. He stares Gunnipuddy down for a long moment, then lowers his arm and storms off to the tap room, not even looking at me. But every other guy in the place sure is.

* * *

Monday morning Gunnipuddy packs his belongings into a U-haul. Nobody helps him. The brothers toss a football in the front yard and make him walk around them with his crates and boxes. It's another warm day for January, and mud is getting on his night table and bookshelf, which he drags across the lawn to the truck. To make a show of it, John fixes us stupid-looking drinks. He doesn't know how to mix drinks, so they've got a lot of competing liquors that taste like hell. We sit on the front porch in our coats and John clinks his glass against mine and says, "Cheers," then asks me if I'd like to go with him to Los Cabos for spring break. His treat. He's talking about romantic hikes and surfing lessons and a beachfront suite with a hot tub, and I have this fear that when we're there, he's going to propose.

I want to get in my car and drive away from John and Phi Delta Mu. I want to go home but I'm terrified of what I'll find there. So I sit and watch my stranger get into the U-haul, and I listen to John prattle on about humpback whale watching, and I down my disgusting drink, and I wish to God I were that woman in the stolen sports car heading west. The woman who beats all the odds, blocks every punch, fears nothing. Which reminds me that I never wrote the damn story that's due later today. I'll be handing in the old one after all.

As Gunnipuddy puts the truck into gear and the tires rub against the curb, I decide that if we're about to part forever, and if I'm his stranger just as he is mine, then it's my duty to exit his story with some style so that when he thinks about it from time to time, it won't be only bad memories. I set down my drink, run up to the truck, and motion for him to roll down the window.

"This dump is only a stopping point for a guy like you," I tell him.

"If you say so," Gunnipuddy says.

I step closer to the van, practically stick my head in the window, and lower my voice. "It was a good kiss, if you were wondering. I'm talking first rate."

Gunnipuddy can't help smiling a little at that.

"But John and I are planning to get married. Understand? That's why it could never work between us."

He glances at John and nods. "Okay."

I step away from the van, and he rolls up the window and drives away.

Does he find my words heartening? Comforting? Who the hell knows? But they are two truths and a lie, and they feel like the parting words of an important stranger. Words that a guy like Gunnipuddy, facing the odds, needs to hear.

Joyriders

Jodi Varon

"Judas Priest!" was how Louis's life-long friend, Sol Klein, had summed up the vandalism in the Mt. Nebo cemetery, where both of their wives were buried. Because the phrase ran the gamut of harassments, "Judas Priest!" was on Louis's lips as he let himself into his daughter's farmhouse with the spare key she kept hidden underneath the loose floorboard on her back porch. "Judas Priest," he said, "look at all the volcanoes."

Louis scanned calderas and cones in Shosha's living room, lava in primeval gushers, sparks like haywire fireworks, wild turkeys drowning in a mudslide along the Toutle River after Mt. St. Helens blew its top in 1980. Mt. Pinatubo, Mt. Etna, Kilauea in Hawaii with its lava fields creeping into neighborhood backyards, all of them were photographs his son-in-law Michael had taken of the world's natural disasters wreaking havoc on human populations.

If Michael wanted more current pictures of destruction, he could dig out the morning paper on almost any day to see all the unrehearsed catastrophes men heaped on top of one another. A volcano with its top blown off had predictions of magnitude, and its unlucky recipients had a tacit respect for the forces of democratic magma and mudslides. But the pressures of men were more insidious, their desecrations a vicious one-plus-one. Take Chaya Klein's busted headstone, for example, the angel with trumpet, head, and one wing missing, the Rosenburg mausoleum bashed with sledge hammers and splattered with red paint, the Lustig onyx tombstone broken and jagged as a saltine cracker snapped in two.

Louis looked out the window at his white van parked in the dust of Shosha's yard, all along the strip of driveway a line of pear and peach trees he'd said would never grow when Shosha and Michael had planted them fifteen years before. The peach boughs were propped with long strips of one by two's, notched and angled to support the weight of heavy, ripening fruit. Behind the pears, bantam hens clucked inside their pen—squawking, smelly, nasty things Louis was certain the coyotes would have made short shrift of, not to mention the snakes who liked their eggs. "You're crazy to live in this wasteland!" had been his shibboleth ever since she returned from a summer on a kibbutz in Israel, crazy to try her hand at horticulture. Now, all around her farmhouse, with its windbreak of poplars and choke-cherries, her fields of organic produce fed the locals, who shelled out more than a little pocket change for a bag of greens.

Seven steps and Louis could be out of his daughter's house undetected, pivot on his heels without compromise, without further messing up his daughter's life or sullying his already muddy reputation. But Louis couldn't leave. He'd given Sol his word. He lifted the photo on the coffee table and turned it over—Shosha, the boys, Michael, behind them the bull ring in Seville. The boys looked bored, Shosha looked like she was baking in the sun, and Michael had that wise-ass smirk Louis had never liked. He couldn't recall when they'd been in Spain, but from the size of his grandsons Ned and Jake, it hadn't been too long ago.

Louis berated himself for not keeping his mouth shut when Sol started moaning about the money to replace the angel on Chaya's headstone, but that look—Sol's droopy eyes with their puffy red circles underneath, the pouty lips that merged with the wattle underneath Sol's chin—when Louis suggested replacing Chaya's stone with something cheaper that he could afford—nice red granite with sand-blasted roses or a rhymed poem—a gorgon couldn't have done a better job in turning Louis's tongue to stone. And the swaying, and the way Sol took his fists and pressed his knuckles hard on top of his shiny bald head until red welts formed there like Miss America's tiara— Louis couldn't stand that, either. Besides, what difference could a little more groveling to his only daughter make? Louis had crawled to Shosha when his life fell apart after Evie's death. First he'd lost his life mate, then the business he'd owned with Sol, and now he couldn't even offer to give his daughter muslin curtains let alone his hallmark custom-made damascene drapes in return for her help.

It wasn't only his inability to give a gift that made Louis slink around when Shosha wasn't home. A warehouse of drapes—Italian cottons or Chinese silks—couldn't cover what Louis owed his daughter. Even in his di-minished world of tit-for-tat, what would one more bad decision matter to the captain of the Titanic? He could pretend that he and Sol were happy where they landed in their apartment after all the attorneys' fees were paid, that he liked driving the white company van with their logo painted over, that they relished living on thin air, sun, and coupon tuna, that he didn't really need his daughter or his grandsons, but even Louis Hazaz wasn't that skilled in self-deception. "Judas Priest!" could not cover, exactly, everything.

Not that Shosha didn't give willingly to her father, but when she gave, Louis forgot the "thank you," swore, or cuffed the boys too hard. After Shosha's last loan several months ago, while Michael was in Sicily photographing smoke and genuflecting people praying near Mt. Etna, Louis had walked out in the yard and shuffled in the gravel, smoked so fast he made his head spin, and stepped too close to the boys' old lookout tower, part of which he launched like a rocket from the tip of his shoe. Words were exchanged and a few regrettable threats were made, Shosha's farmhouse dubbed "a dump that some rich bastard was going to scrape off anyway."

To be honest, all Louis's visits boiled down to catastrophe and asking Shosha for a ten spot or a Franklin. How could he have promised Sol anything when Shosha was so intimately involved? She wouldn't even speak to him. Not even if his strategy began by recounting the razing of Mt. Nebo Cemetery and Chaya Klein's busted headstone could he make all the years of deception and neglect accumulated like clay on his soul dry, crack up, and fall away. What was Chaya to Shosha? Sol Klein's wife? Her deceased mother's closest friend? The first woman in her family to go to college, study Chemistry, work at Target in the pharmacy?

Louis had promised himself to look only in the tin bank on Shosha's mantle for spare change, but who was he kidding? He needed at least a grand. He lifted the tin bank, a narrow rectangle just a little wider than a pocket flask and opened the lid with the smooth edge of the key to his apartment. The tin still had a dent in its side from where Louis had thrown it when he was a younger man, wrenched from its spot in Evie's buffet drawer among all the other charity tins, the Tree Fund for Israel, Relief for Ethiopian Jews, charity for all the Russian *cheders* that never got built before Glasnost. This particular tin had been Evie's personal one for the circular driveway that he never built in front of their house. It used to make him so mad to think of that damn driveway tearing up the lawn. Shosha took the tin when they sorted Evie's things after her funeral two years ago, and Louis sometimes found a few good-sized bills in it, but lately, only quarters.

Evie's menorah sat on the mantle next to the tin bank, and Louis leaned up against the cold, stone mantle rim, everything going dull inside as he traced the menorah's curving silver branches with his finger. What an Eden life had been when Evie was alive. Who could have known she was the one, with her quiet, iron will, who kept everything in balance. He rubbed his fingertips on the tacky drops of colored wax. Blackened wicks twisted up from mounded dabs of wax inside the candle cups, the round base covered too with wax drippings and dust, untended since Louis's last visit to his daughter's house at Hanukkah eight months before.

There was a bay-colored Stetson like his son-in-law never wore on Shosha's bed, and on the easel in the corner a charcoal sketch of his daughter, though Michael was a film-and-shutter man. A pair of worn and cracked black cowboy boots were kicked off in the corner, their small size like nothing Michael could squeeze his Bozo flappers into. Louis sat down on the bed and ran his fingers over the top of his wavy hair. Come to think of it, Shosha hadn't mentioned Michael lately, and Louis couldn't pinpoint any news from Shosha about Michael's return from Sicily, not a date or an incident, nothing. How long had it been, a week, a month, she'd talked like a yes/no android in a voice purposely low so that he couldn't hear a word she'd said.

A wiry pluck, pluck, pluck kept time with the sweat rolling down his back along his spine, the cat clawing at the bedroom screen wanting to come inside. He stood and lunged, trying to swat the cat off the screen. His left leg buckled, and before he could grab for the edge of the dresser, he was down, flat on his back. An orb of white light filled his head and made him think he saw the purple robe of God. He rolled over onto his stomach and tried to push himself up with his palms flat on the floor, but all he got was handfuls of lint and strands of Shosha's long black hair. There was a dog-eared copy of *V.* near the edge of the bed, Shosha's black eyeglasses case, and underneath the bed frame a mound of balled up clothes.

Louis closed his eyes. Little sunbursts exploded behind his lids. He thought about what the doctor had told him, that he needed to calm down; he needed to breathe like he was smelling a field of daisies or he'd be pushing them up. He needed to eat more peas or lettuce or some damn thing. "Pushing up daisies" had been one of Evie's warnings, "you'll be sorry, Louie, when I'm pushing up daisies." Sorry for what? When he thought about his marriage, all he could summon was forty-five years of bliss peppered with minor bickering about how to raise Shosha. The money problems hadn't started until Evie was gone, thank God, but by the time of Evie's headstone's unveiling just before the first anniversary of her death, he and Sol were in over their heads. How could their small-time operation compete with Pottery Barn and Wal-Mart? As for his moral dissipation, he closed his eyes again and whispered a promise to get himself under control once he'd helped Sol to replace Chaya's headstone.

On the floor underneath the night stand, a familiar blue brocade pouch with black, twisted piping caught Louis's eye. He hauled himself onto his knees to reach for the pouch and put his hand through the grey tangle of a spider's web. The hair on his arms bristled, his fingers tingled, and he snatched for the pouch quickly, thinking to cheat the spider from its catch and save himself a bite. He felt around the pouch, Evie's pouch, hoping to feel the familiar sphere of Evie's ring inside. He'd paid two grand for it in 1967. It's just like Shosha, he thought, to leave her mother's treasure in a heap. He put the pouch in his pocket for safe-keeping and got back up onto his knees. Craning his neck, he cocked his head to tilt his good right ear up toward the ceiling. What was it—maybe a dirt bike off in the arroyo behind the farmhouse? One of his grandsons? The man with the Cinderella feet who was cuckolding his son-in-law?

* * *

Louis drove twice past Wedgle's Pawn Shop on Broadway, trying to decide whether to stop, weighing the possibilities of ever being able to redeem Evie's ring once he pawned it. Shosha didn't wear it, and from the measure of dust on the pouch, it had been underneath her nightstand for a long time.

The glare from the summer sun spread a puddle of mirage-water on the pavement, all the bumpers in front of him merged into a sheet of searing light. He hated being outside at this time of day, with the sun beating down directly on his head, though he'd just paid a visit to Evie's grave. Hers was one of the few stones in the cemetery's new section vandals hadn't toppled. He'd tried asking her for guidance or a sign that he could hock her ring, but just as he'd stooped to kiss the roses chiseled into the top edge of her stone, he saw Sol Klein shuffling toward him with a potted purple mum for Chaya's bare plot. Sol flicked his wrist at Louis and offered a string of "Judas Priests!" to the hot air. When Louis tried to pat him on the back, Sol turned his shoulder away. If he were going to channel Evie, now was not the time.

On the third trip around the block near Wedgle's Pawn Shop, Louis scraped his wheels against the curb and yanked on the emergency brake. He sat there staring at the ring, gold filigree with lovebirds and roses wound around a heavy gold band. His business had been worth a mint when he'd bought it.

At first Louis was confused when he walked into the store. "Mr. Hazaz!" a young woman said. He didn't recognize the short and wiry woman, even when she shook his hand. "Nikki," she reminded him, "Arkie's middle daughter. I'm the one who did the belly dance with Shosha at the prom that got us kicked out of school."

He looked at her again, her smooth dark skin, blue eyes, a long and pointed nose that must have been from her mother's side of the family. He tried not to stare at the cleavage above the scoop neck of her black cotton tee shirt. "Nikki?" he finally said, "Arkie Wedgle's little Nikki?" It hardly seemed possible that an old warthog like Arkie could have such a beautiful daughter. And Shosha? Belly dancing? Suspension? He didn't remember any suspension. All he remembered was a swim meet he caught hell for not attending. She must be confusing Shosha with someone else.

Awkward silence followed as Louis weighed whether to be stately and judicious as Shosha's father, pull out the ring to hock, look around, or simply revert to debonair banter. Suddenly, he felt happy with a few choices he could handle, rather than trying to interpret the range of Sol's gloomy "Judas Priests." Nikki straightened the silver and gold rings in the glass display underneath the cash register as she explained that Arkie only came down to the store on Saturdays, and they'd been having some problems lately. She didn't say what kind. She folded her arms over her chest and Louis inhaled like he was sniffing that field of daisies petal by petal, just as the doctor ordered. "Do you want to look around?" she said. "Are you looking for a radio or something?"

"Nah," Louis said. "But sure, I'll look around." He raised the black plastic lid on an old turntable and spun it. He felt Nikki's gaze on his back, and wondered if his white shirt had soaked through with sweat.

"How's she holding up, Mr. Hazaz?" Nikki finally asked. Her palms were pressed flat on the glass top of the cabinet, her red mouth turned serious and hard.

"Who?" Louis said.

"Shosha."

"Shosha?" He was startled. "Shosha? Shosha is a wall." Louis tried to read the look on Nikki's face, but he couldn't, quite. 'Holding up?' Holding up to what? The last time he'd talked to Shosha on the phone, she'd been distracted, jumpy, but he figured she was still angry that he'd wrecked the boys' tower along the gravel driveway and then called her place "a hovel." Maybe he'd said, "Worse than the ghetto." Admittedly, they had both lost their tempers, and he'd said growing lettuce for rich yuppies was like flushing her life down the toilet, but she'd provoked him by calling him a "two-bit bum." At Hanukkah they'd treated him like a stranger. No. Worse than a stranger. Louis put his chin on his chest and shook his head, looked at his watch and twisted the band around his wrist, remembering how they'd all stood around Shosha's living room holding cups of eggnog like Presbyterian ladies at a tea. There was no delicious fragrance of Evie's fried potato latkes coming from the kitchen, no applesauce, no Klezmer music blasting from the stereo in the background, no Evie singing off-key, just five grieving people shuffling their feet on the dirty beige carpet.

Nikki walked to the aisle of electronic equipment where Louis was standing and tapped him on the forearm. "Shosha said she might stop by this afternoon. Maybe around two. With Jeff." Louis puckered his lips and rocked slightly in his torso and shoulders, trying to demonstrate what he imagined as guarded approval, or at least tacit knowledge of this cowboy, Jeff. Jeff, he thought, a crumb could have a name like Jeff. A gigolo could have this name. Jeff.

"Do you want me to look at something you have to sell, Mr. Hazaz?"

"No." Louis shook his head. "No. Of course not." He made a little laugh that came out like a gasping snort. "I came in to shoot the breeze with Arkie." He flicked his hand backwards to demonstrate his nonchalance and fought the sudden pain from a knot in his gut. "I'm out for a joyride." He hesitated, then he stuttered. Did Nikki notice? He cleared his throat again. "I haven't seen your father for a while, so I stopped in to say hello." Louis strolled over to the pop machine as slowly as he could, as straight as his lower back would allow, with a slight swagger in his gait. He lifted the lid on the vintage red pop cooler chest, pumped in four quarters, and slid two small glass Coke bottles down the narrow metal column to the opening. The shop bell sounded as the bottle caps clinked into the receptacle, and Sol Klein walked through the doorway with a wet handkerchief sticking out of the top of his tennis visor.

"Louie!" Sol said as he limped past a shelf of western saddles. "Judas Priest!"

"A man your age shouldn't wear Bermuda shorts," Louis said, watching the blue veins pump around Sol's knobby knees.

"A man my age shouldn't be alive," Sol said. "What are you doing here, besides buying me a Coke?" Sol reached for one of the small bottles in Louis's hands, drops of water condensing on the outside of the clear glass.

"He's out for a joyride," Nikki said above the din of the fans mounted by thick wire hooks from the ceiling.

"Who are you?" Sol said.

"This is Arkie's little Nikki," Louis said. "His middle daughter. Shosha's belly dancing friend. What are *you* doing here?" He raised his voice then tried to disguise his shout by pretending to clear his throat.

"I asked you first." Sol puckered his lips and frowned, his wide brow wrinkled into a dozen folds that stopped in the middle of his crown. He drank the Coke, belched quietly out the side of his mouth, and handed the empty bottle to Louis.

"You going to sell something?" Louis asked.

"What have I got to sell?" Sol took off his glasses and wiped the lenses with his handkerchief. "I came to see Arkie. I'm meeting his beautiful daughter, Nikki. Who belly dances. You buy me a Coke. A million places to go in Denver, and we both end up here." Sol put his hands on the small of his back to help himself straighten up, then limped as he walked to the washroom at the rear of the store.

The buzzer sounded again and a man carrying a child's bicycle with pink plastic fringes on the handlebars walked into the pawn shop. His greasy blonde hair was pulled back into a rat-tail, and he looked around the store as though his neck were stiff, scanning the aisles for other customers, estimating Louis's age with a quick once-over head to toe.

"Put the bike over there." Nikki deepened her voice and pointed to the far corner of the store near the front window, where a row of boys' and girls' bikes stood on display.

The man tossed his head, "like a wild horse," Louis would later say. "I'll leave it here," he said, "by the door." He curled his lip in an attempt to smile, revealing broken and discolored teeth. He wore torn jeans and a bleached-out torn jean jacket, though it was hot outside. He put down the bike and put his right hand in his jacket pocket.

"It will be in the way by the door," Nikki said. "I said to put it over there." She spoke to the man firmly, with little tact, not yet angry, but getting there. She uncrossed her arms and went to stand behind the glass case that propped the store's cash register. The man didn't move.

"Go somewhere else," she said, turning the key on the cash register drawer and depositing it in her jeans pocket. "I'm closing early." The man hesitated. The toilet flushed in the back of the store.

"Judas Priest!" Sol shouted as he threw opened the lavatory door, "it's hotter than hell in there!"

The man looked at Sol's scrawny form hovering crow-like as he walked slowly down the aisle with a wet handkerchief tucked underneath his white tennis visor. He picked up the bicycle, turned, and walked out the door.

"Who was that putz?" Sol said.

"No one special," Nikki said. "Just another junkie who wanted a handout from the till."

Sol took his handkerchief and wiped it around his face. "Louie! Call the police on that piece of crap cell phone of yours and maybe they can catch the guy."

Nikki smoothed her hair back from her forehead and fastened it with an elastic band. She tried to smile. "Thanks, Mr. Klein, but I don't want the police here. They're more trouble than the junkies. We don't keep much money in the till. And don't tell my father," she said, waving her hand toward the door.

"You think men like that don't walk around with loaded guns? He could have shot you for a drawer full of change. Just like that." Sol snapped his fingers.

"The guy stole a kid's bike and wanted some cash." Nikki pursed her lips. "It's a pawn shop, Mr. Klein. Our customers aren't rocket scientists. And usually, they're cowards." Nikki punched numbers into her cell phone. With her dark hair pulled back into a ponytail, Louis could almost imagine Nikki as a teenaged girl, but her voice had an edge he'd learned to steer clear of. "I've told my dad a hundred times to sell this place. We don't need the trouble." She tilted her cell phone towards Louis. "Do you want to talk to Shosha? I'm going to close up, so I won't have a chance to see her here."

"No." Louis could feel pin-pricks around his lips. "And if you don't mind, Nikki, don't mention that I'm here." Sol raised his eyebrows. "And don't give me that look," Louis said to Sol, rubbing his hand around his face as if checking to make sure he still inhabited his familiar body. "I've got my reasons."

Louis sat in his van. He could feel the hard gold band of Evie's ring in his pocket pressed against his leg. He waved as Nikki got into her car and drove away. He watched Sol in his rear-view mirror, got out of his van and walked over to Sol's rolled down window.

"You had lunch?" Louis said.

"Why are you standing in the middle of Broadway like this? You haven't had enough brushes with catastrophe?"

"It's like a morgue on this street now that they blocked downtown for pedestrians. I could do a dance," Louis said.

"Don't do a dance in the street on my account," Sol said. "I don't want your death on my conscience." Sol looked straight ahead at the traffic light on the corner, then sat back in his car and flipped through the pages of the greyhound race form. "I don't want lunch. I want a headstone for Chaya. What kind of husband lets his wife's grave lay in a heap?" Sol put both of his hands at the twelve o'clock position on his steering wheel and pressed his head to his knuckles.

The curve of Sol's back moved slightly. Was he just breathing, or crying? Had Evie been hunched over in the driver's seat, Louis would have chucked her softly underneath the chin, and if she didn't push his hand away, he'd know she'd forgiven him for at least a fraction of his sins. But as it was, all Louis could do was to stand by the side of Sol's car, the hot sun reflecting off his door.

* * *

In the early evening, Louis stopped back at Shosha's farmhouse before he picked up Sol to take him to the greyhound racetrack. The driveway was still empty, but the front porch light was on. Jake and Ned were probably going to be out late. Evie had done the same for Shosha, turning on the porch light and the reading lamp next to the sofa in the living room to guide her daughter back into the safety of their dark house after she'd gone carousing with her friends. Louis walked around the house to the back porch to pick out the spare key, though the door to the mud room was un-locked. That was Shosha, asking for trouble when she didn't need it.

A picture on the refrigerator caught Louis's eye—Evie, propped up on pillows in her blue hospital gown. She tried to smile at the camera, but she looked so tired, so bothered by the tube of oxygen leading to her nostrils, the instruments and towers of fluid right by the bed. Louis was bent over her by the side of the bed, pecking her lightly on the cheek, and he remembered telling her he had her dancing shoes waiting for her in the van. He'd kept the doctor's prognosis to himself, and made Shosha promise to do the same. Almost to the day, Evie slipped away from them six months later.

The boys had been back too; there were dusty running shoes on the living room floor and empty Coke cans on the coffee table next to the photo of the family standing in front of the bull ring in Seville. Little bits of lettuce and a sliver of cheese sat on a chipped white plate. Cinderella's cowboy boots were gone, but the Stetson was still on Shosha's bed, looking comfortable and at home. It was clear Shosha's family was living quite well without him poking into their lives, that Shosha came and went and the boys roamed the arroyos near the house, that this Jeff didn't need his hat for his next cattle drive. The house had that kind of crushing silence of the recently occupied, a feeling that the essence of talk and laughter was still gathered up in all the vectors of air and held a gaiety unavailable to him. He could even smell their scents, the dusty, sweaty, but not unpleasant odor of the boys and Shosha's scent, a mix of fruity lotions and the henna she used to bring out the reds in her hair.

Louis took the blue brocade pouch from his pocket and turned it around and around in his hands. There was nothing of him in this house, just the one picture on the refrigerator, no knickknacks on the mantle, nothing except for the genes running through his daughter's and his grandsons' bodies. He opened and closed the black drawstring cord on the top of the blue pouch, making the fabric pucker like a pout. How could he fix something as big as the mess he'd made, without Evie there to guide him? He slipped her gold ring on the pointer of his left hand, but it got stuck at the second joint. A quick underhand toss, and the ring could be back under Shosha's nightstand again. He rubbed his hands slowly, massaging each knuckle, and turned Evie's ring around his finger, the band hard to turn. His fingers were swollen because he'd been retaining too much water, and even at the second joint, the band was hard to turn.

Louis played out a little fantasy in the silence of Shosha's room—Jake was in the bathroom and came out to find his zayde sitting on his mother's bed with a family heirloom in his big, hairy paws. Or Ned burst through the front door with a basketball tucked underneath his arm, his zayde on all fours routing around in the dust and cobwebs underneath his mother's bed. Or Jeff burst into the bedroom with his six-shooter drawn, wary because there was a white van he didn't recognize in the driveway. A meeting between a cuckolder and a thief. He did not conjure Shosha in his apparitions, because he couldn't face her, even in his imagination.

* * *

The two men sat in silence as Louis drove Sol out to the Cloverleaf Greyhound Club. There was nothing said about their running into each other at Arkie's, nothing about Shosha or Nikki or Shosha's marriage, nothing about dangerous men or the menace or deceit they were capable of. While Louis looked for a place to park the van, Sol complained about the heat and two or three things the president had said that day that irked him. Louis was thinking about how Nikki had calmly handled the junkie when Sol interrupted his thoughts to ask how it went with Shosha and the loan.

Louis rubbed a knot at the base of his neck as Sol opened and closed his fists. He looked at the frayed collar on Sol's polo shirt and remembered how Sol had liked to wear a suit and tie every day, gold cufflinks when they had been partners at the Mill End Drapery Shop. "She wasn't home," Louis said, "so I couldn't ask about the loan."

A jackrabbit dove into the tall brown ditch grass at the edge of the asphalt, kin to all those unnamed eyes he'd seen along the highway the many nights he and Sol drove home from the dog track. He'd been lucky never to have hit anything, though years ago when the four of them, Sol and Chaya, Louis and Evie were returning from the track, Sol had a collision on the road. The evening was still hot, Sinatra crooned on the car radio, and they had all the windows rolled down as they found their way on a back road to town. It was so dark the stars lit the sky like a ballpark, and a cool, sweet smell from the irrigated corn fields spread through the car. Louis held Evie's hand, and he slipped a heavy gold filigree ring with love-birds and roses next to her wedding band. She looked at it in the starlight, holding it close as Louis embraced her. "*Kine-ahora, kine-ahora,*" she whispered, until Sol turned around and said, "Hey, you love birds, keep it clean." That's when the antelope decided to run out on the road. Sol had quick reflexes in those days and swerved away, but he clipped the antelope just the same. Louis could even remember the thud of the animal hitting the bumper on the car. Sol pulled the car to the side of the road, and all of them had climbed out, but by the time they looked, the antelope had hobbled off on its three good legs. Louis told Evie the antelope would heal, though all of them knew what really happened to wounded animals in the wild. Evie and Chaya. Who would have thought the women would be the first to die? Who would have thought that he'd be left alone to try and console his daughter with gestures that amounted to so much nothing?

The third race had already been run by the time Louis and Sol found their favorite spot in the first level grandstand. Sol balanced his cardboard hot dog tray on his lap, pushing the relish back inside the bun with a flimsy plastic knife. When he took a bite, a coin of mustard splattered on his white polo shirt. "Judas Priest!" Sol said. Louis offered him a napkin, but Sol knocked it to the ground.

Sol made his way slowly up the bleacher steps to the men's room as Louis looked around in the crowd for some of their other cronies. It was a slow, weekday night, and men lay sprawled out around him leaning their backs on the bleacher above, their arms splayed, waiting for the breeze that would pick up by the fifth race at dusk. Louis sucked the salt from peanut shells as he added long shots to the headstone deficit. He watched a man with silver teeth studying the raceform; and another one, stocky, black hair crawling on his knuckles; and a man hunched over with a grease-stained ball cap pulled low over his eyes. Everyone in the crowd looked like a criminal. A short man with a bay colored Stetson moved down the bleacher steps, and Louis felt his heart pounding in his throat. The man scowled and squinted, and when he got closer, Louis could see scar tissue covered the man's left cheek as though he'd been caught in a fire. Thank God his cowboy boots were brown and large.

Maybe his ex-son-in-law was onto something with his interest in volcanoes and their unambiguous lava, ash that covers everyone and bakes whole cities like a plate. No one could out-run a belch of heat and smoke, not even the fleetest greyhound or the rabbits that they chased around the track. With volcanoes, there was less mess to clean up.

Sol limped back down with his weight on his left foot, still hurting where he'd kicked at a tree near Chaya's broken headstone. Louis gave Sol half his cherry fruit pie and watched Sol staring blankly as the greyhounds chased the mechanical rabbit around the dog track. "I've got nothing to bet with," Sol said, turning out the grey cloth of his pocket. "I bought Chaya mums this afternoon. Now I got three orange juice coupons and a rain-check for cream cheese."

Louis watched the dogs, not wanting to look at Sol's face or show him his own. Evie's ring was like a hot coal in his pocket. Now he knew what his father had meant when he'd said some things you do in life make you feel like crawling into a hole.

When the dogs rounded the last curve on the track, the three in the lead looked as though they might actually catch the mechanical rabbit. Louis and Sol had seen that happen once—the dogs went wild tearing their teeth into cloth, stuffing, ball-bearings, springs. The two friends had laughed while they tore up their tickets for that race, pounded each other on the back, even though both of them would have been winners if the dogs had merely run as they had been trained to do. Who could begrudge the dogs what they chased without catching night after night after night?

"We'll pay it off," Louis finally said. He double-checked the results of the race when the numbers flashed on the scoreboard, pocketing three tickets to cash in later.

Sol hunched over on the bench, forearms resting on his knees. He picked at the sugar glaze on his fruit pie. "I want another angel for the headstone," he said, taking the gold ring off his pinkie. "Like the one those bastards busted."

"Keep your ring," Louis said, closing his fist over Sol's hand. "We're not a couple of mavens, playing for coupons."

"You wouldn't pawn your own rings?" Sol looked quickly at Louis, then bowed his head and wiped his mouth with a handkerchief. "Louie." He shook his head. "I don't know what I say. Forgive me. This time, I feel it in my soul." Sol pursed his lips, swallowing his sour words. He squinted up at the scoreboard. "You check my tickets. I can't see. I need new glasses."

Louis pulled the winning tickets out of his pocket and put them in Sol's good fist. Sol turned his face away, nodding, holding on so tight the tickets got soft in his palm. Louis turned left and right, the din in the night air suddenly deafening, the announcer's voice melting into the buzz of cars from the freeway. A man standing a few feet away turned to look at them, two old men out enjoying the evening breeze without a care in the world.

Services Rendered

Terry Dalrymple

My conniving little psyche turned on me when I was thirty-seven, right on time according to touchy-feely books about mid-life crises. So I ended up staggering out of my own front door at midnight, yelling back to Marilyn, my wife, who was asleep and so couldn't hear me anyway, "Farewell, stranger. Nevermore shall I cleanse thy spit from a chrome faucet." I drove to our bank's all-night automatic teller and, after several attempts, managed to insert the card correctly and withdraw four hundred dollars, practically our whole life's savings. Then I drove until my bladder threatened to explode, which wasn't long. I skidded to a stop in front of a bar with no name just north of town.

In the bathroom, I held my breath so I wouldn't vomit from the stench as I stood in front of the urinal. On the wall just above the urinal, where I placed my hand to steady myself, I noticed a neatly penned message. I squinted to unblur it: Kayleen, Various Services Rendered, Hourly or Nightly. The careful printing, the business-like tone, and the lack of vulgarity amused me, and I considered the message as I staggered to a table. I ordered a rum-and-Coke, which the big-lipped, big-hipped waitress brought quickly.

Various services rendered. Services. That's what I needed, I thought. As near as I could recall, Marilyn and I hadn't rendered services to each other for at least the last three weeks. I sat there, a man about to lose a job he hated, with no prospects of finding anything better—or even equivalent. A man who had lost his identity. A man who had left his wife and children. A man who didn't know what he was doing, where he was going. Services, I thought. That's what I need. Services rendered.

I motioned for another drink and squinted around the room trying to spot a likely Kayleen in the candle-lit dimness. A peroxide blonde made ugly faces at some hairy ape with a cowboy hat who pawed at her shoulders and breasts; a fiftiesh looking woman blew cigarette smoke toward the water-stained ceiling, stood up, tried to re-inhale the smoke, then sat again and stared blankly at the slumped sleeping figure across from her; a young girl, perhaps nineteen, sat crying in a corner by herself. There were others. But none looked to me like a Kayleen rendered services hourly or nightly.

I watched the waitress as she carried my drink to me. Unattractive, she still seemed the most likely candidate. I studied her broad, hard face, the too-large curves her breasts made in her sleeveless V-necked blouse, the slight bulge of her stomach just above the waist of herLevis, her broad hips and thighs.

"Can you sit?" I asked as she set my drink down. She glanced around the room, shrugged, sat opposite me. "Your name wouldn't happen to be Kayleen, would it?"

She slid two fingers down the V of her blouse, brought a cigarette out between them. "It would."

I tried to smile. "Your name's on the bathroom wall."

She didn't smile. "I know."

"You know?"

"I put it there."

"You put it there?" She shrugged, lit her cigarette, stared at me apathetically. "Well then," I said, mildly stimulated by the question itself though not by her, "how much by the night?"

"Honey," she said and then paused to blow smoke in my face, "I wouldn't sell you five minutes." She stood up.

"Hey," I said, grabbing her hand. I forgot what I meant to say next. I just held her hand and looked up into her broad, expressionless face. She shook her head—pitifully, I think—extracted her hand from mine and sat down again.

"You're a mid-life crisis guy," she said. "I don't take to mid-life crisis guys."

"Not me," I said, wishing I could say it more assuredly.

I had first heard about and rejected the concept of mid-life crises when I was thirty-two, almost five years after Marilyn and I were married. We had just moved to Marilyn's home state of Nebraska, and it was there that a recently divorced high school sweetheart of hers passed one of those touchy-feely books about mid-life crises on to me with rave reviews. I learned from this book that roughly three quarters of married American males had such crises. Noting that the odds were against me, I considered having mine then and getting it over with. But I soon realized that no valid excuse existed. I had an adequate job teaching history at Mid-Plains Community College in North Platte; I had what our one-armed real estate agent called a "lovely little starter home" for which I had paid cash with an inheritance from my grandfather; I had a wife whom I still thought sexy after almost five years of marriage and one birth; I had a three-year-old son of superior intelligence and manners and, we had recently discovered, a second child in the making. So I ignored the odds, forgot about the crisis altogether.

Now, five years later, I sat drunk in a bar with no name in Texas, rejected by a homely waitress named Kayleen because she thought I was a mid-life crisis guy.

"Not me," I repeated, more for the sake of saying something than for the sake of meaning something.

She snorted, quietly, listlessly. "I can spot 'em twenty barstools away." She blew more smoke in my face, then looked around the room. Apparently satisfied that nobody needed her services, she leaned her elbow on the table and spoke, not as if she really cared about explaining, but as if she had nothing better to do. "My first two husbands was mid-life crisis guys on the rebound. Mel hung around about six months, then took off with this cheerleader from the high school and ended up selling hotdogs on the beach in California." She dragged on her cigarette, stared at me with only the slightest glimmer of interest. "You," she said, "I figure you're more like Haskel. He started sleeping with his ex-wife not three weeks after marrying me. I told him go to hell."

"Look," I said, resenting her classification of me with her ex-husbands, "I'm not asking you to marry me. I just want—"

She snorted again. "It's all the same. You guys are stupid and thoughtless as newborn babies." She stubbed her cigarette out, shook her head. "Mid-life crisis guys are losing hands."

I wasn't about to let her get away with that. I wasn't one of the ignorant slobs she must have known. Not me. I was different. My case was special. I emptied my glass in one slow gulp while I tried to think of a clever, biting reply. I set my glass on the table. "Not me," I said.

She stood up. "Go home, honey. That's a safer bet for both of us."

"Hey." She sighed, rolled her eyes as she looked back at me. "Not me," I said.

She put her hands on her broad hips, smirked. "So you're a gambler, huh?"

"Lady," I said and tilted my chair back on two legs. I almost tipped over, then righted the chair. "Lady, life is a gamble, and the only way to get ahead is . . . ." I lost the thought. Or maybe I never had it.

"Hang on." She walked to the bar and spoke quietly to the man behind it. She pointed at me and he nodded. She pointed to the short dark hallway that led to the bathrooms and he shook his head. She said something else to him. They both laughed. Still grinning, he rubbed his chin and stared across at me. When he looked back at her, he shrugged and nodded.

"Come on, honey," she said when she returned to my table. "We'll see what kind of gambler you are." She grasped my hand and literally jerked me out of my chair.

I staggered behind the waitress named Kayleen who rendered services hourly or nightly, weaving among the small round tables where men and women sat clutching their drinks, staring blankly at their empty glasses, staring blankly at each other, or pressing their foreheads against their table tops, sleeping, or pretending to sleep. I watched her broad hips, her fleshy buttocks, the tight Levis that hugged them, and I remembered Marilyn's tiny pantyhose, tried to remember the last time I had noticed her hips and buttocks. I couldn't remember but still felt sure they were slimmer, firmer, more attractive than those in front of me, those of the waitress named Kayleen.

We entered the short dark hallway and passed the bathroom doors where the caustic smell of urine burned my nostrils, caught in my throat. On the door at the end of the hallway someone with a shaky hand had written PRIVIT in red paint that had dripped from the bottoms of the letters so that the word resembled the title of some third-rate horror movie. She knocked twice, paused, then knocked a third time and turned the knob. Inside, the room was dark but for a single, dim, naked bulb hanging above a round table with a worn felt top. I gasped when the urine smell was flushed from my nose by the odor of the room: the thick, heavy odor of cheap liquor, cheap cologne, stale cigarette smoke, and animal sweat.

"I brought somebody," she said to a hulk sitting at the table in a ragged blue sweatshirt with the sleeves cut out. Then, to me, "That's Moose." He grinned hugely, stupidly, and even in the dim light I could see the dark brown tobacco stains on the few crooked teeth remaining in his yellow gums. To his right was an empty chair and next to it sat a flabby man in a light blue jogging suit. He turned toward me, smiled faintly, extended his hand, which felt thick and soft when I shook it briefly. His name was Clay, which I thought appropriate because, other than his light blue jogging suit and one huge gold ring set with five or six tiny diamonds, he was plain, nondescript, as featureless as an unmolded chunk of clay.

Kayleen pointed across the table from him, but before she could introduce the little man who sat there he whined, "Please, no names," and his long slender neck seemed to shrink until his chin rested between the lapels of his pin-striped suit coat. Walter, I thought, noting how incongruous his presence there was. Walter Mitty living out one of his daydreams.

"Dey calls me Smoke," said the black kid between Walter and Clay. He couldn't have been more than seventeen, a fact he apparently tried to hide with mirror-lensed sunglasses and a smoldering cigarette clenched between his front teeth. "What dey calls you?"

Maybe it was the dizzying atmosphere of the room. Maybe it was the dizzying effect of all the alcohol I had consumed in the past twelve hours or so. Or maybe it was my little traitor of a psyche playing yet another nasty trick. In any case, I couldn't think of my name. I hooked my thumbs in my belt, tried to sound as casual, cool, and cocky as Smoke. "Just call me Résumé," I said, squinting at my own distorted reflection in the curved lenses of his glasses.

Moose grinned his stupid grin; Walter kept his chin between his lapels; Smoke said, "Ray-zoo-may. Shi', man, dat a dumb damn name." He motioned for me to sit in the chair between Moose and Clay and began to shuffle the cards. "Fi' card draw what we play," he said between clenched teeth that held his cigarette. "Nothin' else. Deal rotates. Fi' dollar ante. No limit." He began to deal.

"Kayleen," I said, suddenly feeling nauseated as I watched Smoke's long black fingers smoothly flip the cards to each of us in turn.

"Just play, gambler." She shoved me into the empty chair. I looked up at her, perhaps pleadingly, noticed the way her thick red lips parted, the way her front teeth turned slightly in where they met. I remembered commenting, years before, on the sexy appeal of Marilyn's soft pink glossy lipstick. I wondered if she still wore it, realized I hadn't noticed anything about her makeup for years, felt the urge to jump up and run back to her where she lay sleeping in a house I couldn't afford, probably still unaware that I had left an hour or so before.

"Ante up," Smoke said, but I just sat staring at the door where Kayleen had exited. "Come on, Ray-zoo-may, shit or get off the pot, man."

Clay squeezed my knee under the table. "Go ahead," he said softly. "I'll help you along." I shuddered at his touch and the too gentle tone of his voice.

I turned toward the table, my thoughts shifting from Marilyn to my father.

"Shit or get off the pot," had been one of my father's favorite sayings, and he had ample opportunity to use it on me. He climbed telephone poles for a living in Saginaw, Michigan, and my mother cooked and cleaned so he would share that living with her. When I graduated from high school, I sat around for the better part of the summer listening to rock-and-roll records and wondering what I should do next. Finally, my father, who was always short on words, said, "Well?"

I turned the volume down on Chuck Berry so we could hear each other. "What should I do?"

"Shit or get off the pot," he said. I nodded, not because I knew what he meant, but because the phrase was so familiar. He held up his fist and flipped one finger up for each choice he listed: "College, work, or poverty in the streets."

I shrugged. "What should I do?"

"Poverty?" he said. I shook my head. "College?" I shook my head
"Work, then." I shrugged.

He got me a job in his friend's bowling ball factory, a job that paid fairly
well but that bored me more than sitting in my room listening to
rock-and-roll and wondering what I should do. That was his plan, I suspect, because after almost a year he stood before me in my bedroom again.

"College?" he said.

I started at the university in Ann Arbor the next September. Without
distinguishing myself, I made it to my junior year before the registrar sent
a letter requesting that I declare a major. "What do you think?" I asked my
roommate, a skinny biology major from Illinois.

He shrugged and looked up from a hugely fat textbook with a photo-
graph of a dissected frog on its cover. "You like history."

That was true. I had a good head for facts and used to store obscure
historical facts away to spout at parties, mainly in defense against the
masses who spouted sports trivia. So I chose history.

I finished my bachelor's degree and, for lack of any better ideas, stumbled through a masters and the better part of a doctorate. My problem continued to be one of synthesis: I never managed to see—in fact, it rarely
occurred to me to consider—the connections among facts, the relation-
ships, the continuity of history. Thus, when I got married I decided I had
a good excuse for postponing the dissertation, which would require a great
deal of synthesis, and getting a real job.

* * *

I lost consistently at poker as I slowly sobered up and tried to discover
the logic in a game that seemed to me entirely illogical, a game controlled
by chance alone, a game that denied and defied any semblance of reason.
Moose's betting was so inconsistent that I could make no sense of it at all,
but I soon realized that his inconsistency didn't derive from his stupidity.
On the contrary, he seemed to play according to a convoluted sort of logic
obscure to everyone but himself. I think it ran something like this: if your
betting bears absolutely no relation to your hand, or to the way you played
the previous hand, no one can ever figure out what you're up to. In short,
if your system makes absolutely no sense, it's a good system. Apparently
he was right, for although he would lose two or three hands in a row, he always managed to recoup his losses on one or two big-money hands.

Walter always folded at the first bet regardless of his cards. When he
folded, he laid his cards face up on the table, for which Smoke cursed him
furiously. Smoke never folded, always bet big and raised big, throwing his
money disdainfully into the pot and spitting oaths at one or another of us
or, more frequently, at all of us collectively. He lost most hands, but won

just enough to keep from going broke.

Clay was the big winner, the only one in the group to play precisely, cautiously, perfectly. He folded when he should and never lost a hand that he played. As we played, he spoke quietly to me, explaining what he knew about the game, about strategy, about odds. Smoke didn't like that much, but as long as Clay didn't advise me about a specific hard, no serious threats were made. Though I listened carefully, my biggest weakness was that I could never bring myself to fold before the draw or to remain pat with a good hand. Never satisfied with the deal, I'd draw to a rotten hand hoping to make it decent, or I'd split a good hand hoping to make it better. All to no avail. Even when I succeeded in improving my hand, someone else was more successful. Each time I lost, Clay patted my knee under the table, smiled benignly, and whispered an encouraging word or two. I wished that I could move to another chair.

Still queasy after the first two hands, I had passed my first turn to deal, but by the seventh hand, my turn again, I thought I might be ready to take my fate into my own hands. I shuffled clumsily and dealt slowly. I felt pleased with the two tens and two sevens I dealt myself. A good hand. Not great, not a guaranteed winner, but decent, not a guaranteed loser either. I felt pleased, that is, until Moose grinned his stupid grin and slammed his money onto the center of the table.

"Fifty bucks," he said, tobacco juice dribbling down a crease in his chin.

"That's all I've got," I said, hoping the big oaf would change his bet. He raised an empty Coors can to his lips, spit into it, grinned at me.

"If you need more," said Clay. He squeezed my knee and nodded to his sizable stack of bills. I looked at my cards and tried to remember what he had told me earlier. With two pair on the deal, the odds were about two to one that I had the best opening hand; but they were eleven to one that I wouldn't improve the hand on the draw. I had only fifty-two dollars and some change left. If I folded, I could salvage that pittance. Otherwise, I'd have to try for a better hand, which I probably wouldn't get, or I'd have to stick with my two pair, which probably wouldn't win. The story of my life: one losing hand after another.

When Marilyn and I married, my father pulled some very frayed strings with an ex-telephone pole climber turned college vice-president to secure me a one-year appointment at Macomb County Community College in Warren. That stretched into four consecutive one-year appointments before Marilyn got homesick and urged our move to Nebraska. Our time there was brief. At the end of my first year at Mid-Plains, I was fired for, they said, "failing to represent historical facts in such a manner that students might readily and logically assimilate them." Nebraska had had enough of me, and Marilyn had had enough of relatives visiting for days at a time to cure her of whatever sentimentality she once held for the state.

At that time, word was that only a few hundred positions existed in the nation for several thousands of history majors wanting them, so I felt lucky to land the job at Frischmuth Junior College in the Texas panhandle. Lucky, not happy. It was a tiny school, no more than five hundred students, founded in 1933 by an eccentric German immigrant who apparently got lost on his way to Fredericksburg or Boerne or New Braunfels, Texas, all some hundreds of miles south. Convinced that the United States, and Texas in particular, was hurtling into chaos, civil war, and ultimate self-destruction that would make the Nazis' occupation effortless, he insisted that the only way to avoid that fate was through strict indoctrination of future leaders, which could be effected only through higher education. Thus: Frischmuth Junior College, which had all but forgotten its long-dead founder and become a sort of dull vacation spot for area kids too dull to get into a larger school and too dull to understand that they shouldn't be in school at all.

To me, FJC seemed far from a winning hand, but I supposed it was better than no hand at all.

* * *

"Well," said Walter after wiping his palms several times on the lapels of his pin-striped jacket. "I'm afraid I'll have to fold."

Smoke snorted. "Shi', man, we knew dat. When ain't you fo'ded?" He threw his money into the pot without studying his cards. Walter laid his cards face up on the table and looked at Smoke, not fearfully, nor yet defiantly, but eagerly, excitedly, as if he couldn't wait for the verbal abuse we all knew was coming. It came. I didn't listen. I was thinking about my two pair; I was thinking about the waitress named Kayleen who rendered services; I was thinking about Marilyn and the boys.

Marilyn was probably still unaware that I had left. She was probably still sleeping, her lips puckered into the little pout that always formed as she slept, the pout that, early in our marriage, I used to think looked so kissable, the pout I used to study as I lay awake worrying about whether I'd go to sleep. I often ended up kissing that pout, and soon it would be kissing back, and soon Marilyn would be awake, and soon we'd be making love. I tried to remember the last time I had kissed her pout.

"What you eyeballin', turkey?" Smoke said to Clay, who had been waiting and watching while Smoke abused Walter. "I done played my money." He leaned threateningly toward Clay. "You sayin' I ain't?"

Clay looked away, said quietly to me, "I fold." I clutched my little wad of bills in my damp palm, studied my cards, wished I could ask Clay what to do. It was a familiar question, one I had often asked my father, my skinny biology-major roommate, my wife, even my chairman at Frischmuth Junior College.

I'd been teaching at FJC for five years and not liking it particularly well when one Friday afternoon my chairman, whom I also didn't like particularly well, asked to see me. He was late, as usual, but the department's secretary, an ancient crone who couldn't type and who applied lipstick so liberally that it always smeared her dentures, winked at me and whispered that she'd allow me to sit in his office while I waited. She even offered me coffee from his special pot and handed me a styrofoam cup with lipstick prints around the rim. I stood by his plate glass window sipping the bitter coffee from the one white spot on the cup's rim and watching students with snuff-stuffed lips and gimme caps wander in and out of the uniformly square buildings on an otherwise barren campus. I had just begun wondering what man in his right mind would want to teach there when my chairman scurried in, a short, bald man with a bushy beard that swallowed his face and an oversized down hunting vest that swallowed the rest of him.

He plopped into his chair and reached for a manila folder blotched with coffee stains. "I'm worried about you, Spinks."

I watched a boy kiss his girlfriend without first removing his snuff. I shuddered, circled the desk, and sat across from the beard and vest. "Worried about me?"

He made a sucking noise with lips I couldn't see, then said, "About whether you'll make first string."

"First string?"

"First string. It's a sports expression."

"I'm not big on sports."

"Everybody's big on sports."

"I'm not."

"You should be."

"I'm not. How about another expression?"

"You're fired. That clear enough?" I think he smiled, though I could never tell through his wad of black beard.

For lack of any better ideas, I laughed. "It's a joke, right?"

He made the sucking noise again, reached into his down vest for a cigarette. "Just barely." He lit the cigarette, half of it disappearing into his beard. "We're underfunded and overstaffed. Somebody's got to go. I'd say the odds were against you."

It was the first I'd heard of it. One side of my brain celebrated my potential excuse for leaving a place and a job I didn't like particularly well, but the other side had serious doubts about what I'd do next. I looked past him and out the plate glass window at the cud-sucking students, the square buildings, the flat landscape, the flat, dreary horizon. I sipped my coffee, forgetting to watch for the lipstick. "What'll I do?"

Without extracting it from his beard, he drew on his cigarette and blew smoke out his nose. "Probably not much." He flipped open the manila folder. "Look at yourself," he said and tapped the top sheet in the folder. I recognized my résumé, and beneath it the ten-year-old research paper I had sent when I first applied for the job.

Look, you little smartass, I wanted to say, *that's not me. I'm a lot more than a manila folder with a résumé and a ten-year-old research paper.*

"Look at myself?" I said.

He continued tapping the résumé. "No Ph.D., no publications, no committee work, no—"

"That's never mattered."

"It does now."

I shook my head, tried to see if he smiled, tried to see his eyes through the smoke that trailed into them from his cigarette. "Do you enjoy this?"

"It's my job."

I tried to set my coffee down and stand up at the same time, spilled the coffee, watched it puddle on his desk, one thin rivulet of it flowing onto my résumé. "Look, you little smartass," I said and knew I'd regret it later, "that's not me." I jammed my finger toward the folder, glared at it rather than at him.

"Okay," he said quietly, and it was a question: what are you, who are you, if not this?

I stared at the liquid brown streak across the top of the page, tried to remember what the page said. Name, address, one wife, two kids, B.A., A.B.D., three previous jobs. The end. My life reduced to the size of a sheet of typing paper and it fit—with wide margins. I felt dizzy.

"My God!" I said and stumbled out of his office, leaving myself behind on his desk.

* * *

"What it is, Ray-zoo-may?" Smoke said as I sat clutching my little wad of bills and wondering what to do. "Make up you damn mind."

I studied my hand. Ten of hearts, ten of diamonds, seven of hearts, seven of clubs, six of hearts. With two people out and three remaining, the two pair had a fair chance. But how could I be sure? I knew what cards I held, but I had no clue to their relationship with what others held or what remained in the deck. The only sure thing was to fold. Yet it seemed to me a mistake to give up on a relatively decent hand when I was already so far in debt, so deeply committed as it were. I laid fifty dollars on the table, the bills crumpled and wet from being clutched so tightly in my hand.

I remembered the damp bills I had handed the clerk years before when

I paid for our marriage license. The clerk had looked at the soggy bills, frowned, looked at me, asked, "Are you sure you want to go through with this?" I had looked at Marilyn. She had nodded, kissed me. I had nodded to the clerk.

Moose drew one card, which I assumed meant he, too, had two pair. Smoke drew two, a bad sign since it might mean he held three-of-a-kind; then again, he might be pulling hard   for a straight, or even a flush. I stared at my cards, concentrated so hard that I couldn't hear Smoke even though I knew he cursed me to hurry. Moose might have started with two pair; he might have drawn a full house; his cards might have been higher than mine so that even if I pitched my six and drew a ten or a seven I'd still be beat by his full house. Smoke might have started with three-of-a-kind and drawn a fourth, or he might have pulled the straight or the flush. In any of those cases—and several more—my two pair were losers. The safest thing was to pitch the six and hope for a full house. But it was possible—just possible—that I could split the two pair, draw to a straight, or a flush in hearts, or even a straight flush, virtually unbeatable. What should I do? I felt confused, terrified, just as I had felt when I left my chairman's office and rushed home to Marilyn.

"Marilyn," I had hollered as soon as I shoved open the door to the house I couldn't afford. "Marilyn, I need you." I stood in the entry hall, suddenly unsure whether I had entered the right house. I tried to remember why we had gotten the awful abstract painting that hung there, when we had begun repainting the walls, why we hadn't finished, where our bedroom was.

"Of course you do, sweetheart," said Marilyn, walking into the entry hall and kissing me. "And I need you. Would you like a drink?" She was in the kitchen before I could answer.

I found the boys' bedroom where I thought our bedroom was, ours where I thought theirs was. "You're not listening to me," I hollered. I threw my briefcase onto the bed, only the bed wasn't where I thought it was. My briefcase knocked over a floor lamp, bent its shade, smashed its bulb. "I'm confused!"

"Try not to be," she hollered back. "The Wehners' dinner party is tonight." I found the closet, threw my jacket in, bumped into my desk as I turned away from the closet. I suddenly felt more frantic than ever, began shuffling through the stacks of papers on my desk, dropping some on the floor, shoving others across the desk. "The boys will be with the Hammers all night. Can you be ready in an hour?" Marilyn said, stopping outside the bedroom door. I dug frantically through the papers, found two folders, dumped their contents out. "What on earth are you doing, Donald?"

"Looking for myself."

She chuckled. "Well you're not in there."

"My résumé, Marilyn. Where's the master copy?"

"That old thing? Donald, I just cleaned your desk. Look what you're doing."

"Where's my résumé?"

"It's there."

"It's not here."

"Oops," she said and headed for the kitchen again. "Maybe I threw it out."

"You threw out my résumé!"

"You can write another one, sweetheart."

"I can't write another one. I don't know who I am!"

"Of course you do," she hollered from the kitchen. "You're drink's ready."

I drank three rum-and-Cokes while she changed for the Wehners' dinner party. I didn't change. I just sat and drank, wondering if I should tell her I was probably losing my job, wondering what I would do, wondering how she could throw out my résumé, which was me.

The party was terrific, as usual, with more people than the table could seat, more food than the people could eat, and more wine than the whole neighborhood could drink in a week. Somehow, everyone squeezed in at the table; the leftovers were whisked off to a fat dog named Liza; and I drank the wine. Afterwards, at home, in the bathroom, my vicious little psyche struck its decisive blow.

A double squirt of toothpaste on my brush, I scrubbed vigorously at the thick, sour taste of too much wine. While I brushed, I studied the mirror and tried to remember if I had ever before noticed the minuscule brown dot in my otherwise blue left eye. I didn't think I had. When I leaned over the sink to rinse my mouth, my eyes, minuscule brown dot and all, immediately focused on Marilyn's unmistakable mark: a white, bubbly blob of toothpaste spit puddled in the center of the chrome faucet and oozing grotesquely over its edges.

I had asked her time and again to watch where she spit. She always called me silly and promised to clean it in the morning. And she would have cleaned it this time, I was sure, but there was something about bubbly white toothpaste spit on our chrome faucet in a house I couldn't afford that threw my already ragged sensibilities into chaos. I splashed a handful of water over it, enough to wash away the blob but not the slimy film it left behind. The slimy film took a swipe of the hand, which made me cringe and reminded me of Vienna sausages. Marilyn always kept them in the refrigerator so that the juice they were packed in congealed into something like thick snot. I hated them that way. I hated her keeping them that way. I hated her spitting on the faucet. I hated her throwing out my résumé. My

God, I suddenly thought, I hated her.

I turned away from the sink, the thought, or perhaps the wine, making me stumble forward. My shins banged against the bathtub. I tried to wipe the cobwebs out of my face. But they weren't cobwebs; they were pantyhose, the tiniest pantyhose I could remember seeing, like a doll's. I wondered why our daughter's pantyhose hung in our bathroom, and then, remembering we had no daughter, I gasped, momentarily couldn't breathe. Oh, God, please no, please not one of the boys.

No, of course not. Jason was only five, and David, eight, had already discovered the worlds of *Playboy* and *Penthouse*, a stack of which Marilyn had recently found underneath his collection of Superman comics in his closet.

Marilyn's pantyhose, then. I pulled at the waistband, tried to gauge how wide it stretched. I pulled at one knee, then a foot. I dropped the pantyhose. I didn't hate Marilyn; I just didn't know her. Jesus, I didn't even know what size pantyhose she wore. How many more things, how many more important things did I not know about her? I tried to make a mental list of what I knew, but all I could remember was that she threw out my résumé, spit on the faucet, and refrigerated Vienna sausages.

I didn't know my wife, and what I did know I didn't like. It shouldn't be a surprise, I thought. After all, with billions of people in the world what were the odds that a man and a woman would find their right partners the first time around? The chances were slim, even with a long engagement, which we had not had.

We had met at a Save-the-Whales demonstration on campus in Ann Arbor. That was the tail end of the sixties. Wishing to identify with my generation, but terrified of confrontation, I had picked a cause that seemed to have the flavor of the back-to-nature-and-peace-for-all-humankind-and-animals-too recipe for salvation that my peers espoused; and yet a cause that also seemed innocuous enough that it would attract little opposition. Unfortunately, someone became inspired enough to locate a half-butchered whale—God only knows where they found it—and haul it via eighteen wheeler to the center of campus, where it was dumped. It stank something awful. Our spokesmen refused to move it. The authorities were not pleased. A ruckus began. I tucked my *Encyclopedia of Little Known Civil War Soldiers* under my arm, clutched the Coke can I had filled with beer before arriving, and tried to escape. That's when Marilyn and I ran into each other—literally. I spilled my beer on her blouse; she spilled her Coke on my shirt. I offered to buy her another Coke; she offered to wash my shirt. I asked her out; she accepted. The next thing we knew, we were claiming to be in love.

I stared down at those tiny pantyhose. I didn't know my wife. *What should I do?* I wondered, and my little imp of a psyche replied, *Leave her, leave her!* And so I stumbled out the door hollering, "Farewell, stranger. Nevermore shall I cleanse thy spit from a chrome faucet."

* * *

"I'm talkin' to you, sucker!" Smoke said, leaning across and banging his fist on the table in front of me. "Play 'em or lay 'em, man. I'm tired of waitin'."

I focused again on my cards, on all the possibilities there. As I considered each possibility, I wished more and more that I could ask someone what to do—my father, my skinny biology major roommate, my wife, my chairman, even my dastardly little psyche. But most especially I wished I could ask Clay, who seemed to know this game so well. But, of course, that would be bad form, and the others probably wouldn't allow it anyway. For the first time in my life I was faced with making my own conscious decision. I felt terrified. And yet I also felt a certain thrill at suddenly understanding a game that had baffled me all evening. Play them or lay them, Smoke had said, and he was right. The odds were everything, and they were nothing. The important thing wasn't *what* decision I made as much as it was *that* I made a decision fully aware of the odds I faced, and then stuck with it until pure chance proved me right or wrong. I couldn't make myself draw a better hand, nor could I make my hand a winner if it were a loser; but I could make a decision and then follow through with it as if I knew it was the best decision.

All night I'd been dumping one hand for another and consistently losing. Here was the hand I had dealt myself, the tens, the sevens, the useless six. It wasn't a bad hand. Whether I were to win or lose, why not win or lose with what I knew I had rather than with what I might draw. And if I claimed to be pat, maybe I could even bluff one or both of the others into folding.

I looked at each of them in turn, calmly, steadily. "I'll keep these."

Clay grabbed my knee. "Are you sure?"

I looked at my cards, nodded.

"Fifty bucks," Moose shouted.

"And fifty mo'," said Smoke. He tossed a hundred dollars into the pot, leaned back in his chair, flipped his cigarette onto the concrete floor without bothering to crush it out.

If I stayed and Moose stayed, the pot would be four hundred and seventy-five dollars, counting antes. Seventy-five more than I had started with minus the hundred I'd have to borrow from Clay would leave me only twenty-five dollars down for the night. "I've gone this far," I said and looked at Clay. He placed the money in the pot for me. Moose called, too.

"Hell, man, you white son'bitches," said Smoke. He had drawn for a straight and ended up with only a pair.

I laid my damp cards on the table. Moose grinned, dribbled tobacco juice, showed his two pair: fives and threes.

Maybe I was in shock. Maybe I was still a little drunk. Maybe my blithering psyche was making one last effort to maintain its mad reign. Whatever the cause, I couldn't reach the money. The nerves in my arms simply wouldn't respond to the message my brain tried to send them. I stared at my cards. Two pair. The cards I had started with. The cards I had stuck with. The cards I had won with. Not a terrific hand, but one worth betting on. It had been a good gamble. I wondered what Kayleen would think. I wondered what Marilyn would think. I wondered if I would even tell her.

"Come on, Ray-zoo-may, take you damn money."

My arms finally moved. "Donald," I said, looking across at Smoke while I pulled the money toward me. "Donald Spinks." I stood up, thumbed the bills.

"Where de hell you goin'?" His question sounded like a threat, but I answered calmly, looking straight into the mirrored lenses of his glasses.

"Home," I said. I handed Clay five twenties, thanked him, turned to leave.

He grabbed my hand in his thick, soft one, smiled benignly, softly said, "There's the matter of interest."

"Interest?"

"Interest." He squeezed my hand until I winced. "Fifty dollars will do." Smoke chuckled. Moose grinned. Walter pulled his neck in. I paid.

I walked out into the bar, dodging the small round tables where men and women sat clutching their drinks, staring blankly at their empty glasses, staring blankly at each other, or pressing their foreheads against their table tops, sleeping, or pretending to sleep. Kayleen lounged against the bar, smoking. I interpreted what little expression her face showed as surprise when I handed her twenty-five dollars.

"For services rendered," I said. She shrugged, tucked the money down the V of her blouse.

I went home.

Eyes Closed

Eugene Cross

Bars and pool halls were not places you went to turn your luck. Evan knew this. He was not fiercely realistic, but he was aware there was only one ending to those stories of people who drove to Las Vegas with their last penny in hopes of altering fate. But Evan also knew that occasionally some event, small as it might seem, could take place in a man's life and set off other events, positive in fashion, that might place him on the right track, or at least a better track than the one he was currently traveling. And with both of these realizations firmly in place Evan walked into The Gold Crown with six hundred dollars in his pocket, almost all the money he had left in the world, and took a seat at the bar.

On his way in, a few people nodded at him or mouthed his name silently, and this recognition filled him with a swell of pride he'd not felt in some time. It was nice to be known somewhere. He removed his wet coat and set it on the stool beside him. Outside a light hail was falling from the sky. It exploded against the pavement like shattering crystal.

On his way into the bar that night Evan had seen a woman being shoved out of a car parked in the Crown's lot. The woman was crying, struggling to remain inside, but finally the driver, a large man, pushed her out. And once he did he sped away quickly, the door still half open as he swerved onto Liberty Avenue. The woman, who hadn't noticed Evan staring, stopped crying while the car was still in sight and yelled, "It's a goddamn shame is all." And then she gathered her purse from where it had fallen and walked off in the opposite direction the car had taken.

Now inside, Evan tried to put the whole thing out of his mind. He had more important things to worry about.

The bartender, Thomas, was a wiry man in his fifties. He appeared old and fragmentary behind the high mahogany bar, but Evan had watched him break up fights with the strength of a man twice his size. Old-school strong with a concrete handshake, he was always indifferent to Evan. He'd bring him a drink or mention to him someone at the end of the bar who might be looking for a game, but that was the extent of it. He never perched himself in front of Evan and talked about the way things had changed in the bar like he did with the older men. He walked over to Evan.

"Railbender please," Evan said.

Thomas brought the beer. Evan paid for it and then rotated his barstool until he was facing the rows of tables behind him. The pool area was separated from the bar by a waist-high wooden divider. You had to be over twenty-one to enter the bar, but anyone over eighteen could get a table. The pool room had its own entranceway as well, a glass door right next to the bar's entrance. It was a Wednesday night and so both the pool room and the bar were fairly empty. On the weekends, local college boys would bring their dates here. Those were the nights you could make a quick score off some frat boy trying to impress a girl. They'd rarely play for anything over fifty, but it was fast and painless and you could stay in their good graces if you didn't embarrass them during the payoff, if you made sure to say loud enough so their date could hear that they were the best player you'd squared off against in weeks. Evan was always sure to be gracious to those types, the ones who knew they were almost certainly giving their money away. He'd probably gotten dozens of them laid. The dates loved the daring gambling boys. On weekdays though, it was just the old crowd, the guys who'd played here for years. They all knew about the bumpy slate on number fourteen, always complained about the bad leveling job on the upstairs tables, and wouldn't go near the Gandy's because of the loose felt in the corners. These were the men Tonya had warned him about. "In this world there are producers, and there are thinkers," she'd said, "and those shiftless sons of bitches fall into neither category."

Evan took a sip of his beer and lit a cigarette. It had been nearly a month since Tonya left, and he still couldn't kick the habit, show her he was changed, or at least changing. Smoking had been one of her peeves. He'd promised for a long time to stop, but in the end promising was as far as he ever went. Tonya was a smart girl, and she never made any bones about telling Evan exactly what was on her mind. This had been good for him while she was still around, he'd since decided. She was direct with him. "I work, you should work," she'd said. And so he started. He found a job doing late night snow removal during the harsh Great Lakes winter. All night he'd listen to his Guns n' Roses and Van Halen tapes, sipping coffee from a Thermos she'd prepared for him while he tore a beat up S-10, plow down, through endless parking lots and driveways. He formed huge mountains out of the powder that had blown in off the lake. That job had been good. He felt like he was building something, even if it was only temporary. Something inside of him felt right when he saw those mounds of snow after he had finished at a site.

But now it was the beginning of spring, and Tonya was gone and most of Evan's mountains were just dirty piles of ice. And even with a job, Evan had still come to the Crown to play. It wasn't always for the money. Although money, winning it anyways, was nice. It was better than getting a paycheck, in the same way that catching a fish was better than buying one at the market. But that was just a part of it for Evan. He was twenty-six and had been coming to places like the Crown since he was eighteen. He liked the idleness of the regulars at the bar, the way his jeans smelled like cigar smoke the next morning when he held them close to his face. He liked knowing that at any time you could come here and choose to place yourself, or at least some part of yourself, on the line.

Evan looked across the rows of tables along the back wall and met eyes with his friend Jonathan. Jonathan was in his late thirties and a welder for one of the trucking companies that had a hub in town, down near the lake. Jonathan never played for money, and for this reason was a friend to almost all of the Crown's regulars. He had no old beefs, owed nobody, and was in general a sub-par player who mainly came to drink and talk. Evan walked over and joined him at his table.

"What brings you to the Crown on such a lovely night?" Jonathan asked. He smiled, flashing a row of smoke colored teeth. His t-shirt had short blue sleeves, and the veins of his forearms ran towards his wrists like complicated circuitry.

"Looking for a game," Evan said.

"On a Wednesday? I thought you only played weekends."

"Usually," Evan said, "But I'm looking for something a little bigger tonight." Behind them there was a crash of balls as someone took the break.

"How's that girlfriend of yours?" Jonathan asked. "It's been a while since you've had her in here."

"That's over."

"Oh yeah?" Jonathan said. "Sorry to hear it." He lit a cigarette then handed one of the house cues to Evan. Evan took it. It was old and warped, but Evan bent down and lagged the nine ball with it anyway. The first shot of the night always felt right to Evan, as though he were just picking up where he'd left off the last time he'd played. To him, shooting pool was like getting back to a good book he hadn't read in a few days. It was simply the world he preferred to be in.

The cue's tip struck the ball with a gentle thud. Evan watched the ball hit the bottom rail and roll back to almost exactly where he'd struck it from.

Evan disliked when people asked about Tonya. Especially people at the Crown. He'd brought her here only a handful of times, but she was the kind of girl who made an impression right away, straightforward in everything she did. The first time they'd met had been like that. Evan was at Sherlock's, an Irish place right on the lake. He was drinking with a friend of his when he felt a tap on his shoulder. When he turned around there was Tonya, a pretty brunette with the slyest smile Evan had ever seen, like she knew his deepest secret. She was holding a Jameson neat.

"I don't know if this is how you take your whiskey," she'd said, handing it to him, "But it's how I drink mine." And that was it. Tonya had picked out the songs on the jukebox, and they'd danced drunken clumsy for the rest of the night. A month later she moved in.

Jonathan took another cigarette from his pack and handed it to Evan. "So what happened there man?" he asked.

Evan considered the question for a moment. "Same fight, different round."

"What fight was that?" Jonathan asked.

"Coming here. Places like here. She said it shut me off from everything else. Said I didn't really know her." As Evan spoke he could feel the anger heating the pockets of his cheeks, stealing the luck from his now unsteady hands. "I knew her better than anybody," he said. He allowed himself to calm down for a moment. "I knew her that well."

Jonathan gave him a sympathetic look. "Don't sweat the small stuff," he said, "And it's all small stuff." Jonathan raised his drink towards Evan's and they touched glasses. "Stolat," Jonathan said, "May you live a hundred years."

Evan listened for a while as Jonathan talked about how things were at the shop. He heard Jonathan describe the falling orders and his declining hours, but he couldn't concentrate. He'd purposefully neglected to tell Jonathan that when Tonya left she'd also taken her half of the rent money. Evan knew that when he finished talking Jonathan would spread the word that Evan was looking for a game, and he didn't want to play with the pretense of necessity. Jonathan would not tell any of the others, but even he alone knowing would be too much. The number one rule, the one everybody claimed but few religiously followed, wasn't that you should always play sober, or always watch your opponent in action before the money was on the table. It wasn't even to make sure that you were having an "on" night before you bet, since even the best of players occasionally appeared to be amateurs for no conceivable reason. Pure and simple, it was to bet only what you could afford to lose, and as Evan pinched the tight roll of twenties, solid as a cue between his thumb and forefinger, he knew that the six hundred it made up was nowhere near expendable.

After a while Jonathan walked away. Evan watched him move through the smoky room, dodging players and waitresses effortlessly. Evan walked back to the bar and ordered another Railbender. He glanced down the long wooden surface and saw Augie Mitchell sitting alone at the far end. Augie was a staple at the Crown. He was a burly man with an expressionless face and a sprout of blackish hair combed across the pale expanse of his large pate. In his day, he had been a player of formidable talents, but over time it became the drinks that he returned for. Evan had started coming to the Crown towards the end of Augie's playing days. He had watched him once, practicing nine ball alone at a corner table. For a large man he had a remarkably graceful stroke. The cue slid through his thick hairy fingers like a snake through tall grass. Only on the break did he reveal the power that resided in his heavy arms. He'd fire the cue ball towards the rack as though it were a cannonball exploding from the side of a battleship.

Eventually though, Augie lost his job as a foreman at the brewery and sold his Harvey Martin cue to a traveling hustler for cash. Evan heard that it got to be that Augie had to be drunk to play, and then he would miss things, shoot at the five when the four was still on the table, rack like he'd never done it before. And when he wasn't drunk his hands shook too bad for the long shots, for the delicate ones that he'd once been an expert at. He couldn't cut or put English on the cue ball the way he once could, and he tore the felt when he tried to jump. It was rumored now that he was collecting for a bad element in town, that for a price his services were available to anyone. Evan nodded at him and Augie raised his glass slightly. Since Augie no longer played, they'd never exchanged more than a simple hello.

* * *

Evan was almost finished with a third beer when he felt the man standing behind him. He turned his stool and instantly recognized him. He was not a regular, but Evan had seen him in the bar several times drinking or practicing alone at one of the tables.

"You Evan?" he asked. His large eyes darted from Evan's to the ground. The man was pear shaped with a sizeable stomach and a narrow chest. He wore a green sweatshirt with an oil stain on its left side. He leaned on one of the house cues and Evan thought it might suddenly splinter and break under the man's weight. Evan finally nodded.

"Jon says you're looking for a game."

Evan nodded again and held out his hand.

"I'm Frank." The man smiled uncomfortably as if he were not at ease with the formalities. "I just got here. I'm back on number seven."

Evan peered over the man's shoulder. Resting on the green felt was the half wooden crate in which the balls were stored. Next to it sat a black, leather, shoulder strap case. Evan looked back at the man and noted his sloppy appearance. His hair was a stringy blond nest, and his unshaven face looked almost dirty in the bar's dim lights. The Crown had rules on appearance and conduct. Ball caps were to be worn to the front, not backwards or to the side like some of the college kids had taken to doing. Cut offs and ripped clothing weren't allowed, and chewing tobacco was strictly forbidden. But as slovenly as he looked, Frank wasn't in violation of the code.

"I don't know, Frank. You pretty good?"

The uncomfortable smile on Frank's face gave way to an irritated gaze that seemed to fit it much more naturally. "You want to play or not," he asked, jamming the butt of the cue impatiently into the bar's wooden floor.

Evan smiled. When he played the college boys he let the balls speak for themselves. But when he was facing another player it didn't hurt to work in a jab now and again. A little grind helped you to always seem in control, even when you were down.

"I'll play," Evan said. "Let me grab my cue and I'll meet you."

Frank nodded and left.

Evan placed a couple singles on the bar for Thomas and walked through the wooden divider to the back of the pool room. Along the back next to the bathrooms was a wall of lockers. The face of each one was only about as large as a postcard, but they were deep enough to fit a two-piece cue that had been taken apart. Evan had rented number thirty-four for years. It was along the bottom row, and he knelt to face it. He entered his combination, twenty-one, three, seventeen, and felt the gentle pop and then resistance as the lock released. He removed his cue. It was a McDermott Sedona made of birdseye maple. It had a triangle leather tip and sixty-eight inlays made of everything from ebony to oak. Evan had bought it about a half-a-year after he and Tonya had gotten started. He'd managed to save seven hundred dollars and hadn't thought twice about spending it on the Sedona. Tonya had wanted him to buy a car.

Evan screwed the ends of the cue together and held it out at arm's length like a sword. He peered down its curved surface and checked its trueness. He twirled it in his hands and admired its smooth finish and rough wrap for grip near its butt.

"How will you get to work?" Tonya had asked him after he'd shown her the cue for the first time.

"I'll walk," Evan had told her.

"You better watch it, Evan, or you'll be walking your whole life." In truth Evan still did not own a car, but he wouldn't have traded his cue for anything.

Evan walked into the bathroom with the cue and entered the stall. He counted out the six hundred dollars. He would never have played with a penny less than he had. He had lost money before. He had awakened hung over and broke in the morning, unaware for just a moment of what had happened the night before, free from the memory as if it were not his. But it always found him, and then he became certain. And with his pockets empty he was forced to begin answering all those questions he so easily ignored such as how he'd pay the rent and his bills and the numerous friends he owed. It had been the same way the morning after Tonya left. He'd awakened, not realizing at first she was gone, but then past his cotton mouth and splitting head, the cursing and packed bags had returned to him. But that morning had been worse because for a long time Evan had lay in bed and tried with all the truth he could find to convince himself that it was all part of a nightmare, that Tonya was simply at work. But even that was pointless.

Evan patted the money through his jeans. No, he would never play with just words and promises of funds. Waking up broke was one thing, but there were certain rules for welchers, and Evan knew them well enough to never take the chance. But tonight he could win. He walked to the sink and splashed his face with cold water. He held out his right hand, his shooting hand, palm down, and watched its stillness. He seemed to himself ready, certain. Tonight he could jump tracks, and as he took his cue from the stall he felt the rhythm of his heart churning steadily within him.

* * *

At the table, Frank was practicing his draw, trying to leave the cue ball exactly where he desired as if he were some kind of magician. Evan saw that the ten through fifteen balls were still boxed, as he'd known they would be. Nine ball was the only game anyone at the Crown ever played for money.

"So what do you say, Frank," Evan asked, "A race to five for two notes?"

Frank pulled back his cue and studied its joint. It was a nice stick, a vintage Brunswick, and Evan admired its precise inlay work. But he could tell Frank was impressed when he laid the McDermott on the table. Frank began to rack the balls.

"Sounds like a plan," he said after a minute. "Hope you're wearing your running shoes."

Evan won the break off the lag and took the first and second games easily, but in the third he misjudged a bank and watched the nine ball bounce off the inside point of the side pocket. Frank won the game and pulled ahead in the race three-to-two before Evan had another chance to shoot. In the sixth game Evan had a chance at a combination shot that could tie things up. The seven was sitting about an inch off the side rail, and Evan saw that with a good enough cut he could use it to put in the nine, which was near the edge of the corner pocket. Evan leaned down and eyed the balls over the expanse of green felt. He envisioned an imaginary line, the same line the ball would have to travel for him to make the shot. He straightened up, chalked his cue, and ran his left hand over the white cone of chalk on the divider behind him. It would help the Sedona run smoothly over his coarse skin.

Evan leaned down once again and spread the fingers of his left hand over the table, before pulling the felt tightly between them, stretching it just slightly from the slate. He placed the end of his cue between the knuckle of his pointer finger and the inside of his thumb. He held the cue as softly as a woman's hand and ran it back and forth over his fingers. The shot was all finesse, and Evan watched as the nine dropped smoothly into the far corner pocket.

After that the games seemed effortless. In the next one, he sank the nine off a rocket break. And to win the race, he capitalized off a miss by Frank on the three ball. He sank the three through nine, counting each ball as it dropped like a child learning his numbers. After that they played a double or nothing and Evan won that race as well, five games to one. He could not remember the last time he'd played so brilliantly, the balls rolling as if they knew and respected him, the cue sliding through his hands like a piston.

* * *

In the bar Evan bought Frank a bourbon and one for himself as well. He tried not to smile, but when he ordered the drinks, Thomas gave him a slight nod acknowledging his victory. Evan sat down across from Frank at one of the bar's tables and handed him his drink. His eyes still darted from Evan's face to the floor, as if they had yet to play. Frank pushed a sweaty wad of fifties and twenties across the table, and Evan pocketed it without a word. The money looked as crumpled as Frank. Evan hoped that all four hundred was there, but he wouldn't count it until he arrived home.

"It's all there," Frank said as if he'd read Evan's mind.

Evan looked down with embarrassment.

"You play well," Frank said.

"Thanks. I had an on night I guess."

"Yeah, well cheers." Frank lifted his glass and hit it recklessly against the side of Evan's. "So how about one more?"

Evan looked at him. "I really don't think so. I just got started on this one," he said, raising his glass.

Frank smiled. "I wasn't talking about another drink," he said.

"I know," Evan said, "but it's getting late, and my luck can't last forever."

"That's what I'm counting on," Frank said. He gave Evan a smirk.

Evan didn't want to play again. It had already been a good night, and he thought for a moment that he might call Tonya, tell her how well he'd played.

"Maybe another time," Evan said. "I'm around."

"I know you are." And with that Frank stood from his chair and walked back towards his table.

Evan lifted his cue from where he'd rested it against the wooden divider and walked to the back wall. He began to unscrew the McDermott. When he undid the two piece cue, the top half slid out of his hand and hit the floor with a crack. He bent down to pick it up but found someone else facing him as he squatted. He looked over and saw Augie, his hulking form, kneeling beside him. He held the top half of Evan's cue between his fingers like a toothpick. He handed it to Evan, and the two of them stood at the same time.

"It's a beautiful cue," Augie said.

"Thank you," Evan said, surprised by the way the large man spoke. The words came out as nothing more than a whisper, his voice as soft as felt.

"I saw your combo in that last game. That was a nice cut."

Evan nodded. "Maybe we could shoot around some time."

Augie peered down at him. "I don't really play anymore," he said, "I've kind of retired. But I'm sure I'll be seeing you around." He walked back to his seat at the end of the bar.

Evan slipped both halves of his cue into the locker and shut it.

Outside the hail had turned to a light rain. A warm wind was blowing in off the lake, and Evan felt all right walking home. He zipped up his jacket and moved quickly. It was after midnight and the streets were empty. Only a few cars rolled slowly past as he walked. Halfway to his apartment he thought he heard a set of heavy footsteps trailing his, but when he turned he found he was alone.

At home he went straight to the kitchen and took Frank's money from his pocket. It was all there: ten crumpled twenties and four fifties. He straightened them against the table top and then added them to his own six hundred dollar roll.

In the living room he left the lights off and took a seat on the couch. He thought again about calling Tonya. He could tell her about his night. About the money. He could tell her that things were looking up. But it was late and the thought of her not answering at all was worse than anything.

His apartment was on the second floor and outside his window a Maple branch shook beside a streetlight, throwing shadows onto the dark walls. Evan watched them and remembered an early morning shortly after Tonya had moved in. It was a Sunday and they had just made love. Outside the sky was beginning to lighten. They were lying together on a mattress in the center of the floor, and Tonya had her head cradled on Evan's chest. They both stared at the ceiling, silent. Evan couldn't remember now why he had said it. Perhaps he felt he should offer her some compliment, show his affection. And so with the day's first light casting shadows above them he told her he loved her eyes, that they were beautiful eyes.

Tonya quickly squeezed them shut and brought her face to rest near his. "What color are they?" she asked.

Evan laughed.

"What?"

"You heard me. What color are my eyes?" She smiled and burrowed her face into his neck, hiding from him. Evan tried so hard to think, to place them in some context, to find the answer in a memory. But even with her head on his shoulder and with all the luck in the world, he could never have guessed.

Sunrise at the Aladdin

Jean Copeland

"Nickels please," I shouted through the din of singing slot machines and raucous cheering from a nearby crap table of college students on a Saturday night junket. After offering a professional courtesy nod to the two chain-smoking Asian men I'd just squeezed between, I slid my last two Benjamins across the green velvet trim of the roulette table toward the greasy-haired dealer. As his fingers curled around the remaining pawn shop proceeds from the sale of the necklace my parents had given me for college graduation, it hit me that my plane ticket home was the last thing of value I still owned. Funny thing about landlords and auto loan companies, they run pretty short on patience where money's concerned. Only days earlier, as I lowered my beloved diamond pendant into the shop owner's hairy hand, I thought, No biggie, I'll just pay the rent and buy back the necklace after I clean house in Vegas this weekend.

So there I stood, distributing ten five-dollar chips over the table, a conservative bet by my usual standards, placing two on my birthday, eleven, and watching the magic white ball make its fortuitous revolutions around the spinning wheel. My heart hammered my chest as the ball skipped and sputtered across the slots until it landed abruptly on number eight.

"Shit," I soloed among the chorus of other losers crowding the table. "No problem," I then said to the Asian man to my left as his cigarette smoke burned my eyes. "It's good luck to get the bad luck out of the way on the first spin."

He ignored me as he fanned out over the table and deposited fistfuls of yellow dollar chips with painstaking precision as though it made even the slightest difference.

I fondled the next set of ten nickels and kept to the same strategy, covering all my favorite numbers with one chip apiece and plunking down a double-decker on my birthday.

The ball skipped across the wheel. "Come on, baby; come on, baby," I chanted. Eleven, eleven, eleven, come on. "Fuck," I shouted as the ball rested comfortably in slot twelve.

The dealer dragged my fifty dollars in nickel chips over the fuzzy red and black numbers and let them tumble down into the giant abyss before him. I shot him a menacing look, but he didn't even glance my way. I could never decide what I hated more about dealers, phony empathy or unabashed indifference.

The next spin was mine; I felt it in my blood. I drained the last of my free rum and Coke, which was mostly Coke, and blinked away my watery-eyed parents sitting on the sofa a few nights earlier. It was pathetic how they hung on every word of Joanne, the purse-lipped intervention facilitator, as she drilled me with every clichéd guilt trip she could pull from her knapsack. What a huge waste of time. Did she honestly think I couldn't see the impact my favorite pastime had on my parents? If anything, she should've counseled them about overreacting.

"Okay, this is the spin. I feel it," I announced to my Asian friend at the right, only to discover it wasn't my Asian friend pressed against my arm but a warm, sparkly woman presiding over several stacks of turquoise dollar chips. She shook lush golden-brown hair from the collar of her silky blouse and brandished a dazzling set of veneers framed in a nectarine complexion gleaming from a day's pampering at the salon. She wore the aroma of wealth the way a frat boy wears the residue of a stripper's cheap perfume, and I couldn't spare the energy it required to determine if she was checking me out or simply marveling at the calculated approach I took to a sucker's game.

"You seem like a pro," she observed. "What's the secret to roulette?"

I couldn't help but scoff. "Are you psychic," I replied without looking at her.

"No," she giggled.

"Lucky?"

She giggled again. "Sometimes."

"Well if now isn't one of those times you might as well save yourself the aggravation and dump all those chips down that little hole in the table over there. It'd be a shame to ruin that perky mood of yours just 'cause the number right next to your favorite friggin' number comes up instead." If that pithy retort wouldn't get her off my back, nothing would.

"Mind if I watch you to get the feel of it," she asked, leaning unnecessarily close to my ear.

I continued positioning my third round of chips. "Look, I'm down to my last hundred here, and it's kind of pissing me off at the moment, so maybe—"

"I've got plenty," she interrupted and placed petal soft fingers on my forearm

"Show me with my money, and I'll give you half of what we win."

Finally gracing her with my full attention, I was struck by her vast, green eyes and spidery black lashes as she studied my face.

"Be with you in a second." I winked and turned just in time to see the dealer place the glass dolly on top of number twenty-seven.

"Yes," I growled with a quick fist-pump.

"You won?" she asked.

"Only a hundred and seventy-five dollars, but now I can add it to my last fifty."

"How fabulous," she purred. "I'm Andrea, by the way."

"Liz." I quadruped up on eleven and twenty-seven, covered the basket with two just to be safe, and piled my winnings on the third set of twelve. "Let me guess, Andrea, you're staying at the Bellagio, right?"

"How'd you know?"

"Maybe I'm a little psychic," I teased as my eyes twirled around in pursuit of the white ball. "Un-fucking-believable." It landed nowhere near any of my bets.

"Maybe not so much." Andrea smiled playfully, oblivious of the dire consequences of that last bankrupting spin.

"You know what a cooler is, Andrea?" I managed to resist the impulse to shove her exfoliated face into the tower of chips stacked before her well-publicized cleavage.

"Isn't it something you put cold drinks in?"

After determining she was serious, I smiled at her. What else could I do? She'd saved me from exploding into an obscenity-laced rant that would've got me escorted out of yet another Vegas casino by freakishly thick-necked security guards.

"What are you doing slumming it at the Aladdin anyway?" I asked. My eyes darted between her luscious racks of chips.

"They have the most adorable mall here. Isn't that little thunderstorm they do a pip?"

"It's why I never stay anywhere else," I drawled. "Come on, Andrea. Do something with those chips, will you?"

"I've been waiting for you," she said with a grin.

"Let's get it on," I roared, and I was back in the game again, doling out Andrea's dollars like they were someone else's money.

Three hours and a variety of chip denominations later, Andrea loosened the shimmering TAG Heuer watch sticking to her wrist. "Oh my, is this right? Three-thirty a.m.," she chirped. And just like that, my free ride screeched to a halt. It's entirely possible we blew through four grand in that time, but then who was counting?

Given my familiarity with roulette, I probably should've advised the ritzy broad to put away her change purse while we were ahead by a grand, but then again, as my mother was always quick to point out, I seemed to lack even the slightest understanding of moderation. I suppose that's why that tight-assed intervention facilitator from Seasons Rehabilitation was summoned to my parents' loveseat the previous Thursday evening. A bit of overkill if you asked me.

"Wow, that was exhilarating," Andrea gushed. She fell against me in dramatic fashion as we walked away from the gaming area.

"Hmmm," I agreed. "Better than sex."

"Oooh, now that's not a bad idea either," she replied, engaging me with a giggle.

"Well, it's pretty late." I assumed the comment was less an offer than a side effect of the vat of mimosas she'd downed into the wee hours.

"Oh, now you're not planning to go back to your room, are you," Andrea accused and pinned me with a lusty smirk.

"What do you have in mind," I asked just to confirm my suspicions.

She shrugged her shoulders and flung back her hair, and I flashed to Ann-Margret in *Kitten with a Whip*.

I felt my face get hot with indignation. "What did you think you were doing back there, buying yourself a whore?"

Her eyes grew overcast. "I wanted to buy you breakfast. I'll bet you haven't eaten anything since yesterday."

Suddenly, I felt like an even bigger lowlife than I ever thought humanly possible. "Andrea, you've done enough for me. I think we should part ways before I charm you out of any more of your hard-earned money."

I picked up the pace, but she wore Kenneth Cole heels like Jordan wore Nikes.

"My money isn't hard-earned, Liz. It's Daddy's money, and if I can't at least have the fun of spending it, on someone I'm incredibly attracted to I might add, what good is it?"

I stopped dead in my tracks. "So you do want to have sex with me."

"Of course I do, but I'm not trying to buy you. I'd been trying to attract your attention all night, but you're quite the little table hopper, so engrossed in your gambling. I could've set off a bomb or flashed my boobs and you still wouldn't have looked my way."

"That was the complaint of most of my ex-girlfriends," I said, admitting to something I had no idea was true until that moment.

"Not that I expected someone like you to go mad for me."

"What do you want my attention for?" I asked.

"You're a doll." She brushed my chin with her paraffin-dipped hand. "Not to mention you teaching me to play roulette was the biggest thrill I've had in months."

Before I knew it, we were knocking ankles in a booth at a retro diner on the strip devouring western omelets and bottomless cups of stale coffee.

"I must say, Liz, it seems a bit peculiar that a lovely young woman such as yourself would be staying in Las Vegas alone," Andrea pried. "Are you from around here?"

"No, Sandusky, Ohio, born and raised." I rinsed down the vintage coffee with ice water.

"Is this your first time here?"

"No," I said primly, deciding the only thing that was going to be grilled in that joint was the bacon. "Let's just say the city and I have had a rather intimate relationship over the past year, and I just came out here for the weekend to break it off with her, and take back what's mine."

Her playful smile encouraged the game. "Why do you need to break it off with her?"

"Some affairs just get a little too intense and need a cooling off period, if you know what I mean."

She sighed. "Sadly, no, I don't."

"Trust me, you're not missing much. Just a lot of stress and frustration."

Suddenly, her eyes widened with fascination. "Liz, do you have a gambling problem," she nearly shouted across the entire diner.

"No, Andrea," I answered patiently. "Do you? You're here by yourself, too."

She smirked. "I'm sorry. That was terribly rude, wasn't it? Actually, I've never been to Las Vegas before, never even set foot inside a casino."

She then scrunched up her face and lowered her voice a few octaves. "Millionaires lose their money in business ventures. Trailer trash lose it in casinos, my husband used to say when I'd suggest a weekend in Atlantic City. He's quite the elitist twit."

I nodded and scooped up the last morsel of egg with a triangle of wheat toast.

"So why does a woman of your wealth and sophistication trudge around Vegas looking for a good time with some stranger, a punk she singles out at a gaming table." I averted my eyes once I realized she was drawing me in.

The diner's bare fluorescent lighting seemed to reveal a side of Andrea previously concealed by jewel-encrusted fingers waving handfuls of cash around a murky casino. Not only was she beautiful, she had one other irresistible quality about her: she seemed worse off than me.

"I'm alone, Liz," she confessed. She then stabbed at a piece of diced ham with her fork. "I'm a forty-eight year-old, divorced heiress excommunicated from my social circle for coming out as a lesbian and disgracing my husband, P. Warren Vansberger, shipping heir and Kennedy cousin, five times removed. My father, the venerable Jacob Wellsley of Wellsley Pharmaceuticals, supplies the money as long as I keep to my Manhattan penthouse and don't pop in at the Hamptons while he's entertaining Republican royalty." She glanced absently at a crooked autographed photo of Joey Bishop hanging at our booth. "Sometimes I don't know where I fit in anymore."

With that revelation, we were no longer strangers. I raised my chipped cup from its coffee-pooled saucer. "From one misfit to another."

Andrea smiled and chinked her cup against mine. "Here's to the mysterious and wonderful forces that brought us together tonight."

"You mean the forces of vice and excess? What does that say about us that we both chose Sin City as the place to seek acceptance?"

She shrugged defiantly. "Conventionality isn't for everyone. It took me long enough to figure that out."

"Look, I'm sorry I blew all your money earlier."

"I already told you I don't give a damn. I booked this trip because I wanted an adventure. I wanted to feel like I could do something on my own, and I'm doing it. Hell, you're the icing on the cake."

She flashed a naughty grin, and I imagined nibbling her Chanel-scented earlobes, making her feel desired, fixing her broken life for one brief moment. For months, my life had been in a perpetual spinout, but with Andrea Wellsley, I could feel in control again. As her French-mani-cured toes started crawling up the leg of my jeans, I wondered how much cash was still suffocating inside her Gucci wallet.

She gazed at me with tentative eyes. "Earlier you accused me of trying to buy you."

I looked down and caressed the silverware. "I know. I'm sorry about—"

She ushed her platter of crusty hash browns aside and leaned toward me with an unrepentant stare. "I want you, Liz. I'd buy you if I had to, I'm not ashamed to confess, and I wouldn't have to think twice about it." She stood, appearing taller than I first thought, and threw two twenties on the table to cover the twenty-three dollar tab. "I'll be waiting in the lobby of your hotel. If you want me, come and get me. If not, just keep walking. I need a lot of things, but a pity lay isn't one of them."

After Andrea cleared the exit, I glanced around for Ruby, our elderly, sun-baked waitress, and with a slight of hand smoother than Lance Burton, the twenties were in my jeans, and I was out the door. Sorry, Ruby. I'll catch ya next time.

* * *

"I need a shower, honey," Andrea drawled. It was just before noon when she crushed my cheek with a hard kiss. She pranced into the bathroom from the bed, naked and floating on clouds, humming a high, off-key rendition of Streisand's "Evergreen."

I replayed various scenes and sound-bites from our uninhibited sex-athon in the orangey glow of sunrise and reassured myself that if you find the person attractive, it's not prostitution. I may still owe large sums of money to every human being I know, but I'd surely never sink low enough to exchange sex for cash. Only desperate addicts on A&E do that. I would've gone to bed with her even if she didn't subsidize my last bid in Vegas to stop the repo of my Honda Accord.

After the shower jets hit full throttle, I meandered over to her purse and rummaged through the clutter until I located the famous Gucci wallet still bloated with cash and discovered a payout better than anything Las Vegas Boulevard recently had to offer. I slipped out seven of the nine hundred dollar bills she had the nerve to still possess in a city that left everyone flipping over sofa cushions for one last, lousy quarter. I stuffed the wad in the pocket of my knit shorts and telepathically hurried the princess along so I could get downstairs and reclaim my lost fortune at the roulette wheel.

An hour later she finally emerged, gathered up her bedazzled wrap and purse and headed for the door, my anxious palms on her shoulders hastening her exit.

"You know, Liz." She whirled around in the threshold and gazed at me through two verdant fields of innocence. "I wish you could know what meeting you has done for me. You've given me back something money could never buy." She scoured her mind to retrieve the precise words. "A piece of myself I thought I'd lost. Hell, a piece I never knew I'd had. I feel good about being me. It's a nice feeling for a change." Her honesty jabbed me in a place I thought had shriveled up and died.

She grabbed my face and riddled my lips with a barrage of vigorous pecks. I fingered the money in my pocket and almost pulled it out.

"Good-bye, sweetie," she said. "If you're ever in the Big Apple, you better look me up." She fluttered her spidery lashes, and as she padded down the mute hallway toward the elevator, I dismissed shame once more with one swift swing of the door.

She'd come back when she had to buy something, and I felt queasy about having to face her. But I had a six o'clock flight out that night and wasn't too worried about making myself disappear.

* * *

As the 747 roared out of McCarran International Airport, I bade farewell to the dusk-lit plains and taupe mountain ranges embracing the city that had seduced me like a married lover. My mouth was pasty, my stomach as empty as my wallet. I hadn't eaten a thing since the breakfast Andrea bought me before sunrise. Was Andrea thinking as low of me as I was at that moment, buckled in my window seat, salivating over the measly bag of pretzels and cup of ginger ale soon to be wheeled my way? She didn't need the cash I stole from her or the betrayal I left in its place. But knowing her, whatever she was thinking, it wasn't unkind.

The next morning I'd be checking into Seasons Rehabilitation, and my stomach withered even further, my soul, too, in the wake of surrender. I glanced out the window so the plump grandmother beside me with magenta fingernails and thick eyeglasses wouldn't notice the tears creeping down my cheeks. I closed my eyes as the jet ascended. Andrea's face streamed through the darkness, exuberant and free, illuminated when she won seventeen dollars on a street bet during our roulette all-nighter.

I'd long ago become accustomed to exploiting the generosity of vulnerable, well-meaning people. But for some reason, perhaps the betrayal everyone left in Andrea's life, I wished I'd told her what meeting her had done for me.

O'Kaye in the Ninth

Adam Berlin

Pulling his cap a little more snugly over his head, Moe followed Oggie into the off track betting parlor. Oggie didn't wear a cap and his ears always looked pinkish in the winter but as he told Moe, "If you put a little more meat on your bones maybe you wouldn't be so cold." Moe thought he'd be cold even if he had meaty bones and even if he was as big and strong as Oggie.

It was Saturday afternoon. The Port Authority OTB was crowded. Moe looked up at one of the closed circuit television sets that hung from the four corners of the room and saw the list of horses. Next to each horse were its odds of winning. They had seven minutes left to bet on the first race, five minutes to bet on the exacta and three minutes to bet on the first daily double which they had decided not to do. Oggie walked to the back of the room and put the *Daily Racing Form* on the counter, folding it back to the day's Aqueduct Racetrack listings with a perfect crease. While Oggie took out his glasses, Moe pulled the paper closer to his side of the counter and began to read. Oggie finished adjusting the black rims on his nose and slid the paper back to his side.

"What are you doing?" Moe asked.

"I'm looking at the form," Oggie said.

"But I'm trying to figure out the first race."

"I already know who's going to win the first race," Oggie said. "So stop figuring."

"Maybe I know something you don't."

"Like what?"

"Like something I know."

"If you're so sure who's going to win, why don't you tell me?"

Moe kept quiet. He didn't want to upset Oggie, especially today. There would be enough tension without an argument, and Moe reminded himself that he didn't need the aggravation either. He'd started taking his blood pressure pills again since his headaches had returned.

Oggie pulled a pen from his overcoat pocket and tapped the felt tip on the corner of the paper so that the black ink bled. His other hand rested squarely on the counter, solid with fingers spread.

"So who's your pick for the first race, anyway?" Moe asked.

"Glasgo Native."

"He's my pick too." Moe picked up a betting slip. "I figured I'd put two bucks on him just for fun."

Oggie stopped tapping the pen and circled the number two and seven horses in the first race. He did things slowly and with care and his circles were perfectly round. Moe never circled anything in the paper. Not just because Oggie didn't like him to touch it but because his circles never came out as neat and professional as Oggie's. After all, they weren't just a couple of bums off the street. They took their horses seriously. They'd been playing the racetrack for years. When Oggie drew a circle it meant something. Moe respected Oggie even if he was eccentric sometimes, always talking about the future and always figuring some scheme in his careful way like the one they'd finally decided to work today. Oggie's ideas weren't always the greatest, Moe knew that, but sometimes they sounded real good. Especially when Oggie explained them and all their angles. They would do it together the way they always did things together, like brothers, only "better than brothers" like Oggie said because they were together by choice.

"What are you circling the number two horse if we already decided that the number seven horse is going to win?" Moe said.

"Who's riding number two?"

"I don't know. I can't see the paper," Moe said, pulling the racing form toward him. "Sal Donado."

"And who's riding both horses we're staking in the double?"

Moe looked at the paper. Sure enough, Donado was riding both horses. Lazette in the eighth and O'Kaye in the ninth. Moe wondered why he was never able to pay attention to details like Oggie was.

"I just want to make sure Donado is having a good day," Oggie said.

Moe slapped Oggie on the shoulder. It was thick and still hard with muscle. Moe watched Oggie carefully fill out the betting slip. Oggie took out his wallet, removed two singles, and handed the money and the slip to Moe.

"Here," Oggie said. "We'll take our two bucks and put it on Glasgo Native to win the first just for kicks. Then we'll go get some lunch and make the phone call. That way we can get back around the sixth race and have plenty of time to get our bet in."

Moe stood on line at one of the cashier's windows. As he waited he looked around the OTB parlor. There were a couple of Spanish fellows he recognized and an old man with a cane who was always here. There were the other regulars too. Flaherty with his white hair and red complexion from drinking too much, Ray who used to be a cop, the skinny guy who always wore a beat-up Yankees cap with the front flipped up. In the middle of the room, leaning on one of the raised formica tables, was the guy everyone called Big Pete, a big black man who was always shooting his mouth off as if he knew for certain which horse was going to win every race. After Oggie had told Moe he didn't like this man, Moe had watched Big Pete more closely and decided he didn't like him either.

The line moved quickly. Moe pushed the two singles and the betting slip under the glass. The cashier punched the bet into the computer and returned the slip along with the yellow ticket which shot out of the computer machine. Moe went back to where Oggie was.

"Okay. I got us a ticket."

Oggie took the ticket, looked it over, and pocketed it. He liked to hold on to everything. The money. The tickets. The paper. Even the pens.

"I think we'll stick around for the second race," Oggie said. "See how Vasquez does in his first race of the day."

"How come he's not riding this one?" Moe said.

"His horse got scratched."

"No kidding. I didn't have a chance to look at the charts."

There were eight minutes left until post time. Since Oggie was going to be studying the paper, Moe decided to take a little walk around the parlor and stretch his legs. His legs always got all knotted up whenever it was cold out. The temperature reading on the billboard at Times Square had been thirty-eight degrees. The wind made it seem even colder, and it looked like it was going to drizzle again, just like they had predicted on the eleven o'clock news last night. Moe walked around the table where Big Pete stood. Pete had large gold rings on his fingers. He had dark glasses and a neat moustache that almost touched his sideburns. He was telling the people around him how Glasgo Native was favored to win because he'd won his last two races but the horse had run on a fast track and today's track was too wet and slow for the sprinter.

"I'm taking him to place behind Marooned," Big Pete said "That track's still damp from yesterday and Marooned knows how to handle the slow stuff. You watch. Marooned first, Glasgo Native to place, I win the exacta and put my money in the bank."

Big Pete started laughing. Moe walked away.

Marooned was a good horse, that was true, but what did it matter? They only had two bucks on the race and if Glasgo Native lost it wouldn't make much of a difference because the races that mattered were the last races of the day, the eighth and the ninth. So the track was damp. Moe hadn't thought about that. When he looked up on the television screen, sure enough, the racing condition was listed as slow. He had forgotten that there had been a light snow yesterday and that they usually got more snow at the track and Moe wondered if Oggie remembered this. Moe made a mental note to remind Oggie that the track was slow even though he was ninety-nine percent sure Oggie knew the track conditions. Oggie always kept on top of things like that.

Moe stepped out of the parlor and into the hallway of the Port Authority where many of the bettors overflowed, waiting for the start of each race to go back inside. Moe lit up a cigarette and looked down the hall to the main area where all these people were bustling around or lining up for their buses. Maybe he and Oggie would be taking a bus trip soon, or a train. Moe pushed these thoughts out of his head and took a long drag on his cigarette, warming his lungs. He felt a little tired. Through the glass walls of the parlor, where the OTB letters were stamped in green, Moe could see his friend. Oggie had been looking drawn and preoccupied lately and this morning he'd been in a bad mood on the walk over. But they'd go out for lunch soon and Oggie's spirits always picked up when he ate. Moe dropped his cigarette on the floor and pressed it flat with his shoe and went back inside to Oggie.

There was a moment of static before the announcer's voice came over the speakers to announce the line up.

"The horses are now on the track and heading for the gate. Horse number one is Strawberry Fields ridden by Juan Cardo. Horse number two, Swing Easy, ridden by Sal Donado. Horse number three, Marooned, ridden by Frank O'Keefe. . . ."

"That's my man," Big Pete yelled so everyone could hear. "Leave them in the mud, O'Keefe."

There was some laughter.

Oggie turned to Moe, "Bastard."

The announcer's voice continued, "Talisman, ridden by Frank Pearl. Horse number seven, Glasgo Native, ridden by Ward Massili. Horse number eight, Shalamar, ridden by Alex Perez. Post time in two minutes."

The speakers went off. The room began to shuffle. People were getting impatient for the day's races to begin. Up on the television screens the final odds were posted with Glasgo Native a favorite by seven-to-five and Marooned the second favorite at two-to-one. Sal Donado's horse was one of the long shots at fourteen-to-one. Oggie continued studying the paper and Moe looked up at the screen every few seconds to see if the odds would change but they didn't. Moe started to pace a small piece of floor as he always did when a race was about to start. When the race began, Moe would create a picture in his mind of how the race looked using the announcer's call to help him. The few times he and Oggie had gone to the races by subway, Moe loved to watch the strong horses as they made their way around the track, so beautiful to watch and so powerful.

"They're in the gates," the announcer said. More static, then a thumping sound. Moe never knew if that was the sound of hoofs or just a different kind of static that came over the speakers before every race.

"And they're off. At the start it's Swing Easy taking the lead on the inside with Mondo just behind and Glasgo Native third. Then comes Strawberry Fields, Marooned and Shalamar. Careola and Talisman are back."

The announcer's voice kept pace with the action and Moe could picture how the race looked. The quarter was run in twenty-seven seconds, the half in fifty-five, and soon the horses were approaching the finish and Moe listened to the announcer's voice.

"And now Marooned is passing Strawberry Fields on the inside and here comes Glasgo Native moving on Mondo and Swing Easy."

"Stay in there, Mondo," someone yelled.

"Come on, baby," yelled Big Pete.

"And Marooned is on the inside. It's Marooned coming on strong on Swing Easy. Glasgo Native holding on by a length. And down the stretch they come. It's Marooned and Glasgo Native head to head followed by Swing Easy and Mondo. Now it's Marooned by one and at the finish it's Marooned, Glasgo Native and Swing Easy."

The speakers went off. Up on the screen the three, seven and two horses were listed unofficially in the Win, Place and Show columns. Big Pete was laughing and telling all his fans around the table how if the afternoon was going to be this easy he'd be able to retire. Big Pete laughed long and loud.

"If he knows so much, what the hell is he doing in this dump?" Oggie said. He slicked his hair back with his right hand.

"I thought Glasgo was gonna pull it out at the end there," Moe said.

"Forget about it. It's only two bucks. Besides, Donado did good."

"What do you think? He's an experienced jockey."

Oggie smiled. "You think today will be our lucky day?"

"I hope so, Og. That would be something, wouldn't it? I'm getting nervous just thinking about it."

"Yeah. Me too a little. Are you getting hungry?"

"I'm okay. What about you?"

"Let's stick around for the second race to see how Vasquez does. Then we'll go eat."

"You want to bet this race or just listen?" Moe said.

"We'll listen. We'll be doing plenty of betting later on." Oggie glanced at the paper. "Vasquez is riding a pretty good horse."

"What's the horse?" Moe said.

"Alarum."

"Oh yeah, that's a good horse."

Up on the screen Moe saw that Alarum was a four-to-one, third in a pack of nine. Moe wondered why he was no longer able to keep track of these horses like he used to. In the past months he was having a harder time concentrating. Oggie told him not to worry about it, that everybody forgot things now and then, and wasn't it only last week that Oggie hadn't been able to find his glasses. But Moe didn't like having such lapses in concentration. Maybe he wasn't sleeping right or something. Moe thought he'd go out for another cigarette but his thought was interrupted by the sound of the bugle call over the loud speakers and the official results were posted on the screen. In the first race at Aqueduct, Marooned paid $3.90 to win, $3.30 to place and $2.70 to show. Big Pete had won twelve bucks on the exacta.

"Twelve bucks on the exacta," Moe said out loud.

Oggie went back to tapping the felt tip pen on the newspaper. The whole top corner was wet with black ink. Big Pete was laughing about something he'd said, and Moe felt like going over there and slamming his fist on the table in front of Big Pete's face and telling the loud mouth to shut the hell up because he was trying to concentrate on his betting. Moe thought that if he was as strong as Oggie, he'd go over to Pete and see if the big shot wanted to step outside. Moe sometimes felt like telling Oggie to start up with Pete but he didn't want any trouble, especially now. Besides, Pete had his friends and this area wasn't a good one to start a fight in. The television switched pictures and the odds for the second race were back on the screen. Vasquez's horse Alarum was still at four-to-one. Moe remembered he was in the mood for a cigarette.

Since they weren't betting on the second race anyway, Moe decided to take another walk. Post time wasn't for another twenty minutes and Oggie wouldn't want to talk with all the studying he was doing. So Moe left the OTB and went down the hall, then took the escalator to the main floor, almost missing the step at the bottom. He pulled a cigarette out of the pack and lit up. He had to cup the match against the draft moving through the open space of the station. There were so many people around, some coming into the city, some going home holding bags and packages.

A mother holding the hand of a little girl walked by, and Moe winked at the little girl and smiled. The girl looked at him, and her head turned as her mother walked on. The pom pom on top of the girl's white hat bounced around as she was pulled forward. The girl smiled at Moe. Missing her front teeth, her smile was so sweet it made Moe smile again. Moe loved kids but he'd never had any of his own.

"How come you never got married and had kids?" Oggie used to say. "You seem to love them so much. Why don't you find a wife and have some?"

"Leave me alone," Moe would say.

That questioning always put Moe in a thoughtful mood, but in a bad way, and sometimes when he felt a little depressed and didn't know why that question popped into his head. Moe thought how it was funny how life turned out and how the time seemed to speed up every year until it all got away from you. How many years had they been together? How many afternoons had they spent at the OTB betting the races with nothing to show for it. A few ups. A few downs. Some good times. The little girl was out of sight. Moe dropped the cigarette near his foot and pressed it against the tile floor of the station.

* * *

Oggie was in the same position where Moe had left him. When Moe walked up to Oggie he saw that Oggie had circled horses in every race.

"What are you figuring every single race for, Og?" Moe said. "I thought we were just going to wait until the last two."

"Just passing the time," Oggie said.

"You thinking of betting on any of these horses?"

"I was just looking at them."

"You hungry yet?"

"Yeah. You?"

"Yeah. You still in the mood for delicatessen?"

"Sure."

"You getting nervous, Og?"

"Not bad."

"I'm getting a little nervous," Moe said.

All pools closed for the second race. The horses were introduced and the race started. Moe watched the people in the room. He always found it interesting to see how differently people reacted while a race was going on and since they weren't playing this race he had a good excuse to just look around. Moe was watching the man with the Yankees cap when Alarum crossed the finish line in first place. A few yells went up, a few Damns and Shits and slapping of hands. Then the bustle of the OTB started again as people began lining up to place their bets for the third race. Alarum. Moe remembered that was Vasquez's horse. He was a great jockey that Reuben Vasquez. Tough and experienced and the best rider on the circuit so far this year. That would help the pay-off during the daily double because Vasquez was favored to win the ninth. Moe walked back to Oggie. They decided to leave and eat a leisurely meal before returning to bet the last two races of the day.

* * *

Posters of Broadway shows Oggie and Moe had never seen lined the walls of the restaurant. The waiter in front pointed to a booth in the middle of the floor near the dessert cabinet. Mirrored images of cream pies and layer cakes made Moe want a slice right now but he would wait. They picked up the large plastic-coated menus and looked through the items. Oggie munched on a pickled tomato while he read.

"What are you getting?" Moe said.

"I don't know yet."

"I think I'll get a pastrami sandwich. I'm in the mood for something spicy."

"This corned beef, turkey, swiss and Bermuda onion combo looks good to me," Oggie said.

"Which one is that?" Moe said, scanning the list of titled sandwiches. "The Elizabeth Taylor?"

"No. The Spencer Tracy."

"That does look good. But I'm staying with the pastrami. Should we split an order of fries or potato salad?"

"Fries is good."

The waiter came over and took their order. Moe reached into the pickle dish, picked out a green tomato, inspected it, didn't like the brown bruise mark near the stem, and put it back in the dish. The waiter brought back two glasses of ice and put down the two bottles of soda. Moe poured his cream soda into the ice. Oggie left his Cel-Rey soda alone and picked out another pickled tomato.

"When are you making the phone call, Og?"

"After we eat. Before dessert."

"Do you think they'll tell him?"

"You mean Vasquez?"

"Yeah."

"They'll tell him."

"I don't mind letting you know I'm still a little nervous about this whole thing. What if it don't work?"

"We already discussed this."

"I know but I'm still a little nervous."

"Look," Oggie said, putting the tomato down and looking straight at Moe. "What are we doing with our lives?"

"I don't know. Nothing much I guess."

"That's right. Nothing much. And that's what we'll keep doing if we stay in New York. I'm sick of it, Moe. I'm sick of the cold weather, I'm sick of the hustle, I'm sick of living in the neighborhood off a little social security, having to watch every move we make. How long has it taken us to save fifteen hundred bucks after food and rent and going to a restaurant a couple times a week?"

"A year and a half."

"A year and seven months. And what's that going to buy us? Suppose we don't bet it. What could we get?"

"I don't know."

"Come on. What could we get?"

"I don't know. A couple of good meals. Maybe go to one of these here Broadway shows."

"Come on, Moe. What are you afraid of? If we lose we lose. We'll go back to living the way we are. And if we don't take this chance we'll be living like we are anyway. Fifteen hundred bucks isn't going to change nothing. But if we win, Moe. If we win that daily double and it pays off like I think it's going to, then we're out of here. We'll catch the next bus out of that damn station for Florida and buy us one of those condominiums we got the pamphlets about. Century Village or West Palm Beach or whatever. And we'll go swimming and sit in the sun, maybe go fishing, maybe even meet a couple of widowed ladies or something. Didn't we already talk about this a hundred times?"

"I know, Og. I want to get out of here as much as you do. But remember what happened the last time we bet a lot of money in Atlantic City? That was it. In less than an hour."

"And this will be in less than two minutes. But it's our only way out. We can save for the next twenty years till we're dead and we won't make as much money as we could today. If we lose we lose. It won't change nothing. But if we win it's a whole new life, a whole new ballgame."

"You're right, Oggie."

"I know I'm right."

"No. I mean you're absolutely right. I'm with you one hundred percent. Let's just enjoy our meal, and you'll make the call and we'll bet our money. That's the way we planned it. And if we win . . ." Moe stopped. He took a sip of his soda. "Wouldn't that be something? Boy would that be something."

The waiter came with the sandwiches and asked them if they would like anything else. Moe said he'd like some ketchup for the fries, and the waiter pointed to the bottle of Heinz on their table. When they were finished eating, Moe well before Oggie, Oggie got up to make the call.

"You want me to go with you?" Moe said.

"No. I'll be right back."

"I'll see you in a minute then."

Oggie started for the phone booth, which was upstairs next to the bathrooms. Moe yelled good luck.

It was a good scheme, Moe thought. One that only Oggie could come up with. Oggie would call up the track, tell whoever answered the phone that Reuben Vasquez would be killed if he rode in the ninth race and hope that the message got through to the jockey. Vasquez wasn't riding in the eighth race, and Sal Donado had a good chance to win that one atop Lazette. But in the ninth and final race, the second half of the daily double, Vasquez was riding the favorite horse while Donado was riding a long shot named O'Kaye. O'Kaye had potential. She wasn't well known because she had injured her foot at the beginning of the season. But Oggie had a hunch that she was all healed up and that Donado could get her to run hard at the end of the race. They hoped the phone call would throw Vasquez's concentration enough to jeopardize his horse, Gulden Medallion. The way Oggie explained it, all sorts of factors figured into a race and a death threat was a pretty big factor. Of course, even if the threat got through, the chance of Donado winning both races was almost impossible, but if they did win, and O'Kaye remained a long shot in the betting, then the pay off would be something else. They didn't know exactly how much yet, they would have to see how much the daily double would pay and that would only happen if Donado won the eighth race. But if they won the double on a fifteen hundred dollar bet . . . well, that would be all they'd need.

Moe wondered what it would be like leaving New York. Oggie was right though. It was their only way out and if they didn't do it now they'd never do it. Moe remembered saying a long time ago when he was still a younger man that this city was no place for old people. How many times had he seen an old person walking down a busy street with a cane, helpless to the attack of the rushing crowd, so helpless and small and frail. No. This was no place for old people. And the cold. The winters seemed to be getting worse and worse and here it was only December and already Moe was getting the pain in his legs. Then again, fifteen hundred bucks was a lot of money and they had spent the last year and a half saving everything they could and wasn't New York . . .

Oggie was back from the phone booth, and he sat down.

"Well?" Moe said.

"Well."

"Well, how did it go?"

"It went fine. Just like I thought."

"Keep your voice down. Someone will hear us."

"No one's going to hear us."

"So what happened?" Moe asked. "Tell me what happened."

Oggie screwed the top of the ketchup bottle back on and slid it to the side of the table. "I made the call. Some guy answered and I told the guy I was going to shoot Vasquez in the ninth race if he ran and that if Vasquez wanted to continue his career he better stay put in the locker room and take a rest. The guy asked who I was and I told him not to worry about it, that he better go tell Mr. Vasquez about our conversation or he'd have the little fellow's death on his conscience. Then he tried saying something but I hung up."

"I can't believe you did that."

"I did it. Now let's hope it works."

"You sure no one's going to suspect us? What if we win? Won't they know it was us who called?"

"Are you kidding? This city's full of nuts. I bet they've gotten death threats from guys who've lost their money before. Besides, there's no way they can prove it was us. Don't worry about it. You want some dessert?"

"Are you having some?"

"I think I'll get a slice of cheesecake and coffee."

"That cream pie in the mirror looks pretty tempting," Moe said.

* * *

Moe and Oggie got back to the OTB parlor just as the bets for the sixth race were closing. When the race was about to begin there were no lines in front of the cashier's window. Moe followed Oggie to the window and watched him push the betting slip under the slot along with fifteen one hundred dollar bills. The man behind the glass inspected the bills, looked at the two men for a moment, then punched the bet into the computer. Oggie put the betting ticket in his wallet.

When the sixth race was over Oggie went back to studying the paper. Moe was going to say something but didn't since Oggie was probably just trying to keep his mind off what they'd just done. Moe wondered if there was any way of returning the ticket and getting the money back. He decided he wouldn't even ask Oggie. It would only get Oggie upset and Moe didn't want to do that.

The odds were posted for the seventh race, then the bugle call sounded as the pay-off prices for the sixth were listed. Big Pete was still talking away to his friends. Moe tapped Oggie on the arm and said he was tired of listening to Big Pete shooting off his mouth and he was just going to take another walk around the station. Moe figured he'd just have a cigarette and come back for the start of the eighth race, the first half of the daily double. Oggie said okay, that he was going to wait inside and look over the paper.

Moe walked back to the main part of the station and smoked another cigarette. He promised himself that if they did win, and if they really did get to Florida, that he'd try his hardest to quit smoking. Maybe he'd even try getting himself back in shape. After all, he'd been a pretty good swimmer when he was younger and Florida was full of places to swim. He stopped thinking about it because he didn't want to jinx their luck. Moe found himself near the entrance of the station so he walked outside to finish the cigarette. He stood on the corner of 42nd Street. Crude movie titles and pictures of half naked girls stuck out from the theaters. The street was always so crowded and seedy looking but today, in the cold, it didn't look so terrible. The street had a nice misty quality as Moe looked at it through frozen breath. Moe tried to imagine if he would miss 42nd Street if he never saw it again. He decided he probably wouldn't. He'd been in New York all his life.

His hands were getting cold, even his cap wasn't keeping the stinging chill from his ears, so he went back inside the station. He shivered when he felt the warmth. Inside there were so many people rushing around. Moe wasn't sure when the eighth race began. The clock on the wall said 3:40 and Moe wasn't sure if post time was at 3:45 or 3:55. He thought it was one of those two times. He took the escalator back upstairs and saw that the race started in two minutes. Moe went over to Oggie.

"Did they announce the horses yet?"

"The odds are three-to-one on Lazette."

"It's freezing out."

"Look here," Oggie said pointing to the paper. "She's been a close second in her last two races and Donado knows how to ride the slow stuff. We got a real good chance in this one."

Moe remembered he was supposed to tell Oggie that the track conditions were slow and was glad Oggie already knew. He had been meaning to bring it up at lunch but had forgotten. The speakers went on and suddenly Moe realized that this was it. The first half of the daily double was about to begin. They had bet all their money. Moe's stomach got nervous as he heard the static or the hoofbeats or whatever it was.

"And they're off," the announcer said.

Lazette. Lazette. Lazette. Moe just kept repeating the name of the horse in his head until it blocked out the announcer's call. Lazette. Lazette. Lazette. Lazette. He couldn't concentrate on what was going on. The horses were around the first turn and Lazette wasn't even being mentioned. Moe felt dizzy. Lazette. Lazette. Lazette. Lazette. They were at the third post and the announcer's call penetrated his head and he heard Lazette's name. And the horses were moving hard now and coming around the final turn and Moe tried to clear his head and listen. It was all happening too fast and he had to listen. The horses were coming down the stretch and Moe heard Lazette's name along with another horse High Nessy and it was going to be close, it was going to be between these two horses. And then the fast paced voice of the announcer slowed as he called out the names of the first three finishers because it was a victory by more than two lengths and there was no doubt in the announcer's voice that Lazette had won the eighth race. Big

Pete gave out a yell across the room and Moe knew that they had bet on the same horse this time. Oggie was staring up at the television set waiting for the unofficial results and finally Lazette was posted as the winner.

"That's one," Oggie said.

Moe looked around the room. He felt dizzy. It was possible now. They had won the first race in the daily double. Now it was down to one race, one single race, just like if they had decided to bet on one horse, the long shot O'Kaye to win, and that was possible. Like Oggie said, no one knew O'Kaye but now that her foot was better people would see what a fine horse she was and she wouldn't be a long shot again.

The odds for the ninth race came on the screen. O'Kaye was a twenty-three-to-one shot in a field of twelve horses. Moe could imagine what it looked like out there on the track. It was probably overcast and the ground was still wet from yesterday's snowfall and muddy from the pounding of hundreds of hooves. The bugle call sounded and the official results were posted. Lazette paid $5.40 to win. Big Pete was telling someone in his usual loud voice how he was going to win the double because he had bet on the favorite Gulden Medallion to win with Reuben Vasquez on the mount and how Vasquez could ride the soft stuff better than anyone.

"I wish he'd shut up," Oggie said.

"He'll never shut up. I'd like to go over there and punch him right in that big mouth of his."

"He knows how to play the ponies though," Oggie said. "I got to give that to him. He's come up with a lot of winners through the years or at least he says he has."

A rush of voices interrupted them. When Moe and Oggie looked up at the screen they saw what they had been waiting for. Listed were the predicted pay-offs for each possible combination of the daily double with Lazette. Moe's eyes ran down the list to the number five horse, O'Kaye, where the estimate of a $114 return on a two dollar bet was listed. Oggie went right to figuring the amount a fifteen hundred dollar bet would pay, putting the numbers down on the margin of the newspaper with the felt tip pen. When Moe looked at the figure he thought Oggie had made a mistake. If they won they'd collect $85,500. Oggie drew a circle around the number.

"No kidding?" Moe said.

"No kidding," Oggie said.

$85,500. If O'Kaye won. If Vasquez lost. If Donado was able to handle the soft track. If an unknown horse with a foot that might be healed could beat out Gulden Medallion and the other ten horses. If this and if that and still it was possible. Moe calmed himself. He wondered what would happen if Vasquez got scared and pulled out of the race. But Gulden Medallion stayed the favorite at five-to-three and there was no announcement about a jockey change. And when the announcer welcomed the horses onto the track, sure enough it was Reuben Vasquez atop Gulden Medallion and Sal Donado atop O'Kaye and Moe imagined himself at the racetrack.

There was Sal Donado. Small and wiry riding out on this unknown horse O'Kaye. Moe saw O'Kaye. He pictured her as a brown horse, strong and sleek, alert ears, nervous eyes. Right in the center of her forehead was a white streak which made her stand out among the other horses. The air was so cold that O'Kaye's saliva froze on her bit as Donado led her in a trot toward the starting gate. She blinked her eyes in the wind.

"Post time in two minutes," the announcer's voice said after all twelve horses were introduced. Then the static went off.

O'Kaye was being locked into the gate now. Her hoof gingerly tapped the metal grate in front of her. Donado was rubbing the side of her neck, soothing her so she would relax, so that she would keep her strength for the race.

Moe saw Vasquez too, three gates down. He was a little on edge, maybe thinking he better not get out of the pack too far or some nut might get a clear shot off at him. Underneath him was Gulden Medallion, a dark and powerful horse, nostrils flaring, ready to run. Then the static pulled Moe back into the OTB parlor which quieted as the loudspeakers were switched on.

"They're in the gates," the announcer said.

Oggie was staring down at the newspaper. His face was stone. Moe could see where his jaw was biting down. The felt tip pen continued to bleed on the top corner of the page.

"Come on O'Kaye," Oggie said, not knowing that Moe was watching him.

It was the first time Moe had ever heard Oggie say something before a race. Come on, O'Kaye, Moe thought. Then the static changed. It was the roar of the hoofbeats, Moe was sure of that now, and he was back at the track, the green starting gate had popped open and the horses were off. And the announcer's voice helped Moe form a picture of what was going on.

It was a slow start for O'Kaye. She was behind most of the pack which was okay because Donado was just holding her back for the final turn. In the lead were three horses, Gulden Medallion among them. Vasquez was keeping his horse in the pack for now. Gulden Medallion was holding strong but he wanted to go faster and it was a strain for the horse to hold himself back. The horses were past the first post in good time. Sal Donado began his move. He let the reigns out and O'Kaye started passing one horse, then another, as she worked her way up the field. She was beautiful to watch, her long strides so graceful and smooth. Even in the mud she was beautiful. O'Kaye. That was a nice name, Moe thought. For a moment he saw the little girl who had smiled at him in the bus station.

"And at the third quarter it's Gulden Medallion and Foolish Dancer with Port Pleasant, Fade to Black and O'Kaye three lengths back," the announcer said.

O'Kaye. Moe saw her picking up speed now. Donado was letting the horse control herself as he eased his body all the way forward, the wind whipping his green and white jersey into a puff. Donado's breath was coming short and fast and raspy in the cold. O'Kaye was running so easily, just as the announcer said she was doing. She was so beautiful and her muscles were staying warm and loose despite the cold and she was moving faster and faster and faster, opening up, Donado letting her go free.

"Come on. Come on, baby," Oggie said.

Moe was back inside the OTB. He realized that in Oggie's mind, O'Kaye was having a harder time.

And the horses were coming down the stretch and the room went quiet for the announcer.

Moe saw them approaching the finish line. The announcer kept repeating the names of O'Kaye and Gulden Medallion and a horse named Foolish Dancer moving up on the outside. Moe couldn't picture Foolish Dancer too well because he kept seeing O'Kaye straining for the finish line. Donado was leaning all the way forward with his chin practically touching O'Kaye's head and they were coming to the finish and the announcer's voice kept mentioning the three horses and it was Gulden Medallion holding on near the rail and Foolish Dancer on the outside and O'Kaye was between them, pushing forward, pushing forward. Moe formed a picture to the announcer's voice and the horses ran hard and at the finish it was too close to call and too close to see.

Shouts went up all over the room. No one was sure if they had won or lost. Even Big Pete was quiet after yelling out it had to be Gulden Medallion that won. Up on the TV screen the word PHOTO was printed in bold computerized letters. They would have to wait for the winners to be posted. They would have to wait to see if they were going to Florida. Moe tried to picture it in his head. He tried to slow it down so he could see the winner and he thought he saw the white streak on O'Kaye's forehead passing the finish line ahead of the rest. She was a beautiful horse and the muddy track hadn't hurt her stride at all.

Shouts went up. Moe forced his eyes to look at the TV screen. He tried to clear his head. His stomach was turning over and he felt dizzy and he couldn't make out the print on the screen. He looked at Oggie. Oggie had snapped off the tip of the felt tip pen and it bled freely. Oggie's eyes were still on the screen as he folded the *Daily Racing Form* in half with a perfect crease and tucked it under his arm. Moe looked back at the TV and forced himself to focus. Foolish Dancer had won the race. O'Kaye had come in second. Gulden Medallion third.

"Let's get out of here," Oggie said.

"What happened?" Moe said.

"Nothing happened. Let's get out of here."

"But O'Kaye was in front."

"Let's just get out of here," Oggie said.

As Moe followed Oggie out of the OTB, he could hear Big Pete yelling how these soft tracks screwed up everything.

They took the escalator down and walked out of the Port Authority. It was already dark and the wind had picked up. Moe pulled his cap a little more snugly over his head. When the bugle call sounded and the pay offs for the ninth race were posted, Moe and Oggie were making their way down 42nd Street, like brothers, only "better than brothers" like Oggie said because they were together by choice.

Beer, Poker, Pool

Jerry Bradley

"This is good," Red said, taking a pull from the bottle.

"You think all beer is good."

"That's because all beer is good—for a fact."

"But your statement implies that some beer is better."

"Well, some beer is better."

"Not that you could tell."

"Of course I can tell. Just because I'll drink any beer doesn't mean I can't tell the difference."

"Yeah, right."

"See, I drink Bud. But the fact that I drink Bud and not Pabst proves I can tell."

"No, it only proves that you can read."

"What?"

"I'm saying that, if you couldn't see the label, you wouldn't be able to tell the difference between brands."

"I bet I could."

"Five says no way."

"You're on—but you buy."

Watley returned from the bar with three bottles and three glasses. He arrayed them before Red. "Here's a Coors, a Bud, and a Miller. Now let's see what you know. Turn around."

Red angled his chair toward the dance floor while Watley poured, putting an equal measure of Bud in all the glasses. He then placed all three bottles beneath the table.

"Okay, turn back around."

Red studied the glasses. He took a sip from each, then drained each glass in turn.

"Well?" Watley inquired. "Which is which?"

"One of them's Bud."

"Duh! I told you you could read. We know that."

"And one of them isn't Pabst."

"We know that too. I didn't buy any Pabst, smarty pants."

"But you said I couldn't tell the difference, and I just did. I told you I could tell Bud from Pabst, and that's what I did. Pay up."

"But you didn't say which beer was which. Which one was the Coors? Which one was Miller?"

"The Coors and the Miller were the ones that weren't the Bud. Pabst isn't Bud, Coors isn't Bud, and Miller isn't Bud. Get it? Now pay up."

"You're trying to cheat me," Watley protested. "I'm not paying."

"Welcher!"

"Gyp!"

"You owe me five."

"And you owe me five. So we're square."

"At least give me one of those beers you bought."

Watley retrieved the bottles from below the table.

"I'll take the Bud," Red asserted.

"There is no Bud. There's only Miller and Coors. You drank the Bud."

"Oh, I guess we see who the cheat is! Let me have the Coors then."

"I can't do that," Watley explained, "because you drink only Bud."

"I didn't say that I drank only Bud. Obviously I drink other beers. That's why I know the difference between Bud and Pabst. Why would I bet on being able to tell the difference between them if I drank only one brand?"

"Because you're stupid."

"That's what you think. So who paid for the free beer I drank?"

"But who won the bet?"

"Settle it over pool?

"Five a game?" Watley asked.

"You're on," Red said, "but I break."

"You broke last time."

"What do you mean?"

"I said you broke first last time."

"But I didn't break last."

"What's that got to do with it?"

"If you broke last, then it's my turn to break."

"No, you broke first last time, so it's my time to break first this time."

"So we're alternating?"

"Yeah, but not like you think."

"How do you think I think?"

Watley stared at Red. "Maybe you don't."

"If I don't, then how could I have developed a plan about alternating? So my plan proves that I think, and my thinking proves that you don't know what you're talking about."

"I don't have any idea what you're talking about."

"Are you going to talk or shoot?"

"Just break."

"Eight ball, right?"

"That's a slop game. Nine ball."

"That's dumb. We can't use all the balls. We get fifteen balls; we've paid for fifteen balls. We might as well use them all."

"Hey, genius, we could hold six back for the next game and save quarters."

"Then we would be playing six ball in that game."

"We could, or we could put in three more quarters."

"How does that save money?"

"You wouldn't because I'd still be clearing $4.25 a game off you every time I beat your ass."

"Let me ask you something. If we play nine ball, does the fifteen become the nine ball in the second game?"

"What?"

"The object is to make the nine ball in nine ball. Is the object to make the fifteen ball in six ball?"

"The six ball probably won't be on the table."

"I know that."

"So what's your point?"

"Is the highest ball the six ball?"

"No, the fifteen is the highest ball."

"So the fifteen is the nine ball in six ball?"

"Wanna shoot eight ball instead?"

"Break 'em."

Watley drove the cue ball through the rack of balls, smirking as the last came to rest. "My choice," he said. "I sunk a stripe and a solid, so I'm either."

"No, you made the stripe first, so you're a stripe."

"That's not the rule. It's my choice."

"You've got a choice as long as it's a stripe. If you shoot a solid, you're shooting my ball."

"Suppose I had scratched?"

"Then it would be my turn."

"But what color would I be?"

"You wouldn't be any color. You'd be through. It would be my turn."

"What would you be?"

"I wouldn't be anything until I made a ball."

"So you could be anything you like?"

"No, I'd be whatever I made."

"So why can't I be what I made?"

"Because you made a stripe and a solid. You can't be both unless you plan to make all the balls."

"If I can't be both, then I get to choose to be something."

"I told you you don't get to choose to be something. You either are something or you're not."

"So what am I?"

"I told you. You're through."

Three turns later Red sized up a cut shot on the eight.

"How can I be expected to beat you when I have this big sore on my wrist? Doesn't it bother you to take advantage of me that way?" Watley asked.

Grinning, Red stroked the cue unhurriedly. Ever so slowly the white ball eased past the black. It missed it narrowly but nevertheless altogether.

"I win," Watley announced.

"What?"

"I win. You scratched on the eight ball."

"I didn't scratch on the eight. I just didn't hit it."

"Same thing. That's a scratch."

"A scratch is when you sink the cue ball."

"That too. But if you miss the eight ball, it's a scratch as well—a table scratch."

"And what kind of scratch is it if I sink the cue ball?"

"That would be a pocket scratch."

"But you scratched earlier on the four, and you didn't lose."

"That's because it wasn't on the eight."

"You still didn't lose, did you?"

"No, you don't lose by scratching on the four. If this weren't a bar table, I would have to pull one of my balls out of the pocket and spot it."

"So you got to scratch for nothing?"

"What do you mean?"

"Did you pull a ball out of the pocket?"

"Of course not. How could I do that on a bar table? You don't get the balls back."

"So you scratched without any penalty whatsoever?"

"Not really. I had to watch you shoot. That's penalty enough!"

"And now you get to shoot. Same same. Why should I lose when I scratch, and you don't get penalized at all when you do? Do make up the rules to every game you play?"

"How about a compromise?"

"What do you mean?"

"Let's say that, when a player scratches and can't put a ball back on the table, then the other player gets to take one off. Okay?"

"Okay," Red agreed. "So you owe me a ball for scratching on the four. I'm taking one of my balls off the table now."

"But you don't have any balls left. You just have the eight."

"I know." Red picked up the eight and dropped into the side pocket. "You owe me five."

"Say, what is that sore on your wrist anyway?" Red inquired.

"Feel it," Watley said. "Go ahead. Feel it." Watley raised his forearm toward Red's face. A marble-sized swelling was visible above the wrist.

"Spider?"

"No."

"Wasp?"

"Nope."

"Bee?"

"Unh-uh."

"What then?"

"I don't rightly know."

"The how do you know it wasn't a spider?"

"Would've felt it. I didn't feel anything."

"Do you feel something now?"

"A knot. I feel a knot. See? Touch it." Once again Watley extended the swelled flesh toward Red.

"No, thanks. That's all right. What are you going to do about it?"

"Watch it I guess."

"What do you mean?"

"I'm going to see if gets any bigger."

"And if it does?"

"I don't know. I hope it doesn't."

"What if it doesn't get bigger?"

"But it's likely to. They always do."

"So you've had one before?"

"No, but I've heard about them."

"Heard about what? I thought you didn't know what it was."

"I don't—but I've seen things like it. And they're dangerous."

"How dangerous?"

"Dangerous enough to warrant looking after."

"But what good does looking do?"

"You know, the watched pot thing."

"Or in this case a watched boil."

"Same difference. If I watch it, it might not grow. But if it does, I'll notice."

"Then what?"

"Then I suppose I'll have someone take a look at it."

"But you've been looking at it. Even I've seen it. Will one more person do any good?"

"I'm not talking about just anyone. I'm talking about a doctor or somebody."

"I'm somebody."

"Not when it comes to this thing on my arm, you're not. You're certainly no doctor. If you were, then you'd know what this thing on my arm is."

"So why did you show it to me then?"

"Because it's the kind of thing that everybody should watch out for. And while you're not somebody, not in the doctor sense, you are someone."

"Wouldn't it make more sense to keep this a secret until you know for sure what it is? You don't want everyone getting upset over nothing, do you?"

Watley was puzzled by Red's remark. "What if it isn't nothing? I can feel it. That proves it's already something."

"But if only one person needs to watch it, then why tell everyone – unless it's contagious? It's not, is it?"

"Why, are you afraid to touch it? Admit it, you're afraid. Or jealous!"

"You can't be jealous of a sore. You have to be jealous of a person."

"I'm a person."

"Yes, you are, but I'm not jealous. If I were, it would be envy anyway, not jealousy."

"But you are curious. Admit it. You're stumped and don't know what it is."

"No, you're the one who doesn't know what it is. I think it's a spider bite."

"But I told you it wasn't."

"No, you said you would have felt it if it were a spider bite. And you admitted that you could feel it, that everyone could feel it. You offered to let me feel it. So maybe it's a spider bite."

"Maybe it is, and maybe it isn't. Want to settle it at cards?"

"Yeah, let's cut to see who deals."

"What's the point in that? Why not just cut for the money you owe me?"

"You'd like that, wouldn't you, particularly since you got to break at pool?"

"All right, we'll cut to see who deals. Then what?"

"Then we play."

"Play what?"

"Poker – a man's game. I guess I shouldn't be surprised you're not familiar with it."

"I suppose now you'll be telling me that stud is the only game to play."

"It's what I'm accustomed to."

"I'll bet you're accustomed to studs. Is that why you took so long in the rest room?"

"Watley, you'd play strip with a nun just for a glimpse of heaven."

"Nun? Why bring up your sex life? None is the only sex you've had."

"Just get the cards."

"Right here," Watley said, opening the pearl snap on his shirt. The cards had blue backs, but they weren't Bicycles, and they were worn too much to shuffle easily. Watley didn't offer Red a cut.

"Just make sure you deal clockwise," Red admonished.

"There's only two of us, so there is no clockwise."

"Of course, there's clockwise. Lookie there." Red pointed to the clock behind the bar, its red second hand sweeping in standard fashion. "That's clockwise."

"So if a clock runs ten minutes fast, that's clockwise? That clock's stupid."

"What I'm saying is, clockwise won't change the cards I'll get or you get—unless you try to cheat—but it will change the direction the cards come to me."

"What are you talking about? You couldn't find north with an atlas and a pocket full of lodestone."

"I'm not talking about that kind of direction. If you deal clockwise, then your right hand leads. You can't hide it behind the deck and palm a card as easily. If you come at me counter-clockwise, your left hand leads, and I can't be sure what you're dealing."

"All right, cry baby. Have it your way?" Watley made a grand gesture with the deck, then peeled off the first card awkwardly with his left hand.

"You did that for spite," Red said.

"No, I'm going to kick your ass for spite."

Watley dealt each two cards face down. Then he dealt another for each of them, this time face up. Both received jacks, two nearly identical nudes except one was blonde.

"You're a sick puppy to look at her that way," Watley asserted.

"Well, you're a suck puppy. Bet."

"How do you figure?" Watley asked.

"Your jack is lower. It's a club. Club is the lowest suit. Low card brings it in, so you go first."

"The first jack dealt has the right of way. And the lowest suit I ever saw was the one you got married in. How'd you make it shine like that?"

"I know you're wrong," Red countered, "but we can't cut the cards to decide because we're already using them to decide who won at pool. But since I'm eager to get my money, I'll speed things along. Pass," he declared.

"Check. It's called check."

"What?"

"Pass is for bridge. Check is for poker."

"There's no passing on a bridge, idiot. Everyone knows that. And I'm not accepting any of your checks at poker either. Only good old American greenbacks."

"If you don't want to bet, say, 'Check.'"

"Roger. Check."

"Why didn't you say that right away instead of dragging this out?"

"Because of the rules. Rules are important. They're what separate us from the savages. Without them dogs and cats would be dancing in the streets. Without them how would we get anything done?"

Watley was unprepared to debate whether dogs were savages. He checked Red's check, and both stared impassively at one another for a moment.

"Speaking of rules," Watley explained, "there is a special rule on the fourth card. If either one of us has an exposed pair—"

"I've got an exposed pair," Red interrupted. "Look at the ones on my jack."

"I'm not talking about that kind of pair. If either of us shows a pair, then that person can double the bet."

"But neither of us has bet," Red observed.

Watley shrugged. "Nevertheless, those are the rules." He dealt Red a deuce and himself a king.

"Wait, wait. Hold on!" Red said. "You're supposed to burn a card. You didn't do that. You should have burned the two. So that king is rightfully mine." He slid Watley's king—a naked brunette dressed only in what appeared to be a gold cardboard crown—over to his side of the table. "Deal yourself another."

Red may have been right, maybe not, but he didn't argue the point. He turned over an eight for himself.

"Check," Red said.

"You've got two face cards, and you're not betting?"

"I don't need to bet to the win the money; I just need to win the hand. Besides, I spent all my quarters at pool."

"So you're not going to bet on any round?"

"Street. They're called streets, aren't they?" Red corrected. "So why don't you bet?"

"On what—a lousy eight against your king?"

Watley burned and dealt alternately until each had six cards. Neither man showed a pair, but a gallery of eight nudes in exotic poses smiled before them. "The last card," Watley explained. "The river."

"Streets, rivers—now who's playing bridge?"

"Bridge is a girl's game."

"It sure was the last time I played. And I had a good time too until the policeman shined his flashlight under the bridge."

Watley couldn't hide his smile. He dealt Red a card face down and then one to himself. It was clear that neither intended to open. Both men studied their hands.

"Okay, let's see 'em. What have you got?" Watley demanded.

Red turned over his hole cards and pushed his best five forward: two jacks, the king he'd taken from Watley, a nine and a seven. Then Watley turned his.

"Flush," he said, pointing to five naked blondes, two with dimples.

"Nice try," Red said, "but color isn't the same as suit. And the way I see it, these women aren't wearing suits of any kind."

"But they're the same suits." Watley reassembled his hand, laying down his jack, a queen, a king, an ace, and a two. "Straight," he declared.

"How so?" Red asked.

"Well, an ace can be both high or low."

"Yes . . . but it can't be both high and low."

"Who says?"

"Hoyle, I guess."

"So who said you won at pool?"

"I did, I guess."

"But you didn't. I did."

"I did."

"No, you scratched."

"So it's one apiece. Let's settle it. I'm thinking of a number."

"Perhaps you should start with a letter instead of a number."

"Double or nothing?"

"M-i-s-s-i-s-s-i-p-p-i. That's three double letters to your nothing."

"But who has the sore on his wrist?"

Both men sat back in their chairs. There was nothing more to shoot or cut, nothing left to drink. Nothing to decide. Nothing to consider but the swelling on Watley's wrist.

Spider.

Flash

Gayla Chaney

Alone in the darkness of a motel room, on the eve of our nation's birth-day, at the end of my six-year marriage, I close my eyes and pretend to burrow deep into this pillow, burying myself like a seed in the cotton sheets. I have come to Las Vegas to avoid being in Dalhart, Texas, where my former in-laws throw their annual Fourth of July party, to which, this year, I am not invited. Thus, I have decided to throw my own private party, eight hundred and forty-seven miles away from home, in a place famous for good times.

Some folks might say I'm suffering from a psychological sequela of irrational gambling resulting from my recent divorce. Others might say I'm exhibiting the same illogical behavior that contributed to my former husband's departure. They might omit his new, younger love interest if they were only focusing on my role in the huge fiasco that ultimately led to our break-up.

But enough of what some folks might say. If they'd said less when I was there, I might have stayed in Dalhart and tried to put myself back together again. I might have acted more responsibly with my portion of the divorce settlement instead of experiencing a somatoform disorder, which is a term I learned from my ex-husband, the x-ray tech with a medical dictionary. In the wrong hands, a little knowledge can become a dangerous weapon.

Rory, my ex, diagnosed me as depressed. The man is nothing if not astute. He determined that I suffered from magical thinking. I told him I wasn't the only person who owned a rabbit's foot, read horoscopes, or analyzed dreams.

"Dream analysis," I reminded him as he was boxing up his possessions, "was considered very important by both Freud and Jung." I waited for a response and when there wasn't one, I added, "Paramount, in fact." Rory sighed and shook his head, but he didn't argue. He just kept on packing.

His departure triggered some of my more bizarre behavior. I did some childish things I'm not proud of. Rory's car took some abuse. His new girl-friend's place had some raw chicken parts sprinkled in her flowerbeds. There may have been an obscene phone call or two. But I don't think those incidents prove I'm crazy. They merely show that King Solomon knew what he was talking about when he said, "Hell hath no fury like a woman's scorn."

Maybe if I'd made more of an effort, I could have found a way to deal with my divorce in a less destructive way. Maybe I could have avoided some self-sabotaging behaviors that led to my job loss, the alienation of some former friends, and my unpaid house payments, which led to a notice of foreclosure. Maybe I could have behaved with a little more maturity and emerged from the aftermath of our separation and divorce as a better person. But, of course, that's not what happened. Instead, I came to Las Vegas.

Rory claimed I thought my life was a movie. He found it annoying when I refuted his remarks with lines from my favorite films. I informed him I was a cinema fan, which was no different than being a sports fan, such as he was, except for the object of obsession being celluloid instead of pigskin.

I sometimes dream movie scenes, varying them to suit my needs. I star in them and direct them from the comfort of my own bed. I call this practice "somatic cinema." When Rory and I were still together, I shared my dreams with him. "Big name stars played opposite me, and they worked for free!" I remarked to Rory on one occasion. Of course, I was kidding, but he told his lawyer and it wound up in court testimony. That's the kind of guy Rory is. But I left all that back in Dalhart. Tonight I am in Vegas and what happens here, stays here, so I can dream whatever I like.

This evening, I was on a losing streak that I couldn't seem to break, despite trying for nearly twenty-four straight hours. Exhausted, I returned to my hotel room and as my head hit the pillow, I gratefully drifted off, escaping from the reality of my losses, both in the casino as well as back home. I hugged my pillow in hopes of a pleasant scene from *It's a Wonderful Life* with my own personal angel, Clarence, when suddenly, a beanstalk shot up in the middle of the bed.

The absurdity of its appearance paled in comparison to some of my other fantastical dreams, so I watched and waited, bemused only by the ra-pidity of the stalk's growth. Abruptly, one of the stems from the stalk wrapped around my waist and yanked me out of bed, up to the ceiling and through the roof of that cheap motel, propelling me like a rocket into the night sky.

Thud! I landed in a place so far removed from the physical plane I normally occupy that any drifting smoke from a backyard barbeque pit could not possibly be seen, even with a high-powered telescope. I scurried to my feet and found myself standing in a cornfield, amid acres and acres of ripe yellow ears, ready for harvest.

Under normal circumstances, such a dream might be terrifying, but alone in Las Vegas in a strange motel with my whole life in turmoil, I felt only mildly curious. I was undaunted by a beanstalk appearing in my motel room. Landing in a cornfield seemed as natural as sunshine. That may be the greatest thing about letting go of realistic expectations. The strange and bizarre produce interest instead of terror.

Thus, I remained unfazed when a Louis XIV style chair suddenly appeared, exquisitely upholstered in blue and gold fleurs-de-lis brocade, trimmed with a matching gold fringe. Its appearance seemed to offer an unspoken invitation to take a seat. As though I was accustomed to being beckoned by beautiful furniture, I sat down.

The chair began to glide on an unseen track, moving with precision between the rows of this magnificent cornfield. It was better than a ride at an amusement park for there were no crowds, no distracting noise, no price to pay; there was only the serene motion of that divine chair as I traveled effortlessly through the fields, surveying the panoramic view of corn.

The cornstalks parted magically as I passed through, their amber ears tilting and the green stalks bending in what appeared to be choreographed unison. I was not the slightest bit alarmed by my situation. I felt unconcerned about possible repercussions that could occur from damaging a farmer's cash crop, or absconding with someone's magical chair. This is bliss, I said to myself, smiling, aware that I was dreaming, but determined not to wake up.

Instead, I began to ponder if my chair and I were possibly creating crop circles amidst the corn. The thought intrigued me. Perhaps it had been me all along, circling the globe in my dreams, mystically carving designs in farmers' fields in the middle of the night, leaving strange, artistic creations that have baffled the scientific world for years, and I never suspected my own involvement until now.

I could feel the cornsilks brush against my cheeks and their touch was as soothing as a child's kiss. This whole world is magic, I mused, and I wanted to stay there forever, but even as I had that thought, I spied a large oak tree growing in the middle of the cornfield with its branches spread out on either side of the trunk, reminding me of a patriarch blessing his children. Perched on one of the high branches was a man in a brown suit with a stethoscope around his neck, and he was smiling down at me benevolently. On his extended arm, rested a blue, velvet hat with a short, delicate black veil. I noted that the man bore a striking resemblance to the late actor, Burt Lancaster.

"Am I...in Heaven?" I stammered, thinking he might be God appearing as Burt Lancaster in order not to scare me to death, unless I was already dead.

The man laughed and shook his head. "No, this isn't Heaven, and it's not Iowa, either." I hadn't actually thought of Iowa, despite the cornfield clue. As a Texan in self-imposed exile in Nevada, temporarily unhinged from every rational thought, I hadn't even attempted to determine where my dream cornfield was located, or if there was some symbolism I was supposed to grasp that would give me a clue about my future. I was simply enjoying the ride.

The man in the tree released his hold on the beautiful blue velvet hat and it dropped slowly in a floating fashion, as though unaffected by gravity's pull before landing gently on my head. The man cleared his throat to get my attention. "Young lady," he spoke in a kind, yet authoritative tone. "You might need that hat where you're going."

I wanted to ask him where that might be, if not Heaven or Iowa. Church, perhaps? A funeral? Or will I time-travel back to the early 1950's when hats such as this one were actually worn? Maybe W. P. Kinsella has written me into one of his stories.

I had questions, lots of questions, such as will this corn ever be harvested for cattle feed or human consumption? Or will it grow eternally, gracing the dreams of people who somehow manage to find this incredible Louis XIV chair? But before I could get one single word out of my mouth, the cornfield and Burt Lancaster vanished, and I was awake in a dark motel room, and I knew that I was not in Heaven or Iowa or anywhere close to a Kinsella-esque field of dreams.

Las Vegas is not my city; but my city is not mine, either. It belongs to my ex-husband or to our former marriage, or to some other dimension that I inadvertently slipped out of after my divorce and now am unable to find the portal back. I'm a refugee from Dalhart, Texas. My former city no longer claims me. We are estranged.

At this point, I might declare a personal Declaration of Independence and set out in search of a new home. I would like to find a place like the farm in *Field of Dreams*; a place where dreams can grow taller than corn and anything is possible, even resurrecting the dead. I am willing to bet on my future. It may be a gamble, but isn't that why I came to this town? Looking for some kind of salvation in the form of an undefined "it."

It, it, it. I contemplate the word as I lay in my motel bed. There are endless possibilities inherit in that word. "It," possesses its own form of magic. *If you build it, they will come.* I mentally quote one of my favorite movie lines. Indeed, I am willing to build "It," just like Kevin Costner does in the movie *Field of Dreams*.

Although not experienced with a tractor, I'm the determined type. I could do it. However, building baseball diamonds in cornfields may be reserved for sports fans, which would exclude people like me. What about a cornfield for film lovers? Something that could be turned into an old drive-in movie theater where folks could come to watch *Casablanca* or *Sleepless in Seattle* or *Field of Dreams* on a big, outdoor screen. I like the idea that "It" could manifest differently, depending on the contractor.

The Louis XIV chair surely indicates that my cornfield will not involve baseball at all. Who sits in a Louis XIV chair to view baseball? My dream definitely indicates a variation on Kinsella's theme. And what about the hat?

In actual fact, I've never worn a hat. My head is larger than the average woman's, yet this blue, dream hat fits perfectly. Surely, that means something, which reminds me of another movie, one I can't recall at the moment. Still, I believe in signs, and I think everything happens for a reason. I believe there must be some benevolent force out there, beyond the troposphere that sends dreams and visions to help out those of us marooned on Earth. I close my eyes and manage to doze off again, despite the neon light flashing outside the motel window.

I slip easily into another movie scene. This time I find myself at the dinner table with Richard Dreyfuss. He is wearing a yellow hardhat and piling mashed potatoes in the middle of the table, sculpting them into a white, lumpy mountain as Teri Garr, his movie-wife, looks on. The suspense is building as Richard turns to me and whispers, "This means something. Grab your hat and let's get out of here."

I glance apologetically at Teri Garr, but she just shakes her head and hands me my blue velvet hat. It is apparent that the dinner scene is over. I rush after Richard while waving good-bye to Teri, swearing I never meant to steal her movie-husband. "No problem," she assures me and slams the door.

My Louis XIV chair is waiting. I sit down as Richard clings to the back like it was a dog sled. The wind howls so loudly that he has to shout, despite the fact he is standing right behind me. I expect him to holler, "Mush," but he surprises me with his command.

"On, Donner. On, Blitzen!" Richard cries out and immediately my chair rises into the air and flies toward some strange, distant mountain that resembles the old Astrodome. As we approach the mammoth structure, I think maybe that is where my new home abides. The baseball players have deserted it for a newer stadium. It was pronounced obsolete, but it looks fine to me.

There is something fickle about a baseball team that would leave a perfectly functional baseball stadium for a younger, fresher field. Based on that one fact alone, my ex-husband should have been a baseball player, but that's no longer any of my business. I am with Richard now, and I am filled with anticipation of what awaits us inside the Astrodome. I feel Richard's breath on my neck and he whispers something that I can't quite hear because of a distracting noise, but the thought of his lips so close to my skin excites me.

Someone is banging on my motel door saying something about housekeeping, but I am absolutely positive that it has nothing to do with Richard or the Astrodome, or my flying Louis XIV chair. I refuse to answer, hoping that whoever is there will go away so I can find out if someone has left me a Holy Grail inside the Astrodome, or a road map, or the slightest little clue that might explain what I am supposed to do *now* with my life.

But real-life people are never as cooperative as the people in my dreams and whoever is outside my motel door is obnoxiously determined. "Housekeeping!" A shrill voice calls out, and I hear keys rattling in the door. I apologize to Richard Dreyfuss, telling him and his invisible reindeer to go on without me. They vanish instantly. He'll probably never call, I think, and then I open my eyes.

"Just a minute!" I yell, cranky at having to end my adventure, although I realize from the light coming through the window that I have slept longer than I'd planned. I know motel employees have jobs to do and time schedules, but that doesn't make me any nicer as I throw on my clothes from the night before and swing open the door.

"Housekeeping," the woman, standing next to a large, overloaded cart, repeats her pronouncement. I want to respond with, "I heard you the first time," but I don't. Instead, I pick up my purse and room key before letting her in.

"Are you checking out today?" She asks as she leans on her cart.

"No, not today," I reply, escaping before she asks, when. I am not certain of the answer myself, having arrived last Thursday with twelve hundred dollars, my last twelve hundred dollars, hoping, insanely I see now, that somehow I might turn it into twenty-three thousand dollars in time to prevent foreclosure on my small, pathetic house, all I have left from my former marriage, my former job, my former life.

The bank will get my house. Why I thought it so important to hang on to a nineteen-hundred-square-foot house with aluminum siding, a privacy fence and a broken gate that lets all the privacy of the backyard come and go as it pleases, is not clear to me now that I've lost most of my money in a town that never sleeps, where everyone seems either manic or desperate, but unwilling or unable to leave. I should probably check out today. I have enough money to fill up my tank and drive back to Dalhart, collect my belongings, and surrender up my house keys. After that, I'm destitute.

First, I will get some breakfast. There are slot machines everywhere and even before I have my morning coffee, I deposit four dollars worth of quarters. It pays off. I end up with twelve dollars and twenty-five cents, and I head for the dining room with a smile on my face.

Maybe things are going to turn around for me. This is my third day here, and I suddenly feel lucky. Lucky, lucky, lucky. I start saying things in my head like, third time is a charm, three wishes, three is a magical number, three wise men, three blind mice, three strikes— you're out. I don't like that one, so I switch to singing a song about three companions: You and me and a dog named Boo, traveling and a-living off the land. I pause, not liking the "living off the land" part.

My coffee arrives and I cut the "three" stuff out and try to act like everything's okay. No problem here. Nothing is hanging by a single, fraying thread. I'm just taking a little summer vacation, and then I will go home, like Dorothy did after her visit to Oz. Though I'm not wearing ruby red slippers, I still lightly tap my heels together as I recall a young Judy Garland clutching Toto to her and murmuring, "There's no place like home." Home. Home. Home. The word resonates of baseball, which reminds me of my dream.

Maybe there was a secret signal in it, a hint, like dreaming the name of a horse before you go to the races. I remember Burt Lancaster in that tree, the cornfield, Richard Dreyfuss and the scene from *Close Encounters*, which is what I feel like I am having at this very moment, minus the spaceship and the baldheaded, naked aliens.

Could I write a self-help book? *How to Fuck Up Your Life in THREE Easy Steps*. It might sell. I might write myself out of this mess. Is that any more of a long shot than what I've been doing for three days? I think about it and decide that it is. I head for the slot machine with its bars and cherries and lemons.

By the end of the day, I'm one hundred and seventy dollars ahead of what I was at breakfast, but instead of feeling exhilarated, I'm annoyed. It's too little. I'm still nine hundred dollars short of what I arrived with, which was over twenty-one thousand short of what I needed. All I can think about is getting back in my motel bed and escaping into my dreams where I feel no pressure and I get to wear a blue velvet hat and hang out with movie stars.

As I drift off, I try to think of cornfields, believing I can set the stage. But like everything else in my life, I have little control over where I end up. I find myself sitting in my third grade classroom, watching Mrs. Starner make big, looping, cursive letters on the blackboard. She explains that we will do our spelling in cursive and anyone who prints will be bludgeoned to death right after recess. Terrified that I have already made that mistake, I almost wet my pants as the recess bell rings.

I bolt up in bed. The dream was horrible. I am sweating from the sheer memory of Mrs. Starner as the neon lights flash outside my window. It's

113

still dark, and I fear that it may never be light again. If only I had somewhere to go, some driving compulsion to find the Astrodome, some purpose, some mission, some all-consuming cause like a missionary or a revolutionary, or a waiting companion with whom to share the adventure.

Yet at 2:42 a.m., I'm at a complete loss. My head falls back on the pillow with my eyes open, gripped by the terrifying realization that I'm alone. This is the same bed, the same motel, but my dreams have turned to nightmares. I promise myself when morning comes, I will check out. I will pass by the slot machines in the lobby, I will get into my car, and I will leave this sick city before the ghost of Mrs. Starner finds me.

And if there happen to be any cornfields along the way, perhaps one with a lonely tree in the middle, I will stop my car and search the area for an abandoned farm house where I can store all my stuff after the bank takes possession of my house in Dalhart. Sometimes you can find such a place.

It wouldn't have to be permanent. I wouldn't be stealing anything; just squatting, so to speak. A behavior as American as apple pie or baseball or fireworks on the Fourth of July. And I'd only stay there until I could figure out what to do next, which shouldn't take that long. It's not as though I don't have any options. After all, this is America, a place where dreams can come true. Even long shots.

Then I remember. I have one hundred and seventy dollars that I won earlier, plus the one hundred and thirty left in my wallet. I'm out of bed, reaching for my clothes, dressing hastily before I grab my purse and motel key.

I smile to myself, imagining all the possibilities that life offers. Anything is possible! Is this what Burt Lancaster and Richard Dreyfuss were trying to show me? Thank God I pay attention to my dreams. I feel intensely grateful for the three hundred dollars I have left to plant like seed corn in this city where fortunes can spring forth overnight. I am fearless in the face of statistical odds. In fact, I am practically euphoric.

Heading in the direction of Caesar's Palace, I recall a Louis Pasteur quote my high school French teacher made all her students memorize: "Dansleschamps del'observation, le hazard ne favorise que les esprits préparés, Chance favors only the prepared mind." Quickly, I begin preparing my mind with positive thoughts, the lever down, three cherries up, a jackpot win!

Thinking of all the presidents' faces I have in my pocket, I am struck with a patriotic fervor imploring me to believe in the American Dream, rags to riches, Horatio Alger! Dare to risk it all, I challenge myself. Suddenly, I don't feel alone at all. I am surrounded by a revolutionary army, and I am enlisting. I start to hum the "Star-Spangled Banner."

The gleaming, neon lights of the casino remind me of bombs bursting in air. I stop humming as I join the throng drawn in by the flash of marquees and machines. As I reach in my pocket for a quarter, my mind sings out, "Oh say, can you see."

I drop my quarter in the nearest slot and hold my breath. As the national anthem crescendoes in my head, I pull down the waiting lever, believing that tonight it just might be my lucky song.

The Numbers Angel

Sheila Thorne

My daughter Lorelei was everything I'm not. Smart. Successful. Not like her ma, no factory job for her—she was headed somewhere. She went to college and graduate school and then she walked right into a good job, software designer for a top company.

At work I'd always boasted about her to the other women on the line. Lorelei won this award and that award. Lorelei won a scholarship. She was pretty, she had plenty of dates. Every one of my friends knew about her. "Hey June, what's Lorelei up to now?" they would ask. There's probably a whole generation of kids out there who hate her for hearing from their mothers all the time, "That June's Lorelei is first in her class. What's wrong with you? Why can't you be like her?"

I was tempting fate. I said to myself, be careful June, trouble will come, she's too good. *Did I make it happen?* That's what I wonder in my worst moments.

I still can't recall the day she telephoned without a stab in my heart. She'd never given a thought to a mole that appeared just below her shoulder, she said, until she got a bad case of bronchitis and the doctor noticed it while he was listening to her chest.

"You had that mole before?" he asked. "You should have it checked out."

So she had a biopsy and some tests, and they diagnosed it as malignant melanoma and feared it had spread to her lymph nodes.

I couldn't believe it. She was only twenty-six.

"Now Mom, I'm tough as nails, you know that," she said. "I'm a fighter. I'm going to survive this. I know it deep in my gut."

She was right about being a fighter. She'd always known what she wanted and gone after it tooth and nails. I had hope. I would look for the luck signs.

I wondered if it was the water she drank while growing up: I've heard on the news how some of the aquifers are contaminated by all the chemicals dumped out in Silicon Valley and there's more cancer around. I should have paid the money for the bottled stuff. I worked with some of those chemicals myself when I was on the wafer fab line, and I know how bad they are.

Then Lorelei explained that her doctor said billions of blood cells get reproduced daily, and they have to be exactly according to spec with all the defective ones rejected.

"There's no second optical inspector like you sitting inside my body checking them all out," she said. "It's all chance, pure chance. It's just my bad luck."

"Luck! Well now, I know a thing or two about luck, don't I? But you never listen to me."

"That's the thing you've never understood, Mom. There's nothing to know about luck. Luck is the same thing as chance. You come up with the short straw or you don't."

"Uh huh."

I struggled to move away from that particular subject, a dead-end. "Listen, eat lots of broccoli," I finally said. "I heard somewhere that's good for fighting cancer."

Lorelei had always made fun of me for believing in good luck and bad luck signs. She didn't like it that I gambled, it was a sore spot between us. I'm not a heavy gambler, I do it mainly for the company. I told her that again and again but she'd snort or make sarcastic remarks. I don't think she ever understood what I go through every day.

All day I sit hunched over a microscope, zipped into a gown like a body bag and wearing a shower cap and gloves, in a sterilized room where the air blows through the vents so loudly you can hardly talk to the woman no more than a foot down the line from you. I scan the rows of silicon chips lined up on little blue trays till I'm dizzy, inspecting circuits that glow green and yellow and pale red, looking for screw-ups, the misalignments and broken connections, and plucking the faulty chips out with my tweezers. Behind me the foreman glides up and down the line, peering over our shoulders with his hands clasped behind his back, checking our output. I'm the fastest second op inspector they've got. To keep my job I've got to stay fast, and what keeps me fast is the games I play while I work. I used to play games like, if I finish five trays before lunch break, I'll have a piece of cake for dessert. Twenty trays this afternoon, I'll stop at the Glo-worm for a beer before I go home. If I was dealt a lot of transistors I could do it easily, but if I got nothing but the big processor chips I didn't stand a chance. The not knowing was the game, what kept me awake and focused on my work.

Then some of the women on my line hooked me up to a numbers game. This was before the state lottery. I would pick three numbers from my totals at the end of the day to bet on. I'd buy my tickets at the Pink Elephant grocery store, just a few blocks from my house. The very first time I played I put up one dollar and won five hundred. Sometimes I bet on the number of rejected die instead of the total, or sometimes I'd pick numbers from the total of passed die instead of the net total. I bet small, just chump change, but whatever way I played it, it made the work more interesting, gave a little excitement to the day.

After a few months of this I was about a thousand dollars ahead. Then—back when Lorelei was still a toddler—a girlfriend convinced me to go to Reno for a weekend. I'd never been there before. I'd never even thought about gambling until I started playing the numbers.

Another mom from Lorelei's day care center agreed to take care of her for the two days. This was the first vacation I'd had since Tommy took off on me, and it was magical: the flashing colored lights, the tingly sound of money pouring down chutes, drinks on the house. I felt like a queen, like I was wrapped in all that plush velvet that surrounded me. I played the slot machines and keno and ate all I could at the buffet. Later, I learned to play blackjack.

Then I started stopping at the Four Hearts Card Room off 101 on my way home from work. Since I clocked out at two forty-five and Lorelei usually didn't get home from school until three-thirty or so, or sometimes later if she had band practice or softball, I would play for a little while to relax and enjoy the company after work. As soon as I walked in I could forget the assembly line and all the pressures. I was in my own special world. I liked to sip a tequila sunrise or a beer while I played my cards. No one at the table talked much, but there was still a connection that felt good. I just played to stay even, I always held with a stiff. It's the company I like even more than the excitement. It's not that I expect to win a pot of gold, but it's nice to ride on a little bit of hope every day. It's a way to keep going. When there's so much luck around, why can't it be me that turns up aces once in a blue moon?

After Lorelei grew older I took her with me to Reno and let her play in the video arcades. But Lorelei was always different. She was serious. She liked to read books—old dusty books from the library, not the kind you buy at the grocery store. Me—after I've been inspecting circuits through a microscope all day, the last thing I want to do is look at little squiggly words on a page. Sometimes I thought Lorelei was trying to make a point of being as opposite to me as she could. As a little girl she ran to me when she hurt, wanted to take baths with me. When she grew older, with all those books she read she got beyond me. If I had an opinion about anything she would frown at me and say, "Well what can *you* know? You don't even read the newspaper." Sometimes I felt like she was ashamed of me.

During her first year of college she said to me, "Mom, you have a sickness. You're a compulsive gambler. You're throwing money away instead of saving it up for something nice or useful."

"Oh yeah, like what?" I shot back.

"Like taking a trip on your vacation time, for instance. Or taking a course at the community college."

"Oh, that's a laugh," I said. "Where is all this vacation time? Who's worked her butt off every minute to support you? And who came through with the money to help you in college?"

Her father Tommy had once promised to help her, but when it came down to the wire he wrote from Seattle, where he's living now, that he didn't have it. She'd won a full tuition scholarship, but she still needed living expenses. All those years I'd been putting a little bit of my paycheck into a CD I could fall back on, and I gave it to her instead.

That shut her up, though I was still sore.

I'm not compulsive, and I think I've been a better mother for a little gambling, frankly, because it's kept my spirits up. After I've been to Reno, or the card club, I'm relaxed. I think without the gambling I would have done a lot more yelling at her. Because after an eight hour shift on the microscope, I sure did feel like yelling sometimes. But she never knew that.

* * *

Lorelei's lymph nodes under her right arm had to be taken out. After surgery I sat with her in her hospital room on the seventh floor. Green lines wiggled across the monitor that was attached to her, the same sickly, glowing green of the circuit pathways I inspect all day.

Seven's a potent number—for good or for bad. All that week I watched for more signs, but I didn't see any.

A huge picture window looked out on the bare, brown east foothills. The glass pane, flecked with dust, made everything outside look flat, like a giant, grainy television screen. The real world was that sealed-in hospital with its fluorescent lights and muffled noises, with the doctors on their rounds wearing dark suits and name tags, milling about in hallways like casino pit bosses and bunching in the elevator, eyeing me silently.

I went to see her every day. She acted chipper. "Actually, it's convenient I have all this time to think now," she said. "I've come up with plans for a whole new design project."

When she got out of the hospital, the chemotherapy started. I took her to the clinic for the hits, sat with her while the red poison dripped into her arm, drove her back to her apartment and stayed with her. She'd be sick during the night, and then we'd both get up in the morning and go to work.

* * *

The chances of recovery were about twenty percent, the doctor told me. One to five. When the first tests came out well, the good cells seemed to be winning. The doctors were cheering.

"What did I tell you," beamed Lorelei. "I've signed up for scuba diving lessons. I'm going to take my three weeks next year in Mexico. How does that sound?"

She looked pretty in her wig.

"Wonderful," I said, but right away I worried. You should always keep quiet when anything good happens. And sure enough, after a long spell of this good luck, a period where life seemed almost normal, they found tumors in her brain.

After that I have no clear sense of time or order. At some point she moved in with me. At some point she could no longer work and went on disability. Her hands trembled and she had spells of dizziness. I stopped socializing, never went to Reno or the card clubs anymore, barely managed to play the numbers now and then. I took a leave of absence from my job but I was worried sick they wouldn't let me come back. There's no union and they do anything they want with you, it's not a job like Lorelei's where they treat you right. Her they couldn't fire while she had this sickness because it's against the law. At my place they'd fire you anyway, assuming you didn't know your rights. And then you'd have to go through a big law case, which most of the time they'd win somehow or other because they have all the money.

In the low-ceilinged basement of the hospital, a long maze of corridors with red and green arrows painted on the walls led to a metal door with a sign on it reading "Department of Nuclear Medicine." This is where I took her to be zapped by a linear accelerator while I sat in a small white, windowless waiting room in a row of straight-backed chairs. The door would open and she'd stagger out into my arms. On the way home she'd be burning up. She'd lower the window and hold her mouth open to the rushing air to cool her insides.

But here's the worst part, the part that I don't like to tell. There was a small portion of me, just the tiniest, that was glad to have her back home again and *needing* me, my little girl, my angel. And this meant that in one way I was glad she was sick, or faintly glad, like having a memory of gladness, really, like a shadow of a memory, because that's what had brought her back to me. She no longer criticized me or looked down on me. She wanted me there for her.

I'd tell myself I mustn't feel this way, I *can't* be feeling this way, I'll pay for it. Then I would think about her pain and suffering, but that was unbearable. There was no way out.

My girlfriend Rhonda finally said to me one day, "June honey, why don't you come away to Reno with me for a weekend. You sorely need a break."

I said I couldn't go unless Lorelei went too, because sometimes her brain short-circuited and she collapsed. Rhonda pointed out that the change of scenery might do her good, might give her spirits the little boost she needed to keep up the fight. So I checked with her doctor and he said it would be all right. Then I had to convince her.

"Come on, you don't have to play. We'll go to the shows, sit by the pool. You can do whatever you want. You in the back seat, the buffets, it'll be like old times."

"Those are your old times, not mine," she said.

"Sweetheart, I'm not going to spend hardly any time gambling. I'll stay by the pool with you," I promised. "It'll be good for both us to get far away from that hospital."

Eventually she consented. Rhonda drove us in her car and we sang along with her tapes all the way up to the mountains. I felt lighter and lighter as we ascended. Even Lorelei giggled and hammed it up.

We splurged and got a two-room suite at Harrah's. I stretched in a lounge chair beside Lorelei, ordered a gin and tonic, and smeared my body with suntan lotion. I said to Rhonda, "Go ahead. You're on your own."

Then I lay back in the sun while Lorelei flicked through the pages of a magazine.

"Aah, isn't this the life now," I said.

That was the wrong thing to say.

"Maybe it's the life for you, Mom. For me it's not the way I want to die," she replied.

"Oh honey, don't think that way. Let's make the best of everything."

"You're right. I'm sorry," she said.

Squirming in the hot sun, I couldn't help but think of the excitement going on six stories below me and how I was missing it. I wanted just a little of it so badly. Finally, at around four o'clock, Lorelei went to take a nap, so I dressed and rushed downstairs.

For a while I sat with a cup of quarters in front of the slot machines, slowly unwinding as I watched the sevens, bars, and cherries spin around. I won twenty dollars, put it into silver dollars, and won a hundred more. It was a good sign, I thought, maybe it meant something. Then I found Rhonda and we went to the coffee shop, where we both bought eight-spot keno tickets. She had been losing all day, but she was happy for me. While we sipped our iced teas we watched the screen, and lo and behold, six of my numbers came up, for another six hundred dollars. We screamed. I leapt up and sprinted for the keno counter, hearing Rhonda's voice trailing behind me, too loudly, "You're hot June! Your lucky star's finally shining on you."

That night, instead of eating at the buffet, we splurged on lobster and champagne in the Steak House Restaurant.

I said to Lorelei, "Don't you want to play just a little bit tonight? You'll see, it'll take your mind off things. Maybe some of my luck will rub off on you."

She shook her head. "Sorry, I don't feel lucky. And anyway, what about the shows you promised?"

"Oh yes, the shows," I said. "We better find out what's playing."

She fixed on me her old narrowed, faultfinding eyes. "Yeah, sure. What you really want to do is gamble. Why don't you go ahead and admit it?"

Rhonda popped in, "I'll go with you, honey. Shit, I'm out of luck today anyway. I'd love to go with you."

"No, that's all right," said Lorelei. "I'd just as soon watch TV and go to bed early anyway."

"No, don't do that," I said. "Let's all go. Let's all go to a show together. Come on, let's see where we can get in right now."

"No. I said no," Lorelei repeated. "I don't want to."

She turned and looked directly at me. "When I was little, I used to hear you come into my room at night and take the money out of my piggy bank. Did you know I could hear you?"

I felt the blood pumping through my face and burning in a pool behind my eyes.

"But I always put it back, sometimes more than I took out," I said.

She smiled sarcastically. "Yeah, that's true. That's why I never said anything."

"I never cheated you, not once," I said.

She nodded. "Never mind. It's okay, Mom."

I felt so low. She might as well have slapped me outright. I had wanted this to be a good time for the two of us, our best time together, something to cherish and look back on, and it was all going wrong.

Rhonda patted my hand. "I'll go with Lorelei and you go down and enjoy yourself for a while, Junebug. You deserve it."

I didn't refuse because I needed to forget my troubles and there was nothing more I could say now to Lorelei anyway. So I sat a while at the blackjack table, and in spite of the disastrous dinner my winning streak kept right on running its course. I play blackjack pretty much by the book, basic strategy. But tonight, something felt different. I can't explain it, but I had a sixth sense—somehow I knew when to stand on hands you're supposed to hit and when to hit when you should stand. It was like I'd been given the gift of prophecy. I won a couple more hundred dollars. Yet I stayed depressed, for Lorelei's bitter words kept playing over and over in the back of my brain. One part of me was moving the cards along with surefire instinct and raking in the money. Another part was crying.

Then a grand vision floated into my head. While all this luck was finally on my side, this magic coursing through me, I ought to go for it and make Lorelei a great big present. That would show her. Like the extra money I used to put in her piggy bank, but much more this time, thousands, enough for her to buy anything she wanted or take that trip to Acapulco. Maybe she wouldn't ever scuba dive, but she could still spend a few days in Acapulco. That wouldn't be too much for her.

Craps is where the odds are good and you can make a lot of money fast. I'm usually just one of the small-time bettors at the table, not really in on the action because I've never had big money to throw around, but I've learned a few things about the game over the years. I said to myself, what can I lose? Lorelei's worth any risk.

So I started out cautiously, making a pass-line bet for ten dollars. The shooter rolled a seven. I pressed my bet and won again on another seven come-out roll. Pressed again, then took full odds when the shooter rolled a four. This table was getting hot, so I bought all the numbers across and kept my bets up as I raked in my winnings. The magic was still with me. For once, I was going all out for a pot of gold.

Everyone around the table was whooping and hollering as people crowded in to place their bets. By the time it was my turn to shoot, I was one of the high rollers I'd always watched before. Everyone was cheering me on. The bets mounted higher and higher as I kept rolling winners, betting on the come-out and hitting the points, backing them up with full odds. Now hundreds of dollars were being won on the rolls, and I saw my dream, my offering to Lorelei, the proof of my love which she would have to acknowledge, in the center of that table. I felt a surge of power like a rocket roaring straight up into the sky. Everyone at that table was riding on my magic.

I held those dice a long time, and I could feel the money burning in my pocket. Like a movie, I saw Lorelei lying on an Acapulco beach in the sun and me beside her, plain as daylight the two of us together stretched out like a number eleven. That was my sign. Put it all on the eleven and get back to Lorelei. I knew I'd win. So I asked the dealer to take down my bets. "Yes, sir," I said, "I'm going for the gold." Then I stacked all my chips up in little piles on the table, eyed the dealer, and said, "Eleven." He looked at me like I was out of my mind, so I nodded and said, "This is the big one. The one for my baby."

Then out of the crowd steps a man with slicked-down black hair and a thin line of mustache, sloping shoulders, a round belly hanging over his belt. He glides up to the table like a wound-up motorized toy robot and plops down two black chips on the don't come line. Who the hell is this Mr. Bad Vibes guy? A lot of people had money riding on my roll. I gave him a dirty look. His arms were folded, his face absolutely blank. And then I felt the air and the empty space all around me, in the hollows of my feet, raising the hair on the top of my head, a chill wind that prickled my skin into goosebumps and drained away my power. I threw the dice with trembling hands, and one landed fast and hard on three, while the other spun around. Seemed like it zipped around forever, finally swiping against the other dice and flopping down right beside it. Four.

"Seven out," the dealer said.

It was Lorelei I lost in the roll of those dice. The sign and the show of my love. The money had never been real, I'd won it and lost it and never held it in my hands. But I'd held Lorelei, felt her heart pumping against my breast, smelled the salt, like an ocean, of her hair pressed into my face. My hands could still feel the shape of her back, her thin shoulders, as I nuzzled her to me.

With my winnings lost, I dipped into the money I'd come with. I played the pass line and the don't pass and the field and kept on losing. The table had turned cold after that blank-faced robot man won on my roll, and he walked away. But still I stayed and kept trying one bet after another, place bets, proposition bets, big horn, hard ways, big eight, any craps, even any seven. And with each roll of the dice, my stack of chips got smaller and smaller. I lost them all and kept reaching into my purse, until it was empty.

* * *

The next morning I couldn't look Lorelei in the face. I had to borrow from Rhonda to pay my share of the hotel bill. She was good-natured about it.

Without a word Lorelei plopped herself into the back seat for the drive home. Rhonda did her best to make cheery conversation, but feeling the weight of Lorelei's presence behind me, I hardly responded. As we came down through the pines I stared out at the slats of sun and shadow on the road, like railroad tracks, I thought, and I wished they could take me far away.

Three weeks later Lorelei woke up one morning and said to me, "My head, Mom. It's time to go to the hospital."

"What do you mean, it's time? What are you talking about?"

"Please mom, just get me to the hospital."

She couldn't get out of bed or raise herself enough for me to dress her, and I had to call an ambulance.

I spent most of each day sitting beside her in the hospital. Nurses slipped needles into her, took her vital signs, tried to make her comfortable with concerned, perfunctory smiles on their faces. They didn't speak of cure any more, merely of "less pain."

I thought I should call Tommy, and he came down and sat by her side, crying now that he'd never paid enough attention. He could only stay a day. "Call me," he said, leaving out the "when."

Lorelei drifted in and out of consciousness. Sometimes she knew I was there and smiled at me, sometimes she thought I was someone else. I tried to be everyone for her. I only left the room when the nurses drove me out at ten o'clock, or when they forced me to eat something in the cafeteria. At home I felt like I was drowning in the emptiness and silence. I'd turn on the TV to have something to hang on to until I fell asleep on the couch.

* * *

I wondered about all the things I might've done wrong. What if I hadn't taken her to Reno, what if I hadn't had that little bit of wicked secret gladness, what if I'd gone to church and prayed, what if I'd fed her different when she was a child, fewer processed foods maybe? Was it all really just luck?

Then she no longer spoke at all. The room was gray in shadow and filled with the sound of her labored breathing. The nurses let me stay with her all night. Through the final moments, the sudden stillness in the room, the nurse's pronouncement and the withdrawal of the monitor and tubes, I kept squeezing my eyes shut, hoping to open them to a different scene and place, but it was always the same.

Only the obligations of death lifted me out of the chair and carried me along. I had to make funeral arrangements, phone calls. Somehow I walked out of the hospital and across the street to the parking garage, the sound of my own footsteps echoing in my ears. I hurt all over, as if a fist had plunged right out of the blue sky and socked me in the gut. As I drew up to my car, I was startled to see that the car parked next to it had the numbers 714 on the license plate. That was the same number as Lorelei's hospital room.

I drove home and forced myself to go into her empty room to choose the clothes to take to the undertaker. I started touching all her things, lifting them one by one and pressing them to my cheeks, not thinking about what I was doing. On the lower shelf of her nightstand I saw a Bible, which I picked up and aimlessly opened. And do you know what? It opened to page 714.

Then I knew. It was a message, a message from Lorelei in heaven. 714. Lay a bet on 714.

Cassidy's Gamble: A Palimpsest

Clay Reynolds

There had to be something wrong somewhere. Cassidy had been playing the same poker with the same bunch of assholes for six months, and he had never, never drawn four-of-a-kind. There was nothing else showing in the seven-stud game. Nothing.

Seven-stud was all they ever played. Cassidy preferred other games where he believed the odds worked better for him. But this gang of mental misfits wasn't smart enough for hold 'em, and they didn't have the guts for five or three-card games. Seven-stud it was. Nothing wild. Nothing fancy.

He looked around the table. Two fives here, a jacks-possible there, but nothing like a boat or even trips indicated. Most everyone had squat, not even another pair showing. He had two sevens showing and two down and two cards to go. Just enough to bet on, but not enough to look like much. Hellfire! Maybe his luck *was* changing.

He bet cautiously, trying to keep a serious but casual look on his face, trying to stop his hands from shaking. Friday after-work pots were never large. The most he'd ever seen was near two hundred, but this time, for some reason there was a good start already. The players studied the ten-spot he'd carefully put onto the pile. They knew him to be a cheap bet, easy to bluff. Ten bucks was heavy for him. He regretted the mistake. One turned over his cards, then another did the same. The others furrowed their brows, inspected their hole cards—no, you don't, you motherfuckers, he wanted to scream, you're not bailing out on me for a sawbuck bet. Instead, he tried to look casual, disinterested. He drew a cigarette from his jumper's pocket and put it on his lip. The jacks-possible and the fives stayed. The Okie with zilch raised ten more bucks, grinned around the table like the idiot he was. "No guts, no glory," he said as if he just made up the expression.

Cassidy studied the mound of money on the center of the wire spool that served as a table and fired his smoke with a wooden match. What could be sweeter? The jacks-possible called, and the fives raised twenty more. That was a surprise. He sucked the smoke deep, blew out the match with a stream of smoke through his nose and inspected his hole cards, shook his head as if in woeful self-pity for his own foolishness. This was *too* good. The pot must be damned near four hundred by now. Four sevens! Shit! He crumpled two tens and dropped them in the pot, calling. Two more cards—two more chances to build.

His next up card was a king, and he felt good about that. His hand still looked only fair and hid dynamite. No help for anybody else showed up. He bet twenty—holding the bill for a moment over the pot before letting it fall, as if he was struggling with the decision. The jacks-possible, a heavily freckled, nose-picking red-headed punk from somewhere back east, claimed he had done time in Attica, called, and the fives raised fifty. Cassidy stared at him in mock disbelief, although he really wasn't faking. What the hell could he have down? He was a big guy, black and ugly. His face looked as if something stepped on it when he was a baby, flattened it out, spaced his eyes too far apart, gave him the look of an idiot. But Cassidy knew better. The guy was from Fort Worth, had gang tattoos. He was smart, slippery and hard to pin down. He was also built like a dump truck and had a mean streak that could turn ugly quick. Cassidy had made a point of staying on his good side.

The Okie called—no raise this time, and no comment—and Cassidy studied the table. His attention stayed on the fives. It didn't matter what he had in the hole—sevens beats fives—nothing to do but follow the plan, build the pot. The sweat under his arms trickled down in spite of the near-freezing temperatures outside the unheated drilling shack. One more card and he could quit winners. Quit rich! It was so close he could taste it. He flicked ash into the floor, called.

He didn't need to look at his last card, but to keep up the bluff, he raised the corner carefully, pretended to peek slowly. He had planned to groan loudly, curse, really suck them in, but when he saw the card he stared at it, then groaned for real. What the hell? Another seven! A club! He had to force himself to hold composure. What the hell was going on here?

He casually checked his other hole cards, tried to focus. Two sevens down—a spade and a heart—two sevens up—a diamond and a club. Now, another seven of clubs down. He almost laughed out loud, but instead, he sucked in the last of the cigarette. "Jesus," he breathed out in a smoky rush and fingered the cards.

"You going to bet those cards or jerk them off?" the Okie asked, then laughed his falsetto, tinny bark.

"Don't rush me," Cassidy said. "Lot of money out there."

"That's for goddamn sure," the fives said. "And most of it's mine."

Cassidy looked around the table, inspecting faces, hands. The jacks-possible had been playing and losing steadily all along—for months. No way he could be a cheat. He was too proud of how tough he was, how he could take anything. The fives was dealing, had given him the bogus seven—in fact, all five of them—but he knew the guy, he thought. He'd needed a friend on this job, and the fives had been it. He had a temper, but he was honest, Cassidy thought, and he only won from time to time, never getting a really big pot too often. He *could* be that careful, that smart. But it wasn't likely. Any whiff of a challenge could get you a broken neck. Besides, he was betting into him. If he wanted to give him money, he could just hand it over.

The Okie was too stupid to double-deal or cheat. Besides, he always stayed in so long as he had anything showing—even just a face card with an ace to match it—and so long as he had money, which he always did. He was the head engineer's nephew, was called "acting foreman," which was bullshit, since it only meant that he never had to do any actual work. He made more than the rest of them put together. That's why they let him play with them.

The two folds were sitting, quietly watching, smoking. One was a redneck from East Texas, used to work for the phone company, he said. Got laid off, came out here to make a buck, then he was headed for California. The other was a Cajun from Louisiana. Good guy, for the most part. Kept to himself, mostly, had an ugly scar running down the side of his face. It wasn't that old, Cassidy noticed. Got the shit beat out of him two days after he arrived on the job. He called the fives a "'groid" to his face and learned better, quick. Since then, he'd been quiet, kept to himself, walked around trouble. Even if they'd slipped an extra card into the deck earlier, why? No one had won with sevens or any combination of sevens all afternoon. It made no sense.

"You gonna bet or what?" the fives asked.

Cassidy shook his head, rubbed his chin. The others shifted their weight, almost together, impatient. Even if the move was to suck him in to with too good a hand to fold, hustle him into a sucker bet, who could beat him with any combination showing? What was the point? He wanted to jerk them each up by their collars and ask each one to his face. Instead, he chain-lit another cigarette, thought hard.

The sweat under his shirt turned cold, and he began to see himself accused of cheating and unable to deny it—convincingly, anyway. Maybe that was the game. Maybe it was a set-up to give one or more of them an excuse to beat him half to death, take his money, fuck him up for good. He could call a misdeal right now, he thought, or just fold the hand. But that would mean he'd lose that pot. It was too much money to just walk away from, and nearly two hundred of it was his own cash, wages he'd busted his ass to earn and planned to save most of. He needed that pot. It was time to move on. He had been there too long. Without that money, he'd have a rough road ahead.

The jacks-possible snorted, leaned over, blew snot out of his nose onto the floor. "Shit or get off the pot," he said, wiping his face with his sleeve. "I'm growing whiskers sitting here."

"You'd have to have hair on your balls, first," the fives said. The jacks-possible gave the big black man a narrow look. "To do that, you'd have to *have* balls," the fives added, then laughed. The others chuckled nervously. The jacks-possible sneered briefly, but put his eyes back on the table. Angry tension seemed to warm the room even more.

Cassidy slid twenty dollars out onto the table and waited breathlessly. The jacks-possible scowled down at his hand, cursed, then turned over his cards. Good, that cut down the odds. If everyone would fold, Cassidy thought, he could claim they'd been bluffed, never show his hole cards. Damn! He suddenly thought. That would be sweet!

The fives didn't hesitate, though. He raised fifty—it *must* be him, Cassidy thought—and the Okie called, no raise. "I'm all in," he said with a grin. "Nothing left but my underwear."

"You wear underwear?" the Cajun asked, snorting. "Didn't know Okies wore such." He laughed. "Thought all you Okies went *au natural*, specially them little injun gals."

The Okie looked confused. "I'm not an—"

"My mama's from Oklahoma," the fives said, steady. "And she's half Cherokee." He swung his big head around, looked at the Cajun. "You want to make something of it?" The Cajun looked down at the floor, shook his head, shut up. "Bet," he said to Cassidy. "Or chicken out. I'm tired of fucking with this."

Call the fifty and get the hell out, Cassidy said to himself with an urgent internal voice. That was the smart move. He sucked his smoke, nearly gagged, then fingered the few bills remaining in front of him. Hell no! he heard the same voice shout. Up a C-note, and fuck you! He shoved the last of his bills into the middle of the spool table.

The others stared at him for a moment, disbelieving, then started cursing and muttering. He grinned slyly, then ground out his cigarette and lit another. Too late to worry about a bluff. He was all in. The fives fingered a wad of bills from his shirt pocket and, without counting it, dropped it in, calling. The Okie stared hard at them, then pulled out a nice wallet and from a thick sheaf of notes, extracted two crisp fifty-dollar bills. He smoothed them out in front of him, then fingered them over, holding them by the edge, as if they were hot. "Call," he said.

Cassidy took a breath, then flipped over two of the sevens, leaving his final card—the fifth seven—down. He sat back, folded his arms and smiled. He never took his eyes off the last hole card—the extra club—but he was boiling inside, waiting for the storm to break.

The Okie cursed, as he always did, and pretended to fall back off the crate that served him for a chair. The jacks-possible snorted, blew out his nose again. "Figures," he said. He leaned forward to rake in the cards, while Cassidy began stacking up the cash. The fives stared at the pot, shaking his head, then looked up at Cassidy with a grudging complimentary expression. "Had me by the short and curlies," he said. "Played me like a fucking fish."

Cassidy grinned and said nothing, but his heart was pounding a rhythm in his ears. He pulled the stack of bills toward him, straightened them in an elaborate exaggeration of organizing them, and at the same time scooped up the bogus seven of clubs. It was a gamble, but he had to take it. With as much stealth as he could, he stuck it under his watch's wristband.

"Easy come, easy go," the Okie said, sitting down again.

"It ain't that easy," the fives said. "You'd know that if you were worth a flying fuck."

The Okie stared at him for a beat, tried to assess the comment. Then he grinned. "Wise guy," he said, smiling, looking around.

"Asshole," the fives muttered. "Somebody deal."

Cassidy stuffed the bills into his pocket, then pulled his jumper's cuffs down and buttoned them. "I'm done," he said, standing and buttoning up the front of the coat. "Quitting winners for once." He stood and waited for the reactions he knew would come.

"You can't quit winners!" the Okie yelled too loud. "It's not fair."

"Chickenshit, you ask me," the jacks-possible added, stacking the cards for a shuffle. Cassidy swallowed hard. "Just typical Texas chickenshit." He halved the deck and fanned it.

The others joined in, but the fives stopped it. "He's lost enough, past few weeks," he said and cut the cards. "Don't blame him." He flipped a five-spot out to the middle of the spool table, and looked at the jacks-possible. "Deal," he said.

"Later," Cassidy said.

"Where you going?" the fives asked, his wide eyes narrowing. He was their ride to town.

"Take a shit," Cassidy said, "you want to watch?"

"Not so you could tell it," the black man said, faking a scowl. "He's probably going to go jerk off the hard-on he just got from finally wining a hand," he said, then laughed. The others joined in automatically. Then, to

Cassidy, "I'm leaving after couple more," he said, glancing around. "Less I lose again. You want a ride, be around."

Cassidy nodded, pulled his hardhat down low over his eyes and slipped out and closed the door of the drilling shack behind him. He sighed deeply in relief. He felt as if he'd been holding his breath a long time.

Outside, the wind cut across the gray sky in one final effort to make winter a permanent state of affairs on the Texas plains. He flicked his butt away, watching the red coals scatter and disappear in the gale, then lit one more, cupping the flame of the match in his hand as he contemplated what had just happened. It was still unreal.

He studied the darkening sky. They'd quit early that afternoon because of the wind and the threat of rain, maybe lightening. But once the cold front passed, they'd be back out here, punching another hole in the gravel, trying to coax out a few more barrels of oil from a rapidly depleting underground sea. It was nasty, dirty, hard work. No talent required, no knowledge or ability. Just a willingness to show up on time and risk a finger or a hand to make some asshole millionaire richer.

He looked at the shack's single opaque window glowing yellow against the gloom. There was no percentage in hanging around here, he thought. The red-headed jacks-possible once claimed he could feel a "light deck," won two bets Cassidy was aware of by proving it while blindfolded. Could have been dumb luck, but still. He thought hard. They were bound to figure it out soon, and they'd want a replay of that hand. Or worse, he thought, they might just decide to tack a piece of his ass to the drilling shack wall. They were a rough crew. Two guys had already been beaten badly enough to make them quit, and that was over nothing. The fives held them in line, for the most part, was a kind of unofficial foreman, since the Okie wasn't worth a tin shit. But not even he could stop them if they thought they'd been cheated out of the largest pot they'd ever had, especially if he was the one who thought he'd been cheated out of the most of it.

Leaning against the rig platform, he pulled out the wad and quickly counted the money. After subtracting his bets, there was more than seven-hundred-fifty bucks in big bills, maybe sixty or eighty more in ones. He mentally added that to the two grand or so he had stashed in a cigar box in his room in town. His rent was paid through the first, and he didn't owe a dime to anybody. His landlord had a ten-year-old Jeep—no top, bashed in door, but it ran good, had decent tires—he said he'd sell him for a thousand. That left plenty for gas, food, even a bottle and a woman down the road. For the first time in years he had money to travel on and, he thought with a glance toward the shack, a motivation to go. For once, there was no woman to say goodbye to—or to feel guilty about not saying goodbye to—and nothing to hold him there. He considered Las Vegas. Maybe his luck had changed. Or there was Reno. That was a better idea. Safer. He'd been headed there when he stopped off here to work up a stake.

Cassidy glanced at the trailer office, but it was dark. Goddamn Calhoun, he thought. He already split. Fucking bookkeeper for the company, he ran a nice operation on the side. He showed up every Friday, handed out their paychecks, then offered to cash them on the spot—taking ten cents on the dollar just to keep them from having to wait till the bank opened on Monday—but he usually hung around to see if anybody needed a loan against the next week's wages. He was a tough, mean son of a bitch, Cassidy thought. Wore a black suit, black hat, big black pistol in a shoulder rig under his coat. He held out a whole week's pay from the start. Said it was a deposit against any equipment they might damage or steal. Truth was, it was to keep them from doing what Cassidy was about to do—run out on him. He always said they could have it any time they wanted to quit, but he wanted to pay them off, make sure they didn't leave with anything other than what they showed up with. "That don't count fingers and toes," Calhoun laughed. "Them you can leave. No charge."

Cassidy looked around at the tools and drilling equipment, junk and rusty chain and pipe littering the area. There's nothing here I want, he thought, nothing but my fucking money. He looked again at the trailer office. Goddamn, Calhoun, he thought. That was damned near six hundred more.

Well, he decided, it was too damned bad. He put his hand into his pocket and fingered the role. That more than made up for the wages, and he didn't have to waste time listening to Calhoun try to talk him out of leaving. "We're short-handed," he'd say. Yeah, Cassidy thought, that's why you hired my sorry ass in the first place. You run short-handed, he wanted to tell Calhoun. It's the way you make money on these wildcat operations. He could send an address, hope the son of a bitch would mail the check, which he probably wouldn't. Calhoun was banging the little brunette waitress at the truckstop in town, and she was probably taking every nickel she could pump out of him just to keep it from his wife, who was probably the only person in the world he was afraid of.

He looked at the sky again. Beneath the lighter gray of the late afternoon clouds a darker front was moving in. Snow there, he thought. Sleet and snow. A good time to travel. After this, the season would change, spring would come on, then summer. It would get goddamn hot out here. Give me the cold, Cassidy thought, pulling his hardhat down lower over his eyes. I'd one hell of a lot rather shiver than sweat. He was tired of being a roustabout, anyway, tired of hard labor. Rodeo season was starting up. He'd been a pretty fair horseman at one point in his life. Maybe it was time to try that again.

He stuffed the wad down deep into his pocket and turned his coat collar up against the wind and began moving toward the highway. It was a five-mile walk and mostly into the wind, but he'd walked farther and harder in the past few years. He focused on getting back, grabbing a bath, getting the money, buying the Jeep, then hitting the road north. He had clean clothes, there. He looked down at the greasy jumper, the stained overalls. He'd burn these.

The wind was so stiff, he had to lean into it. It stung his eyes. As he approached the blacktop, he spotted a car moving slowly against the wind. It was an old, plain Buick sedan. Probably a preacher, he thought. Nobody out here but preachers drove Buicks. He waved and began moving at a more rapid pace. When he lifted his arm, the wind cut under his jumper's cuff and caught the card. It scraped against his arm.

If they discovered the deck was off, maybe they'd figure it'd been that way all along, he thought. The redheaded jacks-possible had brought the cards with him. Always did. Maybe he mixed up two decks. It was pretty worn out. Maybe they wouldn't notice it at all. They might quit in another hand or two. He started to trot against the wind, so maybe it wouldn't be missed. If the deck was light, now, maybe that wouldn't seem so odd, either. His mind was suddenly alive with possibilities. Maybe the deck had been "heavy," not light. He hadn't noticed anything about it when he dealt. The extra seven could have been there all along. Just one of those things.

It really didn't matter. He was through with the oil patch no matter what. He'd rather hose shit out of cattle trucks, he decided. He looked back at the drilling site. The light was still glowing in the shack window. They were still playing. Any minute now, they'll figure it out, he thought. They'd kick his ass if they thought he cheated. That had been the biggest pot he'd ever seen on that table, probably the biggest any of them had ever seen on a Friday afternoon. A thrill of panic raced through him. They'd kill him, he thought.

For a moment, he almost turned back. He saw himself going back inside, telling them what happened, showing them the bogus card. Laughing it off and tossing all the money on the table. Big joke, and all on him. Then he shook his head and the vision evaporated in the wind. That wasn't going to happen. There was no way that could happen. If they didn't kill him for cheating, they'd probably just kill him for being a damned fool. General principles.

He finally reached the shoulder of the highway, about fifty yards in front of the approaching car. He was breathing heavily and barely able to lift his arm. The dude ranches up around Reno would be opening in a few weeks, he considered. Maybe he could use part of the cash to get a cowboy outfit and a job up there. Those rich Yankee divorcees were always hanging around the casinos, looking for a cowboy to play a little "buckin' bronc" on their pampered backs. And some of them were willing to pay for the ride.

He'd never seen himself in such a role, but then he'd never won at anything before today, either. Maybe his luck *was* changing.

The Buick passed him, slowing, weaved a bit, as if unsure, then pulled over and stopped to wait for him. He almost fell over, running against the wind. He would be damned glad to get out of Texas and the goddamned wind for a while, anyway. He didn't think it blew like this in Reno. The more he thought about it, the better Reno sounded. He wanted to get away from stupid oilfield workers who thought that because they had grease all over their clothes and under their fingernails they had to fight anybody who didn't. Since he got here, he'd spent his time hanging around this jerk-water town that mostly closed down at dusk. They had one rundown honkeytonk on the outskirts, where he usually wound up trying to lay some overweight, overaged, overdyed retread who probably had a half-dozen ugly kids in a mobile home parked on the other side of town and a husband with a full arsenal stashed behind the seat of his pickup. Shit, he thought, Reno was sounding better and better all the time.

The Buick had a preacher in it all right. He could tell by the thick Bible on the front seat. Cassidy moved it over and slid in with a smile at the old minister behind the wheel as he steered the car back into the wind and pushed it hard to regain speed. The car's heater was blasting, and Cassidy, overheated from his run to the highway, unbuttoned his jumper, rolled up his sleeves. The car was fighting to stay on the road against the cold front that was now howling a steady stream of angry wail, assaulting whatever dared to rise above the sandy ground along the highway.

Cassidy settled back, made himself relax. He fished out a cigarette and lit it.

"No smoking in the car," the preacher said, then added apologetically. "No smoking, no drinking, no cursing. Them's my only rules."

Cassidy flipped the smoke out the window, stared into the darkness after it. They rode along in the silence beneath the wind noise for a while.

Finally, the old man glanced into Cassidy's lap and smiled. "Lucky in love?" he asked, nodding.

Cassidy looked down at the card protruding from his watchband, and new sweat broke out on his forehead, something in his chest hardened and dropped into his gut like a rock. Lying in his open palm was the seven of hearts.

He stared at the seven with the same sense of disbelief he had before when it first appeared in his hand. Somehow, in his confusion, he had picked up the wrong card. There was no way, now, that he would have time to get into town and clean out his gear, make the deal on the Jeep, and get on the road before those idiots found the deck had two club sevens and put the whole thing together. It would be no good trying to explain what had happened. They'd never believe him, even if they heard him out before they killed him, or tried to. He wondered how long it would take for them to figure it out.

"How far you going?" the old man asked him.

Cassidy thought briefly about the money in his room, about the Jeep, his clothes—everything, in fact, he owned.

From behind them a pair of headlights suddenly flashed, and the preacher moved slightly over to allow them to pass. The fives' GMC crew-cab roared past them. He could see dark figures in the backseat, with the redheaded jacks-possible riding shotgun. Shotgun, Cassidy thought. That's about right. Their taillights quickly faded into the windy darkness, barreling toward town and, he knew, the rooming house where he lived.

"How far *you* going?" he asked.

"Why, Amarillo, if this norther don't blow me off the road." The old man shook his head. "Got to preach a funeral up there. Old friend of mine." He peered out of the windshield. "Bad time of year to die, I guess, but the Lord don't wait for time or weather."

"Mind if I just ride along with you?" Cassidy's shoulders sagged with the weight of resignation and loss. Fucked up, again, he thought bitterly. He wouldn't get far on the winnings alone. He needed his stash. Hell, he thought, he couldn't even cheat to keep from cheating.

"Welcome the company," the old man declared. "Radio don't work. Don't see too good at night. Might ask you to drive here in a spell, you got a license."

"I've got a license," Cassidy said, sighed. "Just no car."

"I figure eight hours, give or take," the old man said. "Like to make it by late tonight."

"Fine by me," Cassidy said.

"Ain't none of my business," the preacher said, at last, "but I don't hold with card-throwing. Never found there was much percentage in gambling." He nodded down at the seven of hearts in Cassidy's hand.

Cassidy crushed the card and wadded it into a ball. "Me, neither," he said. "Me, neither."

Smoke

Maureen A. Sherbondy

"Raise five," says Bill, the bail bondsman/bodyguard sitting beside Teresa at the oval table.

Teresa hesitates, wonders if he's bluffing, studies his suited eight, nine, ten, and king. She tosses five chips into the pot, then peeks at her own down cards again. Ace, king, ace. Yesterday, her first day in the poker room, she wasn't discreet enough; she caught the loser next to her looking at her hand. At least there's no smoke in this room. There's enough of that in the casinos and outside.

It takes every bit of control not to smile at the ace, king, ten, four she has up. Her goal is to keep from giving away her hand. It's hard to stifle a smile when she has a flush or a straight, even three of a kind.

For hours she's been making tough decisions: when to go out, when to stay in, when to bluff, when to raise. Glancing at her plastic rack of chips, organized in neat rows of twenty, she realizes she is only down four chips, and if she wins this pot, she'll be up by about fifty.

Teresa feels very brave, playing at the seven-card-stud table with the others. It's sort of like the World Series poker tournament she'd seen on television recently, only this is just a game, not a tournament. Even though it's the low minimum one dollar/five dollar table, it is a few steps up from her monthly poker game with the girls.

The guy next to her, Bill something, the guy with many jobs, seems friendly. He's been talking to everyone for the last two hours, but mostly to her. He asks where she's from and what she likes to do. He smiles at her whenever she raises him. In Richmond, she wouldn't normally socialize with a total stranger, especially one who probably carries a gun. Her heart pounds in her chest. Something about the guy excites her. He has a cocky but adorable grin. Bill lifts his beer glass, empties it in one swig, beer drips over his full lips. He wipes it away with his large, tan hand. He reminds her of someone she once knew. She twirls a long strand of hair, trying to conjure up who he looks like.

When she was single, she met lots of guys, flirted every weekend at bars and dance clubs. But for some reason, she can't remember how to flirt. Did she smile, look at them, then look away? Why can't she remember? It's as if seven years of marriage has erased that part of her memory, banished it to the desert.

A cocktail waitress, all legs and short skirt, arrives as if psychic, and replaces his empty glass. Bill tosses two chips on her dark tray, while keeping his eyes on the growing pot.

Bill is telling her all about the criminals he catches in LA, informs her that the relatives who put up the bond with their house, or savings, usually let him know where the criminals have escaped to. Teresa rolls her eyes at the information. He flashes his bulky silver watch in front of her face, proudly announcing, "Legal Time, for when I take them in."

Loud off-key melodies belt out from the next room. Women singing at the top of their lungs "Bye Bye Miss American Pie," " Girls Just Wanna Have Fun," and "We Are the Champions." She recognizes the tunes, but the words are all wrong. Teresa tries to focus on the folks at her own table.

She finds Bill's conversation more interesting than Irving from Jersey City, or Ruth from Detroit, who keeps asking for poker advice and distracting Teresa from her own hand. Teresa raises one last time, then proudly announces, "full house" as the others flip their cards down in defeat.

She gathers her purse and rack of chips, smiles, and says good-bye to the table. Bill places his warm hand over hers. His words beginning to slur, he says, "Don't leave." She pulls her hand away quickly as a strange vibe runs through her body. Feeling her cheeks blush, she leaves the poker room.

In the casino, she is flooded by the loud trio of sloshed twenty-something year old women, sitting at the boring wheel. They are going through a whole medley of pop tunes from the early nineties, belting out songs. It's too much for Teresa; she can't stay here another minute.

She can't find her friend, Libby, who promised she'd meet her at one o'clock. Just as well, she supposes, they aren't getting along . Last year's trip went smoothly. But this time Libby is upset about being dumped by her fiancé and losing her job. She's been snappy and bossy, moody. This morning Libby yelled at Teresa for getting up at seven instead of eight. What could she do? Leave? Get a different room?

Away from the singing women, Teresa makes it to the conveyor belt walkway that leads her outside. She chokes on the fire-scent in the air. The California fires have blown smoke into the area and her eyes now hurt. She hopes it won't affect the flight home tomorrow. On the street, three short Hispanic men snap cheap brochures against her hands. Trying to ignore the naked men and women on the covers, she pushes her hands in her pockets, looks away from the men. She nearly bumps into a transvestite, wearing a skimpy tiger-striped dress and too much eye makeup. The man is so tall he towers over her like a giraffe in this Las Vegas jungle. He flicks a long pierced tongue at her. She turns toward the dirty sidewalk.

She crosses the lit-up street, amazed at all the people walking around after one in the morning. She's not sure if she should stay up and play some table games or hit the sack early. The tall buildings and colorful, red, blue, green flashing neon signs still amaze her, as do the restaurants and casinos open all night. How does anyone sleep here?

The Brooklyn Bridge, the New York Skyline, the Italian themed Venetian with elaborate columns, the Eiffel Tower, all thrown together in one street, a bizarre montage of places that don't belong together. This fake world plunked down in the middle of a desert.

She'll need a vacation from this trip. She is not used to keeping such late hours. Crossing the street she notices a young couple pushing a stroller. The baby is asleep, oblivious to the lights and smoke-haze around her. When she returns home James expects her to begin a family. He told her it's time; he is twenty-nine, he is ready to be a daddy now.

Something suddenly tugs at Teresa; both a warm maternal feeling and a scary, queasy feeling. She wants and doesn't want a baby. She doesn't feel ready yet to be a mom. She likes the neat order of her life, working eight to five, getting nine straight hours of sleep a night. She enjoys her morning jog, and the slow Sundays, waking up late, lounging around, reading the thick *New York Times* until three in the afternoon.

She loves coming to Vegas, the thrill of the cards, the probability of getting certain hands in poker. The gamble, trying to beat the odds. If she has a baby, when will she get to come here again? When will she get to do what she wants to do?

Will she end up like her sister, Jill, two kids later and thirty pounds heavier? Jill never goes anywhere fun anymore, just soccer games and preschool plays and celebrations. Teresa retucks her shirt into her slim waist, flattens out the puff from her shirt.

James expects her to quit work when a baby comes. She loves her job as an actuary. She's good at it, and even got a raise last month. When the paycheck arrives on her desk, she still gets a kick out of it. Sometimes she smooths her fingers over the raised blue ink on her business card, proudly feeling the letters that spell out her name and title.

Not yet sleepy, Teresa sits down at a let it ride table. Only one other person, a boring one, is playing. She has two classifications: the dull ones who play and have no interest in talking, and the animated ones who share their life story in three hands. The animated ones make playing interesting, even if she is losing; at least she gets free stories for the price of a hand. Yesterday, a friendly one, who was a little shaken, told her about the fireball that just missed his car on the way here. He just made it through before the freeway was blocked off.

After three bad hands in a row, she says, "Give me some good cards."

A familiar voice sneaks up from behind, "There you are." Bill plops his large body down. She hadn't noticed he was six-four when they were at the low poker table. His bond escapees probably take one look at him and offer up their hands to the cuffs without protest.

"Why'd you leave the Mirage?" he asks, spitting beads of beer into her face.

"Oh, just wanted to quit while I was ahead," she answers.

"Flock of Seagulls is playing. You like them?" Bill raises his long face, as if trying to find the speakers.

"Yeah, I used to. Eighties?" She says unenthusiastically as possible, even though she loves the song. Now it clicks, the eighties—Bill reminds her of Carl, a boyfriend she dated for three months years ago. Like Bill, Carl knew how to have a good time. He was impulsive and inconsistent, but excitement swirled around him like mosquitoes near flesh. Girls and trouble followed him everywhere.

Has he followed her? How does he know she left and came here? She suddenly sees him as a fireball coming at her, and she doesn't know where to go. It's exciting and scary at the same time. She feels his breath on her face, hot as fire.

Leaning in he says, "Yeah, eighties. Hey you know, I'm also a bodyguard."

"You told me," she says, staring at her cards.

"Want me to be *your* bodyguard?"

Her wedding band catches the light. She thinks of the slogan "Everything that happens in Vegas stays in Vegas." Is she really thinking this? Could she really mess around and leave it here? She tries to focus on her pair of fives, sets her cards under her chips.

"Put it over *here!*" The dealer scolds her.

His tag says, *Arvis, New Mexico*. Arvis seems grumpy. Maybe he doesn't like this late shift, maybe he misses New Mexico. Teresa glares at Arvis.

"Hey, chill out Arvis. Ease up on the lady." Bill winks at Teresa. Teresa smiles.

"Yeah, like I'm Clint Eastwood's bodyguard next week. Me and Clint go to parties, hang out. I keep my eye on things, you know, *things*."

Arvis pushes chips towards Teresa. She piles them into a neat stack, on top of the other five-dollar chips, as if trying to gain control over this night through neatness. Bill is so different from James. Bill smiles a lot, James is so serious. Bill seems fun; she misses having fun, excitement. Keeping a house, paying bills, planning a family—is so serious. So adult.

Between the smoke and the cards coming her way, she looks to the right and sees Bill sipping his beer. She can't remember the last time her own husband looked at her like Bill is looking at her right now. He wants her. He isn't even playing at this table; no chips in front of him. She tries to spot his gun. He wears jeans and an untucked black shirt. Where could he hide a gun? She wonders what a gun would feel like in her own hands. She wonders what his body looks like under that shirt.

A wall is crumbling inside her, the firm wall of marriage that keeps men away. Her husband isn't here, and she doesn't even miss him. Where the hell is Libby? A voice screams in her head. She checks left to right, beyond the blackjack tables and the roulette wheels, towards the entrance. It's too cold. Cool fire-smoke air seeps through the open doors. The loud shriek of a shocked female winning at slots rises in the background. Heavy silver dollars clank against a metal bin. Everything seems fuzzy with cigar and cigarette smoke. She quickly picks up her neat pile of chips and leaves the casino, walking as fast as she can.

Libby would keep her out of trouble. Libby would be the voice of reason. She'd say something like, "Hit the road, Mr. Bill!"

What should she do? She makes a list of choices in her head, just like she and James do when they are trying to make important decisions. One, call security and have them walk her to the room; two, find Libby; three, try to lose Bill, then go up to the room.

Even if she makes it to her room, she'll be afraid to stay there alone. What if he follows her and wants to come in? Will she want to keep him out? Number two is the only option. With each step, she wonders what has she done to deserve this. Finally, at the entrance to the Mirage, she looks over her shoulder and doesn't see him. Her heart slows down. She wipes the sweat from her palms into her jeans.

Pausing in front of the tiger's glass partition, she cranes her neck up at the TV overhead. It's the image of the two tiger trainers, one of whom is supposedly in a hospital recovering from an awful tiger attack. Today she passed a shrine of flowers and notes from well-wishers placed in front of the hotel. Maybe he is really dead. Nothing seems right here: the fire smoke, the advertisements for this tiger show duo, the big man coming on to her. The tiger is inside her head when she closes her eyes. Who is the Tiger? Her husband? Bill? Is she really married? Or, is she back to her single days when this kind of thing happened all the time. This could be a first date.

Someone taps her shoulder, she jumps, her eyes spring open to see Bill just inches away.

"Found you," says Bill with a huge smile. He pushes a strand of blonde hair from her shivering mouth. His eyes are blue like James's, but warm blue, not cold and distant. He moves his long fingers over her lips, then pulls her face towards his. Her head spins, she chokes on the smoke, or something else that is hanging in the air.

She shakes her head back and forth, slowly. "No, no, I can't. I'm married."

As if the words are a red light that will stop him from moving forward. Reflexively, she pushes her hand into his stomach. She feels his firm muscles. Her hand lingers.

"I'm *married!*"

"Really? Where's your husband then? If he's not here, you're single, right?"

"He let me come here. I come here every year."

"He let you? If you were my wife, I'd be here with you. I wouldn't let you be away from me for a minute."

She wants to close her eyes and be back at her safe home in Virginia, but she wants to kiss this exciting man next to her and never go back home again.

She thinks of the road to LA—closed. The haze of fire is stuck in the air, obscuring clarity. Her hotel room seems countries away. She wonders if the tiger trainer is dead or alive. She wonders who would know the truth between life and death in this place of facades and neon signs.

She lets him kiss her. She kisses him back, then pushes him away.

"No, I can't do this. I can't."

Tears cover her warm mouth. When she turns away to run, two cars nearly hit her as she crosses against the red light. Running through the casino she lunges at the elevator button, tears blurring her vision. With one hand she presses the eleven button, while the other hand touches her still warm lips.

The Proposition Player

Ron Gutierrez

Driving the curvy byways of Forest Park cemetery, I thought the same thing I always did when I paid my respects there: I should have done something different with my life. The heavily manicured serenity seemed to demand of me a cleansing of some kind. So I thought about how if I could vote to outlaw gambling in the entire country, I'd do it in a second. But gambling was a reality—one that was a big part of me—and most of the time I was grateful for it. Or maybe I was just stuck. Sometimes I got the two confused. I parked the car and left my window open, the rental keys hanging in the ignition.

The gravesite was a simple tombstone that marked the too short life of the J. B. Hunt trucking man who had raised me until I was twelve. Surrounded by the remains of total strangers, I stood there and remembered those summers of him taking me on long hauls across southern interstate highways, and I knew I'd never forget the geography I learned from him. It was something real that stuck with me, even now, after all those places we'd traveled had changed.

Gambling was illegal in Texas, and maybe for that reason the rest of my family liked to infer a glamorous dark side to my life. If they'd only known. It was a job just like any other except for one thing—it wasn't like any other. Luckily, it was a weekday so no one else in the family was there. I liked those solo visits to my Dad, something I did immediately after picking up the rental at the airport. Since I wasn't comfortable with sentimental thoughts coursing through my head, and at twenty-eight I was long past questioning fate's hand, I settled for the aloneness of touching his name and letting him know I was there. Before I left, I took a chip from my pocket and placed it on the granite slab I'd been staring at. I imagined time was different where he was, and I hoped the chips I left when I was there would help him find me.

A man stood in the shade of a tree while a woman I took to be his wife sat at a nearby gravesite in the sun and fanned herself. Finally, when she could take the heat no longer, she wiped her forehead and stood up. Her husband followed her to an Eldorado and they drove away with the windows up. Even though it was the middle of August, the weather didn't bother me. I'd outgrown that a long time ago. Or rather I'd given it up—my way of making peace with the world. Training your mind was something you had to know how to do if you made your living at the poker tables.

I walked back to the car and headed to my mom's house. On the way I picked up some flowers at Rosie's. I thought their arrangements too multi-colored and round, but my mom seemed to like them. When I passed Houston Savings the temperature said 102, and I continued driving with the windows down.

Mom was making dinner and both of my brothers were already there. Lon came alone and Ben brought his wife and kids. Grace was coming to-morrow which meant we could talk about her tonight.

"She's gonna go broke with that son of hers," Ben said after dinner. He'd inherited dad's green eyes and his dismal assessments of other people's business.

"Stupid company she works for doesn't think about that," Lon agreed. "They just try and save every little penny."

Grace's employer had switched HMOs after she'd just finished paying the out-of-pocket limit for her son's treatment that year: $2,000. The new HMO had its own out-of-pocket she was going to have to pay before the end of the year. Had the company waited a few more months before switching, she would have been home free till next year. We let a moment of silence fill us with the hope that our commiserating might be all the situation asked of us. Grace was a single mother and determined to be a responsible provider. Like the rest of us, she was proud.

As with most of my visits home, the week went by fast in some ways and slow in others. Flying back into L.A.X.. left me feeling wounded, like I had just visited a children's cancer ward. It wasn't just seeing Grace and her son—we had a good time together and she never mentioned a thing to me about the HMO business—still, every time I got back on the plane re-turning to Los Angeles I had the same feeling. I made a point of booking an early return so I'd have time to take a nap before work, just to get my mind back.

I worked as a prop at Hollywood Park casino. Proposition players got an hourly wage plus health insurance. The casino paid me to gamble my own money to get games started, keep them going, and make the other players comfortable so they kept gambling. I usually came out good enough to make a decent living. It was better than waiting tables. I came to LA to be an actor and poker was just going to be my day job till I got my break.

An acting teacher had turned me on to a casino dealers school he knew of, and after a four-week course, I was hired. I started out as a chip runner, changing cash into chips, spent a few weeks dealing, and then started gradually switching sides of the table. I'd worked nights for the past six years and it had been ages since I'd been on an audition. Poker had a way of taking over my life.

"Hey Tino. Good vacation?" It was Elias, an older dealer who rarely showed emotion or got in trouble with management. Everything was by the book with him. But he gambled on his days off and I felt sorry for him not being able to let go. He was addicted, like most of them.

"Cool," I answered, which we knew meant mercifully dull, part of some master plan we'd all somehow agreed to.

"Bixby's gone. Gone to Commerce."

I shook my head. Commerce Casino was the biggest poker casino around. Way bigger than Vegas. All the famous players made their serious money there. "I didn't know the guy was looking," I said. He'd been at Hollywood Park a long time. He'd only dealt, never played. He saw a different side of the game. Having someone who knew all the players was a big help over the years, so when someone like Bixby left, it felt like a rite of passage for players like me.

Evans and T. J. nodded to me from May's table. Unlike most other female Asian dealers she didn't take crap from angry losers. While I didn't like this subservient side of the others, it wasn't my place to say anything. I took a seat and she dealt me in.

"Vacation good," she said. "*Very* good for game." Her inflection had finality, like she was passing out luck. She could do that.

An older couple sat down and I heard the guy tell his wife he would coach her through a few hands. T. J. cashed out so there'd still be two empty seats available. That was the rule. We cashed out in the order we sat down. Sometimes, if you were on a roll, it was hard to walk away. But rules were rules, and you had to find another table with at least three empty seats. Then, when it got down to one, you had to leave again. "Just relax and pay attention to the table and don't try bluffing anyone," he told his wife.

I felt something in me cringe. That was something I could never do—teach someone how to play, actually encourage them into the thing. If I could vote to outlaw all forms of gambling tomorrow, well like I said, I wouldn't think twice.

After a while, a couple of airline pilots walked in. I'd seen these guys before but never played with them. We were close to the airport. They drank while they played, which made me hope they were on their way home from work and not the other way around, but it wasn't my business.

I just wanted to get their money. Pilots were terrible gamblers. They're too tired or too narrowly focused or something. They didn't watch the other players very well. I saw them take two seats at a 20/40 table on the other side of the room where T. J. was propping. Lucky bastard.

About an hour later the guy on my left took off his pullover, and I saw something I didn't see too often. He was a priest. It wasn't the first time I played with one, but usually I knew right from the beginning. I wondered why he hadn't changed out of his collar and where he'd just come from. When someone played in a uniform, or for that matter, priest garb, it was a lot easier to start talking to them and size them up. I waited till the hand was over.

"So what comes after all the angels and saints?" I asked him with a tilt of my head. Priests usually liked to shoot the breeze as much as anyone else. Sometimes you couldn't get them to shut up. This one eyed me like I was a smart aleck in Sunday school. I thought maybe I misjudged him.

"You might be wanting to ask what comes before all that," he replied, tipping the waitress for a margarita. I never met a priest who didn't drink.

"No, really," I said, "Because whenever I think of the prayer I used to hear at mass, you know, when you get to the part about something, something, something, and all the angels and saints—well I forget what comes after so I make up a funny line in my head."

"What phrase would you be referring to, young man?"

"I say 'And all the angels and saints couldn't put Humpty back together again.'"

He tried to hide a smile but then let out a snort that barely passed as a laugh. May paused and shook her head. "Yes, he make joke, but you're down last three hands."

"Humpty together again is it?" he said. "I suppose you're really afraid that if you started laying decent wagers, someone might have to put *you* back together again." He waved the waitress back over. "Get this poor unfortunate soul a drink, now would you."

"No thanks. I don't drink." It was true. Me drinking would have been like a scarecrow playing with matches. I'd seen it ruin too many good gamblers. I didn't touch the stuff and I didn't miss it.

He looked at me like I'd just defaced his church. "Jesus, Mary, and the holy cross of our Lord. *He doesn't drink* he sits there telling me." He threw in his chips for the next hand. "Next you'll be telling us you don't jack off in the morning."

It was my turn to laugh. Now I knew I could win this guy's money. And I did. I took him for about three hundred in the next two hours. Where he got it I didn't know, and to tell you the truth, I didn't care. Casino chips don't bleed. The ones with colored stripes you buy in stores sometimes bleed onto the white spaces. Bixby had always reminded me that casino chips don't bleed and that meant neither should the players, meaning you took your winnings and losings like a pro. Just accept the hand without crying about it or feeling sorry for the other guy.

Some nights everyone wanted to be the star of the table. Like once, every guy at the table was doing chip tricks. Left hand chip shuffle by this fat guy next to me. Big deal. Anyone and his little sister could do that one. Just proved you didn't have arthritis. Then later the guy on the other side of him did a butterfly as he waited for his turn. Like you just knew he was holding that one in during Mr. Shuffle's little show. I knew I could do a knuckle roll, but what would that have proven? That I'm not intimidated? That I've had too much time on my hands? So I did a back to front and then I purposely messed up a knuckle roll, like I was still learning it. No one ever messed up on purpose, but that was my trick. But it only worked if no one at the table knew me. Sure enough, when I made like I was obviously setting up my bluff early in the game, no one suspected that I actually had a good hand. The river saw some heavy raising and I took everyone's money with a hand they were sure I was bluffing. All because I pretended to mess up a knuckle roll early on.

I wondered if my dad could see me whether he'd have been proud of me, or whether it would have been just the opposite. Bluffing wasn't cheating. It was an important skill, a life skill for me. But still, he was in a better place where deception was probably not considered a good thing. I can't tell you how many times a week I wondered about that, sometimes without even knowing I was even wondering about it.

At seven in the morning, I'd done my eight hours and went home. I took in a little over five hundred. I cashed out and had the cage wire it to my account. I did that with anything that amount and over. At that hour I was tired and who knew what kind of lowlife was watching me and might have followed me into the parking lot. Two years ago someone won eleven grand and was followed home, killed and robbed, and they never found the guy who did it. If you asked me I would call that a loss. How you treated your money was the deciding factor in whether you won or lost.

When I got to my apartment, I called my mom and let her know I arrived home safe yesterday. She could tell I was tired so she said we'd talk later in the week. Still, I could tell she was hesitating. I asked if anything was wrong. She said there was something a little strange and asked if I'd been to see my father while I had been there. Apparently she still felt she had to remind me.

"Why?" I asked.

"I noticed something yesterday that I thought maybe you dropped. But I'm not sure. It's just a plain white chip with an X on it. No colors or pattern or anything."

"That's weird," I said. I had been sure the wind or a groundskeeper would have removed it long before anyone in the family noticed it. It had been a whole week. "It doesn't sound like a poker chip to me." That wasn't a lie. Not technically. Those chips weren't for playing, and you sure couldn't cash them in for anything. We said goodbye and I got myself ready for bed.

I saw my bike against the wall. The front tire was flat. I hadn't ridden in a while and I wondered if the flat was from lack of use or a slow leak. I was out of spares. Biking was my only way of letting off steam and I liked having it ready to go for my days off, so I made a mental note to stop at a bike shop before work. Usually the last thing I saw before I fell asleep was my bike. I'd doze off as I contemplated the spokes, the cogwheels, the brake cables, an entire perfect universe in itself. Yet, whenever I took it for a spin, it wasn't really that at all. It was me. And I was it. And that oneness made the rest of the world more palatable for a time, made it not so important that things didn't always make sense.

I took poker seriously from day one, concentrating on putting together a nest egg while focusing on the 20/40 tables. It took me four years to build a $10,000 bankroll. That was money meant only for poker, nothing else. With that came freedom and bigger wins because it meant, if I was down, I could stay in the game until things turned around for me. Sometimes I could be down for months at a time and without a bankroll to back up my wagers I'd be wiped out. Other props had to take time off and deal for a few months to get some financial stability before going back in. I only had to do that once. Poker's not for the fainthearted. A couple of years ago I lost half my bankroll in one month. That scares you. I had gotten too cocky and was playing the 40/80 tables—way out of my league. I downsized to the lower tables after that.

I had to make between $1500 and $2000 a month just to break even and pay rent, car, and food. Anything over that and I could have some extras and put something away, but when I put money into my bankroll account, that was sacred and I didn't touch it for anything else. There were complicated formulas for figuring out how big it had to be in relation to your wagers, how many big bets you made an hour, risk factor and standard deviation, but for my 20/40 games I had a pretty decent bankroll.

I played at night because my opponents were more likely to be tired and make mistakes. And I never played more than eight hours. That was stupid and I could have lost everything. If I was up by $500 to $800 after three hours, I'd go home—it had been a good night. Likewise, if I was down between $500 and $1,000 in the first four hours, I'd get up and call it a night. There was always tomorrow.

That night Celia was playing. She wasn't in too often but when she was, she played with big money. I X'd her once and she never let me forget it.

Usually when I put out that white chip, it wasn't because someone was cheating, a thing not nearly as prevalent as people think, but because there was something else I wasn't comfortable with. Celia was a black drag queen, very striking, and she had come to my table back when I was dealing. I could tell right away she didn't like me. I tried to roll with it and let her settle into the game. A hostile player was bad for the whole table. But she kept doing things to piss me off like putting her cards at the edge of the table where I had to reach for them, and holding up the game in other obnoxious ways. After she lost a few hands she snapped her fingers and shouted "Pit boss, please!" She said it loud, over and over. When the manager came over she pointed to me and said, "I don't like this dealer." She pulled out a wad of money. "And I won't gamble another penny till you replace him." So I left, but before I did, I took one of the surveillance chips and placed it on the table. She apparently knew what it was for because she said, "Go ahead, put that there, just let me fix my lipstick first," and looked straight at the overhead observation camera like she was looking into a mirror.

Whenever a dealer had reason to believe the casino was being taken, he could put a surveillance chip on the table. Later when they rewound the tape they could tell right away where to stop it and watch what's going on. The cameras caught every square inch of the place, but placing a chip on the edge of the table helped security go back and find a particular point in time. Later that night, when I was dealing at another table, she came up to me and said, "I don't know what your problem is, but I don't need no X on the table when I play. Maybe some of your lowlifes do but not Miss Celia, honey."

I told her that in this casino, what she wore was considered a disguise, and we had to make a judgment call as to why someone was incognito at a poker table. I said I was just doing my job. She looked me up and down. Apparently deciding I wasn't worth slapping and getting her barred from the place, she turned and left.

So there she was again, all made up but still a little frightening in the way that kind could be. She had some friends with her and the only table with enough empty seats was the one I was at. They sat down and she told the dealer, "These here are my friends and now that there's no empty seats, this prop here can go to another table. Then we'd like to play gay poker."

She never gave up. Gay poker, at least according to her, was like regular poker except there were no straights, consequently fewer hands you could win with. She thought that as long as everyone at the table agreed then it would be fine. Everytime she'd tried this we had to tell her the same thing. Elias, who was dealing the table said, "Look, beautiful. The way you play in the privacy of your home ain't our business. But no one can come in here and change the rules of the game to suit them. The casino decides the winning hands, not you. So you can play like there's no straights, but if anyone shows one, that's a valid hand and it has the same value it always has."

"Oooh, you no fun," she flirted back and then resigned herself to the house rules. I took my leave but something made me admire her for at least trying, for foolishly thinking some day she'd change the rules.

When my days off came, I was ready for them. I rode with Midnight Ridazz, a group of about five hundred young cyclists who took over the streets of Los Angeles for a few hours each weekend night. It amazed me how well behaved and cooperative the group was. Everyone was in everyone else's way, but no one got pissed off or territorial. It was like we left car mentality behind. When we crossed an intersection we kept going even after the light changed red. Some of us would stop our bikes in front of the stopped cross traffic till everyone got through. This could last for two or three light changes if we were spread out. The cars were sometimes cool with it since we were a spectacle they were not used to seeing. It was the only time when it felt safe and indescribably good to break the traffic rules and do something as stupid as riding a bike through a red light on a busy street at night. It was a high if there ever was one.

The ride was called Swarm the Pier, a thirty mile jaunt that took us to Santa Monica for some late night partying. At one of the red lights, there was a big rig honking at us, adding fuel to the chaotic noise we were making. It was impossible to tell if it was an angry honk or a honk of support, so I figured, what the hell, it was my father telling me he saw me. So I let out a loud whoop that blended with all the other cheering cyclists screaming out and rushing through the intersection and I raised my fist in a triumphant gesture. The more he honked, the louder I shouted, and I realized I hadn't felt this good in a long time.

We finally got to Venice Beach and the dark boardwalk, normally crowded with tourists, was wide open to us. The ocean had a different reality at this hour, like it had consumed eons of time as effortlessly as it was about to consume this night. I felt a kind of inner strength as I looked ahead at the pattern of bike lights flickering toward the giant Ferris wheel at the pier. Once I arrived there, I made my way to a fish taco stand and my watch said 11:45.

"Hey, I thought that was you, Tino." I turned around and saw Lena with her bike. She was wearing an orange and black striped outfit. A lot of these rides had themes the riders could choose to honor by dressing up their bikes or themselves accordingly. Tonight's theme was "bees" and she was one of several I'd seen that night wearing wings.

"You look good. Do those make you go faster?" I asked. We'd gone out a few times last year till she said she needed someone who didn't have to go gamble after every date. I could be a hard one to get involved with. That part of my job sucked, but it was what it was. At least we'd managed to stay friends.

"They help with the buzz," she said and took out a joint. "Want some?" We walked down to where the bikers were gathered around a boom box and a few guys were gyrating their bikes through some exhibition moves. After a couple of tokes she invited me to a party she was having next week. I said sure. We ate and then joined one of the return home groups. I rode with the faster cyclists and after a few miles Lena fell in with a couple of slower friends.

When I got home it was close to three in the morning and there was a message from my Mom. "Tino, I hate to ask you, but maybe you could help your sister with this thing with her son. Maybe you could send her the money for the HMO deductibles. I know sometimes you win a thousand dollars in a night. Maybe the next time that happens, you can help. OK, bye. We all love you."

I'd brought it on myself. I'd told them how big my winnings were some days, but I never mentioned I might have been down by twice that much the week before. And unless I was up by a couple of thousand at the end of the month, I couldn't pay my rent. And it wasn't like I could touch my bankroll. But they would have never understood that. It would have been like embezzling money from an employer, stealing from a purse in the office lunchroom, or asking the boss for a personal loan. Most people didn't do those things for the same reason I wouldn't touch my bankroll for anything other than gambling. People who did that had no business playing poker for a living. I didn't return her call and I didn't send my sister the money.

So after having that exhilarating experience on my bike, and finally getting to unwind with non-casino people, and getting invited to Lena's party, I went to bed feeling like shit. I pulled the phone out of the wall and thought that would help me sleep, but for some reason it just gave it all permission to finally come out. I thought I'd escape it this time. I thought I'd get away with not experiencing this thing that happens to me every time I return from Texas. This thing where I fall asleep crying and for the life of me I don't know why. I just knew I had to get it out so I could get back to playing a good game.

The next few days were hard. I wasn't my normal self. I was too conscious of the fact that once I sat down to play I had to keep my mind on poker and not on my sister or my mom. Not on anything but the cards, my playing, and the other players. It was a particularly low time for me since I'd never heard back from Lena and I realized I was losing more than I was comfortable with, both on and off the tables. My bankroll was down more than twenty percent and it was tempting to think that I could have given Grace the HMO money and I'd be in the exact same place. But then I'd answer those thoughts by saying I didn't know how much longer I'd be down, and I'd have that much less to get me through this slump. That was the only way to think this through.

Before I knew it, November had come and I hadn't decided if I was going home for Thanksgiving. I needed a break. I'd been wanting to do some traveling, take a drive up the coast or maybe even go over some of the old routes I used to travel with him. That had long been on the back burner. I got on the Internet and downloaded some maps. At least it was a start.

That night, as soon as I walked into the casino, I could see there was a heightened energy in the place. The staff seemed more alive and they were busying themselves more than usual. I sat down at May's table and she told me the prince of India was there. "The prince of India? Here? No way." I said, clearly impressed.

"Oh, you like the others. Know nothing. You been to India?"

"No, I haven't," I said.

"Well, no more ruling families. They can't fly their flags anymore."

I didn't know enough about history to actually know what she was talking about, so I let her continue lecturing me.

"They stripped of power since independence. But hey, someone say the prince of India in the house and everybody like 'Where?'"

Fine, still in power or not, I turned and saw this guy dressed all I Dream of Jeanie, and he had four private security guards and another smaller guy who stayed by his side at all times and I couldn't help staring at him. "Who's that other guy with him?" I asked.

"That's his doctor," May said. "They here last night, on your day off. If they come to table you win big."

The doctor followed the prince everywhere and attended to him like he might cough and die any minute. He had people to light his cigarette and even put it out for him when he was only halfway done. He looked like if he went to the bathroom, someone would go with him to wipe his butt. May told me he lost $40,000 last night, but he had a good time. "First night he don't tip. Tonight somebody tell him why he don't tip and now he tip one hundred dollar every hand." May laughed and looked at me a moment and I realized we had become friends. I hadn't really thought of that before. It made me like poker again. It made me start to like my life again. The world inside the casino glimmered a little brighter and it made me think it might even extend to the world outside for a while.

And maybe that was as good as it gets. Like those long summer days of driving with my father, mapping our own geography, charting our own way. The difference was that now the roads were coming to me. Everyone who placed a stack of chips at my table brought a piece of the world with them. When we looked down at the same felt table, whether they were a priest, a drag queen, or a defrocked prince of India, we were traveling a road together for a while.

An older guy came and sat down at my table and asked for chips. While he was waiting, he got a call on his cell and I heard him say, "Look I'm gonna play for a while, but you need to learn how to handle your business, boy." He hung up and something told me I'd seen him before, but I couldn't place him. Something about the way he said "boy". Not too many people say that. I started searching my mind.

I didn't think I knew him from around here. I remembered visiting my aunt in Chicago several years ago and she took me to State Street where everything seemed more aggressive, a lower common denominator, yet expensive and cosmopolitan. My aunt knew several of the business owners personally and she took me to a lot of stores and introduced me to people. Had this guy worked in one of them? Nothing registered.

May dealt the next hand. I always liked watching her deal. She never painted her nails. She said painted nails distracted customers. I got distracted when I couldn't place someone. The man had a flush with the hole cards. I folded.

"Thank you kindly, young lady," he said to May.

"I be nice first time," she answered.

For some reason I remembered driving my dented car to the supermarket about three years before I moved to LA when a guy had come up to me and offered to do repairs on it for a good price. He looked down on his luck and seemed like he needed the money, so I let him talk me into it. During the course of taking my car to his apartment, I got to meet his wife and his neighbors. Everyone was nice to me, but in a swindler kind of way, and eventually the car was taking one too many visits to fix and I stopped answering his calls. But this man at the table wasn't the same guy or one of the people I met during those visits. I continued replaying episodes in my life trying to place him.

He won two hands, lost three, and kept making small talk with May. Before Hollywood Park, I'd worked about six months at Capitol Records packing CDs to record stores from their warehouse. During that time one of my co-workers son's died in a car accident. He was only fifteen. Someone else had been driving. I wondered what made me think of that now? I didn't recognize this man as one of the employees at that place. Nonetheless, I thought about the others I'd worked with including a co-worker whose father had passed away suddenly and the guy had to fly to Barbados for the funeral. Still, none of these episodes I was rewinding through were helping. I was batting zero on this guy.

He won the next hand. I had raised my bet more than I should have and lost a lot. "Thank you, son," he said to me. I shrugged and smiled. He had good poker manners and I couldn't hold that against him.

"You can't beat luck," I said in admiration. Whenever I said that I remembered I had once acted in a play with that name. It was actually a staged reading, but it had a director and a couple of rehearsals. I started running through every class I ever had, every audition I'd gone on, but I knew this guy wasn't from that world. I finally decided this was affecting my game more than I wanted it to. I was just about to get up and go to another table when he said, "I guess I been pretty lucky all my life. Been a trucker thirty-two years. Not one accident."

And that's when time froze. I could feel it screech to a stop and land on that white chip like it was the end of the world. I tried to tell myself I didn't know any truckers. My dad never had any over to the house that I could recall. Still I saw the X. And it was like the X knew I saw it.

"Ever been to Texas?" I asked. My throat was getting dry. I told myself I no longer cared about him, but still the question came out and I needed to hear his answer.

"Ain't no place I haven't been."

I won the next hand, although I didn't know it till May pushed the chips to me. I was drinking mineral water on ice with lime. I raised my glass to him. "Well, here's to luck." My hand was shaking slightly. It was time to get up and leave.

"I came down here to play a few hours at the end of my run," he said. "Normally I go to Crystal Park but tonight I wanted to check this place out."

I could feel my forehead beading. My glass was empty. "Crystal Park's too slow," I said.

"Probably why it's more my style."

"Who you drive for?" I didn't want to know the answer. My mouth had a mind of it's own.

"Hunt."

"J. B. Hunt?" I tried to change the subject. "The traffic here just gets worse by the day. You must hate L. A."

"It's part of the job. The traffic doesn't mess with me. Haven't ever had a mishap. Now I *have* seen two of my co-workers die in trucking accidents. One of them, hell, was his own son killed him."

The heat was unbearable. It made the road look blurry. It had been two days and I complained about the sun on my arms and legs. Every stop for gas or food was sweltering. At the last rest stop everything was so hot and quiet I thought the sound had burned up off the earth. I touched the window and it was like touching a radiator cap. My dad was going to take a look at something under the truck. I rolled down the window but the air that rushed in was so hot I rolled it back up. I pushed the buttons on the air-conditioner but nothing happened.

"You hold up game," May said to me. I put my chips in but I didn't even look at my cards. This would be my last hand.

"Happened at a truck stop. Eastern Arizona," the man said. "A crying shame is what it was."

How many times had I relived that day? No way could this man be talking about the same thing. Dad got out and told me to wait inside. In the side mirror I saw his lean figure carrying a flashlight. Did he really tell me to wait or did he ask if I wanted to? It seemed important now. He asked if I had to go to the bathroom and I said no. Did he ask if I wanted to stretch my legs? He usually did and I usually said yes. But I was tired and it was too hot to go outside. I don't even remember what we were carrying that day.

"He was hauling steel. He had a full load," the man said, not knowing he had read my mind. "You can imagine how much a load like that weighs. The heavier the load the more agility you have to employ to haul it safely."

I wanted to tell him to shut up but he wouldn't know what my problem was. And it was so damn hot. I wondered if the casino air-conditioning was on the blink. How could anyone pay attention to the game? I stared at the man's rough strong hands and for a minute I could see my Dad's covered in black grease.

"He had his boy with him. The kid didn't know his pa was underneath the truck. So he turns on the ignition so he could run the air conditioner. The truck starts rolling backwards and I hear the guy yelling something, and that's when I see plain as day what was about to happen. I looked inside the truck and you better believe I screamed at that kid to brake."

I heard my Dad scream out and at that moment it was like all the sound came back. The truck started making noise and I heard a banging from somewhere. Then I heard the scream I would never forget. Only back then, it was like my mind wouldn't accept that it was my father. Then I heard another voice from farther away scream "Hey kid! HIT THE BRAKE!"

But I didn't know why the truck had started moving. I was more scared than I'd ever been in my life. I called for my Dad. "Dad! The truck's moving!" But I couldn't see him anywhere. He had to be out there so I opened the window and I screamed again. "Dad! The truck's moving!"

"Of course the kid didn't know how to break and didn't have any idea what was going on. I ran there as fast as I could but the back wheels of the cab already rolled over him. You don't ever forget a thing like that. Stayed in my mind like it was yesterday."

I don't remember if I jumped out of the truck by myself or what, but the next thing I remember I was standing next to the man who had yelled at me. The truck had stopped moving and I could see my Dad's legs sticking out from underneath. The back double tires were hiding the rest of him. "Take it off him!" I cried. I looked up at the man who was standing there. "Take it off!" Foolishly I hoped he might still be unhurt, like if I had seen him trying to move then it would mean he was in pain. The man looked around for help but there was no one else but us.

"Go get inside my truck and stay there!" he shouted down to me. "Do it now, boy! I can't move the truck till you go." He pointed at his truck and his hands were shaking.

"No!" I said. I didn't know why it was so important I go away. It wasn't right for me to leave my father.

He gripped me by the shoulders so hard I thought he'd crush them. "Just do it. Now!"

So I ran. I cried and I ran. And I didn't stop when I got to his truck. I kept running till I got to the hill and even then I couldn't look back, so I kept running. Maybe the farther away I ran, the better it would be.

But part of me knew I had lost my dad. Just like that, all at once. And I wasn't going to be able to run far enough, or scream loud enough, or pray hard enough to change that. I couldn't see straight and I choked on my own breath. I tried to think of a way I could make the day over, erase that it happened, change God's hand. I ran up that hill till my legs were shaking too hard to carry me, and I crashed down into the hot dirt. It was all a terrible mistake and I wanted another chance.

I remember how the sun beat down hard on me and told me I would never, not ever, win my dad back.

The Wann Gambler

Warren Washburn

The spring I turned ten, I spent a lot of time brooding since my dad, when he was around, was always warning me to keep my mouth shut. Old enough to think about things, my main worry was why our Mom left us and never said goodbye. My brothers and I were just simple-minded kids living in Wann, a little village in Nebraska, so how were we supposed to know why she left?

Norman, my older brother, stumbled out of our small house and announced, "Mom's gone. She left us." His mood matched the gloomy April clouds.

"Where to?" I asked. I kept my distance, not grabbing his arms with fear since our family never touched, never. Except of course with the yard-stick or a belt. We did have a family of sorts even though Dad was gone a lot. But Mom?

"Don't know," he said, looking down at the outsized slab of cement that served as an entrance to our rust orange, brick quarters. On the cement slab sat a green paint-peeling icebox, a short red feed barrel, a baby stroller with two wheels missing, a cracked baseball bat, and a softball with its cover half off.

Norman's statement ended the bounce in my walk home from the fourth grade. We attended the Wann Elementary three-room school. It sat about one block from our house, which used to be the bank building in Wann, population no more than thirty adults and kids.

"Where, dammit?" Ignoring the tears in his eyes, I pushed past him toward the door. Where we grew up, it was easy and fun to learn to cuss and swear at an early age. Besides, other kids did it and we were ornery in that way.

I pulled open the rickety screen door, caught a whiff of kerosene from the heater, and looked in. Wearing his usual white shirt and faded blue slacks, our pissed-off dad stood in the kitchen stirring a pan of tomato soup. Him and his gambling. He's the reason she's gone was the quickest notion entering my mind. He gave me a look that said keep my mouth shut unless I wanted a whipping. With light, thinning-out hair, Dad stood a good six feet tall and had large hands and arms. And when he got angry, watch out!

The whistle from the puddle jumper train racing south took my mind off the unfolding heartbreak. I grabbed a quick look at the short train until it disappeared behind a line of stationery boxcars. My gut felt queasy, it was always hungry, and now the kerosene and soup aroma mixed with the feeling of abandonment to make it sting like hell.

An upgrade from the shack we used to live in, our house was built of crumbling orange-red brick. You could open the front screen and see the entire house, the ragged-edged linoleum, scum dirty in spots, the icebox and wooden table and chairs. You could see the small kerosene heater that never did keep the house warm, only served as the centerpiece for two stinking boxes of twenty-five chicks, one box on either side. Yeah, we raised baby chickens in our house, and they stunk and they peeped all night. Straight back was a small kitchen and back to the right was an area that held two beds.

"Where's Mom?" I spied my two little brothers sitting still at the table. By now there were four boys in the family. Maybe it was a wonder Mom survived twelve years of marriage—always scrounging for money, raising four wild-horse boys, no indoor plumbing, and at times very little food in the house. You would think we were living in the depression of the '30s but, for crying out loud, this was 1950.

This woman had continual reasons to shed tears, and her four sons were to blame as much as anyone. We were sickly, lazy, given over to stupid things like eating X-Lax because we were hungry and it tasted like candy. Once when my stomach was yearning for food, I nibbled some and then couldn't stop. Later I sat on the pot for a couple of hours.

Mom had told us that Dad was gambling before they married but she hoped he'd quit and get a job, he was smart enough. But he didn't get a job. He would go to the Omaha bookies, the horse races in Lincoln, and the Ak-Sar-Ben race track in Omaha. In the winter he'd try to raise funds to go to Florida or Arkansas. Getting married and having kids didn't change his habits.

Our youngest brother just looked at me and shrugged his shoulders. Just like me, he was afraid to say much in Dad's presence.

"She's in Omaha for a while, so you can all quit your damn whining," Dad said as he plopped the pan of soup in the middle of the table. Norman and I pulled up our wooden chairs and sat.

"What for?" I just couldn't let it rest. I was starting to try to figure out some things on my own, like at the beginning of each school year what were we supposed to list on a card where it asked, "father's occupation."

"I said 'shut up' or I'll give you something to whine about!"

Watery tomato soup with no crackers was better than nothing. Even one piece of toast at times was something. We had learned to eat slowly; it made food stuff last. Unless, of course, if there were six pieces of fried chicken feet for us four boys, the first two eaters done could grab the last two feet. That was the way it was and no questions asked. We ate fried chicken feet, so what?

"You two oldest wash and wipe the dishes," Dad said. It was our usual chore so we got to it after water was carried in from the outdoor pump. My usual envious thought was why the two little fartnhammers didn't ever have to do any work.

Unlike the previous shack we had lived in, this building had electricity. No indoor plumbing though, not even a pump sink like some of the hovels in Wann had—all water was carried in from the outdoors pump. The outhouse out back provided toilet requirements, unless no one was watching, then we could sneak up close to a tree and take a leak.

The April rain and mud kept us all in the house that day. The radio was left off. Still no TV in this house by 1950. I wondered how could we live without the mother who fed, cleaned, and clothed us. Maybe that's why she left, going without food at times, no indoor plumbing, no money—him and his dammed addiction to racehorse gambling. He wasn't even playing his favorite Little Jimmy Dickens record.

Later that evening, Dad was studying his racing form. We heard the screen door open, and Grandma pushed in carrying a box. Our grandparents, who usually had groceries and lived in a house with an indoor toilet, lived a couple blocks from us. We were quietly sorting out our collection of soda bottle caps, great toys in the absence of the actual stuff.

"Wha'cha you going do with 'em?" This directed to her oldest son. He could sire boys, just had trouble feeding them.

I wanted to rush her to regain some stability, but I was afraid. We had long ago learned free thinking or independent action weren't tolerated in this house. I had learned to freeze up my mouth and thoughts to escape the yardstick.

"Step outside," he said to her.

So, the relatives knew and now the whole damn town of Wann would know. Truth be told and no greater truth than this—everyone, and I mean everyone, rubbered in on the telephone party line. Yeah, this squat brick building did have a wall phone. What about the Wann Ladies Aid busybodies gathering and spreading the news? Of course, nothing takes a trip quicker than small town gossip.

Norman moved fast to look in the box. "Look," he said, "four sack lunches with a sandwich and orange."

"Think they're for us?" I whispered.

Joy upon joy, maybe for one day we could be like other kids who brought their lard pails and paper sack lunches to eat at noon in the big room. We always had to walk home to eat. What would be the use of taking a piece of toast in a sack to school? A real sack lunch sorta took the bite out of going to bed with an incomplete family.

Two beds, Dad alone in one, two little brothers in the other. Norman and I unfolded the lumpy davenport, placed a sheet, blanket, and two pillows on it. Our "bed" extended into the main room, right next to the eating table. Covering Dad's bed was a blanket made from the hide of a horse. That's right, someone had skinned a spotted brown and white horse and made it into a blanket. You could actually feel the horse hairs if you ran your hand across it. It was shabby and tattered, peppered by moth holes.

I had a sick feeling in my gut as I lay on the couch, trying to pass out to sleep and probable nightmares. The room was a lot quieter without the sound of peeping chicks. What we needed, I thought, was a real Joe Palooka, a real Steve Canyon to fight off dreams of Germans and Japs overflowing our Wann town. Where the heck was Dick Tracy when we needed him?

The next morning brought the usual, a bowl of cold cereal with milk. It was better than poached eggs, I thought. Then Dad had a surprise for us.

"Leave the lunches here," he commanded.

"Why?" See, I couldn't control my disappointment or my smart mouth.

WHACK! It was nothing, a sharp blow to my skinny shoulder.

"Cause I said so, that's why," he towered over me. "You boys come home for lunch and share with me."

Right then and there I quit looking forward to anything good. I knew damn well he'd spoil it. I thought about crying to grandma but that would just get me into worse trouble. I wondered why he didn't get a job instead of gambling at the horse races day after day.

As I emptied the remaining Wheaties in my bowl, I said, "It's my turn for the gorilla mask."

"No, it's mine," Norman said. "You got the last one, the Lone Ranger."

"The heck I did."

"Shut up, the both of you," Dad said as he grabbed the box and sat down with a pair of scissors. "Take your shoes off."

So what if our clodhoppers had small holes in their bottoms. A little wet spot on our socks didn't amount to much. He cut the Wheaties box top, the sides, and the mask into oval-sized shapes, then placed the cardboard in the bottom of our shoes. I was pissed I didn't get the mask but my disposition was such that it was a victory over my older brother; he didn't get the mask either.

Another day of memorization at school. At noon we staggered home at different times. I ate my share, kept my mouth shut, then hiked back to school quickly just to get away.

A few guys were waiting for me by the storm cellar. Larry Everman came up to me and said, "Hey, heard your dad started a fight last week over at the General Store. What's wrong with him?"

"Shut up, you son-of-a-bitch."

Larry wrestled me down and sat on my chest. He tried to slug my face a couple times with his fist, but I was too fast. He let me up when the bell rang. Then I had nothing but skinny bones for help which were worthless against farm boys. Never in my years at that school did I win a fight.

Grandpa came over that night. "Here's three dollars for gas, go get her," he said.

"Come out here," Dad said, pulling Grandpa out the screen door while picking up the racing form. I heard him say, "Look, here's a sure thing. Can you spare five more dollars? I can pay you back tomorrow."

It was another skimpy supper, but after going on short rations for a couple years, our stomachs were shrunk. Living scrawny didn't seem like a big deal.

"Boys, I'm going to bet on a winner tomorrow and bring your mom home." Finally he was in a good mood. Therefore, we had to be.

"Now, get your shirts off and take turns sitting up on the chair," he ordered.

Oh, no, haircut time. I have to tell the truth, usually we all cried. He didn't put a cereal bowl on our heads, but the result made us look like hicks, like hillbillies. And because my only pair of jeans, from a week's wear, were filthy, I knew I'd have to wear overalls to school the next day. Why was I born? How much suffering could a kid take?

He didn't have electric clippers; he used a hand-operated one. And it pinched the hairs out of our scalps. If the pain caused us to snivel and sometimes sob, he'd get pissed-off and call us crybabies. So, another night in a dark and lonesome house, with a slight smell of burning kerosene from the stove to further sicken my upset stomach.

The next day when we came home for supper, he was waiting. "Sit down, and shut up. Get a piece of bread and a slice of minced ham."

I sunk down in my chair, fearing the predictable, but still not able to resist really setting him off. "Where's Mom?"

I could tell his face was flushing when he glared at me. "One more word out of you and I'm getting the yardstick. You think you could pick a winner? Just shut up about it."

Norman had some homework, I buried my head in a Bobbsey Twins book, and the two little ones played with Jigger, our family dog.

I watched Dad walk over to the phone, racing form in hand. He pushed in the button and held it down as he gave the hand dial a few vigorous turns. Then he picked up the receiver and gave the operator a number.

"Bomber here," he said.

"Yeah, I know, but you know I'm good for it. You'll get your money next week."

"You going to take my bet or not?"

"Okay, tomorrow at Santa Anita, second race, I want five on Little Red Man to win. That's right, and quit worrying about it."

It's never going to end, I thought.

Now Dad was pleased, whistling around the room, He even turned on the radio. Maybe we could listen to *Gunsmoke* or *Gangbusters.* But no, it was just a music station. "Buttons and Bows" was playing, and then we had to listen to "Red Roses for a Blue Lady."

Going to bed that night I felt a sickness in the gut was worse than a hunger pang. I started thinking how he had lost Grandpa's money on his "sure thing." He probably hadn't paid the ten dollar monthly rent for a while, but he was still trying to pick a winner.

But before sleep it was time for memory homework. "Okay, boys, what does Ak-Sar-Ben stand for?"

I was quick with the answer, "Nebraska, spelled backwards."

"Norman, what's the best five card hand with no pairs?" Dad asked from his position at the table.

"Ace high, then king, then queen."

"What's the next best hand?" It was my turn.

"A pair of anything."

"Wha'll beat a pair?"

"Three of a kind?"

"Oh yeah, what about a straight or a flush?"

We didn't know.

"Boys, what's a flush, and you had better know."

Neither of us knew. Hell, at this time Norman was starting to show an interest in the females, and I had my head in Bobbsey Twins books. If we got spanked for not knowing what the hell a flush was, we just figured the world was unfair.

"Maybe you boys can learn something about horses. Look at this program from Santa Anita. Who's the jockey on Wingover?"

"Willie Hartack," I was sure I got that right.

"Who's the trainer?"

"Hurst Philpot."

"What's a maiden colt?"

We didn't know.

"What's a gelding?"

I ventured a guess. "A male goose?"

"Hell no!"

"Norman, what's the purse?"

"Four thousand."

"Okay, go to bed. One last one, where's Santa Anita?"

"Mexico?" Norman guessed.

"Oh, hell, hell and damnation," Dad sputtered.

"Get ready, you're not going to school," was all he said the next morning. He put on his gray hat, and we watched through the screen door as he walked the two blocks over to Grandpa's.

On a misty, gray morning we pulled on our threadbare jackets and trooped out to his black, stick-shift '45 Chevy. He had bought it used a year ago. He stopped at the Wann General Store to pump in a few gallons of regular gas, and then off we went down the muddy roads for Omaha.

"Dammit, dammit," he cried as the car slid sideways into a mud-spattered ditch. The steering wheel had locked up. Thirty minutes later, after old man Larson had pulled us home, Dad told him, "I'll get you a winner at Ak-Sar-Ben next month."

"Car broke down, maybe come and get you tomorrow," we heard him say into the phone.

"You boys stay home till noon, then go back to school."

By this time I could tell he handled problems by getting pissed off. A year earlier I had discovered a little secret. I would clam up until I could "take his temperature" so to speak. If he had won money, we could all be happy—laugh, raise hell in our words and actions, ask for a nickel so we could walk a block over to the General Store and get a soda pop. But if he lost, he'd stomp in the house and cuss someone out because they'd used or lost his lucky pen, or put a hat on a bed, or opened an umbrella indoors. These were all bad luck omens, and someone should catch hell over it. Get out of the house then was our best bet.

Dad was after-the-fact superstitious. Of course, a bird getting into anyone's house was a definite warning of a death. Listening to the adult's discussions on this, it could mean a family death in the past or foretelling one upcoming.

Another day of hell, but when we came home from school, there was Mom in her flowered, cotton house dress. She was standing with her back to us, leaning against the icebox, and crying. We stood slack-kneed, mouths open, scared to say anything. And then I noticed the floor of the kitchen, almost so black with mud you couldn't see the linoleum. I guessed we had been living like pigs.

After a few minutes she recovered and said, "Norman, go out and catch an old hen. I'm going to fry chicken for supper." She fired up the old kitchen stove and started to heat water to scald the chicken, which would make the feather picking easier. Mom's fried chicken, I thought. How could any meal be any better than that?

I went out back with Norman and watched him grab an old broom from the lean-to shed. Then we chased a white hen around and around until she tired out and just squatted by the backyard cottonwood tree. We grabbed her and fought off her struggling and flapping wings and feathers. Ten years later, on a friend's farm, I was shocked to see that not all people killed their chickens the way we had been taught.

I held the hen down with one hand and stretched out her neck with the other. Norman laid the broom handle across her neck then stepped on it, one foot on each side of the neck. I let go, stood up, and moved away. He then grabbed each of the hen's feet and gave them a backward jerk. The body separated from the neck, and he gave it a toss away from him. I leaned down to watch the hen's eyes close; it always gave me a strange feeling. We watched as the now headless body jerked and jumped and kicked and spurted blood from the neck cavity.

Mom then appeared with the pail of scalding water. She held the chicken by its feet and dipped it up and down in the hot water. We helped her pull the feathers off and scatter them in the yard. Her fried chicken pieces were manna from heaven.

I had frozen up my insides so bad I'd been constipated for three days. Gradually happiness settled inside our house later that night. Before bedtime, she mixed us hot lemonade with baking soda so our glasses fizzed at the top. For the first time that week we could go to bed without fear. We could relax, forget about the kerosene smell and have a little skip to our hearts, inwardly at least.

No school on Saturday. Dad got a call after eating his two poached eggs. Seems as if Little Red Man had placed, now he owed more. The house grew quiet as he slammed the door.

He returned in the early afternoon in a good mood. "Get your jackets; we're all going to town, I picked a winner!" He had been to the bookies in Omaha and had won enough to pay his bills and more. "Here, boys, you get a quarter each so you can go to the movie."

Mom got twenty dollars for groceries, so at least for a week we would eat like we imagined rich people would. A week of nightmares had been erased.

When Dad went out to start the car, it died. He walked over to Grandpa's and soon returned driving their old panel truck. The truck had only two seats up front. The four of us boys sat on two planks, each resting on two cement blocks. We didn't care if it was a bumpy ride, we were going to town!

Just think—Ashland on a warm spring night! Silver Street crowded with cars, no place to park. Sidewalks full of people, clusters out in front of the hardware store watching the black and white TV through the window, beer joints waffling out the smoke of a hundred cigarettes and sweet beer smell, the sound of snooker balls banging into each other, carry-out boys hauling groceries from Harold's Grocery in the middle of main street to the farmer's car, the wife stocking up on another week's food supplies.

And now to spend the quarter. Taking home any change for savings was unheard of. We lived for the moment and when the boom moments hit us, we knew how to make the most of them. First the movie—western, sci fi, gangsters, Fred Astire tap dancing—we didn't care; magic was in the air. I sat with my two little brothers and Dude Vosler, a classmate from Wann. Norman hung back, talking to older boys, looking, looking, and looking at those giggling girls. I glanced at them once, but the mystery of what was under those skirts and blouses was more than I wanted to think about at my age.

Thirteen cents for admission, leaving twelve. Movie popcorn was too expensive.

After the movie, I cried, "Come on, Dude, let's go."

I hustled across the main street trying to ditch my little brothers. They could go find Mom, I wanted some independence. So Dude and I ran across the street to the old ladies' popcorn stand, only five cents, and we could shake salt from her shaker. She lived on the outskirts of town in an abandoned gas station with dogs and cats roaming about everywhere.

Up and down the main street we walked while we ate the popcorn, taking in all the sights. Hoffman's IGA with a donut making machine, the barbershop open late for the fifty cent haircuts, and then, the last seven cents squandered at Harris's Drugstore for penny candy to eat on the way home. It took us a while to make our major decisions, since some candy was one cent each and some were two for a penny. We always went for quantity since we had the scant times forever marked in the back of our memories.

Finally, Mom and Dad rounded us up. Mom had shopped for groceries and visited with friends and relatives. Dad had sat in the back of the Town Tap for poker or pitch games, for real money, of course. The seven mile ride back to Wann on the gravel roads crossing at least three old steel bridges put my brothers and me to sleep until bumps jerked up our heads as the hard candy started its business of rotting our teeth.

At the end of these visits to town, we would fall into bed at once in the bank building. Then Sunday we could do whatever. Sunday night Dad was in a good mood. When we were in bed, he allowed the family to play his favorite game. He would whistle a tune and we would see who could name it first. In the dark there would be the whistle and then quick calls from the first to identify it. I would lay there in a fit of tension since our family grew up on competition. I desired to beat my brothers and my Mom.

I didn't understand how Dad did it, but it seemed as if we competed for his attention. I know I wanted his approval even though at times he put us through hell. It seemed as if I would do something ornery at times, if I thought I wasn't getting enough attention. After the whipping, I had a strange feeling like I didn't despise him, but I knew I was on his mind.

With Mom home, life seemed back to normal by Monday. The gambling man had taken off for the race track, and life was a bit calmer. By the end of a week-and-a-half, we were once again on emergency provisions. Norman and I wandered over to see if a kind truck driver delivering supplies to the Wann General Store would hand out a free sample of anything to a couple of skinny boys with cereal bowl haircuts and wearing washed-thin overalls. It was great to see the look on Norman's face as he ran home to Mom with an offering held in his hands and a wide grin covering his face.

So we were Wann kids once again with a mom as the Earth continued its cycles. We existed as a poor man's example of a fool's paradise. Pitiable, hungry, impoverished in all things at times and then acting crazy and out of our ever loving-minds during the boom times. We would line up in order of birth for snapshots, and our faces, our clothes, our tricycles and bikes would be frozen onto black and white photos for all time. And when Dad bet on the phone or left every day, pretending ignorance of that reality was our only means of survival. We were just simple-minded little kids.

Take Some, Leave Some

Michael Croft

Jimmy Stokes worked in a small room with four pasty-white walls, a metal desk, two wooden chairs, and a filing cabinet stuffed with gaming files. At the Jade Black Club, all the action was out on the floor. That's where the lights beamed twenty-four hours a day, and the dealers called the dice with strong sturdy voices, the kind that floated across the floor and spilled out onto the streets of Reno. But for Jimmy, this was home, the nerve center, the place he studied the numbers, where he found out which games were up and which were down.

Scanning the figures once more, everything seemed okay. The tables were holding their own, hovering in that safe middle ground they'd carved out for themselves the better part of this last year. They weren't booming along, snapping up twenty-one dollars out of every hundred that slid across the tables, thus working the count machines down in the basement into a high speed dither, nor were they plunging along in the dangerous depths of only thirteen or fourteen percent, causing the higher-ups on the fifteenth floor, behind the mahogany walls and thick wide doors, to stalk back and forth, while they sized up Jimmy's fate and that of those who worked around him. At around eighteen percent, he would be allowed to carry on, patrol the floors and smile at the customers, eyeing their bank-rolls and making sure the Jade Black Club clicked along, hitting on all the right cylinders as it chugged it ways through the maze of days and nights.

He glanced at the clock again and saw that it was nearly eight-thirty. That meant that his shift was about half over. He had no choice but to look around and laugh. Tonight wasn't an ordinary night at the Jade Black. Not long ago, his old friend Brian Cutler had called and announced his arrival on Southwest Airlines out of Las Vegas. He and Jimmy were once so close, they used to joke about slicing tiny marks into their arms and proclaiming themselves blood brothers. That was until Brian honed into the action with Jimmy's wife, Julie, a cocktail waitress with long legs and killer blue eyes.

This was right before the three of them were set to hightail it to Vegas with plans to run their casino careers up the flagpole and declare themselves dedicated veterans of the scene. Jimmy didn't find out about the little tryst until he had settled into the life of a dice dealer out on the Strip and assumed he was going to be married forever. Yet when the collective dust settled, all three of the participants had taken off in different directions. Julie drove home to her mother in Arizona, Brian took refuge in the arms of an older woman, and Jimmy scampered back to the Jade Black Club, where he began his quiet ascent up the corporate ladder.

After taking the call the other night, Jimmy didn't know what to do, spring into the air and turn a somersault or slump down in a chair and cuss the night away. But after a while, he thought maybe it was time to let it all go, wash the memory bank clean and start all over again. After all, this was Brian Cutler, his friend of many years, the one he had bonded with back in dealer school and soon saw as the link between himself and the world of gaming he'd grown up in. Within months, he and Brian had hit all the right chords. Jimmy had told him about his father, Pogue, a man who skipped around the state of Nevada like a gnat on a hot skillet, jumping from one casino to the next, working the inside or out, playing by the rules when it helped him and bending them when it helped him even more. At their highpoint, Brian would sit and listen like a small child with a bedtime story, never once flinching when Jimmy told him tales of riding around in his father's Cadillac, while his dad gunned the engine and bragged about the coffee cans filled with silver dollars hidden in the backseat and the shovel tucked underneath the spare tire just in case he needed to drive out into the country and dig up his one and only stash.

Jimmy walked out into the hallway, closing the door behind him. Out on the floor, he blinked and waited for his eyes to adjust to the light. Now it seemed the Jade Black Club was all he ever thought about. Love it or hate it or anything in between, it had always been there for him. Twenty stories tall, complete with rooms and restaurants galore, the casino drew players from all directions, almost like it was the Pied Piper of gaming establishments. Almost seventy feet tall in some areas, its ceiling hovered over the casino floor like a giant net, not allowing anyone to escape. Painted a faint blue, it had an almost ghostly appearance before finally giving way to a litany of other colors. Reds, greens, and browns blended evenly with one another to create a rich vacuum-like atmosphere. Behind those colors was an on-going blast of sounds. Jackpot bells, calls for keno, war whoops from the poker room—all hanging in the air as if pasted into place.

Near a twenty-one pit, he stopped and stared. From experience he knew what he wanted to see. He wanted to see a certain type of poetry. At least by the standards set forth by the Jade Black Club. All of the dealers were to be neatly dressed in white shirts, black slacks, and purple bow ties. In near unison, they were expected to stand tall and flick cards around the tables like a constant string of gunfire going off in the night. Each card was supposed to fly over the top of the customer's bet and then skid to a halt on the green felt layout not far from the player's fingertips, almost as if begging for attention.

But Jimmy liked to think he was beyond all of that, worrying about some silly notion of perfection, one that probably never existed in the first place. In his private thoughts, he reminded himself to stay in touch with the humane part of his personality–that piece of him that still remembered what it was like to deal all day and feel the pain that would shoot upward from the bottom of his shoulder to the top of his neck like an unwavering dart. With memories like that firmly in place, he liked to walk the pits and eyeball the dealers, seeing which ones were standing straight up and down and which ones were shielding their discomfort by resting their weight on one foot or the other. When the time was right, he would order his floor bosses to issue more breaks, anything to help them out. Provided he wasn't pushed too hard, Jimmy wasn't above giving of himself.

Later, he was standing in the middle of pit five, the one with all the action. The craps games were fired up and going strong. The dealers out on the stick were calling numbers and barking commands. Their voices echoed through the club, filling it with a cadence of numbers that rang high, then low, like workers out in the fields. On the inside of the tables, the dealers pushed cheques back and forth with the cool precision of watchmakers, each move smooth and easy, all of them a part of the long, hard training. Out of the corner of his eye, Jimmy spotted his friend and turned in that direction. Brian was slicing his way through the crowd like a halfback. Dressed in a dark blue suit and carrying a beige travel bag over one shoulder, he weaved his way through the crowd with sharp cuts, dodging one gambler after another.

Jimmy thought of letting him go, not bothering to flag him down. Let Brian find his own room, then come looking for him, not the other way around. He even thought about turning his pager off. That way Brian would have to wander all over the club looking for him before finding out where their friendship really stood.

Near the escalator, Brian turned and scanned the floor. Their eyes met and Jimmy had no choice but to wave across the casino at his old friend. Brian stuck his finger in the air and waved it back and forth like a signal.

When they met, Jimmy smiled and held out his hand. Brain grabbed it and gave it a good hearty tug, enough so that Jimmy flinched. Years ago, when they would stand around the bar and joke like little kids, Brian would jab Jimmy in the ribs and say, "The only difference between you and me is that I'm stronger in the bones. Other than that, we're just about the same."

"Man, you look good, really, really good," Brian said.

"I'm hanging in, what else can I do?"

At thirty-seven Jimmy was trim and pale-faced. Too many days cooped up inside either in the Jade Black or home, sleeping late hidden from the sun and fresh morning air.

Brian took a step backwards and glanced around the casino. "Busy, busy, busy. That's what we like to see."

"It's all buses. We contract with a firm out of the Bay Area. Bounty hunters, I call them. They round them up and we take them off."

Brian laughed like Jimmy knew he would.

"Sounds good to me," he said.

Jimmy turned and scanned the floor. Like it or not, what it all came down to night after night was hoping that people would blow their wads, one right after the other.

"So what has you winging your way up north?" Jimmy asked.

"I'm here on a little look-see. I'll tell you about it later."

"You mean, the Mission can survive without you?"

"These joints can survive without anyone."

The Mission was the ultra large place in Vegas, where Jimmy and Brian had worked together before their friendship blew out on all sides.

"I'll be here until Thursday," Brian said, "then I have to be back for a meeting."

Jimmy ran the tab through his mind one more time. Three days to be with Brian, three days to be with an old friend.

At a little after one in the morning, the Silver Dollar Café was brightly lit. Busboys scurried back and forth on the far side of the room, loading and unloading their carts along the way.

At 1:15, Jimmy took another look at his watch and saw that he had been waiting for nearly twenty minutes. He told himself one thing. He wouldn't wait for Brian. He wouldn't wait for Brian. The little refrain went off in his head like a mantra. He wouldn't wait for Brian. He took one last swig of coffee and set his cup down in the middle of the table. Just as he did, Brian walked through the wide entranceway and waved and a huge smile spread across his face. Jimmy hated to admit it, but it was nice to see his old friend once again.

"What did you do, get off a little early?" Brian asked.

"I finished up as soon as I could. There wasn't much else to do."

"Man, you ought to see what they put managers through down south. They really give them a workout. Especially with the paperwork. Ten, twelve hours aren't unheard of around the Mission."

"I stay on top of it. A little bit everyday. That's my motto. That way, I can do my eight, then split."

"I hear that. Of course you can get away with it when you're running a shift, but when the whole joint is yours, then you're married to it. Everyday is full bore. Everyday is busting balls and learning how to get away with it."

"So what's it like, having a big time gig down there?" Jimmy asked.

"Me, I ain't nothing. That's what I've learned. There's so many big fish swimming over the top of me, I can't even keep track of them all. And if you don't watch your ass, anyone of them will bite your head off in a split second and spit it right back at you."

"But the action must be nonstop?"

"You wouldn't believe it down there. I mean, the money. It's everywhere. They bring it in in truckloads and spray it all over the place. It's in the pit. In the showrooms. In the boutiques. Even the snack bars are known to rock 'n roll," Brian said.

Jimmy shook his head. He could remember when he and Brian spent all day stretched out over a dice game, taking and placing bets like guys on a conveyor belt and walked home at the end of day with thirty, forty, sometimes fifty bucks in their pockets and thought they were nearly as rich as the owner of the Jade Black himself. Now he wondered if he could have made it down there, been a Vegas guy like his dad or Brian.

"Guys with six figure credit lines are nothing anymore. Last week, a guy blew a half a million bucks and walked away like it was nothing."

"We don't see that kind of money around here," Jimmy said. "Every now and then we get blind-sided, but not too often. Mostly guys out of San Francisco. You know the ones good for ten grand a pop."

"Chumps. That's who those guys are. Chumps. Down there, we throw them a free room and fix them up with dinner and that's about it. If they squawk, we kick'em to the curb and tell them to take a hike."

A waitress stepped up to the table and smiled at Jimmy. He smiled right back and said, "More coffee for me. And give my friend here anything he wants. I'll sign for it."

Brian ordered a small steak, hashbrowns, and three eggs over easy. The waitress scribbled down the order and walked away, and Brian took in her every move, dissecting her right down to her pores. "Nice legs, huh?"

"Not bad," Jimmy said, looking the other way. "So what brings you up this way? You on vacation?"

Brian shook his head. "Not me. I don't take vacations. I'm here to take a look around. I might be moving back to Reno."

"Is that right?"

"The Mission is thinking of making a pitch for the Jade Black Club."

"What? You must be kidding? This place is making a mint. Why would anyone want to cut loose with it?"

"That's how it was put to me. The word in the street is that the Black family isn't up for the daily grind. I guess they never knew how hard Jade worked all his life."

"I hear that."

Jade Black was the founding father of the casino. Settling into Reno in the late forties, he started out when the town began settling into the world of cards and dice. Straight out of the carny world of central California, he dug into this very spot with a poker room about the size of a shoe box and began punching away at the numbers. By the time Jimmy and Brian fell into their jobs handing out change and paying off jackpots, word on the floor was that Jade had stoked away millions and millions of dollars, which meant he was a big-time success, even by Vegas standards.

"You got to promise me you won't say anything. No one is supposed to knowI'm here. Except you, that is."

Jimmy laughed and thought about the dos and don'ts of friendship. There was more than enough irony here to keep him talking to himself and pacing the floors late at night.

"So what's your say in all of this?" Jimmy asked.

"Me, nothing. I'm just worming around the edges. But if everything falls into place, then who knows, they might run me in up here as president of the property. Wouldn't that be something?"

"They said that?"

"More or less. They said it could be part of the deal. That is if I felt like relocating."

"And?"

"For a shot at being president. Hell, yeah."

Jimmy sat back and pondered his ordeal. His friend, Brian, president of the Jade Black Club. In his long litany of bad moods over his friend, he never once thought of this one.

"You'll be in big buck country for sure. They must knock down what, mid-six figures, plus all the bennies."

"You forgot bonuses. The Mission is big on bonuses. That way they can give them or take them away, depending on how they feel about you at the time."

"The way of the world, I guess."

"Down there, it's eat or be eaten."

Jimmy laughed. Maybe getting bounced out of there years ago was a blessing. He wasn't sure being ruthless was a part of his make-up, no matter how much money was on the table.

Brian leaned back in his chair and stared directly at Jimmy like he was sizing him up for the first time. "There might be a little taste in all of this for you."

"How so?"

"Don't be silly. Getting promoted is one thing. Turning a trick is another. And if you don't do the deal, we all know what happens."

"They walk you to the door and say *adios*," Jimmy said.

"You got that right."

"So what's that got to do with me?"

Brian served up his answer like it was hot stuff. "Who knows this place better than you?"

"And your point?"

"My point. I just made my point. If I get duked into being president, you can be my casino manager. You have my word."

Jimmy stared directly at his friend and thought about the offer. Jimmy Stokes, casino manager. It wasn't the first time it had crossed his mind. He had pondered it a lot. It was the personal pledge he'd carried back from Las Vegas. I'll show'em, he used to say. I'll show'em I can hold my own in one of these joints. "We'll see. Who knows what's coming down the road," he said.

"What's coming down the road," Brian said, slapping Jimmy on the back. "We are, dude. That's who. We're going to make this place sing. Just like the old days."

Jimmy shook his head. The good old days, they still resonated with him, the same way a candy bar tastes when the mood is just right. But then he caught himself when he remembered how much venom he carried home with him from Vegas. "Yeah, the good old days. I remember them. They were something, weren't they?"

Naturally, Brian caught his drift. His shoulders slumped and he stared down at the floor. "I'm clean these days, really clean. I could whistle through my nose if I had to."

Believing him came easy, forgiving another matter. What Jimmy really wanted to know was, if it hadn't been for Brian, would Julie and he lasted, tucked away in their small apartment out on the Strip, the place with the pool and what seemed like air conditioning in every window.

The waitress stepped up to the table and poured a fresh round of coffee for both men.

"Thank you, Debbie," Brian said, smiling with a devilish grin.

Jimmy glanced at his watch. "It's getting late. I gotta get out of here."

Brian dismissed Jimmy's comment with a flick of his wrist. "Slow down. The night is young."

"I know when I'm done for."

Brian gazed around the room like suddenly he was bored. "I got a little something I need to tend to down on the floor."

"What's her name?"

Brian laughed. "How'd you know?"

"Lucky guess."

"Her name is Belle. She's a dancer in the show. Do you know her? She's been here about three weeks now."

"I haven't seen more than a few minutes of the show in years."

The revue was the Galactic Showcase, a knockdown, drag-out rendition of aliens from outer space, complete with a flying saucer trimmed in gold and white and showered with glitter that fell from the sky. Around it, an array of good looking dancers pranced in all directions, clad only in revealing commando outfits and carrying toy guns and laser beams.

Brian laughed. "She doesn't even know I'm in town. I'm going to sneak up on her and surprise the hell out of her."

"Are you going out with her?"

"I think so. Least we were until she left town. Who knows, maybe all bets are off."

"What brings her up this way?"

"Her mother isn't doing so well. And besides Belle wants to go back to school."

"So what's wrong with the mother?"

"Something, I forget. Her blood work isn't quite right. I guess it's hard for her to get around these days."

After signing for the check, Brian walked Jimmy outside to the foyer. Brian turned and asked, "Do you ever hear from Pogue these days?"

"About every other Christmas."

"Quite a guy," Brian said.

"Charming is the word."

"He does have style, I'll say that much for him."

"My mother says he's back in Jersey, but who knows."

"There was a guy who really knew how to have a good time."

"My mother said it about right when it comes to him. A rogue by any other name is a Pogue. I must have heard it a zillion times growing up."

Brian leaned over and laughed. "That's beautiful. That's absolutely beautiful. That nails that dude to a tee."

Driving home, Jimmy thought about the mess all over again. The Brian, Julie, and Pogue affair. The scene he zeroed in was the night Pogue stopped by and brought the whole Vegas venture crashing to its knees. He stood in the living room of Jimmy's new place, dressed in black slacks and a red Cartier sweater that must have set him back a few hundred dollars. He asked for a beer and then sat down on the couch, at the opposite end from Jimmy. Before he took a swig, he made his big pitch. "Some friends of mine are coming to town this weekend and we think we can make some money. If you know what I mean. And the really beautiful thing is, you won't have to do a thing. We're going to take care of you. We're going to be in and out in less than an hour."

"Is that right?"

"We're not going to upset the apple cart. We just want to take a little bite for ourselves."

That night Jimmy heard only one voice going off in his head. It was the one that belonged to his mother. It crept to the center of his being and opened up like a sieve. "Pogue ain't nothing but trouble. Always has been and always will be."

The silent rage rang through Jimmy for several seconds, before he gave his father the only answer he knew how to give. "No, I'm not up for that. You knew that coming in."

That's when Pogue really went to work. "There is nothing to worry about. The other dealers on the crew will do all the work. When the time is right, a few people are going to be over payed. All you have to do is look the other way." Pogue said it so many times, the phrase sounded like an old hymn straight out of church. "Just look the other way," he kept saying, "just look the other way."

When Jimmy shook his head for the last time, Pogue stood up and zoned in on him like a fighter pilot sizing up the field below. "What a little schmuck I raised. That's what I get for letting you hang around your mother so much. You never did know the score. You can't even keep things straight in your own home and here I am thinking you could run with the big boys."

"What do you mean by that?"

"You don't even know, do you?" Pogue said, letting go with his biggest bomb of the night. "You're best friend is banging your old lady right under your nose and you don't even have a clue. Mr. Innocent, that's you."

"What are you talking about?"

"I saw them in a lounge out on the edge of town about a month before you guys packed up and made the big move down here to the major leagues. Anyone with a brain bigger than a pea could tell what was going on. And when Julie saw me, I thought her teeth were going to fall out and roll across the floor."

When Pogue finished, he opened the door and casually turned and took one last shot. Brushing a piece of lint off the front of his sweater, he stared at his son and took aim. "We were going to take some, leave some. That's all. Take some, leave some. What the hell's wrong with that?"

* * *

The next night Jimmy walked into the Hideaway Lounge and stood near the bar. Inside the room was dark—very, very dark. The only light whatsoever was a tiny bulb that hung just above the cash register, giving the bartender enough light to make change from the long flow of bills that came flooding his way. Originally meant as a place for people to escape to after a long night of gambling, the Hideaway was quickly overrun by dealers and pit bosses. At the end of every shift, they stormed in—drinking and laughing and, most of all, complaining.

Once Jimmy's eyes gave way to the darkness, he walked across the room. Swing shift dealers were huddled in the corners, drinking in groups of two's and three's. All Jimmy really saw was the whites of their eyes staring up at him, the rest of their faces still lost in silhouette. Behind them he heard the sharp tingle of ice or the pinging of a glass, one against the other.

Near the cigarette machine, he heard Brian's voice and turned. With ease he spotted his old friend. He was in the far corner speaking with Belle. He was sitting sideways with both feet pointed at the door, like he could bolt at any time. When he caught sight of Jimmy, he stopped and yelled, "There's my man, now."

Jimmy smiled and thought about all the times he had gotten off work, then tracked Brian down in a bar, only to slide next to him, pull out his bankroll, and order a round of drinks like he was some sort of man on the move.

"Honey, let me introduce you to the next casino manager of the Jade Black Club."

"Ssssh!" Jimmy said. "What are you trying to do, get me fired?"

Brian dismissed those around him with a flick of his wrist. "Nobody knows anything around here. It's you and me, kid."

Jimmy sat down and nodded at Belle, pretending not to hear what Brian had just said.

"It's nice to meet you, Jimmy," Belle said. "You're the one Brian can't stop talking about."

"Well, I'm sure you know by now, you can't believe a word this guy has to say."

Belle laughed and so did Brian. "It's all good, trust me," she said.

Belle was young, younger than Jimmy would have thought. Twenty-two, twenty-three, maybe more, but not much more. Blessed with baby blue eyes and soft skin, she looked like a school kid. Jimmy had trouble picturing her on stage dressed in black leather and little else, rubbing up against a flying saucer like she wanted to make love to it.

"I've got some good news, brother," Brian said.

"What's that?"

"I was on the horn today with the Mission. They like what I had to say, especially when it came to you. I really think we're going to do us some business up here."

"It's so exciting," Belle said.

"Yeah, that's what I like about the Mission. Big enough to be on the move, yet not so big, they're lost in all the hoopla. They know enough to have a guy like you in place."

"I'm all ears," Jimmy added.

"You better be all brains," Brian said, slapping him on the back. "Because I am sure this is going to happen. They've got their lawyers all revved up and ready to go."

Jimmy smiled. The more he thought about it, the more he liked it, the idea of roaming the floors upstairs, his name on the big oak door just off the elevator, taking a long lunch with corporate types, giving them his ideas on expansion or what new games to bring into the casino. He knew in a weird way, his father would be proud of him and that counted for some kind of perk in the family hierarchy. Not much, but a little.

A waitress with a long ponytail and deep dark eyes walked up to the table and took Jimmy's order. "A gin and tonic for me and whatever my friends would like."

"Yes, Mr. Stokes."

The waitress walked away and Brian laughed. "Yes, Mr. Stokes. Can you believe that? You start running this joint, and chicks like that will be swarming all over you."

"Brian, please, don't talk like that," Belle said.

"Well it's true. That's how it works. We'll have to get our man a fly swatter just so he can keep them at bay."

"That's not very nice," Belle said.

The waitress set a fresh round of drinks on the table, and Jimmy signed for them with a quick flick of his pen.

"To friendship," Brian said, holding his drink up in front of him like a trophy.

The three of them toasted and Jimmy took a look around. What a rut he had been in these last few years. Driving down the same streets, past the same dirty motels and broken down pawnshops, only to retrace the same steps at night. If it weren't for Brian, Jimmy would be home right now, slouched in front of the TV, watching Conan O'Brian crack and whistle his way through another show.

"So Belle, tell me, what brings you to Reno?" Jimmy asked.

A sad pouty look spread across Belle's face. "A couple of things. My mother is not doing so well. The doctor says she has lupus. Plus I want to go back to school. I want to be a nurse."

"All right, what made you think of something like that?"

"It's important to me, taking care of others. It always has been, even when I was a little girl on the way to dance class."

Brian's shoulders drooped. It looked like all of his bones had just lost their mettle. "Must be nice, thinking about stuff like that. Right, Jimmy?"

"All those things we never knew anything about growing up here," Jimmy said, knowing it was always money, money, money.

"To the world we know nothing about," Brian said, holding his glass up in the air. "We should have been humanitarians, you and me. They could have called us the Frick and Frack Show. Acts of kindness on the come-out roll."

Jimmy laughed. "Yeah, happiness at two-to-one."

"Double odds for doing the right thing."

"Nightly payoffs for feeding the hungry."

Brian laughed and shook his head. "Man, it's a wonder we're even alive after working in these joints all these years."

Jimmy knew exactly what he meant. That's why they were friends. They both knew something about a world that was turned more inward than outward, defined only by a spin of a wheel or a flick of a card.

"How about we do one more, then we hit the road?" Brian said.

To Jimmy, the sound of Brian's voice sounded smooth and easy, like a disc jockey on a late night jazz program.

"You two go ahead," Belle said. "I need to run backstage and grab my bag."

"Take your time," Brian said. "We'll meet you right outside when you're ready."

Belle walked out of the lounge and stepped on the escalator. Her balance was soft and easy, like the dancer that she had trained to be all these years.

"Pretty girl," Jimmy said as she disappeared out of sight.

"I think I'm going to try and keep her around."

Jimmy signed for another round of drinks. This one brought him right up to the edge, the one he and Brian used to peer over all the time.

When they finished, Brian stood up and brushed a piece of lint off the front of his shirt. "Let's wait outside."

Near the doorway, he turned and spoke to Jimmy. "Wait up a sec, I'll be right back."

Jimmy stopped and stood near the exit. Softly, he rolled back and forth on the balls of his feet. He liked the way his shoes sunk into the thick cushy carpet and held him in place. Down the way, he saw an older woman hit a $7.50 jackpot and he smiled broadly on her behalf.

After about a minute of basking in the glow of the woman's success, he turned and glanced over his shoulder. Brian was busy, yakking it up with the cocktail waitress with the long ponytail and the dark pretty eyes. She was laughing so hard, she had to hold onto Brian's hand for support. "A Pogue is nothing more than a rogue," Jimmy heard her say. "That's funny. That's really funny. Did you just make that up?"

"That joke is mine, all mine. And guess what, there's plenty more where that came from."

Jimmy looked away. He couldn't bear to hear anymore. Still Brian's voice rolled over him, taking him in and nudging him from all sides. At the top of the escalator, he spotted Belle stepping on to ride down. Smiling, she carried a green bag over her shoulder and appeared to be a woman in love. At first Jimmy thought of reaching out to her, helping her in some way. But the booze held him in check, gripping him much more than he wanted.

Behind him, Brian's voice continued to pour out. The heaviness of it forced him to close his eyes and think about his early days in Vegas, like the day that he, Brian, and Pogue stood around the parking lot of the Mission, trading jokes in rapid fire. At one point Pogue reached into his pocket and offered up a fifty dollar bill, holding it between his thumb and forefinger like a treat at the zoo. "You guys go out and have a good time. Just remember one thing, it's on me." Before Jimmy could budge, Brian had the money tucked inside his pocket until they got downtown where they rolled the dice back and forth on a 25¢ craps game until well after midnight.

Jimmy watched Belle walk into the bar and smile at him. Turning slightly he spotted the cocktail waitress cross the room and place a round of drinks in front of three dealers and pit boss. Belle glanced at Brian and tapped her watch as if apologizing for taking so long getting back from the showroom. Brian shrugged and shot back in a glib way, "Everything's cool. I'm just busy taking in the scene."

Jimmy turned and chose not to dwell on what else Brian might be saying. After all, he was still a friend, someone he had shared part of the world with, one almost secretive in nature, held together only by long nights of nothing else but cards and dice and stories about Pogue winding his way around the state of Nevada like a gypsy.

Over his shoulder, Jimmy caught side of Brian and Belle moving his way, and he braced himself. He saw Brian had his hand wrapped around Belle's and he was pulling her closer to him, reigning her in as they neared the entranceway.

Suddenly Brian called out, "Hey Jiiiiiiiimmmmmmmmyyyyy!" and the sound of his voice swam over the top of Jimmy one last time. He listened until it enveloped the whole of him and that's when he heard it, the hollow bead of sound that ran through the center of it, like a needle coursing its way through a piece of cloth, and he decided to let it pass right on through, not wanting to embrace it, not wanting to stand in its way, knowing that it was much bigger than anything he could ever overcome.

Golden Day

Jeff W. Bens

Mrs. Cashman needed eighty-seven dollars and I became determined to help her get it.

"But you mustn't give it to me, I won't take it," Mrs. Cashman said, her oversized, pearl-like necklace clanking against the edge of her third refill of coffee in our hotel's delicatessen. "You mustn't." Mrs. Cashman was seventy-three. She hadn't touched the third cup, but she would, as it was free, and coffee, though she'd never say this, killed the need for food.

"I don't have it," I said. Her gaze dropped from mine, into the coffee and the swirl of cream she'd poured in, the coffee white, and she brought the cup to her lips.

"It's not for me," she sipped, "but for Mr. Newcomb. He's eighty-four years old."

Mr. Newcomb lived on the eleventh floor, two above mine, beside Mrs. Cashman, though to hear her tell it he would have to soon move, "to a lower floor on account of his legs, what with the elevators always busted; or maybe straight to the funeral parlor, cut out the middle men." The one time I'd spoken with Mr. Newcomb, or rather him to me, he was sitting alone with a cigar in the Carlson's lobby, staring into the wallpaper. He'd startled me, turning and meeting my eyes. "Cubano," is all he'd said. And then he'd smiled and turned his attention back to the wall.

"Let's get more crackers," I suggested, though my tooth was killing me, the tooth I later had pulled, just to the right of the right incisor, and as I was signaling the waitress, Mrs. Cashman covered my free hand with her own.

"He's not well. It's his joints. They ache beyond normal," she said, and, as if to demonstrate, she pulled up the hem of her navy dress and rubbed her knees. This set her coughing and I checked my pocket for change to see if I had enough to buy her a soup.

"I'll buy you a soup," I said as the waitress arrived.

Mrs. Cashman looked up from her knees. "Not too much salt." Her coughing ceased. "And maybe some extra noodle."

* * *

I'd moved into the Carlson, after my breakup with Lacey, to be with my father, who would die six months after my arrival, though only in my mind did the two events go together. I'd stayed on-- living in his front room, on the sofa, not in his bed-- where the rent was controlled and my mother's picture watched over me from the foyer wall. I didn't have anywhere else to go. My jobs weren't working out: first the desk job with the environ-mental clean-up company, then the retail job with the suit I never earned enough to pay for, that at least I wore to his funeral, and then the selling of vitamins and light bulbs for the handicapped. I'm not handicapped, impaired, challenged, no more than anyone else, not counting my tooth, but some of these companies hire out to fill the needs around the holidays, and it was November and the Christmas rush was on.

I have no siblings. I am an only child. My mother died when I was ten. I sat in the oak tree in front of the junior high school the day of her death, and watched the students on the playgrounds, and then when it was dark I climbed down and went back to our house, where my father was watching the news, and when I came in he smiled thickly at me, his lips gone dry and the lines around his eyes deep in the light of the television, and he clapped his hands once as if for encouragement.

* * *

It had seemed natural to stay on in his apartment, though now that he had been gone, dead, for two and a half months, I was beginning to feel uneasy. The moose head made me nervous. The apartment had only two rooms, and they were not separated by a wall, only by a change in carpet, from orange (in the bedroom) to brown (in the living room), and above the two TV's he'd mounted what a client from Augusta, Maine had sent in a crate with the payment that closed out the client's account of twenty-two years.

My father had two televisions, one for picture and one for sound. Near the end, when he was thin and suddenly old, we'd sit eating something I'd brought home, and I'd have the unsettling experience of watching one newscaster while listening to another. The sound up so loud that it dis-torted, my father never seeming to mind. More recently, the picture tube had begun to go, so I'd hear most programs but see very few. Mrs. Cash-man came over sometimes after he'd died, and we'd sit in the glow of the television, and she'd tell me about the successes of her children, and the failures of her grandchildren, a game show on one of the TV's, the other screen blank, the moose up above it all like a big antenna.

My father and Mrs. Cashman did not speak.

"She's a woman you can't get to know," he once said, though I never had any trouble and it would not be until after his death, after I'd had my day with Mr. Newcomb, that I would understand that what he'd said was so, though not in the ways that he meant.

* * *

Sometimes I brought Mrs. Cashman food and she would cook it. Lacey never cooked. In fact, though we were married, I now don't know what I saw in her. "She had a nice chest," my father would say, polishing to his last good day the sample case he kept-- inside the wallets and the key cases, the purses, the letter openers with the leather handles-- and also the unsold attaches. "A nice chest is important." And she did have a nice chest, but this did not seem a legitimate basis for matrimony.

"And she had personality."

"Personality? Dad she left me. She packed up and left me and took our son."

"Still," my father said, turning his attention to the noise from the upper TV. I must have turned my attention to the window, for it was there that I first saw Mrs. Cashman.

Mrs. Cashman, I'd learn from our lunches, left Poland in the back of a mailsack when she was fifteen. She married Mr. Cashman in Toronto and, when he'd died, she'd found a place with her younger sister, Nora, who'd retired to the Carlson in the late 1970's with a pension from AT&T.

I first saw Mrs. Cashman surrounded by fur from a rug she was shaking out her eleventh story window. The effect was startling: the red rug flapping like a tongue, white fur rising around her, my father pale on the sofa, the green glow of the TV. After a particularly vigorous shake, the rug dropped from her hands and for a minute it appeared Mrs. Cashman might float down behind it. She lunged after the rug, her fingers snapping in the air, as if calling it back, and then a small dog appeared in the sill beside her, barked twice, and bit onto her dress. She smacked it.

The red rug caught a breeze and sailed over the four lanes of Eddy Street.

I retrieved it. I retrieved the rug and I brought it back to her, maybe because I'm a sucker, or more likely because the look on her face after she'd dropped it reminded me of Crawford's the time I ran over his tricycle with Lacey's Cabriolet.

* * *

Crawford, my son, was three when they left. We had almost aborted him, but at the last minute Lacey could not go through with it, and now I am of course thankful to her, though she cheated on me and left me and then for a period I did not know anymore for certain how Crawford was.

* * *

I didn't see Mrs. Cashman again until I bumped into her in the laundry where I was washing my father's clothes.

"Spray bleach," she'd said without prompting, and when I turned from my sorting, colors from whites, she was staring at me, two oyster-sized earrings on either side of her loosely swaying neck. "For the shorts."

I'm not one to speak much of personal issues of hygiene. Lacey once said to me, in bed, "I stink, I know, I don't use deodorant," but that was different, as we were of course without clothes, and besides her smell to me was like a damned nectar; but Mrs. Cashman was squeaking toward me, in the building's basement laundry, her feet in blue tennis shoes.

"You spray the front and the back and, if you're a sweaty man, you spray the waist as well." She said this in a way that was perfectly natural, as if it were the weather or maybe that I'd dropped a sock behind the washer.

She snatched my father's boxers before I even saw her arm move. She turned the shorts in her hand, frowning. "What's the matter. You not got a wife?"

"We've separated."

"Big shot," she said.

"She left me."

She paused. "Spray bleach," she finally said. "Front and the back."

* * *

My father often surprised me, with his televisions, with his moosehead, even with the announcement that he was dying. He'd known about the cancer for six months before he'd called, and then he'd only spoken to Lacey, who taped a note to the refrigerator saying that he'd phoned.

One night, my father, after a particularly upsetting viewing of the eleven o'clock news, surprised me by sending me up to check on Mrs. Cashman's sister.

"Ask her if she feels safe."

"Nora?"

"Yes."

"Mrs. Cashman's sister?

"Yes."

"Why don't you just call her?"

"She worked forty years at AT&T. She's had enough already with the telephone."

I did as he asked. Nora answered the door as if it were perfectly normal for me to be calling at half past eleven, smiling as if she were glad to see me, squeezing my arm in gratitude when I asked her how she was.

* * *

It wasn't until after my father's death that I started to see more of Mrs. Cashman. My job at the handicapped phone bank freed up my days, and so I'd often see her at breakfast or at lunch in the hotel's delicatessen where she'd call me to her table. With Crawford gone and Lacey gone and my father gone, I did not mind the company. There were long periods of silence, with Mrs. Cashman maybe eating half my sandwich, and sometimes she'd talk about her life in Canada, about growing up in Toronto with an Uncle and Aunt, about her husband who, like her father, had been a jeweler, and I'd compliment the jewels she wore and she'd tell me how they were only fakes, but she'd blush. I liked that she'd blush. At seventy-three years old. She was graceful. She wore a hat, for instance, whenever she went out of her apartment. And she'd always motion for me to sit with her, there in the lobby delicatessen, by extending a thin arm to the empty chair, her bracelets sweeping toward it. And Mr. Newcomb, the time I'd seen him sitting in the Carlson lobby, just sitting there with his cigar, he wore a necktie. Even my father never left in the morning without shaving twice.

* * *

I started to bring her vitamins. I was stealing them, true, but the phone job paid under the minimum wage, and I could not afford them otherwise. When the clients invariably asked if I was crippled, I could not bring myself to lie. I'd sold only twelve orders in four weeks, and I knew my vitamin days were numbered.

Once I smuggled her out a lightbulb.

"What's this?"

"A light bulb."

"Why?"

"It lasts a lifetime."

"With me, then, you got ripped off."

The vitamins she accepted, though she said they burned her stomach. "Take them with food," I told her.

"They turn my pee extra yellow."

"Spray bleach," I said.

* * *

Lacey was a health nut. I hated to think that I'd been attracted to the vitamin angle of the handicapped job for this reason, but it is true that my vitamin sales outnumbered my bulb sales by nearly four to one, though as I say they were far from providing a steady salary. Lacey went off with the guy who sold me life insurance, which is a good racket to be in, though I wouldn't like it, always fencing people's insecurities. She did aerobics, sometimes twice a day, and some nights she'd go out with her friends from the gym after the dinnertime workout and I realize now that she was probably then with Edward.

There'd be something in the freezer or the fridge. I'd sit with Crawford in our small yard, and to see over our fence, and the fences that made boxes of all the yards, we'd climb the near branch of our oak, and watch the sun drop down behind the old athletic park and the fireflies rise up from the grass.

I could guess where Lacey had taken him: to her parents, or to Edward's house, and I knew the number of Edward's office as I mailed a check there every month, but I figured I'd wait and let Lacey call, that Crawford would need time to adjust, that he didn't need a scene right then, with his mother and father screaming at each other, and this new man with whom he'd have to learn to get along.

* * *

Because she rarely had much to eat, once I bought Mrs. Cashman a fish. A whole fish that was maybe two days old but I'd been assured was fresh enough. My father had left 964 dollars worth of silver dollars-- eleven coins-- in a ladies' handbag that was fastened with a three number combination lock. After paying rent and back rent, I had nineteen dollars left.

"It's a celebration," Mrs. Cashman announced when I arrived at her apartment with the fish.

We sat at Mrs. Cashman's card table and ate the fish she'd broiled. During the entire meal her schnauzer, Alfred, was humping my leg. Whenever I was in the house he lunged toward me with the heat of a pervert. Though small, he was fat, as Mrs. Cashman and Mr. Newcomb often left their apartments' adjoining door ajar, and, as Mrs. Cashman put it, Mr.

Newcomb "was a dog person." I'd knocked on Mr. Newcomb's door after inviting Nora to dinner, but there had been no answer.

"He rests," said Mrs. Cashman.

"He dances," said Nora, and I thought for a moment she was referring to Mr. Newcomb until I saw that she was pointing at Alfred doing a kind of dance on my poor leg.

"About the eighty-eight dollars," Mrs. Cashman said as she spooned a broth across my fish. In it were bits of green and flakes of black and it looked nice. "Maybe your father left you a little money?"

"Halina!" Nora was sixty-six. The sister born between the two of them had, like the parents, as Mrs. Cashman once briefly put it to me, not survived.

"He left me a handbag full of silver dollars," I said.

"Maybe you can cash them?"

"Your father was a nice man, Mr. Nye," said Nora.

"I've only nine dollars left."

Alfred sighed, settled down on the red rug. Mrs. Cashman re-smoothed the napkin in her lap. Nora began to talk about a new man in her life.

"He's a painter."

Mrs. Cashman speared a bean. "Houses?"

Nora frowned. "What about you, Neil?"

"There's no new man in my life," I said, thinking Mrs. Cashman might get a kick out of this but she just frowned, and so they were both now frowning. My tooth was killing me, but I took another bite, packing the left side of my mouth.

"So, Nora," said Mrs. Cashman, "this man?"

"He's divorcing."

"He's a painter *and* he's divorcing? What next, that he's purple?"

"He's a very nice man," Nora said. She flipped Alfred a red potato. "And what about your oldest?"

Mrs. Cashman waved her fork. "He's troubled. He's worried that Julie will take everything. He sent thirty dollars."

Nora spoke down to her plate. "Thirty dollars."

"He's doing the best that he can. I told him never to marry that . . . that *girl*." Mrs. Cashman shook a little, shut her eyes. When she opened them, she was looking at me. "I'd give it to Mr. Newcomb if I didn't have to pay rent. The poor man's legs."

"And where are *his* children?" Nora asked.

"Oh, Nora, where are any of our children?"

I excused myself from the table. Alfred jumped into my chair, and Mrs. Cashman swatted at him but not before he grabbed what he could. He'd choke on a bone and I'd have to take him to the vet and I didn't even have the money to loan to Mrs. Cashman for Mr. Newcomb's weak legs.

* * *

Crawford had something to do with my guts feeling bad. They'd been bad for a while, not at the start, when I had my father to watch over, but lately nothing had been staying in me. I sat on the toilet in Mrs. Cashman's bathroom, and stared into the mirror that was across from me.

I'd hit Crawford once. He'd run out into the road and an ice-cream truck nearly took him, or at least had to brake, its horn blaring, the clown on top spinning, and I overreacted because when I got to Crawford I cuffed him and even though I felt so bad that I bought him two creamsickles I couldn't help feel that this was something he might still think about, maybe at night, alone in a bed that was not yet his own.

* * *

Nora was whispering when I emerged.

"His own son," she was saying.

"His *only* son."

I went through the opened door across from the bathroom and was in Mr. Newcomb's den. I suddenly had a desire to see this Mr. Newcomb and his frail legs, to get his butt over here and tell me why I should give him eighty-eight dollars when I was broke, too. And I was going to tell him, crossing the den, until I pushed open the den's other door and saw Mr. Newcomb spread out in his bed. An old duvet across him, his body barely a wrinkle in the fabric, he could not have weighed 100 pounds. And beside his bed a sandwich, a small bite mark in the half that was left, hardening, and an untouched glass of milk.

* * *

Stealing the money was not hard. Rather than spend what would be my last shift on the telephone, I moved from station to station talking. The supervisors I worked with were never eager to see me, and they would turn to the phone after a couple of words and then I would just grab what I could of their banks. Between three banks, I collected fifty-one dollars in cash. I left whatever checks there were in a pile on my station, headed toward the bathroom, and just kept walking. I did not feel badly that I was stealing from the handicapped, as I was giving to the handicapped, cutting out the middle man.

I phoned Mrs. Cashman before I went to her room and knocked. She hadn't been in the delicatessen, where I'd treated myself to a coffee with the money I had stolen. I felt a little bad doing so, but I was thirty-six dollars short as it was, so I did not feel that seventy-five cents, a dollar with the tip, would affect Mr. Newcomb's legs one way or the other.

I knocked on her door a few more times but she did not answer. I thought about coming upstairs again later, but I did not really feel like going back to my father's apartment. I knocked on Mr. Newcomb's door. I knocked loudly and then louder still. I had the money he needed. He would be happy that I woke him.

"Who is it?" His voice startled me as it had once before.

"It's Neil," I said. "From downstairs."

"Hold on, hold on," Mr. Newcomb said, his voice coming from across the apartment. "I'll be a minute."

When the door finally opened, it opened only a crack, and I saw Mr. Newcomb, a cane in his hand, his body wrapped in a robe. "Yes?"

"I have your money."

"One hundred four dollars?"

"Fifty-one. Fifty, actually."

"You got a car?"

"Huh?"

Mr. Newcomb seemed to look back over his shoulder. "Go downstairs and get me a newspaper, will you? Will you do that, Neil?"

"Sure."

"Thanks, Neil. Thanks very much," Mr. Newcomb said, and as I tried to look over his shoulder, he quickly shut the door.

* * *

He had dressed. He was wearing tan slacks and white tennis shoes and a green v-neck sweater over a cream-colored shirt, and every inch, if baggy, was pressed. His hair was wet and combed and he moved, for a man with bum legs, well enough to take the paper from me, take my arm, motion for me to sit, and get himself into the chair beneath the picture of his wife and a photo from the War.

I was looking at the photo, trying to figure which of the five young soldiers that leaned on a donkey cart was now this old man thumbing through the newspaper, his cane against the cushion of the chair, when Mrs. Cashman appeared in the connecting doorway wearing her red hat.

"Hello, Neil."

"Hello, Mrs. Cashman. Are you just getting in?"

"No," she said. "Did you knock? I must have been napping—"

"Are you going out?" I asked.

"No, dear–"

She smiled at me, and then her eyes briefly met Mr. Newcomb's as she closed the doors that adjoined the two apartments, her red hat the last thing to go.

Mr. Newcomb had the paper in pieces around his chair, was tearing one page in half. "Golden Day," he said. I looked at him, at his face that I'd seen as so frail, and it did not seem now that way at all, but rather seemed taken over by his eyes, which all but jumped from their sockets.

"I'm sorry that I'm a little short with the money," I began, but he cut me off. He was trying to stand. I got to my own feet and offered him my arm.

"Good," he said. "Good. You got a car?"

"No."

"That's OK. Twenty-two times two is forty-four, that leaves six dollars. What's twenty-two times one and a half?"

"Thirty-six," he continued before I could answer. "Thirty-six dollars, yes, that's OK." He was up now, with his hand on his black, wooden cane, and he was heading toward the closet.

"Go into my kitchen, in the cabinet beside the sink."

The kitchen was clean, and as small as my father's, and when I opened the cabinet beside the sink it was empty. I opened the cabinet opposite. Inside were two cans of mini-ravioli, a can of soup, a tin of tuna, and one box of Ritz crackers.

"Nevermind," Mr. Newcomb called. "I've got it here."

I looked in the cupboard for a minute longer, and then turned to see Mr. Newcomb emerging from the bedroom with two glasses and a bottle of Canadian whiskey. He was holding them in the hand that didn't hold his cane and I rushed to him to make sure he did not drop them.

"Fill 'em," Newcomb said.

I poured.

"Three fingers and then we'll go."

I poured about an inch into each tumbler, tumblers that were already wet.

"Pretty thin fingers," Mr. Newcomb said, and then he raised his glass and drank it back and I did the same. "To Golden Day," he said and he smacked his lips.

I thought maybe the Golden Day was a hospital, or a prescription drug or God forbid it sounded like the place that buried my father. "Yes, it is a golden day," I said, "and I'm glad I could be of help."

Mr. Newcomb was fitting onto his head a green fedora with a red feather in the band. "Let's blow out of here," he said, and we left the

Carlson, and twenty minutes later we were on the number 7 bus to the track.

* * *

At six-to-one, Golden Day figured to pay $216 on our thirty-six dollar bet. After bus fare and the dollar admission, we were able to buy two beers and split a knockwurst. Standing in the concrete fairway beneath the grandstand, Mr. Newcomb talked horses nonstop: see the way that one leans, see the way that one carries, that one has rot, that one's ribs are heavy. He had a comment for each horse that paraded past. And then it was the third race, and out came Golden Day.

I hadn't planned on becoming involved in what I perceived to be an old man's last cry at life, and I was a little uncomfortable about his health, but he'd seemed so eager, this seemed so important to him, that I went along, without questioning. And Golden Day was a magnificent horse: her mane lit with the sun, her head held higher than the horses around her. I'd give the old man his thrill, put him back on the buss—I'd been smart enough to buy roundtrip passes—then get him back to bed before his legs gave out completely. When he slept he might dream of his younger days, and I was glad for it.

I was surprised, then, as the two of us watched Golden Day bank back toward the starting gate, to hear Mr. Newcomb say, "So, your wife left you?"

I took my eyes from the horse. "I beg your pardon?"

"Your wife? She up and left with your own son, Mrs. Cashman says."

"That's private. Mrs. Cashman was supposed to keep that to herself."

"People talk," Mr. Newcomb said, and then he elbowed me hard in the ribs and jutted his narrow chin back toward the track. "Here we go—Golden Day!"

The gun fired, the gate—which was hooked to the back of a truck—sped off, and Golden Day immediately took advantage of her position on the rail. Like lightening she bolted off.

"Golden Day!" I said.

"You must miss him," said Mr. Newcomb.

I looked down at the little man, whose right arm was looped through my left, his other hand clutching the knob at the top of his cane. Then the elbow again, and Newcomb was pointing toward the track.

"Look at her take that turn. Golden Day, Golden Day, Golden Day at six to one!"

She was in the lead. The number three horse was closing. The number eight horse, a giant animal that looked prehistoric, was muscling in from the outside. You could see the mad flair of its nostrils, the hatred in it of losing. "She's got to hold the rail," I said, "come on Golden Day, come on golden girl!"

"You were cheating, maybe?" I felt Mr. Newcomb's face near mine once more.

"No."

"You don't like girls?"

"Of course I like girls."

Mr. Newcomb shrugged his frail shoulders. The feather in his hat blew a little in the wind.

"Here, here," he said, suddenly excited again, "half-way in the lead, and she's a closer."

"What about the number eight horse?" That horse's nose was at her tail, and he seemed to be pressing in.

"It's going to be close," Mr. Newcomb said and we inched up toward the rail. The announcer was calling faster now, the race heating up and while the crowd was sparse, a roar began from the grandstand.

Golden Day by half a length, Lightening Strike closing, Golden Day into the turn, fast finisher, dry track, Golden Day, Golden Day, Golden Day—

"Come on, Golden Day," I shouted, "Come on, COME ON, COME ON—"

The horses were streaking toward us, the finish line twenty feet to my right. We were at the fence before the rail, ten feet from the horses, I could smell them, I could feel their approaching heat--

Lightening Strike--Golden Day--Lightening Strike--Golden Day--

A dead-heat, neck and neck, a line of spit behind each horse, the jockies' faces clamped to the streaking necks--

"GOLDEN DAY, GOLDEN DAY, GOLDEN DAY," I was screaming and Mr. Newcomb was pounding at the fence, his teeth gritted together—

"GO-GO-GO-GO-GO—,"he cried. "GOLDEN DAY!"

And they streaked past, the two horses identical, stretching out, every last inch toward the finish line. The crowd's roar, the blur of the announcer's mad call, Mr. Newcomb with his arms raised up over his head—

And then I realized I was crying, big tears down my dumb face, and when I turned toward Mr. Newcomb he was watching me, the horses crossing the finish line, the crowd's roaring blanket, his arms opened wide to me, the sunlight across his face.

The Inevitable Big Win

Kelley Calvert

For Grandma Frannie

When Tina Grove pulled into the parking lot of her neighborhood corner store, she had a list of fifteen things to do. At two o'clock in the afternoon, she was still working on number one: buy cat litter. Admittedly, the pronounced odor wafting from her cat's litter box added urgency to this particular errand (It was only number eight on the list).

She blamed California for her inability to accomplish everything she needed to do: the continuously mild weather, blue or grey skies, and slight ocean breeze gave the impression that time was not passing at all. Today was yet another mild seventy-degree day, clouds whisking past the sun on their way somewhere else. Time was indeed passing, but the chores on her list were merely transferred from one day to the next until the list seemed to take on a life of its own, a cancerous reproduction, an exponential growth from which buying cat litter would only subtract a tiny coefficient.

Tina sighed heavily as she exited her Ford Escort, a late eighties model; its survival was continually the butt of her friends' jokes. The Escort was a Ford after all, not what her union-born and bred father would call a "rice-burner." After buying cat litter, Tina had to go to the laundromat. Actually, she had to change the litter box and then go wash a load of laundry. She'd better add "Call Dad" to the list, too.

The convenience store doors were wide open, allowing the wind to bring in the ocean air, a mixture of life and decay. Tina strolled up and down the aisles as minutes ticked mischievously by. She couldn't find the cat litter until she reached the paper goods section. *Why would cat litter be next to paper plates and toilet paper?*

Approaching the counter, she saw the Vietnamese clerk pointing to stark, Sharpie-printed words on a piece of cardboard: No Checks for Lottery or Cigarettes. An elderly woman supported herself with a cane, leaned over the counter, squinted her eyes at the sign and then resettled them on the clerk, a question mark hanging in the creases between her eyebrows.

"No check for lottery," the clerk explained flatly.

"And, why is that?" The old lady countered. "I need my lottos!"

"Rule is rule." The clerk pronounced these last words with finality while pushing his glasses up the bridge of his nose.

Tina watched the old lady and store clerk stare at one another in a battle of wills. Her list began playing itself in her mind. Change litter, laundry, call dad, buy groceries, check account balance, exercise, budget—What came next? She glanced around. Two people had gathered behind her; their presence added to her anxiety. She exchanged meaningful glances with the man behind her waiting to buy a two-liter. He rolled his eyes. She nodded imperceptibly.

It never fails. Once again, Tina was behind one of *those* little old ladies. She reminded herself of a recent resolution to be more tolerant of others. She had noted that people never so much as look at one another anymore, and she had vowed to change her impatient ways. Tina absent-mindedly scanned the old woman's dark curls and wondered if she dyed her hair; then, she ran her fingers through her own hair, remembering how her grandmother used to struggle to get a brush through it. In those days, Tina ran from the prospect of grooming as though it were life threatening. Her hair responded to reluctance by growing into unruly rats that took her grandmother hours to pick through, hours that could have been spent riding bikes or playing soccer with the neighborhood boys. Grandma Frannie also maintained jet black hair until the day she died, a feat Tina attributed to sheer will.

When, at the wise old age of eight, Tina confided to her grandmother that she no longer believed in God, Frannie looked straight into her eyes and said, "You ain't got nothing to lose by believing. When you're dead, you don't know no different anyhow."

Frannie had a similar view of playing the lottery: you have nothing to lose. When Tina questioned the logic of the inevitable big win, Frannie simply shrugged her off. "You can't win if you don't play," she'd say, reciting her favorite mantra.

Because Tina was at the precise age where human beings know everything, the age just before everything devolves into nothing, she explained, "You have a better chance of dying in a plane crash."

"I don't take planes."

"Fine. You have a better chance of getting hit by a car than winning the lottery."

"Way I see it, I got a better chance of being a millionaire than you since I just bought me a lottery ticket."

Tina would heave a heavy sigh in her grandmother's direction. Lighting another cigarette, Frannie recited a familiar apology: "I'm sorry you don't have a *real* Grandma who bakes you cookies and takes you to the zoo. You got a grandma who smokes cigarettes, drinks beer, and plays the lottery."

Tina's eyes returned to the sign: No Checks for Lottery or Cigarettes. *Who writes checks anymore?* She shifted the bag of cat litter from one hip to the other.

The old woman had apparently grown tired of staring at the clerk as she then turned to Tina and asked, "Do you know what the California Lotto is up to today?"

Tina looked down at her cat litter and admitted that she had no idea.

"Fifty million! Do you have any idea what you could do with fifty million?"

"Well, I probably wouldn't be standing in line at the local market with a bag of cat litter, huh?"

She seemed not to have heard Tina's attempt at humor. "Anything! That's what you could do with fifty million! Anything you want!"

The old lady relayed this anecdote with such intensity that spit sailed from her mouth; holding Tina's gaze, her tone indicated that her words were sacred morsels of truth.

She tapped her rubber-tipped cane on the ground with a thud and returned her gaze to the store clerk who nodded politely but made no comment. "I walked all the way down here with my checkbook. Are you going to make me walk all the way back up the hill to get my money? The drawing's in an hour!"

The old lady's hysteria was clearly misguided; it was the middle of the day. Tina looked at her watch, suddenly afraid that yet another day had slipped by without her noticing.

Tina turned around to see if anyone else had noticed the anachronism and saw that three people were now behind her in line. The man with the two-liter looked wearily at the bottle, apparently contemplating whether it was worth the effort. The old lady seemed oblivious to the plight of those in line behind her.

The woman's dedication to the lottery reminded Tina of her family's reverence of the inevitable big win. She grew up with the refrain that grandma would hit it big one day. Each Christmas, Frannie's seven children chipped in to buy her a hundred lottery tickets, and each year Tina's family had the honor of buying the tickets on their way to family dinner.

Tina remembered her father's smile coming out of the gas station one Christmas. He had on a new sweater, and he seemed to shine, an aura of optimism following him. His aftershave smell hovered in the car as he handed Tina and her mother their tickets.

"Scratch me off a hundred dollar," he said, looking at Tina in the rearview mirror.

While he began scratching off his ticket in a flurry of movement, Tina fumbled around looking for a coin between the car seats. Eventually, Tina yelled, "Mom! Dad! Give me a penny!"

Her dad always seemed to hit twenty dollars right away, which was a good thing because he never noticed her sitting in the back without a coin until he found his first winner.

"What about you?" he finally asked.

Each year, Tina painstakingly scratched off each little box and scrutinized the images underneath. Under her breath, she muttered, *there must be something here, ok, here it comes*, but eventually she accepted the truth: she didn't inherit her father's luck.

"Nothing."

Seeming to doubt Tina's ability to identify three shamrocks or a tic-tac-toe, he asked to see them, encouragement ringing in his voice. Reluctantly, Tina handed her loser tickets forward. Confirming that she had indeed won nothing, he moved on to the next issue at hand—what to do with his twenty dollars.

"Keep it," Mom said flatly.

"Get more tickets," Tina contradicted.

Tina's dad looked back and forth from her to her mother before disappearing from the car. His voice trailed off behind him, offering a compromise, "Ok, we'll be smart and do half and half."

When he got back to the car, the Grove family repeated the ritual until twenty dollars magically became ten dollars and ten dollars magically turned into a FREE TICKET. Pulling away from the gas station, Tina's Dad winked at her in the rearview mirror.

"Just you wait. One day I'm going to hit it big."

Glittering in the white optimism of Christmas morning, Tina believed in her father's luck. They were just waiting for a big break, the luck that would elevate them from indescript middle-American living to care-free extravagance.

At Christmas dinner, her grandmother sat at the table scratching off those tickets, and the whole family was mesmerized by the possibility that she might scratch off $100,000. A running commentary went along with the scratch-off ritual:

"Ok... here we go... hundred dollar!"

"Hm. Two dollars."

"Shit! They tricked me. Nothing."

"Free ticket."

"Almost had a fifty dollar."

"Dollar!"

On good years, she made back the $100. Other years, the little pieces of cardboard barely carried their weight in the price of paper. But Grandma Frannie wouldn't have it any other way. 100 lottery tickets were preferable to 100 dollar bills any day.

Continuing her surveillance of the old lady in the convenience store, Tina concluded that the old lady, like her grandmother, would prefer lottery tickets to money. Tina sat the cat litter down with a meaningful thud while the old lady continued pleading with the clerk. Tina watched her face turn red with exasperation and followed her 70's striped blouse past her baggy polyester bottoms down to her Dr. Scholl's walking shoes. Her hairstyle attested to careful grooming habits. She didn't *seem* to be crazy, senile, or homeless.

That's when Tina knew that she would do whatever the old lady asked. She knew it as clearly as she knew that she would only cross off "Buy cat litter" from her list that day. Tina had a weakness for old ladies. Frannie had practically raised her, and each time she saw an old lady struggle up the notorious hills of central California, she felt a pang of remembrance. Frannie had always spoken of signs—emblems of good luck, symbols of bad luck.

When Tina complained, she would answer, "You wait until you're my age. Then, you tell me who's superstitious."

Tina would do anything the old lady asked out of superstition, out of memory.

"Young lady, can I write you a check and you buy me my ten chances?"

Tina picked up her cat litter, placed it on the conveyer belt and said, "Give me eleven chances. Ten for her and one for me."

The old lady began scribbling out a check, but Tina pushed it away.

"What's your name, dear?"

"No, really. It's okay," Tina answered.

Her protests were of no use. Like it or not, Tina got a check from Joan S. Schmidt with "Lottery Tickets" written in the subject line.

Tina found herself wanting to tell Joan the stories her grandmother had missed since her passing five years prior like the time Tina scratched off a huge prize during her senior year of college. Just like these tickets, the winning ticket was purchased at a corner store down the street from Tina's house. It was a fall day in Boston, the leaves hanging helplessly to the end of barren branches. The air was just reaching crisp certainty that winter was on its way. She had spent that day traversing the city with her Dad and college roommate, Kate. On the way home, Kate suddenly said, "You know, I have the strangest feeling that today might be your lucky day."

"What do you mean?" Tina asked.

Kate giggled as they picked up their pace.

"I don't know," she said with a smile, "I just have this weird feeling."

Tina's dad chipped in, "Yeah, I'm feeling lucky, too. Let's stop at this corner store and get us some scratch-offs."

Tina bit her lip. The optimism that she once felt playing the lottery with her dad had long since disappeared into cynicism. Her days as a newly-born Boston intellectual had taught her that lottery tickets, along with television and religion, were opiates for the masses, tools to keep the working class from revolt.

"Don't waste your money," she groaned, "It could be bus fare," but her dad was already crossing the street.

"Don't be so hard on your dad," Kate said. "It could be fun. And who knows? Maybe you'll win some money."

By the time they managed to cross the street, her dad was already passing a twenty to the cashier.

"Twenty dollars?" Tina complained.

"I'm telling you. I'm feeling lucky today."

Walking home, Tina felt herself suddenly buoyed by the broad implication of her good fortune despite her disdain for the lottery. Her father and her roommate were in high spirits. She joined them, but held back a little. After all, she wanted to make it clear she didn't approve of this venture. Nonetheless, the feeling of an inevitable win settled upon her college apartment as the trio sat down in the living room for the all-too-familiar ritual. Her dad distributed the lottery tickets evenly between them, mixing the "Chasing Shamrocks" with the "Lucky Diamonds" and the "Golden Pyramids" with the "Raining Dollars."

They began scratching off the first round of tickets.

Nothing.

Second round.

Nothing.

When Tina began scratching off the third ticket, a strange thing happened. Two $25,000s appeared right away. She kept scratching, knowing that the third $25,000 would never be seen... and then... There it was.

Tina hesitated. She stared. She hesitated again.

And then, she experienced an emotion she'd never felt. She rose up, possessed by something outside her body, a superhuman energy, a big break, her salvation.

"I won!"

Her dad and roommate laughed in hilarity.

"How much? How much?" They kept asking.

"$25,000!"

The laughter continued as she danced around the house with her winning ticket. Finally, her dad asked, "Where do we need to go to redeem the ticket?"

The tone of his voice inspired slight suspicion, but Tina resisted. In a sudden moment of clarity, Tina remembered a biology reading that discussed how chimpanzees often have violent physical confrontations in which younger chimps have the advantage due to speed and agility. Relying upon experience, older chimps are known to make pleading, sorrowful gestures of apology to get the young chimp to come close again. The young chimp will advance hesitantly, wanting to believe that reconciliation is at hand but weighing the risk of renewed violence. When the young chimp finally advances, he is plummeted by the older chimp. As Tina flipped over the lottery ticket to find out where to redeem it, she felt her monkey brain puzzling through the situation, deciphering evidence of her father's foul play but believing against belief that she had won the lottery.

To redeem this ticket, please visit:

Yo Mama's House
1015 Idiot Boulevard
Dream Island, MA

"What? What does that mean? Dad?"

That's when her father confessed to buying a fake winning lottery ticket at a joke shop earlier in the day. He had mixed it in with the real tickets to add effect. He even recruited Tina's roommate to fabricate the atmosphere of good luck.

Tina decided not to tell the story of her false win. Instead, she handed the tickets to Joan S. Schmidt and said, "I have a feeling that this is your lucky day."

Taking the tickets into her hands, Joan chose one, held into the air and declared, "This one right here is the big winner. I can feel it."

Luck bloomed into a smile as Joan touched Tina on the shoulder. "Such a pretty girl," she said.

With that, Joan S. Schmidt turned her back and began walking up the hill alone.

Walking away from the corner store, Tina began crumbling up the receipt, the check, and the lottery ticket. She stopped at a nearby trash can to toss the wad of paper, but changed her mind. As she slowly disentangled the lottery ticket, her mind traveled to the impossibly high costs of living in California, the seeming permanence of the national deficit, the endless paper trail of credit, all the small and big, the reachable and unreachable desires of the human spirit. And for a moment, a very small instant, it felt as though salvation was at hand. She may have a better chance of dying in a plane crash, but that piece of paper was somehow worth more than the rest of the junk in her pocket. She folded it in half and placed it in her back pocket, allowing hope to propel her steps toward the car. Her to-do list still floating in her mind, she wondered if maybe there was a God. And then, before she could stop them, her grandmother's words flowed from her lips, "You can't win if you don't play."

Redneck Trophy Wife

A. C. Jerroll

Laura Jean rubbed pancake makeup over what she pretended was a purple spot under her eye. Sawyer hadn't actually struck her, though when they argued the night before, his icy words hit as hard as any physical blow. But she'd get even with him, she told herself, all the while admitting she didn't know what she might do.

She glanced again at the yellow Post-it stuck to the mirror: "Call me at 9," the note said. "You know where." Wednesday night, she thought. That means poker at the He Ain't Here Club. "And he soooo loves his precious poker," she told her reflection. He also loved songs about poker, and he had plenty of them. It irritated her that he played such crap on their home sound system. She had begun to sing along with several, something she took as a sign that Sawyer was corrupting her, dragging her down to his low level. He even had a ringtone for his cell phone that played Cledus Judd's poker song "One Jack Off." Disgusting, she thought and peeled the note from the mirror so she could better inspect her makeup.

Satisfied that her face looked good—damned good, she affirmed—Laura Jean wriggled into her tight jeans, put on a turtle-neck that showed the lines of her breasts to their best advantage, and went to her closet for her red boots. As she looked in the full-length mirror beside her bed, she had no doubt the guys in the club would slobber all over themselves. And Sawyer should be furious, especially if he saw her dancing with some of them. Should be. But maybe he liked it when the guys stared at her, seeing as he never got bent out of shape when anyone flirted or even danced with her. Maybe she'll do some bed-hopping, and then tell Sawyer. That ought to get a rise out of him.

Why he was okay watching her tease the guys with her jeans and dimpled smiles was a mystery to her. "Know what I think?" she had told him during their argument. "I think I'm just a trophy wife and you don't care anything about me."

"Trophy wife?" The idea seemed to amuse Sawyer. "Only upper class dudes got trophy wives, not rednecks like me. A guy that grew up in a plumbing shop don't have no trophy wife, no matter how much dough he makes at poker. I never heard of a redneck trophy wife."

She was relieved that he'd at least laughed. Even laughter is better than his usual aloof ways.

But what if she pushed him too far? What if she jumped some guy then told him all about it? A snatch of a Garth Brooks song ran through her head and caused her to shiver:

Papa loved mama, mama loved men,

Mama's in the graveyard, Papa's in the pen.

But she did in fact love men, and if she loved them too much would it be possible to push Sawyer too far? She shrugged off the idea. He never became violent, not with fists—and not violent with angry talk either, though he could sting her with cold words.

Someone once told her that women were hard-wired to out-talk men, but she didn't believe it for a second. Sawyer could talk circles around her, fence her in, belittle her. "Lotsa times," she told him, "you make me feel like two cents worth of dirty ice." He had laughed, twisted her words around, and made her feel even worse. And he did it all with that curl to his lip and that maddening cold, indifferent shrug.

But tonight, he'll be sorry. Or mad. Or something other than icy. She reached for the phone.

Cal answered, as usual. "He Ain't Here. How else can I help you?"

"Cal? Laura Jean. Tell Sawyer I'm heading that way."

"Will do. He's got a run going at the table, so he ain't in no mood for interruptions."

"Tough tiddy," she said and hung up.

Laura Jean liked it that the club was in the tough part of town, just off the access road to the Interstate. It was inside what used to be a mall some forty years before, a small one that had fallen on hard times. A head shop that sold water pipes to the long-hairs and the He Ain't Here Club were the only businesses still renting space in the old shopping center. She pushed open the glass door and looked down the dim hall. The head shop was closed for the day, but judging from the country music that throbbed from the club's door the club seemed busy enough. A couple of Saturday night cowboys lounging against the wall, rolling smokes, ogled her as she walked by, so she turned to them with her best smile and gave them an extra waggle to admire. One looked too short and stumpy to hold her attention for long. The other showed more promise with his broad shoulders and heavy muscles. They followed her into the club. Men, she thought. They're all so predictable, except of course for Sawyer. He had the hots for her back when they first married. She knew that. But now there was only that shrug and that curl of his lip and his words that fell upon her like icy rain.

She wondered if those two cowboys might be part of her getting even with Sawyer. He hadn't been set off that night she'd done the monkey dance with a stranger in the club, she knew that because he had watched and said nothing. But he hadn't seen her let the stranger feel her up on the crowded dance floor, nor had he seen how she had two-stepped the man to a dark part of the floor and French kissed him.

Telling Sawyer hadn't been easy, and she found her breath shallow with fear as she spoke the words. Maybe he'd hit her. Or maybe he'd go after the guy she kissed and pound the dog puckey out of him. "It's not like I was untrue to you," she said when she decided to confess. "It was just some drunken sex play. It had nothing to do with love. I love you and only you, honey-pot."

He had turned to look out the window, turned with a distracted yawn. "Yeah?" he said, then, "I've got a big poker game tomorrow night. I want you to make an appearance in something skimpy and sexy to distract the boys."

His response was worse than she feared. He wasn't angry or jealous or even mildly irritated. The fact is, she realized with a sinking sensation in her stomach, he didn't care what she had done. The memory of his coldness filled her with rage as she gave her best smile to the two cowboys in the club.

She winked at the broad-shouldered one. She could jump his bones, then let Sawyer know. Maybe that would get his attention. "Maybe," she said, surprising herself with the word.

"What'd you say, pretty woman?" the man asked.

"I don't like repeating myself," Laura Jean said.

"I think I know who you are," he said.

"How much more you want to know bout me?"

"You're married to that gambler, Sawyer Giles. Right?" He gave her what she figured was his best smile, though it didn't look all that good to her.

"I'm Sawyer Giles's girl, but he don't own me."

The cowboy smiled and tipped his hat. "Ma'am," he said. "We think that man runs a moving gambling table, putting big bucks up for grabs, and in our state, that ain't legal. You best try to reform him before it's too late."

"So what are you, cops?"

"Texas Rangers, ma'am."

Laura Jean thought that was terrific. Maybe she could hit Sawyer where it would hurt him the most: right in the fat middle of his beloved poker. That would get him plenty mad. "He's gambling in that back room, if you want to know."

"Yeah. We know. They have nothing but plastic chips on the table, and there's nothing illegal about that."

Disappointment washed over her. So ratting him out to the law didn't work. Maybe she should do the dirty deed with this very Texas Ranger. Sawyer hated cops, especially the rangers. The idea of nuzzling up to the man with broad shoulders gave Laura Jean a thrill. "So you like what you see, or what?" She spun around to give the ranger a good look at her figure.

"Thank you right kindly ma'am, but I'm on duty."

"So meet me when you're off duty."

"Much obliged. But I got a date with my wife. A permanent date. And my buddy here says he's given up women for Lent." The two laughed in what felt to Laura Jean a mean way.

Wimps, she thought. Useless. But she'd find a way to get at Sawyer, and now she knew how. Through poker. It didn't matter that the plan felt vague, because she was sure she could improvise something. As she headed toward the back room Cal blocked the way.

"My advice is," Cal said, "to stay outta there. Sawyer's on a roll, like I said, and he's got stacks of chips in front of him that look like New York City high rises."

"So?" With a slow and insolent sweep of her eyes, Laura Jean looked at Cal from his head to his feet. He's wasn't much to look at. Bearded in a scruffy way, a grubby green shirt over an overhang of a belly, food stains on his khakis. Bent with age, though not old. Maybe bent with hard living and harder drinking. Would Sawyer be bothered if she bedded Cal? But it would be like going to bed with a wet manikin. Doing Cal was out of the question. "You stopping me?"

"Nope. Just advising you. His luck's gotta change any minute now, and if you waltz in there just as he loses, he might blame you."

"I would like that."

The statement seemed to astound Cal. He stepped aside.

Laura Jean hoped her entrance would disturb Sawyer, though she doubted it. She went through the door into a room where smoke hung in fuzzy layers over the poker table. Sawyer squinted at his cards. "Raise fifty," he said and pushed some chips toward the center of the table.

One by one the other players said "fold" as they threw down cards, and Laura Jean thought of a line from a Kenny Rogers song: you gotta know when to hold em, know when to fold em. Apparently those guys know when to fold, and she tried not to look at Sawyer with any respect showing on her face, though she grudgingly admitted that she did admire his skill with poker, a game she understood in the vaguest of terms, her knowledge of it coming mostly from Sawyer's music.

"Laura Jean." Sawyer nudged his glass of bourbon and water. He never drank while he played, but he liked to have a drink in front of him, and he refreshed the ice in it from time to time. "Laura Jean, you better leave before you do something I regret. You best get."

She thrust out her chin. "I'm staying." The idea of doing something he could regret got her attention, and she looked around for a hint of what to do next.

All the men at the table eyed her, Sawyer with a kind of unnerving indifference, the other five with curiosity, though she would have preferred they leer at her with some lust on the off chance they might stoke up Sawyer's jealousy. Two of the players sagged in their chairs, a defeated and sad look about them, especially the one everyone called Jimmy Joe. Two seemed disgusted, perhaps for being losers, and one, a fellow she knew as Redbone, looked angry. His eyes merely flickered her way, then returned to the cards. She had met all the men before, and she knew Sawyer considered them all friends, though he made his living playing poker with the likes of these men.

Some friend Sawyer is to them, Laura Jean mused, considering how deep he has his hand in their pockets. In a quiet voice, she amused herself by singing some of John Coulton's "Gambler's Prayer":

So Lord lift me up in your tender embrace,

Lend me your wisdom, your strength and your grace,

Help me to smash my opponent's fat face,

Oh Lord help me take money from my friends.

Laura Jean watched as Sawyer pulled in his winnings and stacked them with loud snaps, louder than she thought necessary, and she figured he was saying "I'm the big cheese, and you're suckers." She felt certain he liked to belittle everyone as much as he enjoyed putting her down with his aloof shrugs and cold looks. The man sitting to Sawyer's left dealt, and Laura Jean edged closer to Sawyer, watching and trying to make some sense of what the men were doing, for she still hoped to find a weak spot where she could zap Sawyer. But it was no use, for she knew little about poker while Sawyer knew everything that had anything at all to do with poker—movies, jokes, music. His favorite poker music was a jazz album by Joe McBride, something Laura Jean didn't like much, though she sometimes found herself humming "Texas Hold'em" as if she did like it.

After all the players seemed content with their cards, the betting began. Laura Jean expected another chorus of *fold*, but no one uttered the word. Instead each one muttered something and threw in some chips. She made out *call and raise*, and she saw Sawyer grow more quiet and still.

The door opened with a bang, and Laura Jean watched in astonishment as the two Texas Rangers stomped into the room. The tall one held up an impressive-looking badge. The stumpy one stepped close to Sawyer. "Sawyer Giles," he said. "You're coming with us."

"We're playing for plastic," Sawyer said, "as you can plainly see. But I have an ego stake in this game, and I can't leave right now."

"Sorry, gentlemen," the tall one said in a tone that said he wasn't at all sorry. "We don't aim to keep Mr. Giles for long. Come on, now, Mr. Giles. We have a few questions we want to ask. Out in the parking lot. Then you can get back to your game."

"Does that mean you fold?" Redbone demanded of Sawyer.

"Hell no." Sawyer stood up and handed his cards to Laura Jean. "You sit right here," he told her. "Guard them chips, and don't you dare do nothing with these cards until I get back. You hear?"

The two men escorted Sawyer out of the room and closed the door. "This makes me a bit jumpy," one of the sad-looking men said.

"The rangers, they got nothing," another said. "To all intents and purposes, this is a friendly game played for chips. Them rangers can't prove otherwise, so we're safe."

"I say we get on with the hand," one of the men said, a disgusted look screwing up his face as if he just bit into a green persimmon.

"Give him," Redbone looked at his watch, "ten minutes."

"Ten minutes?" another man said. "In a game like this, that's practically all night."

Laura Jean looked at the cards Sawyer had thrust into her hands. Though she knew little about winning, she knew enough to conclude that she held a losing hand, and she said the names of the cards to herself: three, five, seven, eight, and a red Jack. The Jack made her think of a song about the Jack of Hearts. She rearranged the cards in a distracted way and sang some of the song, changing a few words:

The cabaret was quiet except for the drilling in the wall

The curfew had been lifted and the gambling wheel shut down

Anyone with any sense had already left town–

She was standing in the doorway looking at the Jack of Hearts.

"So is that a hint about Sawyer's hand?" Redbone demanded. "You best be careful what you say."

"Nah," Jimmy Joe said. "That's Bob Dylan's song about Lily, Rosemary, and the Jack of Hearts. It's just a song."

"House rules," Redbone said. "You don't tell anybody anything about anyone's hand. Not even if you're singing."

"I ain't telling nothing," Laura Jean said. "We should play, no matter about Sawyer."

The men stared.

"She *is* his wife," Redbone said. "I say we get on with it. I call and raise two hundred."

"Call and raise," Laura Jean said. She picked from Sawyer's stacks some chips that looked exactly like those Redbone had pushed forward.

"Fold," Jimmy Joe said.

"Call," the next player said, and the next one called and raised. More chips hit the table, especially when Redbone raised.

Laura Jean squinted at her cards, trying to look worried. "Jimmy Joe," she said. "Since you're out, would you toss in the right chips for me while I play these cards?"

"No help from nobody," Redbone said. "Even if you are a woman."

"I don't want no help. Jimmy Joe ain't seen Sawyer's cards, and he ain't going to. Alls I'm asking is that he toss some chips when I name them, seeing as I got this bum shoulder. And I aim to put a bunch of Sawyer's chips into the pot."

"Yeah?" Redbone said.

"I like it," one of the sad men said, his face brightening considerably.

"Maybe I ain't wise," Laura Jean said. "Fact is, none of you look like suckers to me, and Sawyer once told me something the great Amarillo Slim likes to say. Look around the table, Slim says. If you don't see a sucker, get up because you're the sucker. Maybe Amarillo Slim was right, and maybe I'm a dope for playing out Sawyer's hand. Call and raise two hundred. Jimmy Joe? Put in the chips for me?"

"Do it, Jimmy Joe," Redbone said, and Jimmy Joe threw in some of Sawyer's chips.

When the next player folded, Laura Jean felt plenty worried. She didn't want any of them to fold. She wanted to give back to these men all the money Sawyer had taken from them, as if they might somehow split the pot when they found out what a zero of a hand she held. Mostly, though, she wanted to lose and lose big. Giving back the money was just an extra. Slapping Sawyer with a loss at poker would be sweet, sweeter than jumping a ranger and telling Sawyer about it. In an attempt to keep everyone in the game she raised only a hundred each time it came around to her. Redbone, his face increasingly white with anger, kept calling and raising.

Revenge, Laura Jean thought, touching the spot below her eye where Sawyer should have hit her the night before when she told about the French kiss. Should have but didn't. If he had struck her, he'd truly deserve what she was about to do.

Before long only she and Redbone were in the game, and he was taking cash out of his wallet.

By the time Sawyer returned, slipping into the room with the stealth of a bobcat, Laura Jean had only a few scatterings of chips in front of her. She noted Sawyer's presence with the slightest of nods, and she felt elated that he had returned in time to see her ruin his poker game. It seemed Sawyer took in the table and the events with a single sweep of his eyes, but the eyes showed no feelings at all.

"Call and raise fifty." Redbone tossed a bill on the table.

"Raise two hundred," Sawyer said.

"Now just a cotton picking minute," Redbone said. "The little lady's playing this hand and you know the rules. No help from anyone."

Laura Jean met Sawyer's eyes. What was he up to? Does he want to lose all his money? Does he somehow think that by forcing a big loss he'd be punishing her for having the nerve to play his hand? She laughed at the thought that he knew so little about her. "Three hundred," Laura Jean said. She didn't even try to hide the smirk of superiority she felt in beating Sawyer at his own game.

Redbone stared at her. He folded his cards and threw them on the table. "It seems," he said, "I've underestimated what you have."

Sawyer leaned over the table to reach for the pot.

"But I don't want you to fold." Laura Jean heard the whine in her voice. "You can't fold. I've got–"

Sawyer grabbed the cards from her. "Nobody sees your hand if everybody folded. That's the house rules."

"Rules?" Laura Jean looked around, bewildered at the other players, who shuffled out of their chairs and headed for the door as Sawyer raked in the winnings.

"See you boys next week," Sawyer said. He turned to Laura Jean with the deadest, coldest smile she had ever seen. "Help me get this cash off the table," he said, "before them rangers come back in." He started scooping up the bills.

Queen of Hearts

Laurie Champion

Darlene hates it when her husband and her lover get together, especially when the occasion calls for her presence as well. While she finds the acquaintance between Wayne and Troy peculiar, Troy's love for her is no doubt mystical. It's the sort of magic that transcends tense situations.

"It's just meant to be," she says. "Preordained from the beginning of time."

Of course, her habitual reading of romance novels enhances these touchy-feely sentiments. Troy, she thinks. She imagines his muscular shoulders. Troy standing shirtless, baggy Levi's slouched around his hips. Although she's always been embarrassed to try, she calculates that the jeans might be precisely loose enough for her to pull down without fidgeting with zippers—always practical, sometimes awkward, and never romantic.

She has more enticing things to do, like running her fingers through his hair and feeling his arms around her waist. He stares into her eyes with those incredible green eyes of his and swings her hair away from her breasts. "Forbidden fruit," he once whispered to her, while massaging her breasts.

"Fruits," she corrected. Reading the novels makes her more aware of language, and she wants the affair to be grammatically correct.

Darlene exaggerates Troy's sex appeal to some extent, but most women do find him attractive. No question about it. He's a construction worker, and he works out four nights a week in the garage he converted into an exercise room. His robust body and handsome face are found not only in Darlene's dreams. But glances and coos from other women go unnoticed. In her heart of hearts. Darlene knows she's the only woman for Troy.

Darlene doesn't need to exaggerate her own beauty—she looks like she stepped out of every man's most sensual fantasy. She's voluptuous, with long legs and thick, auburn hair. But more overwhelmingly, she has that indefinable feature—sex appeal. She's got it down. It's something about the way she carries herself--her smile, her strut, the twinkle in her eyes, and God, the clothes she wears to accentuate her attributes. Drives men crazy.

Darlene knows Troy wants her to divorce Wayne, and she's trying to devise a scheme to keep everyone happy. She sometimes feels like an evil person, like one of those demon worshipers she's seen on TV, so she's extra careful to keep Wayne from finding out about her secret life. That way nobody gets hurt.

But lately Troy's putting pressure on her. He's been acting weird when he gets around Wayne, and she wonders if what appears to be Wayne's suspicion is merely her own guilt or imagination.

Darlene plans to do something quickly. She can't take many more incidents like the one last month. She and Troy lie on the living-room floor. Everything was perfect— wearing only her satin panties, she'd met him at the door. They were engaged in the most imaginable passionate moment, against the background of soft music and candlelight. Not once, did they let the fear of Wayne coming home spoil their appetites.

Her plan all along has been to deny an affair, deny it to the end. If Wayne ever comes home and catches them on the floor, she'll say it isn't her—must be someone who looks like her.

So, they lie side-by-side, intimately taking advantage of Wayne's gambling habit—he was at his weekly poker game. Nothing seemed out of the ordinary. Nope, everything was just peachy creamy.

Then, with absolutely no warning, not even a hint of things to come, Darlene felt Troy bite her ear. She knows he has a "thing" for ears, so it didn't startle her at first. But when she felt his teeth again, she asked "What are you doing?" She ran in the rest room and looked in the mirror. "My ear has teeth marks on it. You can't do that!"

"What?" Troy asked from the living room.

"You bit my ear."

"I thought it would be romantic."

"No, you didn't. You want Wayne to find out. This has to stop. I can't take a chance on him finding out. You did it on purpose."

"No," he said.

She marched into the living room and showed Troy her ear. "Look what you did," she said. "Who do you think you are? Mike Tyson?"

"Darlene, come on. Please."

"Please, smeaze. I don't trust you. I'm beginning to think you're a vampire."

"You don't trust *me*? You're the one who's married."

She made him leave but called him the next day and apologized profusely. She keeps telling herself it didn't happen, and she hates even to think about it now. She wonders why stuff like this doesn't happen to

Madame Bovary. Although she hasn't actually read that one, she's heard about the good parts.

Luckily, Darlene has an incredible ability to re-create experiences. It won't be long until she's able to remember that evening as one filled with ecstasy--utopia, right in her own living room.

She's already beginning to weaken her accusations against Troy. Troy loves her. He can't help himself. When he comes over tonight, everything will be back to normal. Like old times. She imagines herself in the new panties she bought last week at Nordies. Or maybe she should do like she did that one time—no panties.

She and Troy get together every Friday night, while Wayne plays poker over at the one-bedroom apartment Clayton and Jim rented for gambling and such.

One Friday evening, she's busy fluffing the pillows on the bed, when Wayne walks in the bedroom.

"Have you seen my plaid socks?" he asks.

Darlene sits on the bed. "What plaid socks?"

"My poker socks?"

"No, I haven't." She searches his top drawer. "Umm. Maybe they're dirty. How about these?" She tosses a pair of plaid. socks on the bed.

Wayne asks her if she wants to go to the poker game with him. "Remember all the money I won last time you went?"

"Yeah." Two or three years ago, Darlene recalls. She starts looking under the bed. "I can't figure out what happened to those socks." She hopes Troy didn't accidentally wear them home. "Did you have them on last week?"

"I think so. Yeah, I remember. I did."

"Whew, I'm lucky."

"Yeah, you are." He repeats his request.

She thinks Wayne's invitation for her to join him sort of strange and worries he might be suspicious if she doesn't agree to go.

"It'll be fun," he says.

"I don't know anything about poker," she says. What about Troy? she thinks.

"Just go this once," Wayne says. "Besides, I might win enough to take you to Galveston."

"Well, okay," she says. "I'll have to run down to 7-11 and get some mascara." On the way to the store, she imagines herself lying on the beach in the Bahamas—number eleven on her list of things to do before she dies. She envisions men staring at her, while she sips a pina colada. A foreign lover. How exotic.

She hops out of the car, pulls her cell phone from her purse, and calls Troy.

"Troy, we can't meet tonight."

"Okay, I need to work out anyway."

"I know you're disappointed."

"Darlene . . . there are other Fridays, you know."

"Wayne wants me to go to the poker game—"

"Poker game. What poker game?"

"The one at Clayton's. I'm afraid to tell him no." She tells him she thinks he should go to the poker game. "That way Wayne won't get suspicious."

"Poker game. Yeah, I'll go!"

Darlene gets the mascara and starts driving home. By the time she gets there, she's convinced herself that Troy said he'd go to the poker game or anywhere else she wanted him to go. She assures herself he insisted, despite her objections. He just can't resist her. He's even willing to subject himself to an uncomfortable situation. "No," she now remembers him saying, "I can't miss my Friday night with Darling Darlene."

When she and Wayne sit at the poker table, she instantly feels tense. Everybody's so serious, and they're playing some game where they deal the cards so fast, declare a winner, and start dealing again so quickly that she can't figure out what's going on. Oh well, who cares? She's only interested in personal aspects of the game. Kind of like Danielle Steel. She's concerned with the "human condition."

Darlene finds it amusing that a young man serves the poker players. She gets up to get herself a glass of wine and asks if anyone wants anything.

"I'll take a beer," J. R. says.

She brings him a beer, and he tosses her a red chip.

She's half-embarrassed, half-flattered. She sees Troy eyeing the men around the table, as if to see if they're looking at him. They're not.

Troy looks around the table again before flashing a wink her way. When she senses it's getting tense around the table, she thinks it's because she's torn between her feelings for Wayne and her feelings for Troy, but it's really because it's always tense. All the men believe they're the best poker player, so of course it's tense. Not only is their money at stake, but so are their egos. Their money, they admit they lose, but they never forfeit self-imposed titles. They're all sitting around like roosters with their tails flashed up in the air. Textbook cases of delusions of grandeur.

Darlene moves to the living room and flicks on the TV.

Wayne stops by on his way to the rest room. "You okay?" he asks.

"Yeah," she says. "You winning?"

"Yeah," he says. But he isn't. He's one pay check down and one on tab, but Darlene will never know the difference. He sits beside her on the couch. "J. R.'s trying to piss me off," he says.

"Really?"

"Yeah, he gave you that chip so I'd get mad. He's an asshole. He wants me to think he's flirting with you."

Darlene doesn't believe him. She thinks J. R. gave her the chip because he *was* flirting with her. "Why does he want to piss you off?"

"So I'll play lousy. Nobody likes him. He's got a lot of money, so he usually schemes it to where he'll win a couple, then he leaves."

"How could he win just because he has a lot of money?"

"He can bet more."

Darlene knows that also means he can lose more, but she decides to encourage Wayne's illusion. "Yeah," she says, "J. R.'s a jerk." She stands up, gets the chip out of her pocket, and gives it to Wayne. "For luck."

Wayne goes back in the other room, and Darlene pretends to watch TV. There's some guy on *The Tonight Show* who claims he can save marriages. He instructs viewers to put their wedding rings on the coffee table, so he can perform the rituals, "marriage miracles," he says. Darlene's interest elevates, but she doesn't see a coffee table.

"What are you watching?" Troy asks from the hallway.

"Nothing," Darlene answers.

Troy approaches her and tells her J. R. gave her the chip to piss him off.

"How would he know about us?" she asks.

"He doesn't. But he likes to make me mad."

Darlene doesn't think his reasoning is sound, and it becomes crystal clear that she's the only one who knows the real reason J. R. gave her the chip. Face it, she's irresistible. She also concludes that J. R. must be winning.

Troy returns to the table, Darlene waits awhile, then follows. She sits beside Wayne and notices he has a big stack of chips in front of him.

He holds up five blacks. "Five hundred."

"How much are the black ones?" she asks.

"A hundred."

She estimates he has about a thousand dollars, but she doesn't know about the tab. "We should leave while you're ahead," she whispers.

"No," he whispers. "J. R.'s left, Clayton's asleep, and Troy can't play poker. Jim and me can get his money."

Darlene observes the three men as they squint at their cards and mumble. Jim's dealing, and they're all acting like someone's life is on the line. Troy has a lot of chips, but Jim keeps borrowing from Wayne.

213

Every hand one of them tosses his cards in the middle of the table and grunts. The other two just kinda look down at the table as they place their bets.

But the next hand that comes around, nobody folds. They all three sit there staring at each other like this was some sort of reality TV show. The stakes get higher and higher. Jim folds. Wayne keeps raising Troy. Wayne taps his foot, like he does when he gets nervous. Darlene thinks Troy wants to win so he can help her get a divorce. The Bahamas is gradually losing appeal. She looks at Wayne's cards, but she doesn't know what beats what, so his hand means nothing.

Wayne shoves all his chips to the center of the table. "All in," he says.

"Call." Troy throws his cards on the table.

Before she has time to consider who wins, Troy shouts, "I nailed your ass!"

On the way home, Wayne explains that Troy knew he'd won without seeing his cards, because he had the highest possible hand. "The nuts," he explains. "No biggie," he says. "I'll win next week or when I get enough money to play again."

Darlene waits weeks for Wayne to win--the Bahamas gradually regains enticement. She hasn't heard from Troy in a while, but she knows the reason, the *real* reason. It's not because, as he'd put it, "I need someone without complications. I'm tired of sneaking around."

No. Time helps Darlene fabricate reasons for the breakup with her lover. She thinks she may even write a book about it. God knows she's got the experience, some *real-life* experience. She could write one of those "based on personal experience stories." Or even better, she could mix fiction and fact: a romance novel based on real life. What a concept. She ponders the closing line:

"When propelled in the position of seeing him compete with someone she only thought she loved, Charlene realized she loved her husband. She had no choice but to break her lover's heart. And break his heart she did, all the while remembering the ring, still laying on the coffee table."

Pigeon

Jocelyn Paige Kelly

The casinos in Las Vegas have no clocks, and Eddie Rhea doesn't wear a watch. He's a twelve-year-old going on thirty. Nearly six feet tall, with a filled-out, muscular Samoan frame, Eddie is more man than child. Last week, the first signs of stubble set in on his face, a five o'clock shadow that made even his father envious. He is too big to roughhouse with friends half his size, too young to play with kids a few years older than him, but not old enough to make decisions for himself. Towering over his peers like a PE coach over a bunch of kindergartners, he walks down the halls of the sixth-grade center, carrying his books like a football he's ready to toss.

The principal takes one look at Eddie. "We need you at the staff meeting."

"I'm not staff," Eddie says.

"Teacher assistants are considered part of the staff," he says condescendingly, stopping Eddie in his tracks with a simple gesture of his hand on his chest. Something his father would do.

Eddie looks down on the principal, a man six inches shorter than him. "But I don't work here," Eddie says, voice still cracking.

"Oh, you have a son that goes here?" he asks, almost like a statement.

"I go here."

The principal pauses and gives him a long look. "How many times have you had to repeat the sixth grade?"

"Never, asshole," Eddie says. The bell rings and Eddie walks past the principal without hearing a reprimand for colorful use of language.

Eddie arrives to class late because time is not Eddie's friend. It takes time for him to walk the hallways, class to class. Crowds of teens, all Eddie's age, giggle and pass him by—angst in ten-minute increments. He struggles to get in the desk and chair, a design meant for his peers, but not for him. The girls pay little attention while the boys mock his overgrown stature, a mouse in the body of a giant.

His health teacher won't give him a pass to the nurse's office and gives him lip for being late to class. He reeks of body odor, like a boy whose parents refuse to admit he needs deodorant. The class is all whispers and stares as Eddie stomps to the back of the room where he slumps over, head down on his desk. Before he can close his eyes, the lights are turned off.

They watch a film on sexual development, and Eddie considers his options. Maybe going to a casino isn't the best idea. He'll have to take a bus, and he'll smell like smoke when he gets home. *It's not like they'll notice*, he reasons, sniffing himself, the collar from his t-shirt covering his nose. He doesn't even have to go far, just away from the people who see him everyday. *Grocery stores have slot machines*. All he has to do is leave the apartment complex, cross three streets and look both ways. It's less than a mile to walk, but he wonders what the clerks might say, especially the woman who works customer service. She's known Eddie and his family forever, and he's pretty sure she wouldn't approve.

When the bell rings, the movie is only halfway through. The teacher tells them they will watch the second half, which deals with sexually transmitted diseases, tomorrow. Eddie picks up his books and on his way out, as the lights are turned on, he makes eye contact with the girl he has a crush on, the brunette with Hello Kitty barrettes. She smells of citrus and vanilla. When she smiles in his direction, her lazy eye staring him in the face, it makes him blush, and then one of the boys who bullies him slams a post-it note on his back. As he walks down the hall to math class, the other kids in the hallway point and yell *Sasquatch*.

Then he hears, "What's a four letter word that describes Eddie?" The girls giggle. Eddie blushes. He worries what the word could be. "I'll give you a hint! The last two letters are N and K." Eddie smiles. *They think I'm a hunk*. They giggle more with hands over mouths.

Eddie wants to be a child, wants the other boys to be his friends, wants the teachers to respect him, to know who he is when he walks down the hall and to see him as one of the other kids and not confuse him with the staff. Every day he hopes that it will be different.

Not one of his classmates has ever seen Eddie smile, but they all know who he is.

"Stink!" one of them yells. Giggle, giggle.

Eddie puts on his poker face.

"Ewwww!"

"That's five letters!"

"Okay, then what?"

The words echo down the nearly empty hallway. A murmur circles around the girls and boys, and the girl with the lazy eye passes Eddie from behind, brushing on the side.

"Tank!" they yell. *Tank*.

His stomach turns before he can make it to the restroom. With his head in a trashcan just inside the entrance door, he hears three girls snicker. "Can't you read? This one's for the girls."

"Girls," he huffs and passes Mrs. Sccachi, his math teacher, towering over her like Gandalf over Bilbo. He blushes, avoiding eye contact. Her presence makes him feel like a golem.

She is five feet tall with the spirit of a Maori warrior. He looks at her and imagines a spear in her hand, ready to attack the restless natives. Everyone is afraid of her except Eddie, who stares at her with a bit of lustful drool pooling in the corner of his mouth. Her class is the only class Eddie looks forward to. He stares at whiteboards with scribbled bits of handwriting, handmade poster art on walls, and *school is fun* spelled out in construction paper stapled onto fabric walls. During class he rearranges in his mind the letters and makes new words, *Mrs. Sccachi is Sccorching*.

Mrs. Sccachi touches on geometry. Eddie's been paying close attention—too close. He draws in the side margins, writes equations that only make sense to him. Things that allude to angles and insertions of A into B. It makes him smile and attracts Mrs. Sccachi's attention.

"Eddie, would you like to share with the class?"

His face is redder than before, and he stammers. The class laughs. His world spins and the Maori warrior comes at him with a vengeance, but he doesn't see it coming—her hands ripping the paper from underneath him, the raise of the eyebrow at his doodling, and the lowering of her eyes.

Mrs. Sccachi crumples up the paper and tosses it in the trash bin without another word, and Eddie is grateful for her silence.

Every other class passes time, and Eddie makes the time go faster by getting back on target. He thinks again about his plan and writes everything out like an equation. Minus the woman, the word listed as an unknown variable. Maybe he isn't meant to know that variable until much later.

He decides during history class that maybe a convenience store would be a prime location to learn how to gamble like a real man. Who really pays attention to the people there anyway? They're all just pigeons sitting on stools, playing with their rent money.

He makes an estimate at the odds in a formula based more on his idea of the world than real statistics. The assumptions he makes are based on false ideas. He believes that even if he's caught, the repercussions will be less than if he's caught in a casino. It's the risk of people worrying about getting fired that he's counting on. There's also apathy. He's figuring that apathy will give him a lot of leeway. He writes in all caps: *MINIMUM WAGE EMPLOYMENT = APATHY*.

The bell rings. Eddie gathers his books and trudges to the next class.

The principal sees Eddie and heads the other way. Eddie looks from left to right, but he is the only person in the hallway. Eddie can't figure out why the principal is afraid of him.

In the locker room, Eddie changes into his gym clothes. The entire room stinks like an armpit, and Eddie smells the worst.

Soon, he's off and running, doing laps around the field, faster than any of the other boys. His gym teacher told him he'd do great on a track team, and that he should consider track as a way of getting a scholarship to go to college. Eddie asked him, "What's the point?"

The sweat he breaks makes two large ovals form underneath his arms and a large triangle on his back. The gym teacher decides to let Eddie continue to run laps so he can let the other boys in the class play football. "You understand, right?" the teacher asks him, standing next to him, the same height and build. Eddie shrugs. He is too lost in thought to care, but every time the ball is thrown closer to him, he has to avoid the impulse to go and catch it.

At a certain point, he begins to walk instead of run, but his mind is still running through his plan. He figures if he travels a bit out of the way, he approximates, to an AM/PM or a Circle K that isn't too close to his house, he won't run into people he knows. This will increase his chances of success. He'll walk there from the bus stop, and wear sunglasses, nod hello to people so he doesn't have to speak. For several days he's practiced grunting and stoic facial expressions. He thinks he can play the role. People already believe he's older.

When Eddie gets on the school bus headed home, he goes over everything in his head. He's got it all planned out, but he begins to wonder, with his head rested against the glass, watching the world pass by, what led him to this point. *Boredom*. He chuckles, remembering his mother's refusal to buy him a PlayStation. "Video games are bad for your eyes," she had reasoned. She controlled every aspect of his life—what he watched on TV, what he read, what CDs he bought, what he ate, and especially the clothes he wore. Nothing over ten dollars, and always from Wal-Mart, because she works there on weekends. She even tried to buy him clothes that were too small for him, as if she could contain his physical growth.

Now he would be taking control.

He gets off the bus, and as he turns into his driveway he decides to ditch his books by the mailbox and run as fast as possible to the AM/PM just off Eastern Avenue with the remainder of his lunch money for the week. He arrives at the convenience store out of breath, asks to buy cigarettes, and prays he won't be carded. If he's asked for his ID, he won't be arrested. This he knows. Other boys at school have tried and failed. A big fat *no* from the clerk and a kick in the ass out the door. He doesn't really want to smoke, but his father complains about how much gamblers smoke, so he hopes cigarettes will sell his image.

Big gobs of sweat drip down his forehead. The back of his shirt is drenched. *Maybe they will think I work hard.* Will he get caught? *Thump thump*, heart pounding out of his chest. *Thump thump.*

"Pack of cigarettes."

"Kind?"

"Marlboro."

He stands outside the AM/PM now. Lights the cigarette the way he's seen others do it and takes a drag. Coughs. Takes another drag, this time with less going into the lungs. He savors it, but the flavor doesn't give him much satisfaction. On the third drag he feels the thrill, the rush of the lungs, like anger exploding inside. Relief. He takes another drag and relaxes against the side of the building, looks out to the streets at the cars passing by, and sees another boy from school, Marc Denning, sitting in the back seat of his mother's station wagon. Eddie nods. *Who's the man now?*

He comes home to an angry mother. "Where were you?" she asks, with a barrage of questions he doesn't answer. "Why'd you leave your books outside? What's wrong with you? Did I raise you not to have manners?" Eddie shrugs, takes his cigarettes to his room, puts them in his baseball glove since he's not allowed to play anyway. Her voice echoes down the hall, "You're grounded, young man!" But Eddie chuckles. His mother had finally called him a man.

At school there is a sense of respect thrown Eddie's way. He's a Malboro man now. He smokes half a pack a day, shares the other half with the boys at school. They all take what he gives them, and none of them say thank you. His father tells him that real men don't give thanks, even if his mother disagrees.

Days pass like quicksilver. His father tells him stories. He tells Eddie that he's still looking for work, but he spends his day smoking weed and watching reruns of Tom and Jerry cartoons, which never cease to make him laugh. He pats Eddie on his head while Eddie sits on the floor, and his father rolls a joint. "Don't worry so much. Things will always work out for the best." Eddie leaves to help his mother with the laundry and hours later after his father has drifted in and out of sleep, and his mother has cooked them dinner and gone to bed, Eddie's father comes into his room and sits on the bed and rambles. He tells him that when he was Eddie's age he had sex for the first time with a woman twice his age, and how all the boys at school envied him and asked for advice. Eddie opens one eye when he feels the grip of his father's hand on his shoulder, his body weight leaning into him to whisper in his ear why using two condoms is better than one because one isn't always good enough. And then, with tears in his eyes, he lingers to describe the beauty of the sunset on the islands and how much he misses surfing. He tells Eddie that he's a good boy because he protects his mom, and rubs him on his head and leaves the room with the door open just a crack, the hallway light still on.

Eddie begins phase two of his plan. He buys cigarettes and begins a conversation, asking for the latest issue of *Hustler*. *A man contains his excitement*, his father told him. He puts on his father's poker face, even though he feels like a kid in a candy store. Eddie is sure he can mimic his father's vacant stare with no problem.

He goes with stereotypes, ones he knows from TV. Things he's heard his father say that he doesn't understand. "Women." "Nice." "Nag, nag, nag." Thump thump. Asks for cigarettes, "Malboro." Gets his money out. Tilts his head. "Is that the latest *Hustler*?" The clerk says yes. Mentions something about the last issue. Laughs. Eddie is on a roll. Smiles. "Pussy," Eddie says. Clerk gives him what he wants. Puts it on the counter with the cigarettes. Thump thump.

"That'll be $8.92."

Eddie peels the money out, one by one, counting slow. This looks cool, Eddie thinks. Just like George Clooney or Brad Pitt in Ocean's Eleven. He gets bold. Asks for some quarters. All he has to do is play now.

He sits on the stool and pretends he's any schmo gambling away his hard earned money, putting quarters into a slot machine and pressing buttons. His heart races seeing the clerk occasionally stare at him from behind the counter. Cherry, cherry, lemon, seven. He worries that his school lunch will sneak up his throat and give him away. Cherry, cherry, cherry, cherry. It's like he's on the top of the Stratosphere on the Big Shot, suspended at the very top, waiting for the bottom to fall and pull him down at enormous speeds.

He wonders how fast the time will fly by, and then it does.

The classroom settles down as Mrs. Sccachi begins to hand back last week's quiz. When he gets his math test back, Eddie reads what Mrs. Sccachi wrote: "Excellent work, Eddie!" Four gold stars. *Jackpot*.

Eddie doodles inside the margins. Cherries, sevens, and dollar signs. Marc Denning laughs, nudges him on the side. He whispers, "Megabucks."

"An amusing anecdote you'd like to share, boys?"

Marc nods *no*, and as Eddie begins to speak, his voice cracks. "Megabucks is up to sixty-seven million."

The class roars. Eddie smiles, a big, wide, goofy grin. Mrs. Sccachi taps her foot and sighs. "Very funny, Eddie. Come here," she motions with an index finger. She is tiny and fearless, and Eddie's knees wobble as he goes up front, his shoulders slumping forward more than usual. She hands him a piece of chalk, and he blushes.

"I want you to write what I tell you."

And Eddie does. He writes down the equation, but he understands it less than he did when he was staring off into space. He writes what he is told, but he thinks different thoughts, and loses track of what he's doing.

"Eddie, that's not funny." But his classmates think so.

He has written $= APATHY$ as the solution to her problem.

Mrs. Sccachi scowls at him. All he can think is $Mrs. Sccachi + scowl = angry\ hot$.

He comes home later to find his mother drunk. "Hello!" says, greeting him with an exaggerated smile. His mother is a greeter by trade. She greets people at Wal-Mart on the weekends to help pay for Eddie's clothes. She greets the mailman, the cable guy, the neighbors who walk their dogs, the strange men who come to see his father at all times of the day. She even greets the fathers of Eddie's friends. Eddie looks at his mother and goes to her purse. "You can't even say hello to your mother before reaching into her purse?" she asks, tugging on his elbow. She falls over her chair and onto the floor. Eddie reaches into the purse and takes out the wallet, takes whatever money is there, all of it, and leaves. He doesn't even bothering closing the door behind him. "Can't you close the door behind you? What kind of man am I raising anyway?"

Thanksgiving, Christmas. The holidays give him a break from school, but they make it harder for him to leave the house and go gamble.

Eddie gambles money he doesn't have. He borrows from his mother's purse, from his father's emergency fund in the shoebox in the hallway closet, from the teachers who leave purses in plain sight or cash inside unlocked drawers. He doesn't take it all though. Small portions. A slice here, a slice there. It all adds up.

His parents start to notice money is missing. Each one blames the other. They argue between drunken rants and stoned arguments. Eddie hides in his room, pulls the Sponge Bob sheets over his head, and waits for them to go to bed. He falls asleep and it comes to him in a dream.

There is no debate this time. He'll take it one step further. He heads to the AM/PM by his house. He likes the thrill of it, how he feels of himself when he beats the odds, but the girl behind the counter makes him uneasy. She keeps eyeing him. It reminds him of the girls at school, but what does he have to lose? *Nothing*, he realizes. *But this illusion*.

Quarters in, clink, clink, clink, clink. Win. Lose. Win again. It's like a roller coaster. Eddie is about to turn upside down. *This is better than video games*. He wonders if he's earned more than enough cash to buy the PlayStation, and then that thought bursts as if it never existed. He is lost in the idea of fruit and sevens.

When the cop walks in, Eddie sits up straight. Puts the quarters in slower, sips his coffee. The cop stops at the door, next to Eddie. Looks at

Eddie. Eddie stares at the video console. The cop leans over. "You must be tired. You keep staring at your screen when you've already won." Eddie nods. "Better go home and get some sleep, buddy," says the cop, who leaves, and so does Eddie.

He oversleeps. His mother frets over him, feels his head. "Maybe you should stay home from school today," she reasons. Eddie doesn't disagree. He grunts, moans, rolls over so she will quit rubbing his back. Later, she brings him tea and two Flintstones vitamins.

The first day back to school after vacation is a drag. The boys at school are on his back about the cigarettes. Everyone is smoking now, and they keep asking him about buying liquor. Eddie doesn't answer. He roams the halls with his eyelids drooping, his feet falling over each other.

His teachers all say to him, "Are you feeling better, Eddie? You still look tired."

Eddie puts on his poker face. "Odds are I'll be fully recovered soon."

The next night, Eddie goes big. He is tired of the AM/PM, and takes a bus to the casinos on the Strip. Leaning against the pole on the bus, Eddie watches the people coming and going. He's not sure exactly where to get off, but decides to follow the crowd. The fear that he may get caught is a big part of the thrill.

He stumbles into a casino where the front is open to the sidewalk. The air is cool, and the lighting is dim, except for the sparkle of the slot machines. He heads towards the ones he knows, pausing at the poker machines and the other games he's never played before. Small steps, he reminds himself and heads to the slots.

Women pass by him, not girls. Women. He's seen women like this before, but he's alone this time. It's different. The women all yell: "Keno!" "Cocktails!" "Cigarettes!" Legs. Cleavage. So much temptation. He tries to focus on the slot machines, but he's nervous, excited, even stimulated. "Cocktail?" she asks. Eddie nods.

She comes back with a gin and tonic, a manly drink, or so Eddie had thought when he asked for it. His father's drink. Like water, only better. Then he wants to try his mother's poison, Daquiri. They taste like Slurpees. Eddie decides he likes girly drinks better.

Cherry, lemon, sevens. His luck is beginning to run out. He can barely put the coins in the slot or feed the machine with his dollar bills. A man sitting at the next machine asks him if he's okay, and he nods yes. He presses the buttons, and everything begins to spin. He can't stop the motion, no matter how many buttons he pushes, how much cash he puts in the machine.

His money is suddenly gone. He digs into both his front pockets and then his back. He takes off his shoes and looks in his socks. People stare and it pisses him off. "What the fuck are you looking at?" his voice cracks.

He regains his composure. *It's time to go.* He fumbles while getting up. He follows some people leaving the casino, and one of them says to him, "You shouldn't be driving, buddy." Eddie finds this hysterical. "I'm not old enough to drive," he says.

The conversation snowballs. Eddie bursts. His secret spills out in the space between the casino and the sidewalk. He's loud. Unintelligible. And angry at anyone who passes by.

It's really late when the cops bring Eddie home. He's half sober now.

His mother is teary-eyed, but Eddie is unmoved. He's thinking about the cool feeling of being served alcohol, how the cocktail waitress didn't even think twice, flirted with him, gave him her number. He was thinking about calling her up just to see what would happen but later decided that wasn't such a cool idea.

His father stares at him, but Eddie is too far removed to realize it isn't a vacant stare. "How could you?" "Where were you?" "What's wrong with you?" "Are you on drugs?" "Is that alcohol?" His parents ask too fast and ask too many, and then blame each other. It's a blur that he can't even understand.

"Losers!" he slurs and points, laughing until he can't control himself just before he pukes on his shoes.

Grounded is the only phrase he understands before he collapses on top of his bed, face first into the pillow. He feels his mother move him on his side, whispering that she has placed a bucket by the side of his bed and telling the scary story of how the drummer of Led Zeppelin drowned on his own vomit.

When he closes his eyes, he pictures a stairway to heaven lined with rows of slot machines. Each level is more difficult than the last, but all the more exhilarating. His mother strokes his head, gently pulling his hair away from his eyes, "Oh, where did my little boy go?"

"I'm right here, Mom," he says. "I'm right here."

Contributors

Jeff W. Bens is the author of the novel, *Albert, Himself*. His essays and short fiction are published widely.

Adam Berlin is the author of the novels *Belmondo Style* (St. Martin's Press, 2004) and *Headlock* (Algonquin Books, 2000). His stories and poetry have appeared in numerous journals. He teaches writing at John Jay College of Criminal Justice in New York City and is co-editor of *J Journal: New Writing on Justice*.

Jerry Bradley is the author of five books, most recently *The Importance of Elsewhere* (Ink Brush Press, 2009), and has published more than two hundred stories and poems. A member of the Texas Institute of Letters, he is a professor of English at Lamar University in Beaumont.

Doyle Brunson is a living legend in the poker world. He has played professionally for over fifty years. He has won prestigious tournaments such as The World Series of Poker, been inducted into the Poker Hall of Fame, and written several books on poker playing strategies. In 2006, *Bluff Magazine* voted Mr. Brunson the most influential force in the poker world.

Kelley Calvert currently resides in Monterey, California, where.she is an Assistant Professor of English for Academic and Professional Purposes at the Monterey Institute of International Studies. When not scratching off lottery tickets or scouring the beach for an inevitable big win, she can be found working tirelessly on her first book, *Hope Walks into a Bar Looking for Change*.

Laurie Champion is Professor of English at San Diego State University. She has edited several volumes of fiction and nonfiction and published many essays and short stories in distinguished literary journals. She spends her time people watching, surfing the net, and hanging out at the beach. She also plays poker, but not very well.

Gayla Chaney's fiction has appeared in literary journals and anthologies, most recently in the sci-fi anthology, *Thank You, Death Robot*, published in 2010 by Silverthought Press. She and her husband, Phil, make their home in central Texas.

Jean Copeland is a high school English teacher and writer whose fiction has appeared in *Off the Rocks*, *Best Lesbian Love Stories 2009*, *Harrington Lesbian Literary Quarterly*, *The First Line*, Hotmetalpress.net, and

Prickofthespindle.com. She is grateful to her father, James, for passing down the writing gene.

Michael Croft, a Reno native, is a senior editor at *Narrative Magazine* and spends his evenings working at Sundance Bookstore.

Eugene Cross teaches creative writing in the Bachelor of Fine Arts program at Penn State Erie, the Behrend College. His stories have appeared in *American Short Fiction*, *Narrative*, *Story Quarterly*, and *The Pinch* among others. He is the winner of the 2009 DZANC Prize for Excellence in Literary Fiction and Community Service. His collection of short stories, *Fires of Our Choosing* is forthcoming from DZANC Books.

Terry Dalrymple teaches English at Angelo State University in San Angelo, Texas. His publications include *Salvation*, a collection of short fiction, and *Fishing for Trouble*, a novel for middle readers recently reprinted by Ink Brush Press.

Andrew Geyer's books are *Siren Songs from the Heart of Austin* (Ink Brush Press 2010), *Meeting the Dead* (UNMP 2007), and *Whispers in Dust* and *Bone* (TTUP 2003), which won the silver medal for short fiction in the *Foreword* Magazine Book of the Year Awards. Geyer's stories have appeared in numerous literary magazines and won many awards, including the Spur Award from the Western Writers of America for best short story published in 2003. He currently serves as Assistant Professor of English at the University of South Carolina Aiken.

A fifth-generation Californian, Ron Gutierrez lives in Los Angeles. His inspiration for "The Proposition Player" came from a pro gambler he met on a midnight bike ride and a tragic news story involving a big rig trucker. Ron loves to take real situations and then morph and twist them into new stories, forcing himself and his readers into lives they'd never otherwise encounter. He appreciates having a muse named Mark, a chow named Leo, and his parents, Louis and Alice, who like playing the slots in Las Vegas.

A. C. Jerroll is a pen name sometimes used by a Texas writer who has published two dozen books as well as numerous short stories, essays, and poems in various magazines. He serves as editor for a literary journal and for several literary presses; and he is a member of the Texas Institute of Letters.

Michael Kardos is the author of the story collection *One Last Good Time*, forthcoming in February 2011 from Press 53. His stories have appeared in many magazines and anthologies and have been cited as Notable Stories of 2009 and 2010 in *Best American Short Stories*. He lives in Mississippi, where he is an assistant professor of English at Mississippi State University. His website is michaelkardos.com.

Jocelyn Paige Kelly grew up in Las Vegas, Nevada. Her work focuses on the use of imagination and altered states while sometimes crossing genre lines between realism and magical realism. She uses her wry sense of humor to bring the best out of her characters as well as the people she meets in her daily life as a creativity coach and hypnotherapist.

Clay Reynolds is an award winning novelist who has published more than 1,000 individual pieces of writing, including thirteen books. A professor of Arts and Humanities at the University of Texas at Dallas, he also is Director of Creative Writing. His most recent novel is *Threading the Needle*, and his next published volume will be *Hero of a Thousand Fights*, a collection of the dime novels of Ned Buntline.

Maureen A. Sherbondy is an award-winning poet and fiction writer. Main Street Rag published her first book, *After the Fairy Tale*, in 2007. *Praying at Coffee Shops* was published in 2008. The collection won the 2009 Next Generation Indie Book Award (poetry category). Her short story collection, *The Slow Vanishing*, was released in 2009. *Weary Blues*, her third poetry collection, will be released in 2010.

Sheila Thorne has worked as a union organizer on factory assembly lines and as an instructor in the California State University, San Jose writing program. Her fiction has appeared in Louisiana Literature, Nimrod, Stand Magazine (in England), and other journals.

Jodi Varon's most recent book is *Drawing to an Inside Straight: The Legacy of an Absent Father*, a 2007 WILLA Award Finalist from Women Writing the West. She is also a translator from the Chinese and an interpreter of the Chinese frontier experience in rural eastern Oregon, with several articles in the Oregon Encyclopedia. She teaches literature and creative writing at Eastern Oregon University in LaGrande.

Warren Washburn is a retired high school business teacher and football coach from the state of Nebraska. He has published a high school football text, several business education articles and several short stories. Gambling was as common in his family as corn in Nebraska during the summer. His favorite poker games are seven card stud, five or fifty-five, and Texas push'em.

www.ingramcontent.com/pod-product-compliance
Lightning Source LLC
Chambersburg PA
CBHW050512260626
47157CB00004B/1297